The Years That Followed

CATHERINE DUNNE is the author of nine novels including *The Things We Know Now*, which won the 700th anniversary Giovanni Boccaccio International Prize for Fiction in 2013 and was shortlisted for the Eason Novel of the Year at the Irish Book Awards.

She has also published one work of non-fiction: a social history of Irish immigrants in London, called *An Unconsidered People*.

Catherine's novels have been shortlisted for, among others, the Kerry Group Irish Novel of the Year Award and the Italian Booksellers' Prize. Her work has been translated into several languages.

She was recently longlisted for the first Laureate for Irish Fiction Award.

She lives in Dublin.

The Things We Know Now

'Catherine Dunne's accomplished, character-driven fiction has gone from strength to strength and locale to locale in eight successive novels. . . *The Things We Know Now* is . . . a deftly written account of the successful, second marriage of a Dublin man, Patrick Grant, to Ella, a psychotherapist, and the heart-breaking tragedy that befalls Daniel, their teenage son. Multi-voiced and painfully dark, it reads like both a Shakespearean, yet quietly feminist, tale. It's also very much a mystery story – with a decidedly brave, if risky beginning, which Dunne brilliantly pulls off against considerable odds . . . What makes this particular mystery story such a gripping read, however, are the lengths to which we readers are kept intrigued and tantalised all the way to the final pages' *Sunday Independent*

'*The Things We Know Now* finds Catherine Dunne in top form, tackling one of the great challenges facing Irish society today while maintaining her gift for exploring complex family dynamics' *Books Ireland*

'Catherine Dunne's moving new novel looks at what happens when tragedy forces one couple to uncover their son's other life . . . Throughout this powerful novel, Dunne shows a keen and compassionate eye for the complexities of family dynamics . . . She writes brilliantly about the [family's] pain and bewilderment . . . Their all-consuming grief and rage is superbly evoked'
Irish Times

Missing Julia

'A compulsive page-turner that held me engrossed deep into the night. Dunne is a very talented storyteller and, as the threads of the tale unravelled and the tension built, I found it impossible to resist the urge to race on towards the revelation and climax . . . There is darkness and suspense aplenty in *Missing Julia*, but so too is there raw emotion in all its stark, vulnerable and fragile humanity . . .' *Irish Times*

'Her writing is captivating' *Irish Independent*

At a Time Like This

'A wonderful and utterly convincing evocation of friendship over the years' *Irish Examiner*

At a Time Like This is an uncompromising read which offers a masterful insight into the complexities that exist between friends, and how forgiveness and understanding are paramount to the survival of any friendship. A fascinating read' *Ulster Tatler*

The Walled Garden

'*The Walled Garden* is that great rarity: a flawless novel' *Express*

'A hugely gratifying book; something to feed the spirit again and again' *Irish Independent*

Catherine Dunne

The Years That Followed

MACMILLAN

First published 2016 by Macmillan
an imprint of Pan Macmillan
20 New Wharf Road, London N1 9RR
Associated companies throughout the world
www.panmacmillan.com

ISBN 978-1-4472-1168-6

1 3 5 7 9 8 6 4 2

A CIP catalogue record for this book is available from the British Library.

Typeset by Palimpsest Book Production Ltd, Falkirk, Stirlingshire
Printed and bound by CPI Group (UK), Croydon, CR0 4YY

Visit **www.panmacmillan.com** to read more about all our books
and to buy them. You will also find features, author interviews and
news of any author events, and you can sign up for e-newsletters
so that you're always first to hear about our new releases.

For Fergus, with love

PROLOGUE

Calista

Extremadura, Friday 14 July 1989

THE JULY HEAT IS AN ANVIL. The sky its usual oppressive blue. The landscape of Extremadura trembles and shimmers, retreating where it can from the unforgiving glare of noon.

Calista splashes cold water on her face, pats herself dry with a towel. She makes sure to pat gently: no point in helping to make things worse than they already are. She raises her eyes to the mirror and stops, as though startled by what she sees there. She leans closer. Her unflinching brown eyes look back at her. With one finger, she traces the sudden circles, the newly wrinkled flesh at the corners of her eyes. All those fine lines, she thinks; they will soon be fissures. My face will one day look like some arid Indian riverbed.

Calista is at once reminded of Maroulla, of how she used to look. The woman seemed to age all at once. It was as though she had stepped straight from youthful to elderly with no gracious hinterland in between. Calista sees now on her own cheeks those same faint explosions of red: tiny veins threading their way towards each other. A premature labyrinth of expired blood. Her breath catches for a moment. Calista hates this: the way she looks so much older than she should.

She replaces the towel on the rail, smoothing its folds. Before she turns away, she runs her fingers through the silver bob of her hair, tucking a strand or two back into place. She's vain about her hair: proud of its thickness and its defiant steely hue. She still wants, still needs this daily reminder, this visual marker of the time when, overnight, her hair had turned from black to grey. The potency of that transformation is not to be forgotten.

And Calista has never wished to forget: dyeing her hair would, in some way, have been a betrayal of Imogen and all that had gone before.

She walks quickly through her bedroom now and out of the double doors onto the upper terrace, where she moves at once to the shadiest spot. The breeze – such as it is – which coils itself round the hills is at its best here; there is, today, the faintest scent of pine. Calista eases herself onto the lounger, which is placed at the perfect angle to catch every current of cooler air. It also allows her an unrestricted view of the gates of the house, while at the same time hiding her from sight. She lies back and rests her arms across her chest, fingers interlaced.

Like a corpse might look once it has been laid out, she thinks. And she smiles.

Tomorrow, perhaps, or the day after, she will drive down to Torre de Santa Juanita and have a glass of rosé with Rosa. *Rosé with Rosa*: it had made the young woman laugh, the first time they'd met. The way that she, Calista, rolled her Spanish 'r's. Just like a native, Rosa grinned.

But I am not a native, Calista thinks. I do not come from here. Sometimes, it feels that she is from very far away, centuries away, and she has merely dropped in to finish some ancient story before disappearing again. She feels sad for a moment, sad for how Rosa and her family will feel when all of this blows wide open, as it surely must. Calista has a stab of something that feels like fear. She begins to breathe deeply, slowly, calming herself.

Calista knows that she needs to hold her nerve: this is no time for confidences. She glances at her watch. She'll rest now, just for a little while.

*

Somewhere in the distance, the phone rings. Calista sits up at once. She looks around her, alert, poised to spring. It is as though she is searching for answers in the bright air that surrounds her. It's too soon, surely, much too soon. Can it be over already?

Calista leaves the terrace and walks carefully down the stairs. She will not rush. She knows that the answering machine has already kicked in; she will take as much time as she needs. Calista makes her way along the hallway, drawn by the machine's winking red light. She hesitates for a moment and rests one hand at the base of her throat. She can feel the rapid, steady thump of her heart, its beat pulsing through her fingers. With her free hand, she presses 'play'. Then she stands back and waits. In that still, single moment between silence and speech Calista savours the feel of the cool sandstone tiles under her bare feet.

There is just the one message, as she'd expected. Very few people have this number. 'Aphrodite,' a man's voice says. 'It is done. The transaction is completed.'

Calista plays the message again. And again. Then she deletes it. She has a fleeting, vivid memory of a man's face in a mirror – a face she would prefer to forget. She presses 'play' one more time to make sure that no trace of this, or of any other message, remains. Then she turns away. Each step she takes now feels new and significant.

So, Calista thinks, as she climbs the stairs. She makes sure to hold fast to the curved handrail as she ascends: it wouldn't do to lose her footing now, not after all this time. She finds that her hands are trembling, that her legs seem to have lost some of their usual strength. I am so tired, she thinks suddenly, surprised by the realization. But at least this new certainty is good.

Every day for four years, Calista has imagined this moment. She has wondered how she'll feel, how she'll begin to shape a new life, how she will fill the years around it: this absence she has craved for so long.

For an instant, the air around her seems to pause. The house holds its breath. Calista stops, allows the evening to enfold her. She will sit for a while on the small chair that nestles in the corner of the half-landing. It invites repose. She can look out over the countryside from here.

Just for a few moments. Just until what has happened begins to become clearer. Until she and the house can breathe together once more.

Pilar

Madrid, Friday 14 July 1989

PILAR STARTLES AS THE DOOR to the street swings shut behind her. She reaches out, tries to grab one of the handles, but the three bags of vegetables she's carrying make her clumsy, slower than usual. The early morning silence ruptures as the door slams; metal clangs against metal. Pilar winces as she feels the sudden vibration under her slippered feet. It is as though the whole building shudders. She takes one anxious moment to watch and wait, in case a pane of glass shatters. But nothing happens.

She shrugs to herself and turns away. So what if the residents complain? What more can she do? She has already called Juan Pablo to fix the closing mechanism: that door has been acting up again since last Thursday. One of those intermittent faults that started up several weeks back. The kind that Juan Pablo keeps grumbling about because they are so difficult to repair. The kind that frustrate Pilar more than anything else in the building.

The sound of the telephone in the *portería* is shrapnel in the morning air. Pilar hurries across the foyer to answer it, struggling to keep the plastic bags under control. '*Sí, señora,*' she says. '*En seguida.*' Immediately. At once. Now.

Sometimes Pilar wonders whether the residents of her building know any other words. Most of them don't even see her, of course – this is what Pilar has come to believe. She is an unseen presence: someone who takes in the post, runs errands, keeps the building secure. She makes sure that the residents are spared those unpleasant daily reminders of all that she does for them. Rufina comes every morning only when everyone has already left: no one sees her mops and buckets. No one stumbles into the silent, moving shadow that cleans the dog-shit off their floors and polishes the chrome handles of their apartment doors.

Pilar makes her way back across the marble floor, heading towards the lift. The cool, air-conditioned atmosphere is welcoming after the furnace that rages outside. Even at six in the morning, the heat at the market had been oppressive. Pilar had felt a slow stickiness crawl between her breasts and underneath the heaviness of her hair. Stallholders fanned themselves; damp half-moons bloomed under the sagging armpits of their T-shirts. There was a musky, animal scent everywhere: sweat trapped by the awnings that had been placed there to defeat the sun.

All the women were complaining, most of them loudly: about prices; about the corruption of their elected officials; about all that public money about to be wasted on the forthcoming elections – who needed politicians and their fancy suits! You couldn't open a newspaper these days without finding out about some scandal or other. Water, planning permissions, taxpayers' money used to fund junkets abroad. The intense heat added a bitter edge to the women's complaints, more fuel to the fire of their satisfied indignation. Pilar had the feeling that even the most stoical of these elderly, black-garbed shoppers had begun to lose their patience. Never mind mid-July, they were all agreed, these temperatures were *still* not right, still not normal.

There are afternoons when Pilar feels that all the oxygen has been sucked out of the air: that it has been replaced by the gritty red dust that is slowly exhaled by long, clammy daylight hours. It settles everywhere around the building, this red dust: above the doors, on the tops of skirting boards. It lurks on the treads of the stairs, too: no matter how often Pilar has Rufina dust and mop and brush all the horizontal surfaces she can find, she cannot defeat its constant rusty presence.

She steps inside the lift now and presses the button to the second floor. Señor and Señora de Molinos live in the apartment on the right-hand side. She is a little haughty, that one, and Pilar believes that her surname suits her. When agitated, the woman waves her arms around, reminding Pilar of a squat, fat windmill. Her husband is quiet, balding, polite. He raises his hat as he passes the *portería*, morning and evening. It is a small courtesy, but a constant one, something that Pilar has come to rely upon. She dumps the vegetables at her feet now, prepares herself to press the doorbell. Her fingers are white and pinched from the stretched, painful handles of the plastic bags. Her right hand tingles uncomfortably.

Señora de Molinos is waiting. She wrenches the door open even before Pilar rings. '*Gracias*,' she says, her dimpled hands already reaching down for the bags at Pilar's feet. Her '*gracias*' is overly sibilant. No matter how hard she tries, Señora de Molinos cannot hide her origins. Somewhere around Almería, Pilar reckons; somewhere in the dirt-poor Andalusian countryside. Pilar has learned how to smell poverty, to winkle it out from wherever it lurks, underneath all of her residents' ruses: she is not that easily fooled. And the woman makes Pilar's point for her this morning: she is dressed – overdressed – ready for the street, at this hour! Her too-black hair is piled high on top of her head, glistening stiffly. The scent of the lacquer mixes unpleasantly with whatever heavy perfume she's wearing: Opium, Pilar thinks. A perfume for dark nights and cold days. A perfume for a much younger woman.

Pilar looks at the señora's summer dress, straining lumpily across her belly. She sees the red nails, the none-too-subtle eyeliner, the smudged line of shadow. She sees the spiky, unsightly clumps of mascara and Pilar cannot but wonder what sort of youth the señora is so valiantly trying to recapture.

'*Gracias*,' the señora says once again, nodding and smiling. But all the while, her eyes have been darting above the *portera*'s head, across the landing to her neighbours' door, watching, always watching, as though she is about to be caught in some indecent act.

'You're welcome,' Pilar says, inclining her head to one side, giving the woman her practised smile. She doesn't linger: the señora never likes her to linger. Pilar doesn't waste her energy, not any longer, in trying to understand the oddities of her residents.

She reaches down and hands the two remaining bags of onions and aubergines to the señora. She'll collect the money at the end of the week, as usual. And she has to be fair: the señora does at least say 'thank you', and adds a little something extra on Fridays. It's not much, mind you, but at least it's a token.

Pilar has always graded her residents carefully. At the top of her chart, there are those who are generous, sometimes more than generous. Señor Alexandros, for example – or Mr Alexander, as he prefers to be called – and his elegant wife, Madam Sandra. Mr Alexander can be arrogant and bad-tempered, for sure, but he is never tight-fisted.

He can afford to be generous, as can all of Pilar's residents: this is not a building, or a neighbourhood, for the financially faint-hearted.

A few years back, Pilar developed a stoop. Not a real one, of course. She is not yet that old. Almost fifty, she has already outlived her mother. Her father is still alive, in his native village of Torre de Santa Juanita, deep in the Extremaduran countryside – or at least he was, three months ago. Pilar still sends money home from time to time, although she has long since stopped trying to influence how her father spends it. Her brothers were supposed to take care of him, once he was too old to work the land. But the older and the more infirm he got, the angrier her father became. He is a man who does not like to be looked after.

Pilar feels sorry for her eldest brother, Paco, who lives in the home place. She has little time, though, for the other two, Javier and Carlos, who still live, resentfully, in that same small village that they've known all their lives. Paco never married: it is he who will inherit the olive groves. The wives of Javier and Carlos are as bitter about this as the olive flesh they help to harvest. Pilar has seen it on too many occasions: the contempt in their eyes, their thinly veiled aggression towards gentle Paco, their endless squabbling over money.

And in the midst of it all, her father, Miguel, who sits like some feudal lord, surrounded by his vassals. Truculent; overbearing; unwilling to hand over the reins. Pilar often wonders how Paco stands it.

As well as her father's rage, it seems to Pilar that the more competent her three brothers became, the more their father envied them. When his sons became adults, it was as though he saw in their burgeoning lives a mockery of his own diminishing one. He refused to leave the farm after Pilar's mother died. He stayed; he still stays. He lashes out, again and again. Once she'd left home, Pilar rarely returned to visit. And if it weren't for the promise she'd made to Señor Gómez all those years ago, she would have stopped going back altogether.

There are days even still when Pilar feels guilty for leaving. Over the years, she often felt that she was living on undeserved time in Madrid. Time granted to her in exchange for escaping her father, her brothers, her village, her mother's fate.

Pilar always knew that her *real* life had been wrenched away from her more than twenty years ago: she knew it even at the time. Whenever she came close to reclaiming it, it slipped away from her again. On those occasions, she blamed herself bitterly for her own lack of courage. She came to know the ashy taste of regret.

But now, everything is different. Life has given Pilar a second chance. All the years ahead are full of luminous promise.

Pilar has learned how to be patient, how to behave, how not to rock the boat. Her greying hair, her hesitancies and her stoop are part of the suit of armour she gathers around her while she deals with all those lives that inhabit her building. Pilar has learned to keep her gaze just below theirs: most of the residents prefer not to have eye contact. She has learned that they like to come and go unnoticed. She lets them believe that they are, indeed, unnoticed.

But, from the small rectangular window in the door of her *portería*, Pilar watches them. Waits until they leave to fulfil whatever purpose they have, to travel to whatever daily destination they have.

In the mornings, she ticks them off her list, one by one. In the same notebook, she keeps a tally of the money that each one owes her. She has learned, in the past, how it is often convenient for people to forget.

She watches and waits, waits and watches.

And she has also learned that with most of them, what she sees is merely surface. Underneath, she is sure, they are all hiding something.

Calista

Extremadura, 1989

IT IS NOW LATE EVENING and the air is glowing. Calista doesn't know how long she has been sitting here, gazing out of the large circular window that captures the landscape below.

This is her favourite time of day. She has always loved the way there is no dusk here. The way the day plunges bravely into night, with no wishy-washy hour of grainy light in between. The crickets continue their nightly racket, the smell of jasmine intensifies, and the great red ball of the sun disappears with predictable efficiency behind the horizon.

Calista knows that if she keeps on looking, she can postpone the moment that awaits her in the room at the top of the stairs, a room now shaded by the dying embers of evening.

From here, Calista can see the lights of the nearby villages, the silvery gleam of painted houses, the serried groves of olive trees. Occasionally, a motorbike stammers along the road below her, punctuating the quiet air. She watches the way night settles across the countryside, the way shapes shift and alter in the rapid darkness. Hills become folded predators; farmers' shacks menace the crouching fields. It is possible to see for miles: in the distance, a butter-coloured moon spills stillness onto the darkness below.

Here, at this vantage point, right at the top of the hill, no approach, no retreat goes unnoticed. Calista had chosen this site so that nothing could ever again take her by surprise.

She leaves the landing now and makes her way up the final

steps of the stairs. She switches on all the lamps, illuminating the vast upper storey – an open-plan living room surrounded by glass on all four sides. The soothing sea-green shades bathe this room in a wavery light during the hot afternoons. Then, it is like being underwater, in a different element, where life ripples along at a different pace. Sometimes, when there is no air on either the upper or the lower terrace, Calista sits here for an hour or two, reading, dozing.

She designed this house herself, along with Fernando, a young, local architect who was keen to embrace her ambitious plans. Above all, he shared Calista's enthusiasm for the work of Frank Lloyd Wright. 'This will be my tribute to him,' Fernando had said, his eyes alight. 'He is my hero.' The curving staircase, the light-filled rooms, the local stone, which made the house seem to emerge, fully formed, out of the landscape: all had been talking points in the neighbouring villages during the year of its construction.

The mad, solitary Irishwoman: Calista had heard the whispers, the rumours, the speculation that animated the night-time conversations in José and Inmaculada's bar. She'd been amused by all of it at the time.

These days, once night falls, one of Calista's more constant routines is to watch with the darkness, and to remember. Once, Rosa asked her if being so visible made her feel vulnerable. 'Don't you mind?' she'd said. 'The way that people can see when you're alone?' The question had surprised Calista. She'd never thought about that, not here. Here, her house was her sanctuary. Within it, life was safe, orderly. Contained. That was why she had chosen the location in the first place. Besides, she was surrounded by so much rugged beauty.

Calista has always wanted to believe that beauty is a protection in itself.

She reaches into a cupboard and takes out a bottle of whiskey.

She pours herself a generous measure and sits, facing the fireplace. No water, no ice in the whiskey. Her father had taught her that, a long time ago. He disdained such frivolous fashions and Calista has followed his example. She allows herself to smoke only in the evenings, and she lights a cigarette now, drawing the smoke deeply, pleasurably, into her lungs. Her head feels instantly light. She sips at the whiskey. Soon, she will feel tired enough to sleep.

As she smokes, she lets her eyes drift towards the gallery of black-and-white portraits that make up the one, startling wall of the chimney breast. They are as familiar to her as her own face. In a way, they are her own face. Her gaze alights on the central photograph: a man, young, dark-haired, handsome, but not in any conventional way. He has a strong, commanding face; clear, brilliant eyes.

Calista has kept this portrait of Alexandros, no longer out of love, but out of the desire never to forget. On either side of this man, satellites orbiting the moon, are the bright faces of two young children. Smiling faces, unknowing faces, gazing off into the future.

Tonight, Calista welcomes the unravelling of emotion that comes as she looks at him, at all of them.

All that I've loved, she thinks. All that I have ever loved.

She cannot put it off any longer. Calista sits back, nurses her glass and allows herself, finally, to remember.

Pilar

Madrid, 1989

PILAR CUTS THE STRING ON the bundles of letters that Jorge, the postman, has just delivered. Juan Pablo is not here yet and Pilar has begun to feel irritated. There is a lot to do today. Above all, Juan Pablo needs to see to the front door, which has once again begun creeping open of its own accord.

Pilar begins to sort the envelopes into piles according to each floor. There are a few thick, creamy envelopes for Madam Sandra: invitations, Pilar presumes, to the cocktail parties that she seems to attend endlessly, and never in the same outfit twice. There are several for Mr Alexander, too, who has numberless social occasions of his own.

One of nature's gentlemen, Juan Pablo likes to call him. Pilar isn't so sure about that: there is a steel to Mr Alexander, a central core of selfishness. Nobody becomes *that* kind of rich by being nice to other people. Pilar has no doubt that Mr Alexander's world revolves entirely round Mr Alexander.

Just like his father, Pilar thinks, the thought assaulting her out of nowhere. Stop right there, she tells herself sternly. Stop it at once. This is neither the time nor the place.

It is almost ten o'clock now and Pilar is agitated. Juan Pablo has telephoned to say that he has been delayed, that there is a traffic accident. He has stopped off for a coffee: the police say that the junction will take at least another hour to clear. He will be there as soon as he can. Pilar hates these sudden changes to her routine. She also hates it that Juan Pablo is lounging in a cafe somewhere chatting and smoking cigarettes while she is anxious to get on with the day's tasks. But at least he rang: at least that.

It feels that events this morning are lining up to conspire against her. There is no sign of Mr Alexander, and neither is there a phone call to the *portería* from Madam Sandra.

Pilar suddenly realizes that she hasn't seen the owners of the top floor all weekend. In itself, that's not all that unusual: Madam Sandra and Mr Alexander often stay home for days on end, but they usually call on Pilar for *something*. They have visitors who arrive and leave loudly, their Mercedes-Benzes and their chauffeurs waiting patiently outside until well after midnight. The couple have always entertained lavishly. Their terrace, which wraps round the entire front of the building, is large enough to accommodate a table for twenty. The terrace itself is like a lush garden. Madam Sandra has filled it with exotic plants and shrubs, and Pilar has often admired the way the sound of cool, trickling water seems to come from every direction.

Madam Sandra is an excellent cook. Pilar knows this because Mr Alexander once told her so: told her the whole story of how he had stormed his now wife's restaurant in the centre of London and carried her off with him, the very first time he had dined there. Madam Sandra was listening to this tale, one eyebrow arched at her husband's effusiveness.

'Don't exaggerate, darling,' she said, but she was smiling. 'You had to storm the citadel a little longer than you like to admit.'

Mr Alexander had shrugged good-humouredly, but turned to Pilar, as though asking her to choose between his wife's narrative and his. 'Mine's the better story, though, Pilar, isn't it?'

And she'd smiled, rightly guessing that no real answer was required.

Pilar has often earned a quiet few thousand pesetas herself before the contract cleaners arrive to clear up after one of Madam Sandra's posh dinner parties – either those that take place in the vaulted dining room or outside on the terrace. Pilar has never been asked to serve, though. Madam Sandra employs young, slim, handsome waiters for that. Never women, and Pilar has always found that interesting. She wonders whether Mr Alexander's wife needs to keep her husband's wandering eye under control.

Like father like son.

On party nights, the young waiters arrive in the late afternoon, are gone by eleven. They are all silent, dark-eyed, watchful; they look like brothers. Pilar is convinced that they, too, are Cypriots, although she has never heard them speak.

All at once, Pilar realizes that not only has she not seen or heard from Madam Sandra and Mr Alexander over the last three or four days, neither have there been any deliveries of food, or wine, or flowers.

Pilar is becoming more and more uneasy. Perhaps they have been suddenly taken ill. Perhaps they are suffering from food poisoning – so much food goes off so quickly in this heat. Perhaps – and here Pilar begins to perspire – perhaps they already made an arrangement with her to look after things while they took a long weekend away and Pilar has somehow forgotten. Mr Alexander and Madam Sandra have always travelled a lot – sometimes at a moment's notice, but they've never failed to let her know when they will be back.

Pilar is sure that she would never forget something as important as that. But she feels a chill flicker of doubt nonetheless and, just in case, she riffles through the pages of her notebook, in a fever of anxiety. Nothing. She gets up from her chair and begins to pace. The golden rule is that Mr Alexander and Madam Sandra must never be disturbed. That has always been clear. That is one of the reasons they live on the top floor.

Pilar can feel her anxiety grow. This Tuesday is also the day for the window cleaners. Madam Sandra never forgets: she is very methodical in her domestic arrangements. She likes to be present when the men arrive, but she never stays. She returns as soon as they have finished, inspects the work and dismisses them when she is satisfied.

Pilar glances at her watch. She will have to call Madam Sandra, if only to enquire whether there is to be any change to the day's arrangements. The window cleaners will be here in half an hour. It's most annoying that Juan Pablo is late. Pilar makes her way back to the phone in the *portería*, easing herself into the old armchair, positioned as usual for optimum viewing of the foyer. She hesitates, then lifts the receiver and dials the number of the top floor. There is no response. She tries again. Still no answer.

Pilar replaces the receiver and sits for a moment, thoughtful. She has no need to consult her notebook to inform herself of what she must do in such extraordinary circumstances. She knows all of the residents' preferences by heart. She will try a third time to call them and if there is still no response, then she will take the lift to the top floor. If the door is unanswered, she has per-mission to use her key and enter the apartment, to supervise whatever work needs to be done. But this has never happened: Madam Sandra has never yet forgotten.

Their phone rings out.

Five minutes later, Pilar is at the heavy oak door that leads to the top-floor apartment. She hesitates before she knocks, pressing her ear to the warm wooden surface. She can hear nothing. She looks down the door's glass eye, imagining herself being seen from the inside: foreshortened, fish-eyed, rigid with anxiety. Then she knocks, twice, waiting a couple of minutes each time for a response. One of them might be in the shower, or still asleep, or they might be . . . When there is no answer, Pilar inserts her key in the lock and pushes the door open.

As she does so, the smell assaults her. She cannot avoid it: the force of its onslaught makes her stagger. For a strange moment, Pilar remembers the mouse, caught in a trap in the corner of her bedroom downstairs. She'd forgotten that she'd set it and the sweet, sickly scent of decay had driven her mad for days until she found the small, weeping, blackening corpse, tracking it down by making her way around the apartment on her hands and knees.

This here, she thinks suddenly, this must be some mouse.

'Mr Alexander,' she calls, standing with one foot just over the threshold, ready, always ready to retreat. 'Madam Sandra?' She can hear the appeal in her voice. There is a stillness to the room that is unnerving. As though nothing has moved here for days. She can hear the low hum of the air conditioning; but despite its coolness, the air is thick with something that Pilar does not have the words to name. She feels her knees begin to tremble. Her palms are damp, the key sticky in her grasp.

She opens the door to the vast living room. Nothing. Frightened now, compelled to move forward yet dreading what she might be about to discover, Pilar puts her hand on the bedroom door.

'*Señor?*' she calls. '*Señora?*'

When she pushes her way in, the overpowering foetid air makes her gag. Her eyes water. The angry, insistent buzzing of a million glassy flies, their bodies fat, their wings blue-veined and translucent, tries to drive her back. Our territory, they say, swooping around her head in a cloud of rage. *Ours.*

Pilar puts one hand to her mouth – she cannot be sick, not here. With the other, she tries to wave away the flies. But what she sees has made her throat close over. She is unable to speak.

Around and around inside her head, the words of her mother's prayer keep pulsating. The holy words seem to mimic the furious rhythm of the bluebottles' buzzing. *Almighty God, have pity on us, help us in our hour of need. Almighty God, have pity on us, help us in our hour of need.* Over and over again it goes.

But Pilar knows that the woman on the bed before her is beyond pity, beyond help. She is naked, her body marble-like against the blood-soaked satin sheets. Her arms are by her sides, her palms facing upwards, as though in supplication. Underneath her breast, there is a single, scarlet wound. Pilar begins to shake, but something drives her forwards.

She moves away from Madam Sandra, trying not to look back. She calls out Alexander's name: 'Mr Alexander, are you here? Mr Alexander?' But there is no reply. Pilar pushes open the bathroom door. At first, she cannot make out what she is seeing. There are signs of struggle everywhere: towels are strewn across the floor, toiletries scattered; shards of glass crunch underfoot. Everywhere there is a buzzing blue cloud of flies: drunken-crawling, sated. A great mound of white stuff in the bath, slumped to one side, looks for all the world like a wash-day bundle, just like in the launderette where Pilar once worked during her early days in the capital. She comes closer, still calling Mr Alexander's name.

And then she sees. Mr Alexander's head, just visible beneath the taps. The smoothness of the skin, the now delicate contours of his familiarity fill Pilar with an agonized tenderness. For one crazed moment, she longs to reach out and touch that forehead in all its vulnerability. She recoils at once, her hands flying to the base of her throat, guarding herself against attack. Mr Alexander is dressed in his white bathrobe, one foot protruding palely at an odd angle. Underneath this foot, the bath is filled with an opaque red-black substance, one that looks both thick and sticky, its surface dotted with the bloated bodies of bluebottles.

'Oh God, oh God, oh God. Jesus help me.' Pilar stands there, rocking back and forth to the heartbeat of her whispered words of prayer. She cannot think of what else to do. The rocking is silent, comforting. Perhaps she'll do nothing at all, just stand here and wait until . . .

Finally, Pilar jerks into awareness: What am I doing? She finds sudden strength in her legs, just enough to flee. And then she runs, weeping, out of the bathroom, through the bedroom, out of the door towards the lift, keeping one hand clapped over her mouth, just in case. She knows that she shouldn't touch anything: something she has learned from all those cop shows she watches on late-night TV. She covers one hand with her apron and pulls the apartment door closed behind her. She cannot shake off what she has just seen. Wave after wave of nausea fills her mouth with a sickly, watery substance. She clings to the metal bars of the lift door. What is she going to do?

The police. She must call the police.

Pilar pulls open the door of the lift, hardly hearing the metal shriek. She tries to push the button for the ground floor, but her fingers won't work properly: they feel like someone else's, someone without strength or endurance. She tries to breathe deeply, to still the trembling of her hands. Suddenly, the lift jerks into life, begins its slow, almost rocking descent. She fumbles in the pocket of her apron, grips the single key to the *portería*, prays that she will not meet any of the residents when she reaches the entrance foyer. All she wants is to get to her telephone: that solid, black Bakelite instrument that will allow her to relinquish responsibility for the horror she has just witnessed.

The lift door opens. The face of the marble hallway is blank, expressionless. Pilar turns with relief towards her door, opens it quickly despite the trembling of her hands, and closes it firmly behind her. She stays standing and calls the emergency number. She watches as the spinning chrome dial of the phone takes a long time to wheel back to where it started. And then a woman answers, with a kind woman's voice.

Hearing her, Pilar is undone all over again. She starts to cry, great hiccupping sobs that make speech impossible.

'It's OK. You're OK,' the woman's voice says. 'I'm here to help you. Can you tell me your name?'

Such a practical request makes Pilar feel more stable. She can, finally, feel her feet upon her own solid floor. She can even see her swelling ankles. Yes, yes, she can do that: she can give this nice woman her name. And as an afterthought she says: 'I'm the *portera* here.'

'Good. That's good,' the woman says. 'Now, can you tell me where you are calling from, Pilar?'

Pilar blurts out the address, overcome again by the fresh horrors of the sixth-floor apartment. She cannot get Madam Sandra's marbled flesh out of her mind, or Mr Alexander's slumped and bloody form in the bathtub. And the flies; everywhere the fat, triumphant flies.

'You're doing fine, Pilar. Really fine. Now, just one more question: can you tell me the nature of the emergency?'

The nature of the emergency. Pilar wants to laugh. Is that what this is? An emergency? Do two dead bodies constitute an emergency? There is hardly any hurry about them now. Pilar stops herself, appalled at her reaction.

She stumbles out an answer: 'I've just found them. And they're dead; they're definitely dead. The smell . . .'

'How many are dead, Pilar? Can you tell me how many?' The woman's voice has changed. Now it is filled with urgency – a calm urgency, but an urgency nonetheless. In the background, Pilar hears other voices – nothing clear, just murmurations.

'Both of them. Madam Sandra is on the bed, and Mr Alexander is in the bath. They wouldn't answer the phone or the door of their apartment, so I had to go in, and there's blood in—'

'Where are you now, Pilar?' the woman interrupts her, but her voice is kind again.

'Back downstairs in my *portería.*'

'Good. That's very good, Pilar. The police are on their way. They will be with you in less than ten minutes. Can you make sure that nobody goes into that apartment? Can you do that, Pilar?'

'Yes, of course,' Pilar says. She feels the first faint stirrings of indignation. She is beginning to be irritated by this stranger's overuse of her Christian name. And she wants to tell this woman that she, Pilar, she too, knows a thing or two about police procedures. 'I'm the only one with a spare key. And I didn't touch anything,' she says.

'That's very good. The police should be arriving at any moment. You've done very well.'

Suddenly, Pilar wants to be off the phone. She needs to be outside in the hall; she needs to meet any of her residents who might arrive back unexpectedly; she needs to reassert whatever control she can. This is her territory, after all. Abruptly, she ends the call and pulls open the door of the *portería.*

Now Pilar is worried about what she will say to Juan Pablo and how she can explain to the window men that they are no longer needed. They are sure to be pissed off: cash jobs are rarer than hen's teeth these days.

What is she supposed to say now to the men with buckets, stepladders and pockets filled with chamois leather?

She walks out of the *portería*, locking the door carefully behind her, as though the words she has spoken on the telephone might somehow leak out and upset her residents. Pilar has the sensation that she has left all feeling behind her, up there on the top floor. It's almost as though the scene she has just witnessed has become unreal. The more she distances herself from it, the less probable it is that it has really happened. She already doubts herself, her own eyes. Then she has another thought, one that annoys her hugely on her own account. Never mind the window men: who's going to pay *her* for all that cleaning she did a couple of weeks back? Who is going to do that now?

Somehow, the question, the annoyance, the sense of the floor beneath her feet, all make Pilar inhabit the space around her again. She hopes that some strength will soon come back to her legs, which are now numb. Slowly, she walks towards the front door, where she stands and waits. In her head, she practises what she is going to say to the police.

They are here, right here, right now: two large, uniformed policemen loom up at her from the street outside. They press the *portería* bell repeatedly, peering in through the wrought-iron decorations on the door, their hands cupped around their eyes, their caps askew.

Resolutely, Pilar makes her way towards them.

She needs to gather together all the densely patterned fabrics that make up her story: she needs to make the seams straight and tidy inside her head. Pilar must make sure that in the telling of some carefully selected truths, she holds back those words that never should be spoken.

Pilar is ready now: she knows what she is going to tell them.

Calista

Extremadura, 1989

CALISTA SIPS AT HER WHISKEY. Her hand, she notices, has become a little less steady. Outside her window, the darkness of Extremadura is now total. The moon has disappeared, bruised by cloud.

Alexandros.

His face, that first time Calista saw him. Glowing, filled with an energy that thrummed beneath the surface of his skin. The smile that creased the corners of his olive-green eyes. Hair so dark it sheened blue in the light. How could she ever forget?

It is a Saturday in April 1966.

The early arrival of summer is made visible by the carpet of cherry blossom on the lawn: a delicate covering of warm, pink snow. Calista's mother, María-Luisa, busies herself in the dining room, folding the white linen napkins, moving the crystal a fraction to the right or a fraction to the left. She straightens the cutlery.

When María-Luisa speaks, the irritation in her voice is razor-edged; it makes her accent stronger, her words more clipped than usual. And when she's like this, she can never remember the difference between 'say' and 'tell'.

'Maggie, please, I say you *two* sets: one for the fish course, one for the meat.' Except that she makes it sound like '*feesh*' and '*meat-ah*', with that upswing at the end of the sentence that shows how close she is to exasperation.

Maggie emerges from the kitchen, wiping her anxious hands on a not-very-clean apron. 'Yes, madam,' she says, but Calista can see how bewildered she is. She is just two years older than Calista's seventeen, but the real gap between them has nothing at all to do with age. Maggie is a domestic, *una criada*, a servant: she hails from Longford, somewhere. Calista is able to find Longford on a map. It's hours away from Dublin and she cannot think of anything that might interest her there.

Behind her mother's back, Calista lifts one of the fish-knives, points to its flat blade, mouths the word '*feesh*' and sees Maggie bite back a smile with difficulty.

'I'll do it right away, madam,' the girl says. She moves towards the table, suppressed laughter brightening her cheeks.

'Are you sure you know the difference?' Calista's mother asks her. Her tone is weary now.

Maggie's eyes flare with injured innocence. 'Of course,' she says with some dignity. She lifts the knife that Calista has been waving at her and holds it out to Madam. 'This one, this is for the fish –' except that she makes the word hover somewhere between 'fish' and '*feesh*' '– and this other one is for the meat.'

María-Luisa sighs. 'Yes, now please try to remember for the next time. Have you started to make the hollandaise?'

Maggie looks at her employer for one terrified moment and flees. María-Luisa shakes her head, pulls at the cuffs of her beige cashmere cardigan.

Calista says: 'Do you always have to be so hard on her?'

María-Luisa looks at her daughter, her eyes sharp as cut stone. 'We have standards in this house.' She matches the tip of her middle finger to the tip of her thumb in that classic gesture of Spanish emphasis that always makes Calista flinch. It makes her think back to a teacher's nails dragging against the blackboard, or the flinty sound of sudden grit in a stick of classroom chalk. María-Luisa moves her hand up and down, up and down, stressing every other word so that her sentences acquire an unpleasant, hypnotic rhythm. '*It* is *one* of the *ways* we *show* our *class*,' she says. 'That *we* are *people* to *be* respected.' Now she spreads her palms wide, a gesture of helplessness. 'How else can your father do business?'

Calista couldn't care less about how her father does business. She doesn't even know what business he *does*: 'import and export' sounds dull and vague to her, as dull and vague as Longford, and she doesn't care to know more.

'Who's coming today?' she asks.

As an answer, her mother looks at her watch. 'A young colleague of your father's. A Mr Alexandros Demitriades, from Cyprus. His family are important people in shipping, I believe. Your father thinks it right that we at least invite him for lunch.' She shrugs. 'I have no idea what he is like: I must do as your father asks.'

Calista hears the words that have remained unspoken: even if I don't like it. María-Luisa is good at this. She excels at the subtle putdowns, the sly removal of the self from anything uncomfortable or unsuccessful. 'Now,' she says, her tone rising a notch. 'Go and let Felipe know. Make sure both of you are down here in twenty minutes. Mr Demitriades will be here at one o'clock sharp.'

Calista doesn't ask her mother how she is so certain of her guest's punctuality. Instead, she turns on her heel, glad that her tasks of polishing the glasses and the silverware have passed her mother's severe, appraising eye.

She takes the stairs two at a time and knocks on the door of the bedroom that leads off the first landing. 'Philip?' she says. Philip is her twin, so like her in so many ways that he could be her other self. Except in this one thing: Philip is as studious as

Calista is indifferent to learning. She does not understand her brother's passion: all those dry facts and figures, stories about long-dead people, the baffling grammar of languages no longer spoken. Calista never addresses her brother as 'Felipe'. He made it clear, even as a seven-year-old, that he hated the strangeness of his foreign name, hated the way it set him apart from others.

Calista, on the other hand, quite likes hers. It is an ancient family name of her mother's, stretching back into Spain's past centuries of knights and warriors and all their chivalrous pedigrees. Calista believes that her name links her to the myths and legends of *The Lady of the Highlands.* Her Spanish grandparents used to regale her with exciting stories about this powerful woman who lived in the mountains of Extremadura. A woman who abandoned her homeland in search of adventure. Calista loved these tales: they were so much better than dull, insipid stories about queens and fairies and frogs turning into princes.

But Philip hates his foreignness. He struggles at school to be the same as everyone else: his Spanish name is an imposition that he resents, bitterly. María-Luisa has, however, insisted: at school, within the family, around the neighbourhood, her son is to be called 'Felipe'. Calista is the only one who defies her. Maggie has told her yet again recently that in this, she's on her own. Maggie refuses to risk the certainty of Madam's steely wrath.

Philip opens the door a fraction. 'What?'

Calista can see open books and notepads, a large dictionary and an even larger atlas strewn about the room. Her brother is buried deep in his studies even on his weekends at home. The school has great hopes for Felipe. He is their rising star, and his teachers can only be illuminated by the trail that he blazes.

'Lunch,' Calista says. 'In twenty minutes. Mamá says to be sure that you're ready.'

Philip frowns. 'Why?' he demands. 'I'm studying. Exams begin in seven weeks' time.'

Calista doesn't rise to the bait of the looming examinations. If she does, it will give her twin the opportunity, again, to give her grief over her poor study habits.

'We're having a guest to lunch,' she says quickly, 'Alexandros somebody or other.' And then it strikes her and she laughs out loud: 'Alexandros the Greek! Or is it Alexandros the Great?' She makes a face, unsure. 'Anyway, doesn't matter – whoever he is, I think his family does business with Dad.'

'Why do *I* have to be there?'

Calista shrugs. This is a well-worn conversation between them. She touches the tip of her middle finger against her thumb, moves her hand up and down for emphasis and says: 'Because we have *stand*-ards in this *fam*-ily –' She breaks off as soon as she sees Philip's grin. She knows how closely she resembles her mother – everyone who meets them says so. She has María-Luisa's height and elegance, her mother's fine-boned hands, her flashing dark eyes. Calista knows, too, that she is skilled at mimicry. And she likes to make her younger brother laugh. Younger by only fifteen minutes, but still.

Philip mutters, 'All right, then, yeah,' and closes his bedroom door.

Calista leaps up the final three steps to the second landing and pushes her way into her room. The light is dim, despite the bright spring bloom outside her window. She believes that her mother has furnished this house as though it belonged in a wealthy Madrid suburb: just like the one in Calle de Alcalá, where Calista's grandparents still live. They'd moved there some-time in the early 1940s, abandoning their home and their land in Extremadura in the wake of the terrors of the Civil War.

María-Luisa had taken Calista and Felipe to Madrid to visit their grandparents, once, when they'd made their First Holy Communion. Calista still remembers the sombre atmosphere. Like here, that apartment was stuffed with heavy furniture: dark, brooding wardrobes; sagging drapes at the windows. Perhaps it's the effect of the sun, shining on the rosewood chest in the corner, but Calista is sure that she can catch the faint scent of mothballs even now, coming from the curved, gleaming drawers.

Calista was about nine when she first began to understand how different her family was from all the other families she knew in Dublin. A Spanish mother, when such foreignness was rare, truly exotic. A father who travelled, who brought gifts back from abroad. A large house, one that stood in its own grounds. High-ceilinged rooms filled with treasures; treasures that made Calista imagine the echoing vastness of Africa, of Europe and of India. Carved wood; silk rugs; the tribal masks that used to terrify and fascinate her when she was a child. It was as though Calista's family was a shimmer of hot colour, a glow of shot silk across the grey and shadowy Irish landscape.

Shortly after Calista's ninth birthday, she was invited in return to Mary Peters's party. She didn't even like Mary Peters all that much, even though they sat close to each other in school. Calista didn't want to go. She was missing her twin, missing his constant, spiky presence: her other half. She didn't want to be with girls; she wanted to be with Philip. He had recently been taken away from her and packed off to some boarding school down the country. Calista went to the local primary, just two or three meandering streets away from home. When she'd asked why Philip had had to go so far away, her mother murmured something about the importance of a good education for boys.

On the day of Mary's party, Calista's mother insisted on driving her there in her smart new Ford, saying that she would like to meet the birthday girl and her mother. 'It is important, always,' María-Luisa told her daughter, as she indicated and pulled out carefully from the driveway, although there was no traffic: there never was in those days, 'to have manners, to show that you have breeding.'

Calista shifted uncomfortably on the back seat. Awareness had begun to wash over her, each new wave bringing with it a sense of alarm and foreboding. None of the other mothers drove; none of the other families had cars. This Calista knew for a fact: a fact that she had absorbed, along with many others, such as the darned elbows of so many children's jumpers, the schoolbooks shared between sisters, the break-time sandwiches that came wrapped in waxy paper, the sort of paper that enfolded what her mother called 'shop bread'.

And then there was the milk that the other girls kept in their schoolbags until it was time for big break. It came in jam jars with screw-top lids that when opened, released a warm, animal sigh into the classroom air. She remembered all these warning signs now as her mother pulled up at the kerb. Three girls, with large pink bows in their hair and hand-knitted Fair Isle cardigans, were standing at Mary's door, waiting to go inside. They turned when they heard the car, turned and gaped.

María-Luisa unfolded herself elegantly from the front seat, her mint-green costume and white gloves a beacon of strangeness in the Dublin housing estate – all grey walls and brown front doors. As Calista followed her mother up the path, she felt mortification prickle across the back of her neck, the stiff fabric of her dress making her hot and angry. *Go home*, she said to her mother silently, her head vibrating with a new and unfamiliar fury. *Why don't you just go home?*

She saw Mary's mother appear suddenly on the step, saw the way she hurriedly whipped off her apron, then ran her hands through her hair. Calista saw how hard she tried to look welcoming, rather than whatever else it was that she was feeling. But then María-Luisa extended her hand, smiled her most winning smile and said: 'Mrs Peters, I am very glad to meet you. Thank you so much for inviting Calista: you are very kind.'

And suddenly, it was all right. Everyone relaxed. The other girls looked at Calista with a new respect.

'Won't you come in?' Calista could hear the uncertainty in Mrs Peters's voice.

'Thank you. But I won't disturb. I will come back for Calista around five, and perhaps I can drive all of you girls home, too, no?' María-Luisa was smiling at the other girls and, miraculously, the girls were smiling back. 'Would you like that?' María-Luisa asked.

Three heads nodded; three pink bows dipped and rose again in unison.

'Good.' The crispness had returned to María-Luisa's tone. 'Then I will see you all later. Thank you again, Mrs Peters. And, Calista, don't forget to give Mary her gift.'

All eyes followed her down the path. Everyone waved as the car pulled away. Calista felt that she could breathe again.

Mrs Peters said brightly, 'Let's go inside, girls. Let's have our party!'

Calista remembers the ice cream and jelly, the fizzy red lemonade, the Rice Krispie buns, solid and sticky with chocolate. All the food that María-Luisa frowned upon at home. The five girls played pass-the-parcel, pin-the-tail-on-the-donkey and musical chairs, although Calista noticed that one or other of the pink bows cheated at musical chairs, every time. She wanted to cry out each time it happened; but instead, she heard her mother's voice inside her head, warning her about breeding, and so she said nothing.

Over birthday cake and more lemonade, Mary's four small guests oohed and aahed over Mary's birthday presents – Calista had given her books, *The Turf-Cutter's Donkey* and *The Bookshop on the Quay* by Patricia Lynch, which María-Luisa had said were appropriate. The others had brought a jigsaw, a *Judy* annual for 1958 – although the year was already half over – and a pencil case stuffed full of colouring pencils. And then it was time to go home.

When María-Luisa returned, smiling, she handed Mrs Peters a bunch of long-stemmed lilies. 'Thank you so much, Mrs Peters – I do hope Calista was well behaved?'

Mrs Peters appeared flustered, unsure what to do with the flowers. She held them at arm's length, clutching at their stems through the damp brown paper. She looked as if she feared they might somehow take her by surprise. 'Oh! Yes, perfectly. Such a lovely girl. Calista's welcome anytime. We loved having her, didn't we, Mary?'

Mary nodded, her thin, eager face still smeared with chocolate.

'May I?' María-Luisa took a Polaroid camera out of her bag. 'I should like very much to give each of the girls a souvenir of this lovely day. Is that all right?'

There were squeals and giggles as all five girls posed for the photographs. There was some pushing and shoving as they watched the photos ghosting into life; the pink bows jumped up and down, beside themselves. Calista was fascinated, watching as each of the girls' faces emerged, one after the other. She saw the way the camera captured their expressions, freezing their sense of mischief, their shyness, their uncertainty forever under the glossy coating of memory. The other girls were awestruck and Calista felt her stock rise on that day. Like it or not, she knew that she owed that to her mother.

She glances now at her bedroom mirror where several photos congregate, their corners tucked into the wooden frame. Each one jostles the other for space, just like the pink-bowed girls on the day the pictures were taken. In there, somewhere, is the fading Mary Peters of eight years ago, with her soft eyes and her sticky face. Calista wonders where she is now, where all those girls are. It is as though they disappeared into some shadowy underworld of hairdressing and shop-assisting and sewing factories. Calista was the only one of her classmates to receive what María-Luisa called a proper secondary education, an education suitable for a young lady.

Calista now drags the brush through the tangle of her dark hair, smooths the front of her dress and gets ready to go back downstairs. Her watch tells her it's almost time. She daren't be even a moment late. She hesitates for a second, but then decides against the lipstick that she's tempted to wear: just a faint pink frosting – she's seventeen, after all – but she judges that given the mood her mother is in, it might be wiser to avoid a row.

Calista makes her way down the stairs to the hallway, just as the clock is chiming one. At the turn, she hears voices, laughter, the sound of animated introductions, her father's booming voice. 'And this is my son, Felipe.' She sees all the heads below her: Philip's, her father Timothy's, her mother's and, way taller than all of them, what must be Alexandros's.

Her mother looks up, sees Calista and smiles. It is as though that one small movement breaks the thread of whatever binds together all of those standing in the hall. Almost at once, Alexandros moves away from the others, turns and watches as Calista comes down the stairs. She sees his eyebrow lift, something in his gaze makes her begin to blush, and she wishes she'd risked the lipstick.

'My daughter, Calista.' Timothy waves his hand in her direction. He sounds satisfied about something. His movements are jaunty, almost arrogant, as though he's showing off his spoils.

Alexandros steps forward, gives the smallest of bows and brings his lips close to the back of Calista's hand, although he does not kiss it. Calista starts. A jolt courses through her, a tingle not unlike the shock she'd got once from a badly wired lamp. As Alexandros raises his head, his clear green eyes look right through her, as though he can see something beyond what she now is, standing there in front of him. He seems reluctant to let go of her hand. When he finally does so, Calista can feel the warmth and the strength of his fingers, pressed into her palm like a memory.

And then she knows; of course she does.

They move into the dining room, where Maggie is hovering.

As they sit, Alexandros's hand brushes against Calista's. The sudden contact startles her fingers into life all over again. His knee presses against hers under the table from time to time, seeming accidental, although Calista is sure that it is not.

She still remembers the certainty of that day: that something about her old life was ending. Something new and electrifying was just beginning.

Calista finishes her whiskey and stands up. She tries not to let her eye be drawn back again towards the gallery of black-and-white portraits. She wants to avoid Alexandros's ancient gaze. She moves quickly towards the window instead, snapping off all the lamps as she goes. Dotted across the inky sky, the stars are small, watchful, light-filled blossoms. They blink at her only occasionally.

For a moment, Calista stands there looking out, still able to recognize some familiar landmarks, despite the blackness.

Montánchez, away to the south. The distant lights of quietening farms: Calista can name all of their owners now, one by one. They all greet her, and she them, when they meet along the winding back roads. Initial wariness on their side gradually gave way to a respectful, guarded affection. Calista made sure to use only local materials, employed only local labour, in the building of her house. She buys only local produce, from the weekly markets or direct from the farmers themselves. These things are not forgotten, not in a place such as this.

As Calista enters her bedroom, she knows that this will be another sleepless night. Not because of what has already happened, hundreds of kilometres away – she has been ready for that for years – but because the potent force of memory has gripped her, and she must give it its due, must see it through to the end, before it will release her.

It is difficult, though, to separate memory from all that it brings with it: love, pain, loss. Betrayal. A mysterious alchemy sometimes makes the remembering more gentle, more resigned. But not tonight.

Tonight, Calista feels that every cell is firing, every nerve ending poised. This is it.

This is what all those years have led her towards: from that first family lunch with Alexandros's knee pressing against hers to the ending that has always been inevitable.

Pilar

Torre de Santa Juanita, 1957

PILAR DOMÍNGUEZ couldn't wait to leave her village.

Torre de Santa Juanita huddled itself into the countryside beyond Montánchez, its houses crowded into insignificance. The mountains lorded over it, the land withheld itself, and the inhabitants dressed themselves in all the resentments of poverty. When Pilar finally left, she did as her mother, María Dolores, had bid her.

'*Vete, hija,*' Mamá had urged her eighteen-year-old daughter. Her tone had been full of an unaccustomed urgency. *Go, my girl,* she said to her daughter. Leave this place and shake the dust off your feet. Don't ever look back. Something in her mother's eyes terrified Pilar. She knew that, more than this *place*, her mother meant her to leave this *life*. She'd watched as Mamá faded away, frail and birdlike, her body barely making a ripple under the thin blanket that covered her, that final winter.

Just before she died, she took Pilar's hand in hers. There was a surprising strength to her grasp. 'Listen to me,' she said. 'If you stay until I am gone, you will never escape. You will spend your life serving your father and your brothers.' She paused, drew one shallow, difficult breath. 'And no matter what the priest says, there is no nobility in poverty, even less in servitude. Go.'

Pilar ran. She still remembers the date: 17 May 1957. Paco took her in the cart as far as their nearest neighbour, fifteen kilometres west of Torre de Santa Juanita. From there, his dark, silent friend, Gabriel, took her to the bus station in Mérida. When they arrived, Pilar stepped unsteadily off the pillion of Gabriel's scooter, thinking that she'd never been so happy to feel the ground beneath her feet as a solid, unshifting thing. She caught a slow, grateful bus to Badajoz, and then took the overnight train to Madrid.

Pilar had her mother's life savings in her purse: the few pesetas that Mamá had managed to keep back from her weekly lacemaking, saved stealthily in a cloth bag at the bottom of the earthenware jar where the flour was kept. No chance of any man looking there, Mamá had said grimly.

Pilar had grown up knowing that her mother had 'married beneath her'. She'd felt this unspoken knowledge, absorbed it as she grew. Nobody had ever said as much, but the understanding hung in the air: chill and blunt, like trees in winter. Her mother's way of speaking, the way she walked with her head up, the way she often answered back, her sharpness igniting her husband's rage: all of these things set her apart from the other village women.

Never marry, she'd told her only daughter, shaking her head. Her brown eyes were alight with intensity, her fists tightly clenched.

Answer to no man.

Everything had terrified Pilar on her arrival in Madrid: the traffic, the noise, the enormous scale of the city and its monuments. The Puerta del Sol: all those hurrying people!

When her mother had pressed the envelope of pesetas into Pilar's hands, dusting off the ghosting of flour as she did so, she also handed her daughter something else. A scrap of paper, many times folded. When Pilar unpleated it, it felt feathery in her hands, insubstantial. She held on tight, afraid it might fly away from her. She sat beside her mother, on the bed, as María Dolores struggled for breath to explain. She laid one trembling forefinger on the faded writing.

'This man, in Madrid, will help you. His name is Alfonso Gómez. He is a lawyer and you can trust him with your life.'

Pilar looked at her, startled, her eyes full of questions. How did her mother know this man, when she had never, as far as Pilar knew, even left her village? And how did she know that Pilar could trust him?

María Dolores allowed her gaze to rest somewhere above Pilar's shoulder. 'I know this man. He is from around here.' She turned and looked her daughter in the eye. 'He is the man I should have married.'

Pilar gasped. She couldn't help herself. Her mother had a *past*? That was even more astonishing than the fact that there had once been another man in her life. Up until that moment, in Pilar's young eyes, María Dolores, *Mamá*, had been simply that: a mother, always present to her four children: three boys and one girl, her youngest. She was a wife, too, of course, but that amounted almost to the same thing. Her life was defined by belonging to other people: to a casually brutal man, to four grown-up children, to some brothers and sisters of her own, carelessly scattered around Asturias and Galicia.

'I was not good enough for Alfonso's family,' Pilar's mother continued. 'Never good enough. They were wealthy pig farmers from close to Montánchez; my father and mother owned a few acres here in Santa Juanita. Alfonso asked me to run away with him to Madrid, but I was too afraid. I said no. It is something that I have regretted all my life. I should have gone. I should have had the courage.'

It was the longest speech Pilar had ever heard her mother make. She did a rapid calculation: Paco, Pilar's eldest brother, was twenty-five, so Alfonso had disappeared from her mother's life at least that many years ago: how did she even know he was still alive? Suddenly, Pilar was struck by a new and astonishing thought. What if Alfonso and Mamá . . . ? What if Paco, gentle Paco – so different from Javier and Carlos . . . ? What if her mother was telling her only half of the truth?

As though she'd read her daughter's mind, María Dolores said: 'There are some things we will not talk about – there is no time. Just know that Alfonso is alive and well and practising law in Madrid. I sometimes have news of him.' Pilar didn't dare ask. María Dolores reached out and took her daughter's hand. 'You must not be like me. You must not be afraid. You must go and make a life for yourself.'

Even at the time, Pilar knew that she would remember those words forever. Her mother's intensity, the urgency of her gaze, the cold, grim bareness of her bedroom: the images were seared at once into Pilar's memory. She watched as the older woman slumped back against her pillow. Talking exhausted her.

'Rest now, Mamá,' Pilar said. 'I will stay with you. Please, you have to rest.'

María Dolores nodded, and closed her eyes. Pilar watched as sleep overtook her. She couldn't help her sense of disbelief. She tried to find a sign, any sign, of long-ago, youthful passion in her mother's weary face. Mamá had loved another man, and she, Pilar, had known nothing about that other life, suspected nothing.

Did Papá know? Surely he must have done. Santa Juanita was small, a tightly wound, suspicious community where need and want and envy made everybody scrutinize their neighbours' every move. This sudden suspicion of Pilar's made sense of her father's jibes, the throwaway remarks that he spat around the room when something had, once again, catapulted him into one of his rages. Pilar felt a swelling sorrow for her mother. Mamá had been an educated girl, one of the few in the village who had gone to school until she was eighteen. The nuns in the nearby convent had spotted potential in María Dolores, encouraged her in her studies. Mamá's own mother, Loló – Pilar's tiny grandmother – had cleaned for those same nuns, making her way on hands and knees up and down the stairways and the parquet floors of the convent, polishing the holy surfaces until they gleamed. Loló adored her only daughter, was determined to give her all the opportunities she herself had never had. And María Dolores had loved school, loved learning.

Pilar still remembers Mamá's wails of anguish when, one inexplicable afternoon, Papá had wrenched tumble-loads of books off the olivewood shelves that Paco had just finished crafting. He ripped the spines off each, one by one, tossing them into the already blazing fire. She remembers little else, apart from the dark, burnished swirls of the wood and the way the pattern had caught her eye. That and her father batting away her mother's flailing arms as though they had been made of string. When Papá turned his rage on Pilar, she fled, through the door, across the frozen yard, where she hid in the byre until her father's storm had blown itself out.

Pilar knew nothing of the circumstances of her parents' courtship – not even how they'd met, or how long they'd known each other before they married. In some of the other village houses, there were one or two awkward, wavery black-and-white photographs on display: the happy couple, snapped outside the door of the village church. The men all looked the same: scrubbed, embarrassed, wearing ill-fitting suits. The women, for the most part, wore pretty dresses: some of them a cut above the rest with a pearl button or two, a little bit of lace, here and there some satin ribbon. But there were no photographs in Pilar's house.

All Pilar knew was her mother's prayer over the years that Pilar's life must not be as hers had been. She'd insisted on Pilar's staying on at school until she, too, was eighteen – a battle she had managed to win: her weapons were years of tenacity and lacemaking, along with the money she'd earned cleaning for the nuns. Just as her own mother had. 'Not for a third generation, though,' María Dolores had warned Pilar, shaking her head, her eyes aflame. 'You must break the cycle. You will clean floors for nobody.'

And so Pilar had left. When she took the overnight train to Madrid, she had two addresses in her pocket: that of the nuns' hostel where she would live for the next eight years of her life, and that of Señor Don Alfonso Gómez, who would help her transform the rest of it.

He comes out of his office to greet her. Alfonso Gómez is a tall man, an imposing one, with elegantly greying hair and kind eyes. This man might have been my father, Pilar thinks, and that strange possibility fills her with wonder. She gazes at him, searching for some memory of Paco, some shadow of resemblance in the face that is now beaming down at her. She wonders if Señor Don Alfonso has ever suspected. She will probably never know.

'Pilar. Delighted to meet you at last,' he says, shaking her hand. His grasp is warm and firm. Pilar feels shy, almost tongue-tied. She can't help but compare him to the man who is her father: Papá's blunt, wiry frame, his bullish strength. His hands, with their bruised and broken fingernails, their rough skin. A life's history of burns and cuts traced across their surface, a whole network of roads and pathways of hardship.

Señor Gómez's hands, in contrast, are soft, white, almost hairless, with two gold rings on his slender fingers. Fingers just like Paco's. Pilar catches herself staring, and blushes. If he's noticed, the man gives no indication.

'Come with me,' he says. 'Let us sit down in my office.'

Pilar follows him obediently.

Once seated, Señor Alfonso begins to relive his memories of Extremadura, rhapsodizes about his favourite wines there, praises, above all, his family's pigs, the superior acorn-fed ham that they produce.

Wonderful indeed, Pilar thinks, sourly: such produce is a luxury only for those who can afford it. But she says nothing. Pilar wants to like this man for her mother's sake. She finds herself carried along by his enthusiasm, the way he barely pauses to draw breath. By the time Señor Alfonso has finished, Pilar is at ease.

'And you, my dear, you have settled in well? The hostel is to your liking?'

Pilar is startled. She has not expected Señor Alfonso to be quite so up to date. 'It's fine,' she stumbles. 'Really, it's fine. And I have a job. At the laundry. The nuns got it for me.' It is work that will do for now. Although Pilar doesn't know how long she'll be able to stand the steaming vats of clothes, the unbearable heat of the pressing machines, the gimlet-eyed supervision of Sister María-Angeles.

Señor Alfonso smiles. 'I think we can do better than that.' He looks at her, over the top of his half-moon glasses. 'You are a well-educated girl. A most presentable girl. We will find you something more . . . suitable for a young woman.' He waves one hand in the air, dismissing her current occupation as not worthy of her. 'And if the nuns are not impressed by that, well, then, we will find you accommodation elsewhere.'

'No, thank you,' Pilar says quickly. 'I am happy to stay there. It is very cheap. And I want to save.' She waits for him to ask.

'For something in particular?' Señor Alfonso looks at Pilar. His gaze is intent. She has the impression that he is measuring her.

'Yes.' Pilar draws a deep breath. Memories of Santa Juanita, of the entire Meseta, come crowding. The cold flagstones of winter. The searing heat of summer. The always-present grief of *not having* and its twin sister, the force of longing. 'I want to buy my own apartment someday. An apartment in a beautiful area, with proper heating and air conditioning. And I want all my own things around me. My own front door to close and open as I like. I never want to be poor again.'

Pilar sees herself that winter she was ten, on her knees on the kitchen's freezing stone floor, picking the weevils out of the last sack of rotting potatoes. She can still remember the stench of decay. Despite Señor Alfonso's comfortable office, she shivers.

He nods and Pilar feels the first stirrings of relief. He hasn't laughed at her or dismissed her aspirations as ridiculous. It looks as though he understands, that he has taken her seriously.

'And I can help you,' he says. 'I can certainly help you with that. Madrid is an expensive city, but there are always bargains to be had, if you know where to look.'

Pilar knows from the man's tone that some of that kind of knowledge must certainly be his. She wonders for a moment whether such bargains are similar to those bargains that can be had in the villages around Santa Juanita from time to time: when someone's bad luck, or bad harvest, or bad management becomes the source of their neighbour's unexpected good fortune. The grief that those bargains cause, lasting for generations, like tribal memory. But Pilar can't afford to worry about that. She has herself to look after now, her own life, separate from all those other diminishing lives in Santa Juanita.

Señor Gómez pauses. 'I understand, and we shall discuss such business again, at our next meeting.' He looks at Pilar. 'You and I will be keeping in touch on a monthly basis, my dear. Should you need anything, anything at all in between, you must call the number your mother has given you. It is my private line and I will always be available to you.' Something crosses his face: a shadow of memory, or sadness. Pilar can't tell, but his voice when he speaks again is quieter. 'May I ask if your family are all well?'

Pilar answers politely: she feels that politeness, rather than information, is all that is expected of her. My father works hard, she says, and my brothers, Paco in particular. Mamá has not been well for some time. The doctor is not optimistic.

Señor Alfonso nods as he receives each piece of information. He says nothing, but Pilar feels as though she has passed some kind of test.

When she leaves that day, Pilar feels older, wiser. And she has a plan. She will work at the laundry full-time for as long as she needs. Maybe Señor Alfonso will find her a weekend job, someplace that will pay her cash, under the counter, make it really worth her while. He has contacts, lots of contacts. In the meantime, Pilar will show him how much money she is capable of saving, and he will help her secure her first loan. It is possible, he's promised, everything is possible.

Mamá was right: Alfonso Gómez is a man who can be trusted. The kind of father Pilar has never had. And besides, helping her will be, perhaps, a kind of atonement for his past sins. Father Ortiz was always very keen on atonement. Pilar has listened to his sermons in her village church more times than she cares to remember. But she has learned something, after all, from those

44

long Sunday mornings. She will remember and use it to her own advantage.

Señor Gómez owes Mamá: even if he doesn't realize it.

Pilar floats out of the lawyer's office that day.

Life has begun at last.

Calista

Extremadura, 1989

THIS MORNING, CALISTA FEELS A strange new sense of
serenity. She lies still and watches and waits as the tranquil world
of Sunday begins to unpleat itself all around her, until the local
farms come alive outside her window.

Life in this part of Extremadura has a different rhythm on
Sundays. Everything outside slows, becomes somehow muffled.
Even the dogs bark more quietly. The landscape awaits the tolling
of the church bell, the call to first Mass. Then the day begins.

Calista has dreamed, again, of Alexandros, of that first time
they'd met in Dublin, almost a quarter of a century ago. She cannot
distinguish any longer between dreaming and remembering. Each
bleeds into the other, laying down layer after layer of the sedimen-
tary rock of memory. The day is clear in every detail.

That day in April 1966, Calista watches Maggie as she successfully
negotiates her way through the fish course, the meat course, the
dessert. Even her hollandaise is a triumph. Coffee is served in
the drawing room, tiny cups filled with the sort of heady, fragrant
bitterness that Calista has never learned to enjoy. She's right
about her father's mood. He is celebrating some joint venture
with Alexandros's father, Petros, something that Calista will learn
about later.

As he says goodbye, Alexandros presses something into

Calista's palm, his urgent green eyes warning her not to react. She closes her fingers around it, making sure it remains hidden from view. María-Luisa has a particularly keen eye. Today, though, her mother's gaze has lingered on Alexandros. Calista realizes that, despite herself, María-Luisa has for once been charmed.

'A nice young man,' she says, once Maggie has closed the door behind him.

Timothy rubs his hands together. 'He'll come in useful,' he says. 'I wouldn't say he's the power behind the throne, but he's a handy conduit to his father, nonetheless. Petros Demitriades and I are going to be making a lot of money together.'

María-Luisa links her arm in his and they walk together towards the drawing room. Timothy smiles fondly at his wife and pats her hand. Calista is struck by the new harmony that surrounds her parents today: an unusual ease with each other, as though they are walking together towards a better future. She begins to wonder just how wealthy Alexandros's family is.

'Glad that's over,' Philip mutters, turning towards the stairs.

But Calista gets there before him and races up to her bedroom. Once safely inside the door, she uncurls her hand. Alexandros has given her a business card, just like the ones her father uses. This one is cream in colour, thick, with embossed blue-black writing in the centre. 'Alexandros Demitriades,' it reads. On the bottom left-hand corner, 'Demitriades and Sons'; on the right, a scribbled phone number in blue pen. Calista turns the card over. On the back, simply, 'Call me.'

How different her life might have been had she not done as Alexandros asked. It does not occur to Calista not to do as he has asked. And not just because he *has* asked: already, this after-noon as she gazes at the card in her hand, Calista can feel the sweet swell of danger, a whole sea of exhilarating possibilities.

She opens her wardrobe door and pulls out a cardboard shoebox. Inside, her transistor radio nestles under a wad of crumpled tissue paper. María-Luisa disapproves of the music that Calista loves. And Calista knows she would disapprove even more of the card Alexandros has just given her.

Radio Luxembourg is Calista's passion. She keeps the volume down low, and listens late into the night. Her ear is always on the alert for one of her mother's sudden, unannounced appearances at her bedroom door.

Calista and Philip had both begged to be allowed to see the Beatles when they'd visited Dublin three years earlier. But María-Luisa would not be moved.

'It's not fair!' Calista had cried. 'You dragged us out to see Predident Kennedy when we didn't want to go! You're just being mean!'

And María-Luisa had looked at her fourteen-year-old daughter, her dark eyes flashing.

'That is not the same thing. Not the same thing at all,' she'd said. 'History was being made by the president's visit. Not trashy music. Go to your room.'

Calista had stamped up the stairs, Philip following in her furious wake.

Now Calista slips Alexandros's card underneath the tissue paper. She feels a renewed shiver of anticipation. Her shoebox of treasures contains yet another secret, and Calista is thrilled by its presence. She feels herself beginning to drown in the song of those green eyes. All the years that follow spring from that one, heedless phone call.

Calista rings Alexandros once the weekend is over. She spends a suffocating Sunday with her parents and Philip, her body taut with impatience. She uses a phone box down the road from school, early the following Monday morning. She doesn't dare use the telephone at home: María-Luisa keeps far too close an eye on her for that. For the next week, Calista leaves the house every morning ten or fifteen minutes earlier than usual. In the afternoons, she arrives home from school only a little later than normal – careful, always careful not to arouse her mother's suspicions.

Each time Calista calls him, the words that Alexandros speaks so softly, so insistently, make the whole world tilt. Calista no longer recognizes herself. Sometimes, she forgets where she is, forgets what Alexandros looks like. His voice is enough.

Her mother thinks that she has had a change of heart about her exams, that this last-minute fever of seeming conscientiousness has been ignited by a sudden desire to do well. Calista feels no guilt about feeding this continuing deception: she feels only defiance, mixed with a sense of elation that the term of her imprisonment at home is coming to an end. Freedom beckons. Freedom and Alexandros.

'Meet me,' he says. He's been urging Calista for days. Alexandros does not understand why she has not come to him, and Calista can sense his growing impatience. She is afraid: afraid that he will lose interest, that he will stop pursuing her unless she gives him something to pursue.

'Saturday,' she says, suddenly. 'I can get away next Saturday, but it will have to be in the morning.'

He laughs, that soft laugh that Calista will come to know so well. 'As early as you like,' he said. 'The time of day makes no difference.'

'Where will we meet?'

He gives her an address off Palmerston Road, right in the heart of the most fashionable part of Dublin.

'Take a taxi,' he says. 'That way, it's more private.'

'But I've no money,' she says, dismayed. Calista senses, rather than hears, his laughter this time. She is glad he can't see her.

Suddenly, she feels very young: misgivings are tugging at her underneath the excited thumping of her heart.

'Come for ten o'clock,' he says. 'I'll be waiting and I'll pay the taxi man.'

'All right,' Calista says. Ten is good. María-Luisa plays tennis on Saturdays, leaving the house around nine.

It is as though Alexandros senses her sudden doubt. 'I can't wait to see you,' he says. 'I've thought of nothing else since I met you.'

Calista hangs up, as though the receiver has burned her. She is glad no one can see her face, that no one knows the reason for the sudden heat she feels, the flush that is only partly guilt.

María-Luisa takes forever to get ready on Saturday morning.

'Won't you be late?' Calista asks, taking the plate of scrambled eggs that Maggie is handing her. She is pleased that her voice sounds so calm: polite, not really all that interested.

'Marilyn has telephoned to say she will be half an hour late today,' María-Luisa says. The disapproval in her voice is eloquent. Calista waits to hear her mother say all that she has said so many times before. That sometimes the Irish have no breeding. That punctuality is a virtue. That one must never make commitments one cannot see through. María-Luisa expects things to be as they should. She sees no reason why an external event should have an impact on anyone's life. She turns to Maggie. 'Have lunch ready for one thirty, Maggie, instead of one. There will just be the three of us: Mr Timothy is at the office.'

Calista seizes her opportunity. 'I'm going to the library at school. They're opening on Saturdays between now and the exams. Miss Holroyd is giving an extra class in essay-writing.' She stops. Best not to over-egg the pudding.

Her mother smiles. 'Very well. Fluency of expression is

important.' She nods. 'Maggie will keep something for you if you are late. I think your brother is having a good effect on you.' She bends down, takes Calista's chin in her hand, kisses her daughter on the forehead. 'A *little* learning is no burden for a woman to carry.'

Calista watches as her mother's Ford pulls out of the driveway. She leaps to her feet. Maggie is watching her from the doorway.

'Library?' she says, grinning. She is wiping her hands on her ever-present, ever-grubby pinny. Another bone of contention between her and María-Luisa. But Maggie is sly enough not to invite confrontation: each time she serves at table, she dons a new, spotless apron, its stiff, square folds still visible from having been recently ironed.

'Excuse me, Maggie,' Calista says, annoyed. 'Can you please get out of my way?' She leaves the dining room, takes the stairs two at a time.

When she reaches the landing, Maggie's Longford voice rings clear and true from the hallway below: 'Library me arse,' she calls.

He is waiting. Alexandros is waiting. Calista is filled with an anticipation that energizes her, makes her feel alert and awake and alive.

He is very proper as he helps her out of the taxi. 'Thank you,' he says to the driver. 'You are right on time. It is good to know that my sister has been in such good hands,' and he tips the taxi man generously.

Calista steals a sideways glance at him as he leans through the window of the car, one arm carelessly resting on the roof. It is true: they could be brother and sister. The same dark colouring, the height, even the elegance. Alexandros's clothes are right up to the minute: his dark trousers, white shirt, narrow tie. Calista can see his powerful shoulders, muscles rippling beneath the white fabric. 'Tennis,' he'd said that day at lunch, in answer to María-Luisa's question. 'I like to play tennis in my spare time.' And the laughter when he'd spread his hands wide, indicating innocence. 'I have no vices,' he said. 'I am a good Cypriot boy.'

'Boy?' boomed Timothy. 'You call yourself a boy at thirty?'

And Alexandros had shrugged, the smile never leaving his eyes. 'I am the boy of my family, sir – with three brothers older than I, I am simply the apprentice.'

That day, María-Luisa's eyes had lit up as Alexandros described the reach and the extent of his family business: Petros's shipping company was tightening its embrace around Europe, conquering smaller enterprises, swallowing them whole as it advanced. And all the while, Alexandros's knee was pressed against Calista's and she tried to keep the white heat of his flesh from showing on her face.

Alexandros leads Calista up the stone steps now towards the entrance to the building. He pushes the door open, flourishes Calista into the hallway with one hand. *My territory*, he seems to be saying. *Welcome to my territory.*

His first kiss bruises her. His hand, grasping its way under her blouse, makes Calista push him away at first. 'Stop!' she says. The strength of her own voice startles her.

Suddenly, he understands. 'You've never been with a man before,' he says. It is not a question.

Calista looks at him, indignant. 'I'm only seventeen,' she says. 'Of course I have not been with a man before. What kind of girl do you think I am?'

Alexandros kisses the inside of her wrist, gently. 'That is nice,' he says. 'I am glad that you have chosen me for your first time.' He murmurs endearments she can barely hear over the singing of her blood. His green eyes are brimming. 'It is an honour.'

Has she chosen him? Is that what this is? Is this how people make choices? Calista begins to panic. All at once, she is not sure that she wants to happen whatever it is that is already happening. Alexandros is tugging impatiently at her clothes. Alexandros is silencing her with his kisses. And it seems that Alexandros is the one to have chosen her and that she is, somehow, powerless to resist.

Calista cries out when he pushes his way inside her at last. Alexandros thinks it is with pleasure. Calista feels his weight, the way his body pins hers to the bed. She watches the play of sunlight on his black hair.

'Ah, my love,' Alexandros says. And Calista feels that the pain is worth it.

Pilar

Madrid, 1965

PILAR IS EXULTANT. She can't help it.

Señor Gómez called her to his office last night. Pilar had been startled when Conchita, the surly housemaid, banged on the door of her tiny bedroom at around eight o'clock. '*Teléfono,*' she growled. Pilar had sped downstairs to the hall, where the hostel's payphone was located. Bad news, she kept thinking. Bad news from home. Her one thought acquired a pulsebeat that set the blood pounding in her ears. *I don't want to go home. I cannot go home.*

'Yes?' she said. 'This is Pilar.' Her voice stumbled across the sharpness of the pebbles that had gathered at the base of her throat.

'I need to speak to you urgently. Can you come?'

Relief washed over her. Pilar struggled to reply. Señor Gómez had never asked to see her like this before – all of their meetings were in the mornings, early, by prior arrangement.

'Of course,' she managed at last, breathless. She sped back upstairs, grabbed her jacket and her handbag, and ran back down again. Only then did Pilar realize that she had not asked Señor Gómez the reason for his urgent summons. No matter: she'd find out soon enough.

After eight years of monthly meetings, Pilar trusted this man with her life. And so she kept on running, ignoring Sister María-Angeles's insistent, irritated calling of her name. If she fled now, without stopping, she had a fighting chance of making it back before curfew. Sister and her irritation would just have to wait.

'Pilar,' Señor Gómez greeted her at the outer door of his office, delight spreading across his kindly features. 'Come inside. I have some splendid news. Our bid on the apartment building in Calle de las Huertas has been accepted.'

At first, Pilar couldn't take it in. And then, Señor Gómez's smile, his steady pumping of her hand, her own sudden tears made her realize: she had done it. After eight long years, she had finally done it. She had left her old life behind. She was now, at last, a grown-up at twenty-six years of age. She was an independent woman, properly in charge of her own present, her own future. She needed to answer to no man.

Señor Gómez was, of course, the majority shareholder, but Pilar owned twenty per cent of the building, with an option to buy out her *business partner* over the next ten years.

Pilar loved how those words sounded: she kept repeating them to herself, silently, over and over, feeling the shape of them on her tongue. They made her want to hug someone, although probably not polite, proper Señor Gómez. Even better, it was as though a million kilometres, a million years, now separated her from the village of her birth. *Gracias, Mamá*, she thought. You made it all possible.

'You must be discreet,' Señor Gómez warned her. A client of his, he said, approaching the rocky shores of bankruptcy. The building was something he needed to offload quickly, unobtrusively, before it became too big a bargain for one of his many business rivals. 'You must not tell anyone.'

Pilar almost laughed. Who, she wanted to ask, would she tell?

'You must promise me, Pilar,' Señor Gómez insisted. 'No

whisperings to your young man, or your best friend: this must fly completely below the radar.'

Pilar had been surprised at Señor Gómez's assumption that she had a best friend. Even more so, that she had a young man. Why on earth would she want a young man? Pilar remembered Gonzalo, his breath hot on her neck, his fingers blunt and awkward, painful and fumbling. That, followed by a baby every year until she was forty, even older than forty?

No, thanks.

'I promise,' she said. 'Besides, I don't have a young man. I don't want one.'

Señor Gómez had laughed at that. 'Well, perhaps not just now,' he said. 'I think you have other fish to fry.'

There were already tenants in the building, he told her. For now, it would be the most practical solution for Pilar to move into the living quarters that came with the *portería:* a kitchen, a bathroom, a living area and one large bedroom – located in one of the most fashionable areas of Madrid. That would mean, of course, that Pilar would also take over the *portera*'s duties – the present incumbent was due to retire. Señor Gómez paused. She could see him weighing up the odds that always remained invisible to her.

So. What did Pilar think?

Pilar didn't need to think. Of course she could do it. The duties that Señor Gómez outlined were as nothing compared to the constraints of a life surrounded by dozens of bickering girls, the demands of the nuns at the laundry, the stress of waiting tables at Señor Roberto's restaurant every weekend. Not to mention the night shift at the neighbourhood launderette, endlessly loading the washing machines, folding other people's sheets. She could be a *portera*, of course she could. She could run errands, manage money, take in people's deliveries. Pilar remembered her mother's words: that she was never to clean floors that belonged to other people.

No, Mamá, Pilar thought: if I ever clean floors again, they will belong to me.

She watched the customary slow smile spread once again across Señor Gómez's face. He nodded his approval. Later, he added hastily, Pilar would, of course, want more space, a better job, a different lifestyle. But this would do for now, he said: this was killing lots of birds with one stone. Take things slowly, he counselled. Cut your cloth to suit your measure.

Little by little.

A month later, Pilar packs her things and leaves the nuns' hostel. Sister María-Angeles is less than pleased. 'It is customary to give notice,' she says. 'So that I can find your replacement.' She fingers the heavy rosary beads that gird her habit, cutting her in the middle like one of the copper hoops that encircle the vats in the laundry.

Pilar looks at her steadily. 'A replacement?' she says. 'Your hostel is already full of replacements, Sister. Many of them fallen women. What better replacements could you get?'

Pilar is conscious that Sister Florencia has appeared in the hallway, her slight figure partly concealed by the late-creeping shadows of the January afternoon. She regrets that: Sister Florencia has been kind to her, always, and to all the other girls who work in the laundry. Pilar would have preferred her not to witness her departure, not like this.

Sister María-Angeles cannot contain her anger. 'You ungrateful girl,' she says. 'We took you in out of the goodness of our hearts.'

'Really?' Pilar takes a step closer. 'I think I've paid very dearly for the goodness of your hearts. I've slaved away for you, one way or another, for far too long. All of us here, we're all badly paid, badly treated, badly fed.' Pilar can see that some of the other girls are leaning over the banister, peering down into the hallway. Their faces are terrified with listening.

Good. What Mamá once did for her, perhaps she can now do for some of them. There are times when it is necessary to be frightened, Pilar believes. Necessary to feel the fear of imprisonment in order to grasp for freedom. She raises her voice. 'If that is what you call the goodness of your heart, you can all keep it. I'll wash your clothes and your floors no longer.'

Pilar has the satisfaction of watching a pall of silence gather around Sister María-Angeles. It is almost visible: another wimple that shadows her broad, pale features. Shock makes her outrage impotent.

Then Pilar turns on her heel and leaves, dragging her one suitcase behind her. As she steps outside, she can feel the eyes of Sister Florencia upon her.

She hopes that the young nun will understand. She hopes that she can forgive her. Pilar decides that she will visit her, soon, in the clinic where Sister Florencia helps out, three days a week. She deserves an explanation. She deserves to have all her kindnesses acknowledged.

And now, it is Sunday morning and Pilar is in El Rastro. Here, in Madrid's biggest flea market, there is everything she could possibly want: an Aladdin's cave of furniture, bedding, ceramics, paintings, crockery, cutlery. Not all of it is rubbish, and Pilar has discovered that the past few years of looking and not buying have helped her develop a discerning eye. The stallholders have got to know her, and now they shout over to her, all of them vying for her attention.

She knows that she looks purposeful this morning: she also knows that she looks pretty. She's had her hair done – a French plait with interwoven scarlet ribbons. And she wears a new skirt and blouse, both bargains from last week's shopping. She stands out from the pressing crowd of tired middle-aged women. They look down at heel, those women, with their disappointed faces and their sharp-tongued observations. They poke about the fabrics, turning tablecloths over with disdainful, grubby fingers, rummaging through the stallholders' careful arrangement of their goods. Pilar wonders how these patient men and women keep their sense of humour.

'Look here, señorita, and look no further! Quality you will find nowhere else! Come, come, look and linger – no charge for that.'

And Pilar does look. She looks and she lingers and she drives bargains that please her. She loves the busyness of the market and goes there week after week. And week after week, she transforms her *portería*.

She buys rugs, wall hangings, pretty sheets, lacy tablecloths and napkins. She spends from her substantial savings as she has never spent before.

And then, just as suddenly, she stops.

Mamá taught her that, too. Decide your budget. Stick to it. Don't be wasteful.

Pilar has already been to a proper shop, though, somewhere that sells real antiques, not the bric-a-brac of a Sunday flea market. A few weeks back, she'd put on her best dress and shoes, along with her most confident air and she'd pushed open the door of Alcocer Antigüedades on Calle Santa Catalina.

If the quiet, suited man who greeted her had been surprised at her youth, or at the unusually good quality of her footwear, he gave no sign. He was courtesy itself. He showed Pilar the ceramics she asked to see, and the nineteenth-century furniture that she had read about in the library, and the pieces of sculpture that she ached to touch. He had even handed her some of the pieces, as though he'd already intuited her need. Her fingers had trembled as she'd touched them. She knew it must be vulgar to ask, 'How much?' as there were no prices displayed anywhere, not on the gleaming furniture, or the jewellery, or the paintings. Just a discreet white ticket, tied on with fine string, with the year, the city of provenance and some symbols that Pilar did not yet understand.

'May I show you anything else, señorita?'

Pilar took this as a polite signal that it was time for her to leave.

'Not today, thank you,' she said. 'But I appreciate your kindness. And I shall be back.'

The man smiled at her. 'Somehow, I have no doubt of that,' he said. 'I look forward to it.'

Pilar is as good as her word.

For the next twenty-five years, the shop on Calle Santa Catalina provides her with all that she needs. Pilar loves the scents of the interior, the quiet intimations of luxury, of wealth. The hush that descends as soon as she opens the door, its small bell jangling.

But what she loves most of all is that this is about as far from Santa Juanita as it is possible to get.

Calista

Extremadura, 1989

MONDAY MORNING.

Calista glances at her watch once more: it is eleven o'clock on 17 July. The previous three nights have been a fever of imagining, the days an increasing agitation of waiting.

When will her son call? When will she know for sure?

The transaction was completed on Friday. Calista knows she has not imagined that telephone message. It is over. Everything is now over. So why has Omiros not been in touch?

She paces the living-room floor, her steps measuring its length all over again. Calista keeps her back to the portraits on the chimney breast. The sight of her son's young, smiling face makes Calista grieve all over again. She knows that she has lost him, too, and somehow, his loss feels more final than ever.

Calista stumbles against the side of the armchair. She looks up and can no longer avoid the child's bright gaze. She sits, facing his portrait, and the day unfolds before her once more.

They are in the swimming pool together: she, Alexandros, Imogen and one-year-old Omiros. It is the summer of 1973, and they are in Petros and Maroulla's house in Platres. The early morning mountain air is pleasantly fresh. The pool is empty at this hour and Calista loves having the children to herself before the squabbling cousins descend and the morning's activities begin in earnest.

It is one of those times when Calista can pretend that her days are almost like other people's. Almost normal.

'Look,' Alexandros calls, 'a real water-baby!'

Alexandros is holding on to his son, one large hand placed lightly under the baby's tummy. Omiros is grinning, his small hands slapping the surface of the water, his chubby legs kicking. But it is clear to Calista even then that his movements have purpose. He is propelling himself forward, little by little, until he seems suddenly to remember that he cannot swim and begins to falter. Alexandros scoops him up then, laughing, and Omiros shrieks with delight.

'He is swimming. Did you see? Look, Imogen, your baby brother is swimming!'

Imogen and Calista both cheer and clap, and Alexandros tosses Omiros's small, sturdy body into the air and catches him again easily as he falls, swooping him towards the water and away again, like a small, strange human bird.

'Look at me, Papa!' Imogen calls. She swims towards her father, managing almost the full length of the pool before she tires.

'Yes, very good, Imogen,' Alexandros says. He places Omiros on his shoulders, and the child grasps his father's hair. His expression veers from delight to terror as Alexandros jumps, weightless, up and down, up and down, in the shimmering blue water of the pool. His powerful legs look foreshortened, distorted in the waves he makes.

'Be careful, Alexandros,' Calista calls. 'Don't frighten him.'

But Alexandros ignores her. Calista sees where Imogen waits for her father to turn round, her small face a study in disappointment.

'That's wonderful, Imogen,' Calista calls. 'You've got even further than yesterday. Now try and swim back to me.'

Crestfallen, Imogen obeys. Calista feels the ripples of her own irritation as the child makes her way back to her. Alexandros is here only at weekends. He and Petros arrive together on Friday evening; they leave at dawn on Monday. Saturdays and Sundays are spent in the large family grouping that always converges on the house in Platres in August. Calista has asked Alexandros, tentatively, to make sure that he pays some attention to Imogen; but he always seems to forget until he is reminded again.

'Well done, sweetheart,' Calista says as Imogen reaches her. She kisses her daughter's cheek, scoops her up into her arms.

Alexandros approaches them. He lifts Omiros from his shoulders and hands him to Calista. He holds both hands out to Imogen. 'Come,' he says. 'You and I will have a swim together before the cousins come.'

Imogen brightens at once. Omiros begins to cry as soon as Alexandros moves away from him, Imogen clinging to his back, squealing as they both rise and fall like a dolphin.

Calista tries to comfort her son, but he wriggles and frets and will not be soothed. 'Come,' she says at last. 'Let's go and find Papa.' She holds him close, happy that he is not struggling against her any longer. Together, they follow Alexandros to the other end of the pool.

Afterwards, watching Alexandros and Omiros together, Calista understands that this is how it will always be. Six-year-old Imogen sits on her knee, content; Omiros's eyes follow his father everywhere. With one of those peculiar flashes of future, of illumination, that Calista can never explain, she understands that she will always have to fight for her son's affection. The child's expression even now is serious, intent, as he watches his father towel himself dry.

It is as though he, too, understands how things will always be between them.

Calista presses the heels of her palms, firmly, to her eyes. They feel sandy, gritty, watery, as though she has suddenly been transported bodily back from that long-ago swimming pool in the mountains. She tries to breathe deeply. It feels as though even the room is waiting for Omiros to call. Calista cannot stay here any longer, imprisoned by all these memories. And she cannot keep waiting for the phone to ring. Inertia has never suited her. She needs to do something now, at once.

It is a few days since she has visited Rosa. She should go, or Rosa will be anxious, worried that something is amiss. It is, of course; but nothing that Calista can tell her about. She decides to go this morning, immediately, before Rosa makes her way to her, her red moped a busy insect along the winding streets that lead from Torre de Santa Juanita to the house on the top of the hill.

Calista, above all, wants to avoid Rosa's coming here. Somehow, she feels that in this house, surrounded by all of the family photographs, the truth will force its way out of her mouth and into the horrified air between herself and the young woman she has grown to care for. Calista cannot allow that to happen.

She makes her way down the stairs and picks up her car keys from the table in the hall. She hesitates, just in case, and glances back over her shoulder towards the answering machine. No red light winks; no further message awaits. Not that she had really expected anything, but still. She needs to be alert to all possibilities.

The first time that Calista had met Rosa and the Martínez family, she'd been charmed. 'Welcome,' Rosa had said, smiling. 'Welcome to Bar Jaime. We are so glad you have accepted our invitation.'

It was Fernando who'd insisted that Calista visit the only bar in Torre de Santa Juanita. 'You never know,' he said, 'when you might need your neighbours, and these are the best anyone could have. Very few people in the village get written invitations – I'd go soon, if I were you.' And he'd smiled. 'They're all dying of curiosity.'

Rosa had taken Calista by the hand that first evening as soon as she'd arrived. She'd introduced her to the couple behind the bar, a tall man and a tiny woman in their early fifties, Calista guessed.

'This is Inmaculada,' Rosa said, 'and this is José, my future parents-in-law.'

'You are most welcome, Calista,' José said. 'Inmaculada and I are delighted to meet you at last.'

Calista started then as the door slammed open and a young man staggered in, carrying two crates of beer. He was tall and thin, his black hair thick and unruly. Calista thought that he would be handsome someday, once his features had grown and matured into his adult face.

'Jaime,' Inmaculada scolded, 'I've told you before – one crate at a time. You'll hurt your back.'

The young man grinned at her. 'Still fussing, Mamá,' he said, 'even after all these years.' He turned to Calista. 'Welcome,' he said. 'I'm Jaime, and Rosa has already told me all about you.' He wiped one hand on his shirt and then held it out to Calista. She shook it, laughing. She couldn't help seeing the sudden mix of embarrassment and dismay on the faces of his parents.

'Jaime!' Rosa said, shocked.

He shrugged, grinning at all of them. 'What? Everyone in the village knows that this bar is a hive of gossip.' He smiled at Calista. 'You should know that. It is the staff of life around here. Rosa thrives on it. One day, I tell her, she will grow fat on it.'

'Never mind that,' José interrupted. 'Calista, please sit down and Jaime will serve you some of our best rosé.'

The bar was light and bright and welcoming. Calista made sure to compliment Rosa on the cheerful cushions, the posies of flowers on every table, the checked tablecloths. 'This is lovely,' she said, and saw Rosa light up with pride.

'We want to put our own stamp on it, Jaime and I. José and Inmaculada are very kind – they allow us to do what we wish. You must come and see us here, as often as you like,' Rosa said, her small face vivid with smiling. 'We will feed you tapas and wine and gossip.'

José and Inmaculada joined Calista at the table. Jaime served wine that came from the family vineyard, and all four raised their glasses to Calista.

'Off you go now, you two, and earn your keep tonight,' José said to his son. 'Look after your inheritance.'

Calista still remembers how their conversation was animated and friendly, taking them well into the night. José told Calista about his vineyard, his pride in their slow production methods. 'No shortcuts for us,' he said. 'We want a high-quality product.'

The vineyard would eventually be Jaime's, he told her.

'But not before he gets his university education,' Inmaculada interrupted.

Calista recognized the motherly firmness in her tone. 'It has been a bit of a battle, but we insist. Rosa and Jaime must have something to fall back on. This is not an easy life.'

That was almost five years ago now. Calista can still remember that first evening, a kaleidoscope of impressions and feelings etched clear and deep into her memory. The warmth of José and Inmaculada; the friendliness of Rosa and Jaime; their enthusiasm as they embarked on their first grown-up adventure together. And then there were the greetings of the villagers who dropped in throughout the long evening for a coffee or a beer, unable to hide their sidelong curiosity.

There was a moment, just one, when Calista was afraid that someone would ask her the most natural of questions: 'Have you any children?' But nobody did, and the kindness of that discretion impressed her.

When Calista left, she took away with her a sense of ordinary, daily happiness. It was a feeling she recognized, one of love and optimism, one that recalled her and Alexandros's beginnings, back in 1966.

The year that Calista seemed destined never to leave.

'I am taking you to Howth,' Alexandros is saying, 'to the sea. All the way across the city –' and he waves one arm as though Howth lay on the other side of the world, across vast blue oceans '– where nobody knows us. We can be private there.'

Calista is glowing. It is Saturday; the May sunshine is at its height. She is sitting in Alexandros's sports car, its red metal gleaming in the noon light. She feels free, grown-up, and she is in love. She has also escaped – for a day on Killiney Beach, she has told her mother, 'with the girls'.

Alexandros reaches across for Calista's hand, kisses it. 'You look wonderful,' he says. His voice is soft, his eyes bright with love. 'I cannot wait until we are together, always.' They take a picnic, a basket that Alexandros has filled. It contains bread, cheese, wine, olives. And baklava. It is Calista's first time to taste baklava. Alexandros feeds it to her, morsel by morsel. Calista loves its sweet honeyed stickiness. After lunch, they lie together among the rhododendrons and Alexandros makes love to her slowly, sweetly. Calista can taste the honey on his lips.

Only once during that perfect afternoon does his face darken.

They are talking of their future, of their families, of a life together that is full of promise.

'What is it?' Calista says. The sudden shadow on his face frightens her.

Alexandros comes to sitting. Calista watches him. She feels something inside her tighten.

He begins tearing at the grass, pulling out small clumps with his fingers. Calista notices how the dry, sandy soil still clings to the tiny roots. For a moment, she is dismayed. How has she upset him?

'My brothers,' he says, finally, the words suddenly accented again. 'I have to fight them for everything.' He shakes his head. 'They will not take me seriously.'

Calista wonders. They will not, or they do not already? Sometimes, meaning and nuance stumble and fall between Alexandros's two languages. 'Why not?' she asks.

He won't look at her, but Calista sees that his frown has deepened. 'They are so much older than I am; they think I am not capable of doing all the things that they do.' He shrugs. 'They keep control of the business between them, all of it. They do not leave any room for me.'

Calista is puzzled. 'But aren't you learning extra skills here? That's what my father said. He said the experience here and in London would be invaluable to you in the future.'

Alexandros looks at her. 'My father has sent me away for a year, to perfect my English, to learn how his colleagues in Ireland and England do business. That is all good, as far as it goes. The problem is that in my absence, I cannot know what is happening at home.'

'But . . .' Calista begins. She doesn't know what to say, but senses that some reply is expected of her. And then, just as suddenly as he has darkened, Alexandros brightens again.

'Come,' he says. 'I want to see the fishing boats in the harbour.

I want to feed the seals. I will buy you an ice cream.' And he jumps to his feet, stuffing the wine bottle, the napkins, the remains of the baklava back into the picnic basket. His whole stance is one of impatience. 'Time to go. Come, stand up.'

Obediently, Calista stands. She takes the hand that Alexandros offers her. Before they leave, he kisses her. 'You make me happy,' he tells her. 'I am happy you are mine.'

Calista smiles at him. 'So am I,' she says.

She wants to return to the subject of his brothers, but Alexandros stops her. He places one finger on her lips, silencing her. 'Follow me,' he says.

And she does.

Calista remembers how all those early days seemed to be infused with light. Her first thought each morning on waking was that Alexandros loved her. Her last thought at night was that Alexandros loved her. In between those two luminous moments, her day seemed to shimmer, filled with joy and promise.

'We will be together very soon,' Alexandros would whisper, as they lay in the narrow bed in his Dublin flat. 'I just need to finish my time here to my father's satisfaction.'

'Do your parents know about me?' Calista asks, timidly, one afternoon.

Alexandros lifts her hand to his lips. 'Not yet,' he says, kissing her palm. 'But soon.'

Calista wants to ask, 'How soon?' but she does not. She has already seen the way Alexandros's face clouds over when she says or does something that displeases him. Calista is never sure what it is that displeases him and so she grows careful. She will do anything to keep the love in his green eyes, the tenderness of his embrace, the certainty of his hand in hers.

She worries, too, about being found out. They are very careful, she and Alexandros: they go together to parts of the city that María-Luisa and Timothy would never dream of visiting. But nonetheless, Dublin is small, tight. Everyone eventually knows everyone else.

In 1966, it is also a city without red sports cars. Calista is afraid that Alexandros's extravagance will get them noticed. But he waves away her fears. He will take care of things, he says.

Alexandros knows what he is doing.

Once, though, before the skein of lies unravels, they risk a public outing closer to home. María-Luisa and Timothy are invited to dinner, somewhere in Rathgar, and Alexandros insists that the city centre will be safe for Calista and him to have their first proper evening out together. He wants to show her off, he says. She is lovelier than ever, he tells her, and he is proud to have her on his arm.

Even her father has noticed a change. Somehow, the secret hours in Alexandros's bed have transformed Calista in a way that can be seen by others – even if they don't know what it is that they are seeing.

'You're blooming, my dear,' Timothy exclaims, casting an appraising eye over his daughter. Calista blushes, terrified that her father can see right through her. María-Luisa, luckily, is not there. But Maggie is. In the midst of serving potatoes au gratin, she looks up sharply, catches Calista's eye across the table.

Calista looks away. 'Thank you, Dad,' she says. 'I think I caught the sun this afternoon.'

Afterwards, Maggie is waiting in the hall. She tugs at Calista's sleeve as she tries to make her way past. 'You be careful,' she hisses, and her eyes are full of warning. 'I seen too many girls where I come from bein' sent away for doin' the likes of what you're doin'.'

Calista wrenches her arm free from Maggie's grip. 'I don't know what you're talking about,' she says, her tone more haughty than she has intended.

Maggie lets her go. '*I* know what I'm talkin' about,' she says fiercely. 'I've been fendin' for myself since I was thirteen. I hear stories, all the time.' She pauses. 'An' all those girls – they thought they'd never be caught out neither. Do you want to end up like them – locked away in a nuns' laundry, washin' other people's shitty sheets?'

Calista runs up the stairs, her anger simmering. How dare Maggie. How dare she. She throws herself on her bed, staring at the ceiling. Alexandros has told her not to worry, that he knows about such things. Nothing can go wrong. She can trust him, he says.

He will look after everything.

And now, Alexandros is waiting for her at the end of the street.

Calista watches until her parents' car has disappeared down the driveway. It is seven thirty: she has three full hours before she needs to make her way home again. She waits until Maggie has gone out into the back garden to put the vegetable peelings onto Timothy's compost heap. Then she eases open the front door and flees.

Calista can feel the thump of desire as she makes out Alexandros's dark head at the steering wheel. He leans over and pushes open the passenger door for her. 'You look beautiful,' he says, as she swings her legs in, knees together in one smooth movement, just as María-Luisa has taught her. Alexandros takes her hand and kisses her fingers.

'Where are we going?' she asks, breathless from running and from love.

'We are going to the Trocadero,' he says. 'I have already booked the table. Do you know it?'

Calista shakes her head. She is glad that she has taken extra care getting ready for this evening. Her maxi-dress is flower-patterned, swishy and daring at the neckline. It is yet another secret purchase: María-Luisa has no idea of how her daughter's savings book has come under attack. Calista removed it from her mother's desk, the desk at which María-Luisa sits to write letters to Madrid, to pay household bills, to sail her tightly run ship of domesticity.

Calista hopes that her mother will not discover its absence for at least another couple of months. She refuses to think of this as theft: this is her money, her post office savings book in her own name. She's seventeen, after all. Surely she has the right to spend her own money in any way she wishes? So Calista has argued with herself.

Now she sees the way Alexandros is looking at her breasts. He can't take his eyes off her. The dress has been worth however much it cost. Calista feels powerful and sexy, grown-up and clever. She sits back into the passenger seat, pleased with herself.

Everything about the Trocadero restaurant thrills Calista: the unfamiliar ambience, the candles and white linen tablecloths, the deferential and unobtrusive waiters. She is sure, too, that she can spot several famous faces from the Dublin stage. Last week, Timothy had insisted on taking the family to the Queen's Theatre in Pearse Street to see *The Shadow of a Gunman*.

'Part of your heritage,' he'd said. 'You should get to know O'Casey.' Calista thought that María-Luisa had been bewildered by the play, but she and Philip had both been star-struck.

'But why?' her mother had asked at the interval. 'Why must we see always the violence?'

And Timothy had looked exasperated. 'The play is part of the commemoration of the 1916 Rising, my dear.' His voice had had an unaccustomed sharpness. 'Our children need to understand the history of their country, violence and all.'

María-Luisa had been silent for the rest of the evening.

Tonight, Calista is amazed to find herself in a restaurant such as this, looking as though she dines out surrounded by famous people every night of her life. Looking as though she belongs. Alexandros smiles at her, amused.

The waiter arrives, murmurs a greeting, places menus on the table in front of them. He starts to say something about the evening's specials, but Calista no longer hears him.

A young man has just approached their table. He is tall, fair-haired, well dressed. He is also clearly tipsy. Calista can see him draw nearer, over Alexandros's left shoulder. He leers at her, his unsteady gaze somewhere below her neckline. Calista blushes, looks away as he passes.

Alexandros is watching her. 'What's wrong?' he asks, his hand covering hers.

She shakes her head. 'Nothing,' she says. 'It's just . . . I think that man is a bit drunk.'

Alexandros pats her hand. His eyes narrow as he watches the man move away from them. 'Don't worry,' he says. 'I will protect you.'

Some instinct makes Calista hold her tongue. She feels a crackle in the air, an electrical current that has turned into something as lethal as desire. The tipsy young man, walking back again, has just now stopped at their table. Calista does not need to look up. She can feel his presence, like a cold sigh across her forearm. The hairs on her arm lift; she sees the instant arrival of gooseflesh. And she is afraid.

'My compliments,' the younger man slurs at Alexandros. 'You are in the company of the loveliest woman in the room.' He reaches out one hand; his fingertips graze Calista's bare shoulder. She flinches, draws back from his touch.

Alexandros ignites. He suddenly towers over her, over the tipsy man at her side, over the waiter, and then things get confused. The table leaves the floor miraculously, scattering wine glasses, flowers, cutlery; shards of glass stun the air. And then there is blood, on her dress, on the white linen napkin that lies across her knees, on Alexandros's knuckles.

In the scuffle, Calista cannot tell who is who. The waiters hurl themselves into the fray; she sees them try to separate the two flailing men – although Alexandros's punches seem to land with a lot more accuracy than the younger man's.

And then she is at the door; they are both at the door, Alexandros's rage still flaming. He drags her back to the car. He says not one word until he has pushed her into the passenger seat.

'Don't ever, ever again look at another man while you are with me,' he says. His grip on her wrist is painful, a burning sensation that frightens her.

'I didn't,' she sobs. 'I did nothing. One minute he was nowhere and the next he was standing there beside me – I don't even know where he came from.'

Alexandros releases his hold on her. He cups her chin with one hand, shakes his head, sorrowful at her lack of understanding. 'This is how much I care for you,' he says. 'How much I love you. No other man has the right.' He grips the steering wheel. 'You must never do that again.' And he starts the car.

Calista cannot speak. So this is what love is; this is how true love feels. All that she has just seen now means something new, something that has been transformed, transmuted, translated into an exciting and unfamiliar language.

The fists, the blood, the brawl – these are now tokens of Alexandros's enduring love, of his protection, precious talismans of his devotion. Timidly, Calista reaches out, touches his hand. 'I love you too.'

Alexandros turns and looks at her, but his eyes don't seem to know who she is, or where she comes from.

Then he nods. 'Remember,' he says. 'You belong to me.'

Alexandros drives them both back to his flat. His driving is too fast, erratic: he wavers all over the road. Calista prays that there are no cyclists about for him to run over.

When they reach the bedroom, he doesn't even wait for her to undress. His kisses are almost savage: she feels that he is trying to devour her. But his endearments are passionate and poetic, even if she doesn't understand everything he says. *Mine*, she hears over and over. *My*. Alexandros does not take his usual care that night. Instead, he lies on top of her for a long time after he is finished.

Calista is anxious to go, to get home before her parents discover her absence. Finally, Alexandros seems to understand the urgency and pulls on his trousers, a careless sweater. He hardly speaks.

'Are you angry with me?' Calista asks. She hates the question, hates whatever the smallness is that she can hear in her own voice, but she cannot stop herself from asking it.

Alexandros smiles. 'No, no,' he says, softly this time. 'Not with you. But we must do something to make our situation more . . . appropriate.'

Calista doesn't ask what he means, not then: she needs to go, now, before her parents get home.

Maggie is waiting. Her expression is a mixture of fear and fury. 'Where have you *been*?' she hisses, dragging Calista through into the hall. Her eyes fall on the blood on Calista's dress, the smudgy black traces of tears on her face.

'Jesus Christ of Almighty,' she whispers. Her eyes search Calista's.

'It's not what you think,' Calista rushes to say. 'There was a fight – it wasn't Alexandros's fault. I'm not hurt – this is not my blood.'

Maggie grips her wrist. 'Go upstairs,' she says, 'change your clothes, have a bath and wash your hair. I'll cover for you when they get here.'

Calista is discovered when María-Luisa runs into Sylvie at the tennis club. Sylvie is French; her daughter, Mireille, is in Calista's class. The humiliation, María-Luisa almost spits at her daughter, of finding out that you were not at the beach, or the library, or shopping with Mireille. You barely know Mireille: you have never once called to her house.

'Where have you going?' María-Luisa screams, her rage making her ungrammatical again.

Calista says nothing. She watches as Maggie begins to walk backwards towards the kitchen, her face white and anxious, suddenly smaller. Calista understands that Maggie is frightened that Madam's fury will soon be directed against her.

María-Luisa is shouting now. She turns to glare at Maggie. 'Did you know about this – about the lies, the deceptions of my daughter?'

Calista's eyes caution Maggie, over her mother's shoulder. She shakes her head in warning. 'Maggie knows nothing,' Calista says. 'Leave her alone. If you stop shouting, Mamá, I will tell you.'

Slowly, María-Luisa turns back to face her. The energy seems to have left her body. Her daughter's tone tells her all she needs to know. 'Who is it?' she asks. 'Wait.' She waves one hand in the air, stiffly, in dismissal. 'You may go, Maggie.' Her eyes do not leave her daughter's face. 'Calista and I will continue our conversation in the drawing room.'

And so Calista tells her. During the telling, the air shimmers between mother and daughter. The room doesn't feel big enough to contain all that Calista now has to confess. And María-Luisa is relentless: she will know it all, unpick it all, down to the last detail.

'How long?' she asks. Both of her hands are tight fists at her sides, the knuckles showing white.

Calista can see her mother calculate something when she answers: 'Just over six weeks. Since the day he was here at lunch.' She hears her own voice grow defiant. Calista likes the feeling. It is time she stood up to her mother: she is, after all, an adult, entitled to her own life. And Alexandros is wealthy, well connected, from a good family: all the things her mother has always told her are important.

'Are you pregnant?' María-Luisa asks this so softly that Calista has to strain to hear her.

'What? No!' she shouts.

'You have been sleeping with a man for six weeks. And for six weeks you have lied.' Each of María-Luisa's words resounds; they slap the air. 'How can you be so sure you are not pregnant?'

Calista is silent. Last month, she was safe. This month, she cannot know for sure, not yet.

'You know that you will have ruined your life if you are, don't you?'

Calista digs deep and finds another reserve of defiance. 'We love each other,' she says. 'We can marry.'

Her mother shakes her head. Her face is sorrowful. 'You have no idea what you are talking about,' she says.

'You married when you were nineteen,' Calista shoots at her. 'That's not so different from me, is it?'

'Exactly,' her mother spits back. Her eyes search her daughter's face. 'You have no idea what is ahead of you. No idea at all.'

Two, maybe three weeks later, just as Calista's exams are finishing, comes the certainty. Her and Alexandros's baby is on the way. Calista cannot feel sad about that: this baby is her way out. To a bright new life with her handsome and romantic new husband who loves her to pieces.

But Calista can still hear María-Luisa's howl, all these years later; she can still hear her mother's words when finally she could speak.

'You've made your bed, my girl. And now you may lie on it.'

Pilar

Madrid, 1965

PILAR IS PUTTING THE FINISHING touches to her uniform. Severely cut black dress, starched white apron, black shoes and sheer black stockings. She puts on her tiny pearl earrings and passes one hand over the smooth darkness of her hair. Not even one stray curl. On the upper floor of the restaurant, Señor Roberto is nothing if not exacting. The informal bistro downstairs is another matter: that business is delegated to a manager. Roberto does not feel the need to be so demanding there.

Pilar pins the frothy white cap into place, still convinced – even after all this time – of its silliness. Pilar is not a fan of frivolity. Nonetheless, she checks in the mirror to make sure the cap is on straight, that the grips that keep it in place are no longer visible. Señor Roberto will examine this, as he examines every detail, before permitting his waiting staff to grace the floor of his dining room. He is, perhaps, the only restaurateur in the city who employs women to serve in his exclusive establishment.

Four days a week – Thursday, Friday, Saturday, Sunday – for more than eight years now, Pilar has arrived at exactly five o'clock in the afternoon to begin the preparations for evening service at Number Eleven.

Alfonso Gómez had introduced her to his old friend Roberto almost as soon as Pilar arrived in Madrid. It seemed that Señor Gómez knew everybody who was worth knowing. Pilar became aware of how small the huge capital city really was – something that surprised her – almost as small, in many ways, as Torre de Santa Juanita.

But here, people seemed to be connected to one another in different ways. They were not yoked together by poverty or envy or long-forgotten family feuds over land. Nor were they held together by the simple threads of friendship. Instead, these men – because in Pilar's experience, they were exclusively men – were woven into each other's lives in ways that spelled influence, mutual benefit, the advantages of business deals well done. Discretion was everywhere: a quiet, well-bred guest, present at every gathering.

'Watch and learn,' Alfonso Gómez had told her. 'Watch and learn. Roberto is the best restaurateur in Madrid.'

When Pilar first started at Number Eleven, Roberto had trained her himself. For almost a year, she endured weekend after weekend of exhausting rituals, of punishing, repetitive tests that measured everything from her knowledge of wine and food to her memory for names and faces. Tests that, above all, assured Roberto he could trust her. 'You are ready,' he'd said, at last. 'Table three is yours.' And a wave of his hand flourished his approval. Pilar had looked at him, afraid to understand what she thought she had just heard. Her? Ready? For table three?

Roberto walked away. 'You know what to do,' he said.

Pilar had been filled with a mix of exhilaration and terror. Hidden from the rest of the room, three was the most discreet of all the tables at Number Eleven. From the street, the building that housed the restaurant was indistinguishable from all the other apartment buildings on either side. There was no name, just the number, carved into a rough-hewn block of olivewood. Some patrons booked a table months in advance: their eagerness was palpable. Some had no need to book: those who were preceded by a hush and a flurry of activity in the dining room; those who were shown to their table by Roberto himself.

Pilar also learned that for others, a table would never become a possibility, no matter how long the supplicants were prepared to wait.

Famous faces were everywhere under Roberto's roof. Politicians, members of aristocratic dynasties, men of the Church. Occasionally, there was a woman or two – but only late in the evening, after hands had been shaken, coffee taken, business concluded.

Señor Gómez was a frequent visitor, along with a changing sea of nameless, faceless men who followed in his wake. Their conversations were always in English, a language that Pilar pretended not to understand beyond a few simple phrases, greetings, numbers. Señor Gómez had told her it was better that way.

She felt grateful, and not for the first time, that Señor Gómez had insisted, when they'd first met, that she take English classes at night. 'It's the future,' he told her. 'The business world everywhere will come to rely upon the English language.' He'd looked at Pilar over the tops of his half-moon glasses as he tapped the desk in front of him for emphasis, his gold rings glinting in the light. 'You don't want to be left behind – you are a clever young woman. Go to it.'

And so Pilar did as she was told. And Pilar is still doing what she is told. She watches; she learns; she waits.

On those evenings when Señor Gómez dined at Number Eleven, he gave no sign that he knew her. Pilar glided around the table, served the courses seamlessly and answered all the questions that the guests might put to her.

Tonight, Señor Gómez will arrive with a party of six. Señor Roberto has already briefed her. At nine, the party will gather in the bar downstairs, where an aperitif will be served. They will choose from the menu at their leisure; dinner will be served at ten. 'Very important clients of Señor Gómez. From Cyprus, I understand. Señor Gómez is most anxious that we give them five-star treatment.'

Pilar smiles at him. Almost a decade of following orders has made her brave. 'Don't we always?' she asks.

Roberto allows the ghost of a smile. 'The highest standards are only maintained . . .'

'. . . by demanding increasing levels of excellence from ourselves and from others,' Pilar finishes for him. For a moment, she wonders if she has gone too far. Roberto has a mask that never slips, not even at two or three in the morning when he invites the staff to sit and have a drink with him after all the guests have left.

But tonight, Pilar is feeling giddy. At twenty-six years of age, she has already achieved more in this city than she ever thought possible. Soon, she will tell Roberto that she is leaving. She no longer needs to work so hard. She is now, after all, part-owner of a building: a fully tenanted, fully operational apartment building, something Pilar still cannot quite believe. She cannot tell Roberto this, of course: Señor Gómez would never forgive her. He likes to keep all the different aspects of his life in their separate compartments.

'Business,' he tells Pilar, 'is mostly a matter of not letting the left hand know what the right hand is doing. Play your cards close to your chest. That way, people do not get the opportunity to take advantage.'

Pilar has always followed Señor Gómez's advice: she has taken it to heart with a mixture of gratitude and respect. He has, after all, looked after her interests and made it possible for her to be financially independent, perhaps even on her way to being rich, one day. There are times even now when she needs to pinch herself.

But lately, Pilar has become conscious of a growing

restlessness. She needs to make some changes, to work a little less, to enjoy herself and her freedom a little more.

Roberto looks at her now. He nods his approval. 'You are correct. Ever-increasing levels of excellence. I have absolute faith in you.' This time, he does smile as he moves away. Pilar feels light and almost happy. She walks across the landing to where one of the junior girls, Maribel, has prepared the fresh flowers for table three. Poppies, carnations and a colourful profusion of anemones in white, pink, purple.

'They're beautiful,' Pilar says. 'A lovely combination.'

Maribel smiles. 'Señor Roberto insisted we have something bright and colourful to remind the guests of Cyprus.' She shrugs. 'He wanted carnations to represent Spain. These men are here in Madrid, after all.' Maribel hands the arrangement to Pilar. 'Be careful,' she says. 'I have only just watered the Oasis. Mind you don't spill any on your uniform.'

Pilar walks slowly back to the dining room and places the flowers in the centre of the table. Using her measuring tape, she places each table setting at the appropriate distance from its neighbour. She makes sure the cutlery is spotless, the crystal gleaming, the napkins folded into soft, white petals.

When she is satisfied, she goes down to the kitchen to quiz the chef about the courses that her guests might choose. There is still plenty of time, but she has a lot of detail to attend to.

The first course is almost done. There is a reassuring buzz of conversation around table three. Pilar moves behind each of the seated guests, checking the wine glasses and the water glasses, on the alert for the smallest sign that something might have been overlooked.

The table has settled into two distinct groups. Three heads, on either side of the table, lean closer to each other as words are emphasized, issues teased out, disagreements soothed. The men's voices have become low and insistent. The man at the centre of these two groups leans back a little and lights a cigarette. He glances to his left, towards where Señor Gómez is seated. Pilar is aware of this man's physical presence: it is almost visible, a haze of clear colour. His silence is a powerful one. She guesses – having witnessed similar scenes before – that the others round the table are doing this man's bidding.

Pilar slides a clean ashtray onto the table to the man's right and removes the used one. She is quick, unobtrusive, but he catches her nonetheless. He turns and looks at her, his eyes keen, inquisitive. 'Thank you for the excellent service,' he says. 'You understand English, I think?'

'Yes, sir, a little.'

He nods. 'I should like to know your name,' he says. He continues to look at Pilar, his gaze unwavering. His eyes are dark. They give nothing away. Pilar can see the sheen of sweat on the broad, tanned dome of his forehead. He is completely bald. His goatee beard is neatly trimmed, with occasional glints of grey showing against the blackness.

'Pilar, sir.' She can feel her face begin to grow warm and is suddenly grateful for the restaurant's dim lighting.

'Well, Pilar,' he says, 'my name is Petros Demitriades. I hope we will get some time later to speak about your beautiful city. I am a visitor here. I'd like the point of view of a native.' He leans forward, taps the ash off his cigarette into the ashtray Pilar has placed at his hand. His eyes never leave her face.

Pilar smiles, inclines her head. 'Of course, sir,' she says. 'It would be a pleasure.'

She moves on, aware that his gaze is following her, and she begins to panic. Men have tried to pick Pilar up before, of course, but Señor Roberto has always guarded his female staff fiercely.

But this is different: she does not want Roberto's protection.

She is, all at once, in the grip of a sexual attraction she has never known before. Barely able to catch her breath, she hears the relentless beating of her heart. It thuds against her ribcage, trying to escape. Pilar retreats behind the lacquered service screen for a moment, and furtively wipes her hands on her uniform dress. She doesn't dare crease her apron and instead becomes engrossed in the orders for the main course. Nobody will disturb her here, at least not for a moment or two. Calm yourself, Pilar says. What is wrong with you? Get a grip.

This man is much too old. In his early sixties, at least, although it is impossible to be sure. Tall, powerful, physical.

Get on with it, Pilar tells herself, sternly. Get a move on and do your job.

Señor Roberto looks pleased as the evening draws to a close. He visits each of the tables personally. Pilar admires the way he has a word for everyone, the way he remembers the saint's day of each of his most famous diners, the names of their children, their successes in business, or music, or film. Maribel and Alicia, both junior waitresses, have always been great for cinema gossip: they have recently whispered to Pilar that the great Buñuel himself once had lunch at Roberto's.

Right now, the air is hazy with the blue mist of cigar smoke. Pilar can smell the fumes of Señor Roberto's best twenty-year-old brandy; she hears the notes of discreet, masculine laughter as business is wrapped up and farewells exchanged. Soon, Señor Roberto will close the doors and invite the staff to have a drink with him before the last clean-up begins.

The men from table three leave Number Eleven together. 'Goodnight,' each of them says to Pilar, politely, and she smiles and thanks them, one by one.

'Goodnight, sir – we hope to see you soon again.'

Petros Demitriades is the last to leave. He takes Pilar's hand in his, says her name softly, as though he is trying it out on his tongue. He holds her gaze for what seems like a long time and she is aware of the warmth and insistence of his touch. He hesitates, as though he is about to say something and then, almost regretfully, it seems to Pilar, he turns away. 'Goodnight, my dear,' he says, and walks quickly towards the door.

Pilar feels the jagged edges of disappointment. The night feels flat now, despite the men's generous tips. For once, Pilar does not want to sit with Roberto and the others. She wants to go home.

As she climbs into a taxi, Pilar chides herself. What's the matter with you? she says silently, as they speed through the city streets. Let it go. He's way too old, too married. You don't need complications in your life.

Pilar watches through the grime-streaked window of the taxi as couples make their way home through the slick October streets from whatever night out they've just had. In the grainy light of street lamps, she sees lovers cuddle up to each other, heads bent against the rain. She watches as an elderly man tucks his wife's hand tenderly into the crook of his arm.

'*Señorita?*'

Pilar starts. For a moment, she has no idea where she is. Has she been asleep? Has she dreamed what she thinks she's just seen? Has she snored? Pilar sees that the taxi has stopped outside her building. The driver is looking at her, one arm draped insolently across the back of his seat. He is grinning.

Pilar is angry. How dare he. She pays him, counting out the peseta coins, one by one, into her gloved hand. She gives him the exact fare, pleased when she sees his face fall.

The taxi man is still muttering as Pilar slams the car door and makes her way home.

*

It is early the following morning when Señor Gómez telephones her. There is something odd about his voice: something that sounds both hesitant and unfamiliar. As he continues to speak, Pilar realizes that what she is hearing is embarrassment.

'It is completely your decision, of course,' he is saying. 'But should you care to meet my colleague for lunch, here is the address of his hotel. Petros asks me to tell you that he will wait for you for one hour.' There is a pause. 'He knows nothing of our connection. He approached me most discreetly, let me reassure you of that.'

Pilar imagines polite, appropriate Señor Gómez at the other end of the phone, weighing up the invisible odds that always seem to inform his judgement. She has no idea what to say to him.

'Should you not care to accept his invitation, then simply don't turn up. There is no pressure, Pilar, and no harm done either way. I want you to know that I am merely the messenger. Please do as you wish.'

'Thank you.' Pilar puts the phone down, her face on fire.

She has cause in the future to remember this conversation. Above all, she will remember the phrase 'No harm done.' Harm – that small, coiled, dangerous word, poised and ready to strike.

She wonders how she ever managed to ignore it.

Pilar has decided to arrive an acceptable twenty minutes late. She slips into the hotel ladies' room and touches up her lipstick, runs a careful brush through her hair. She looks at her reflection for a moment, asks herself if she's sure about this meeting, about this man, before she becomes, once again, impatient with herself.

It's just one lunch, for God's sake. Just a lunch in a fancy hotel with an older man who happens to be wealthy. Or perhaps it's the other way round: Pilar is not sure anymore. Either way, why not?

Pilar leans forward, looks at herself in the mirror once again. This time, she holds her gaze for a moment. It may be just one lunch. It may indeed be with a man much too old for her. But one thing is sure: Pilar is acutely aware of the impact that Petros has had upon her. She's just spent a restless night with his imagined presence: all those wakeful hours filled with the way he'd looked at her, the soft way he'd repeated her name, the way he'd held her hand in his as he was leaving the restaurant.

Pilar shrugs, the movement barely perceptible in the enormous hotel mirror. She sees that it has one of those gilt rococo frames that she finds hideous: a triumph of too much money over too little taste.

Enough, she tells herself. It's too late to turn back now.

I don't want to turn back now.

The truth is, it is not just that Pilar has been feeling restless of late. The truth is that Pilar is lonely. Maribel and Alicia have gone, once again, to visit an elderly cousin of Alicia's, and Pilar cannot bear to spend any more dull, endless afternoons in the confines of an old woman's suburban apartment, filled with cats and dust and the oppressive scarcity of fresh air. Besides, Maribel and Alicia speak of only two things. One is work: finding it, keeping it, staying in Señor Roberto's good books. The other is waiters: the swift, slim-hipped, penniless young men who serve in Roberto's bistro downstairs.

Pilar doesn't need to share their worry about work; but she's certainly not telling Maribel and Alicia that. And she's not interested, either, in the doe-eyed young men who have neither class nor conversation. Pilar has become increasingly impatient with all the limited horizons that she sees around her, hemming her in, preventing her real life from happening to her.

She wants something different. She wants someone for herself. The years are slipping by, after all. In four short years, Pilar will be thirty, a thought that horrifies her: unless something changes, she will step across the threshold of her fourth decade without ever having known love.

It is a thought that has become urgent recently, insistent in a way it has never been before. It seems to Pilar that this thought has been lying in wait somewhere, biding its time, on the alert for the slightest opportunity. An opportunity it has now sensed and lost no time in seizing, its arrival as unexpected as it is startling.

Pilar blots the edges of her lipstick one last time, makes sure her dark hair sits alluringly over one shoulder and makes her way out through the door and towards the hotel dining room.

She prays that Petros will be there, that he will not have changed his mind.

He stands up as soon as he catches sight of Pilar. His face is alight as he greets her. 'I'm so glad you came,' Petros says. 'It is a real pleasure to see you again.' He holds on to Pilar's hand a little longer than is necessary, just as he did last night: holds it insistently in both of his. Pilar feels relieved and regretful when he finally lets her go.

They eat; he talks. About his many business interests in Madrid, his friendship with Señor Gómez, his travels, his desire to see Pilar again the next time he is in the city. Would she do him the honour?

Pilar notices that Petros does not mention Cyprus. Nor does he allude in any way to home or family, wife or children. Pilar sees him glance at his watch and the day suddenly falls away from her. He has to leave: it is clear, even without his confirming it. Petros is a busy man.

He sees Pilar's disappointment and mistakes it for hesitancy. 'Take this, please,' he says, pressing a business card into her hand.

Pilar studies it.

Petros smiles and points to his surname. 'De-mi-tri-a-des,' he says. 'Not unlike Spanish in pronunciation – all the letters equally enunciated.' A month, he tells her. He'll be back in a month. 'If you think you would like to see me, just call this number.' And he scribbles a telephone number underneath the official one – 'My private line' – his blue fountain pen scratching its way across the thick white card.

Pilar tucks the business card into her handbag. She already knows that Petros is far older than she is: decades older. But now she sees the years etched into the deep lines around his eyes. Pilar sees how much married he almost certainly is. She sees how impossible all of this most definitely is. But she doesn't care.

Pilar feels this man's physical presence as a powerful, over-whelming, invitation to love. It makes her breathless: she feels as though she has been captured, carried off somewhere from which she will never return. The speed of her own transformation astounds her. She feels, finally, awake and alert and alive.

Over that long afternoon, filled with the promise of adventures to come, Pilar allows herself to fall headlong into a heedless future. It is a future that banishes her reservations, laughs at her denials, turns her certainties inside out like the sleeves of a well-worn sweater.

Pilar is lost that afternoon, and she knows it.

Calista

Extremadura, 1989

CALISTA HAS DIFFICULTY GETTING her key into the lock. Her hands no longer seem to work properly. When she finally manages to push open the front door, she fumbles at the pad for the alarm, getting the numbers wrong. She stumbles across the threshold and drops her bag as she punches in the code for the second time.

Her perfume bottle escapes from the depths of her handbag and shatters on the tiled floor, sending shards of scent and glass everywhere. The air fills with an over-sweet intensity. Calista swears out loud, her voice high and angry in the stillness of the empty house. She feels the familiar twist of anxiety as she walks the five or six steps, quickly, towards the answering machine.

Nothing. There is no red light; no message awaits.

Calista leans her back against the cool wall of the hallway. She slides down onto the floor as a wave of despair engulfs her. She begins to cry at last, tears that have been lying in wait for hours, days, years, waiting for this opportunity to escape.

Calista has been betrayed. No other explanation is possible. Betrayed, duped, lied to: all over again, once more with feeling. It is now midday on Monday, three days since the phone call that reassured her that the deed had been done, the transaction completed, the nightmare over. She'd left Rosa and Jaime just half an hour ago, filled with certainty that finality now awaited her. But it doesn't.

Calista leans forward and rests her forehead on her knees. She is tired, so tired. And all of this remembering is excruciating: a refined form of torture that has her in its grip and will not let her go. She wants it all to stop.

This day – this very day – twenty-three years ago. She can still see herself. A nervous, beautiful seventeen-year-old girl, newly pregnant, newly married: poised on the cusp of an old, old story.

It is July 1966, and they are standing in departures at Dublin Airport, all of them, making awkward conversation until the time comes for Calista and Alexandros to board the plane. Nothing happens in this conversation: everything that is significant, everything that is important is happening underneath the glazed surface of the words they are speaking.

Calista wants to be on her way, wants to leave this life behind, to fall headlong into her new one. She is filled with a delighted optimism. Her new parents-in-law seem welcoming, and this unexpected kindness gladdens her. On the night before the wedding, Petros – whose resemblance to all his sons, but particularly to Alexandros, is remarkable – spoke at length about honour, family, fidelity, responsibility, duty. Calista felt shy as this man held both of her hands firmly in his, his gaze direct and unwavering. She was conscious, uncomfortably so, of María-Luisa and Timothy sitting stiff and upright on the other side of the room.

'We must always strive to do what is right,' Petros said. 'We must love and protect our families and do what is best for our children and our grandchildren; we must never shy away from our duty.' His large face filled with a sudden solemnity. 'I take this opportunity to formally welcome you, Calista, as the newest member of the Demitriades family. Your parents and your brother will always be welcome in our home.'

And then Petros embraced her, kissing her on both cheeks. Maroulla, Alexandros's mother, barely spoke – her English was fractured, at best, but she nodded and smiled, although Calista was not at all sure that the smiles and the nods were meant for her. Because Maroulla never took her eyes off Petros. Her gaze followed him everywhere. Calista was impressed by the older woman's adoration of her husband. She hoped that she and Alexandros would love each other like that, too, their devotion increasing with the passage of years. Calista longed for that kind of love, instead of the precise, careful politeness that her own parents shared.

María-Luisa was impressed with Petros: she couldn't hide it. She put her icy anger at her daughter to one side for the duration of the festivities – festivities that would have been much more discreet had María-Luisa had her way. But throughout it all, Calista watched as her mother was won over by Petros's charm, his generous gifts and his gestures of public extravagance.

'Our sons,' he said, beaming at everyone seated round his table on the night before the wedding. He signalled to the white-coated waiter to bring more Moët. 'They marry only once, no? We must celebrate, all of us, the Cypriot way!'

And now all of the wedding celebrations are over and Calista is anxious to be on her way. As she waits, surrounded by slivers of conversation, she is aware of her new and unfamiliar appearance. María-Luisa is responsible for this, and Calista has been too afraid to fight her. A great admirer of Jackie Kennedy, María-Luisa has chosen her daughter's powder-blue going-away suit, her pillbox hat, her white above-the-elbow gloves and her low-heeled pumps.

Calista still remembers her mother's excitement when President Kennedy visited Dublin in June 1963.

'So handsome,' María-Luisa had murmured. 'And a Catholic.'

They'd stood outside Kingston's in O'Connell Street the day of the motorcade; her mother, Calista and Philip, cheering, waving flags, welcoming the President of the United States. Even though Calista hadn't wanted to go, she found herself caught up in the atmosphere of hysterical celebration. The city – the entire country – had been in a frenzy of excitement.

But María-Luisa's real admiration was reserved for Jackie. 'So elegant, so beautiful, so sophisticated,' she declared, over and over again, until eventually even Timothy said, mildly: 'I think we all know how you feel, my dear.'

María-Luisa had been cross at the interruption, had retreated into a sulky silence for an hour or so, only to hold forth again on Jackie's sense of style, her grace and her fearless individuality.

For Calista, being so fashionably dressed today makes her feel even more conspicuous on Alexandros's arm, although nobody is looking in their direction. She has already glanced around her as though searching for a friend, several times, a ruse to avert her eyes from the knowledge of María-Luisa's stern gaze.

Calista is a *wife*. The word still feels unfamiliar, formal: a bit like her unaccustomed suit and hat, as though it doesn't fit her comfortably yet. She has tested it many times, but its strangeness still vibrates on her tongue. It is such a full word: a language all of its own. It speaks of so many possibilities. A whole new world flows from its four slender letters, a whole new weight of responsibility.

Yesterday, old Father Callery performed the Rite of Marriage, unaware of the extent of Calista's sin. She had gone to confession on the other side of the city, at her mother's urging.

'Father Callery knows you all your life,' María-Luisa said. Her voice, her eyes were cold as she'd pulled off her gloves, finger by unforgiving finger. 'There is no need for you to disappoint him also.'

Calista felt María-Luisa's eyes burn into her back during the ceremony as Father Callery looked at her kindly and said: 'Who can find a virtuous woman?' He paused, then, turning his gaze on Alexandros. 'Her price is far above rubies.' He leaned forward and spoke softly, so softly that only Calista and Alexandros could hear. 'Take care of each other,' he said. 'Alexandros, be good to your wife and love her. She is indeed a virtuous woman.'

Alexandros smiled his brilliant smile. 'I will,' he said. 'I will.'

Husband. Wife.

Standing in the airport now, surrounded by all those she loves, Calista can barely remember her life before Alexandros strode into it in April. Three tumultuous months ago.

'That's us,' he says now. Calista hasn't heard the announcement, but her new husband begins to move forward with confidence. He makes to kiss María-Luisa's hand, but Calista sees her mother pull back a little and Alexandros's lips reach the tips of her gloved fingers instead. He pauses for a moment, then moves smoothly on and shakes hands with Timothy. Calista cannot read her father's expression and his careful, deliberate distance from her now makes her eyes fill.

She knows, too, by the set of her new husband's shoulders that he is offended: María-Luisa's rebuff has made him angry. Calista glances in his direction, hoping that he will not retreat into sullenness on the long flight to Cyprus. Philip approaches and Calista lets go of Alexandros's hand and puts both arms around her brother. 'It's not the end of the world,' she whispers, 'and Cyprus isn't at the ends of the earth. You'll come and see us.'

Her twin hugs her hard. 'Of course,' he says. 'Of course I will.'

Calista doesn't let go. The strength of Philip's embrace brings a memory rushing to the surface, something she hasn't thought about in years . . .

'Come on, Cally,' Philip is saying. 'You can do it.'

He waits, patiently, at the bottom of the slope – the only proper hill in the whole neighbourhood. Its smooth, paved surface leads all the way up to the local shop and Mr Murray, the shopkeeper, turns a blind eye to the dozens of children who practise their skating skills just outside his door.

Philip and Calista are nine, and Calista is trying out her new roller skates. She hasn't yet managed to develop the knack of marrying speed with balance. Philip has already mastered the art, even though skates are not meant for boys. All morning, he's ignored the jeers and taunts of the neighbourhood kids. Calista sometimes wonders if he even hears them.

'Just watch me one more time,' he's saying. 'Lean forward a bit when you're goin' up. An' do everythin' fast – don't think about it.' Philip speeds once again up the slope. He pauses at the top, then races back down with a fearless, elegant grace. When he reaches Calista, he turns swiftly and comes to a halt beside her on the footpath.

'Lady Philip! Lady Philip!' the onlooking boys call out, their words puzzling to Calista.

Philip doesn't even glance in their direction. All he says is: 'The left skate is a bit loose. We need to tighten it for you. Gimme the key.'

Calista watches as her brother straps the metal skates onto her feet, helping her to stand, to find a wobbly kind of balance.

'OK,' Philip says, still holding on to both her hands, 'all you've got to do is move fast. If you slow down, it won't work.' He grins at her. 'You can do it. I know you can.'

Calista nods, unsure. But her twin's belief in her gives her hope. Philip always gives her hope.

'I'll stand here at the end of the slope,' he says. 'Don't worry – I'll catch you if anythin' goes wrong. I won't let you fall.'

Philip pulls her to the top, making sure that Calista stands safely on the flat part just outside the shop door. Then he runs to the bottom of the slope, both his arms open wide. 'OK, Cally,' he says, 'now!'

And suddenly, Calista is flying. Somewhere between the top of the hill and her twin's open arms, she finds her balance. As she speeds towards him, laughing out loud, all Calista can see is the grin that spreads across Philip's face. She can hear his whoop of glee as she approaches. Then she turns, quickly, gracefully at last and, for the first time, doesn't crash to a halt.

Philip hugs her in delight. 'You did it! You did it! I knew you could do it!' He holds on tight for a moment and then pulls his willing sister to the top of the hill once again.

'One more time,' he says, 'and then you won't need me.'

And once more, he held her. Philip held her then just as he holds her now, today, and Calista suddenly doesn't want to let go.

'Come, Calista, it is time we were boarding.' Alexandros reaches for her hand again, holds it a little too firmly. He begins to walk towards the departure gate. Calista has to hurry to keep up with him. She turns and looks back at where her family is standing. María-Luisa has already turned away. Timothy half waves and then immediately follows his wife.

Only Philip remains, his right hand raised in farewell. Her twin's face is no longer itself but just a memory.

Pilar

Madrid, 1966

PILAR IS WAITING.

She has been doing a lot of that, lately. But this is the kind of waiting that is energized, filled with anticipation. It does not at all feel like the early years, full of empty longing, when Pilar was waiting for something – anything at all – to happen. It is, instead, a certainty that something is already happening, already making its way towards her. All she has to do is be ready, to welcome that something when it arrives.

To welcome him when *he* arrives.

He, of course, is Petros, and this is his sixth visit to Madrid since that first night at Number Eleven last October. Pilar remembers the exact number of occasions that Petros has swooped into her city, into her life, enfolding her in his huge embrace. She keeps a diary of their weekends, cramming page after page with the detail of all that he says, all that they do together. She wants to hold on to every moment. Pilar plans to relive every day that she spends in Petros's company. Part of her understands that she is laying down memories for the future: for that time when he will no longer be with her. She wants to postpone that day for as long as possible. The months since they met have become absorbed, one into the other, slipping past in a hazy excess of fine dining, fine gifts and finer sex.

Pilar is in love. For the first time in her life, she is in love. Being in Petros's bed is very different from that rite-of-passage fumbling in Torre de Santa Juanita. That all now seems like another world: poor, young, inexperienced Gonzalo. Pilar pities him and wonders what has become of his life – although she's pretty sure that she can guess at its limits. A life defined by the poverty of soil and struggle and the unforgiving scrutiny of your neighbours.

It is Pilar's delight that makes Petros laugh. 'You make me feel young again,' he tells her as they lie in the vast bed of his vast bedroom. 'You make me into a twenty-year-old all over again, tireless and hungry – always ready.'

Pilar knows, of course, that this is not the truth – or rather, that this bears no relation to fact. Petros is in his early sixties. He is married, naturally. And he has four sons. 'She is a good woman, my wife,' he tells Pilar at last, because she has asked. 'Maroulla and I married very young, and we married because our parents arranged it. That is all. It was a union that was of benefit to both families.' He shrugs. 'That is how things were.'

He leans over, kisses Pilar. 'So even though I am so much older than you, I have never met anybody quite like you.' He strokes her hair, whispers to her. 'And I have never made love like this before.'

Early in the new year, Petros whisks Pilar out of Madrid.

He does this, often without warning: they've left the city on a whim and gone to Granada, to Seville, once to Málaga, where they spent an entire weekend aboard a yacht. Pilar has learned to make her arrangements well in advance of her lover's monthly visits.

Rufina is glad of the extra money and asks no questions. She goes about her chores of mopping and dusting, cleaning and polishing as silently as ever. The woman never complains. Pilar thinks that she is glad of the peace and quiet of the *portería*, one weekend a month.

'Are you sure you can be free, even at short notice?' Pilar had asked her, back in December.

Rufina had looked at her, a little wearily. 'Yes, Señorita Pilar. I am never busy at weekends. My oldest girl can look after the little ones.'

And so Pilar escapes, to the glorious freedom of Petros's arms.

'We are going to Barcelona tomorrow,' he tells her on the night of his arrival in March. 'First thing in the morning. I have booked us into the Majestic Hotel. I think you will like it.'

Like it? Pilar can hardly speak. All that five-star luxury? 'Really?' she says. She can hear how excited she sounds.

Petros is smiling at her. Pilar sees how amused he is and wishes for a moment that she wasn't so transparent.

'Yes. I have a meeting for a couple of hours in the early afternoon. The rest of the day will be ours, and Sunday, too, of course.'

'How will we get there?' She tries to sound calmer, more casual. After all, it looks as though she might have to get used to this.

'By car,' Petros says. 'My driver will be here at six thirty a.m.' He grins at her, his face suddenly years younger, full of mischief. 'So we'll need to have an early night.'

The driver, Quique, is punctual. He waits outside the front door of Petros's apartment building, and Pilar smiles to herself as the elderly *portera* greets them the following morning and opens the door to the street. 'Good day,' Pilar says, smiling. But the woman doesn't acknowledge her. Her eyes slide over Pilar and she greets Petros, instead. '*Buenos días, señor.*'

Pilar doesn't care. She hopes the old bag is watching as Quique leaps out of the Mercedes and opens the car door for her.

*

Barcelona enchants Pilar. She wanders around Park Güell while Petros has his meeting, her mind opening to Gaudí's work in a way that exhilarates her. She loves the Ramblas, which she and Petros walk down together in the evening, hand in hand, stopping off for hot chocolate to ward off the city's cold air.

But above all, Pilar loves the sense of intimacy that develops as she and Petros talk for hours and she listens to all that he says, absorbing everything she can about this man whom she loves with an intensity she has never dreamed possible.

Over dinner, when Petros is mellow with food and wine, Pilar dares to ask him about his family.

He looks at her, his eyes a question. He hesitates before he speaks. 'Pilar,' he begins, 'I—'

She interrupts, quickly. 'I want to know,' she says. 'I want to know everything about you.'

Petros reaches across the table and takes her hand. 'This is a wonderful gift,' he says, 'the time we spend together. But I am not free to love you in the way that you would like. I need you to understand that.'

Pilar nods. She will not allow her eyes to fill. 'I know,' she says. She is glad that her voice sounds steady and strong. 'I know that. We both understand that. But I still want to know about you, about your life when you are not with me.'

He strokes her hand. 'As long as we are clear, Pilar. I don't want to hurt you.'

'I know. I know. Now tell me.'

And Petros tells her of his four sons. 'I am proud of them,' he says. 'Of all of them. Yiannis is the eldest. He will be head of the family business when I retire. Ari and Spyros are the middle two, very close in age. They run the Athens office. And then there is Alexandros, the youngest.'

Petros pauses for a moment and something crosses his face – a shadow that Pilar thinks might be sadness or resignation.

'What about Alexandros?'

Petros waves her question away. 'Oh, he's always been a bit of a worry. A malcontent. He just needs to grow up.'

'What does he do?'

'Right now, he is spending a year between the United Kingdom and Ireland. He is perfecting his English and working with some international colleagues of mine.' Petros draws deeply on his cigarette. 'I hope he is serving a proper apprenticeship. There is a place for him in the business, of course – he just needs to be ready for it.'

Pilar knows by Petros's tone that he will not say more. Instead, he smiles at her, that warm, mischievous smile that makes Pilar's heart sing.

'And what about you?' he asks. 'Don't you want children of your own someday?'

For a moment, Pilar cannot answer. Of course I do, she thinks. But it's impossible. Because all I want is you.

'Someday,' she says. 'Right now, I have other fish to fry.'

Petros has a lavish apartment in the Calle Santo Domingo: in a building that Señor Gómez has helped him find. Petros is pleased with his purchase. The first of many, he tells Pilar. Although his main business is shipping, he believes that a man must diversify.

'It is dangerous to place all the eggs in one basket,' he tells her from time to time. 'The risk is too great. This is something I like to teach my sons.'

And Pilar nods, as though she agrees. Pilar tends to agree with most of the things that Petros says. Sometimes she understands them. Pilar is very happy indeed with how her building is performing and feels no need to diversify.

She understands, too, that Petros will be with her as often as he can, now and into the future. He has promised a longer time together, sometime this year. Perhaps ten days somewhere discreet and expensive. Pilar longs to remind of him of this promise, but she has learned when not to mention it, when to pull back: usually the moment that Petros begins to frown. Not yet, he says; not yet, but soon.

Maribel and Alicia suspect a boyfriend and Pilar has been careful to tell them nothing. It is easier to be careful, now that she no longer meets the two young women at Roberto's. He, Roberto, was regretful at Pilar's decision to leave Number Eleven.

'I shall miss you,' he said. 'But nonetheless, I understand. Remember, there will always be a job for you here, should you ever change your mind.' To Pilar's astonishment, his eyes filled as he took one of her hands in his and kissed it. Then he looked her right in the eye. 'He's a lucky man, whoever he is.' And then he let her go.

Pilar was speechless. She wondered whether Maribel and Alicia might have spotted something that night back in October. It would have been hard for anyone to miss Petros's imposing presence on that evening. Casually, she made sure they looked in another direction.

'It's just somebody from home,' she insisted. 'Not really a boyfriend. More a childhood friend.' She tossed her head, then, showing lack of interest. 'Besides,' she said loftily, 'he's much too young. I'd never be interested in someone that young.' She saw Alicia and Maribel exchange glances, saw their unwilling admiration of her sophistication, and she turned away, smiling to herself.

And now Petros is here, once again. It is May, and summer is bursting to the surface, all over the city. Pilar knows just how that feels. She and Petros are spending this weekend here, in Madrid. He has been travelling a lot and he is tired. Pilar is glad. She likes looking after him, loves it when he needs her.

When Pilar is with Petros, the great disparity in their ages no longer seems to matter. He has energy, vision, endless ambition, as though these qualities have increased and intensified over the years, rather than diminished. It is as though the accumulated wisdom of each decade stands on the shoulders of its predecessors, driving Petros forward, ever forward. Petros has no interest in a quiet life.

'I will retire eventually,' he says, 'and pass on my business to my sons – Yiannis is most capable. But for now, I enjoy too much what I do to give it all up.'

Pilar breathes again. She does not want to think about what Petros's retirement might mean for her. She is afraid to tell him, in the same way that she is afraid to confess how much she loves him. She takes consolation instead from the fact that he is not yet ready to 'give it all up'. In there, she believes, somewhere between the 'it' and the 'all' is where she, Pilar, is placed. She wants to stay there for as long as she can. The thought of life without Petros is painful, sometimes unbearably so.

From time to time in her small apartment, particularly late at night when the noise from the street keeps Pilar awake all through the endless hours until dawn, she allows herself the fantasy that Petros will marry her someday. For this to happen, his present wife will, of course, have to die.

The first time Pilar thinks like this, she is taken aback at her callousness, startled at the ease with which she despatches this unknown woman. But as the fantasy becomes more insistent, more elaborate, that moment of guilt is all the more easily dismissed.

Old people die, Pilar reasons. It happens all the time. It could happen to whatever-her-name-is – María, Marina, Maroulla – suddenly and without warning. It really could.

And so Pilar lives her life from one weekend a month to the next. She cares for her building and looks after her residents. She writes the occasional letter to her father in Torre de Santa

Juanita and goes to the cinema with Maribel and Alicia when she has nothing better to do.

And in between, she waits.

Calista

Extremadura, 1989

FOR SOME TIME NOW, Calista has made no effort to move. The possibility that she has been betrayed, that Alexandros still lives and breathes, is a possibility that paralyses her. She sits on the floor, surrounded by the air of defeat that insinuates its way into the house as the afternoon stillness intensifies. She looks at the groups of photographs that cover one wall of the hallway: her photographs, her work, the work that had gifted her the first real sense of herself that she had ever experienced.

Calista recalls the patient lessons with Anastasios, the reverence with which he handled the camera, the tranquil air of his studio, where Calista's confidence had finally started to bloom. Back then, she had taken dozens of black-and-white portraits of her children as they grew.

Here is Imogen's first day at school. Here, Omiros's first, faltering steps. There, Imogen on her first bicycle, arms flung wide in triumph as she finally gets her balance. And just below, Imogen on her father's yacht, already steady and sure, a miniature sailor in Alexandros's arms.

Calista stifles a sob as images of her daughter's life come crowding.

It is 14 February 1967.

Calista gazes at her baby's face. She reaches out and takes

one of the tiny hands in hers. The baby lies in the cradle beside Calista's bed, her small fists clenched at either side of her face, as though ready to do battle with the world. Calista is surprised all over again at the strength of her daughter's grip. Only a day old, she thinks, and already she is grasping at life.

'I'll look after you,' she whispers to the dark, downy head. 'I will always protect you.'

Alexandros, Petros and Maroulla are Calista's only visitors after the baby is born. Alexandros had hovered outside the delivery room for hours last night, occasionally putting his head round the door. When he sees his daughter for the first time, his face softens, and then he looks suddenly unmoored, bewildered and clumsy, as though he no longer knows what to do with his hands. It is the first time Calista has ever seen her husband at a loss.

Petros, on the other hand, arrives as if he owns the hospital.

The moment she sees him, Calista feels on edge. He is as jovial as Maroulla is quiet, reserved. 'Well, well,' Petros says, 'a girl.' Calista has only a few dozen words of Greek, but this is one of them. *Koritsaki*: little girl.

Petros says it a few times, as though he can't quite believe it, as though he's expecting someone to contradict him. Calista waits for her father-in-law's congratulations – waits for either him or Maroulla to say something kind, anything at all. But instead, there is a silence, one that not even Alexandros looks poised to break. Finally, Petros claps one hand on his youngest son's shoulder and says, his tone hearty, consoling, forgiving all at once: 'Never mind! A boy next time, eh?'

This, Calista has also understood. Maroulla shoots her daughter-in-law a look. The look says: *It's not worth it. Say nothing*. But Calista can't help herself. She feels indignant on her daughter's behalf – on her own behalf, and on Alexandros's. So what if all of the grandchildren are girls? Isn't Petros lucky to have such a healthy brood? Calista looks towards her husband, about to beg him to respond, but he turns away from her for just a moment, and looks at his father. His face is shadowed by something that Calista cannot read.

Maroulla says something that Calista doesn't catch and Alexandros turns round towards her. Then he begins to translate his mother's words.

'Such a lovely little girl,' Maroulla is saying. Her hand cups the baby's soft cheek. 'Have you decided on a name for her?'

'Yes,' Calista says. She glances over at Alexandros and attempts a smile. 'I wanted something Irish for her – or at least Celtic. My mother called me after someone in her family, from generations back, to remind me that I'm half-Spanish. I want our daughter to know that she is part-Irish. I think we all need to be reminded of where we come from.'

Maroulla nods and smiles as Alexandros translates Calista's words once more. She says something softly to her son and he bends down at last, touches his new daughter on the forehead and smiles. 'Her name is Imogen,' he says. He kisses the baby and takes Calista's hands in his. 'She is wonderful,' he says. 'And so are you.'

At that moment, Calista is filled with love for her husband. It is a love that feels relieved, grateful. This baby will make everything better.

When Calista had first come to Cyprus, almost seven months earlier, a new and glowing bride, she'd been thrilled with the excitement and optimism of this new place.

Soon after she arrived, Alexandros took her away from his parents' house for a whole, delightful, five days.

'Come,' he said. 'We will spend our honeymoon touring the villages of Cyprus. I want to show my island to you. I have booked us a hotel in Lefkara.' And he smiled his brilliant smile. 'Lefkara is special. You will soon see why.'

During those days, the places she and Alexandros visited together cast a spell on Calista. The sun shone out of that blue, clear light that filled an enormous sky. Each village intensified the sense of ancient magic that she felt was still alive all around her.

Lefkara was a tumble of old houses, the local stone glowing and warm to the touch. Crumbling steps led up and down the narrow arched streets; cafes nestled in the shadow of hills. Everywhere there were huge terracotta amphorae, the bright red blooms of poppies and geraniums spilling out of their open mouths.

Women still made lace in Lefkara, and Calista was reminded of her grandmother in that brooding apartment in Madrid, her elderly head bent over the intricate design of the family's tablecloths, centrepieces, christening robes. Here, too, Calista could see elderly women bent over their tasks: their work delicate, the colours light, the patterns exquisite.

Walking hand in hand with Alexandros in the evenings, Calista saw her husband's island as an enchanted place. Ireland seemed grey and flat and dull in comparison. She loved the exotic growth, the lushness of colour everywhere. It was as though life here was lived in harmony, with the volume of some internal music turned up.

But all at once, out of nowhere, homesickness fells Calista. A sense of loss assaults her with a savagery that leaves her reeling.

After their honeymoon, back once again under Alexandros's parents' roof, nothing is familiar. The food feels oily and strange; the heat is hostile. Ari and Spyros, along with their wives, Eva and Dorothea, have all returned to Athens and their absence makes the large house feel empty. Although Eva and Dorothea have only a little English, they are warm and funny in a way that Maroulla and Petros are not. And they gossip, furiously, about their husbands' family.

From them, Calista understands that her parents-in-law are anxious that their eldest son marry. 'Yiannis is old,' Eva tells Calista, shaking her head. Her brown eyes are large with the sincerity of her amazement. 'He almost forty. He must have wife.'

'Why doesn't he?' Calista asks. She has wondered this herself.

Dorothea shrugs. 'He work. Too much.'

And Eva shakes her head. 'No. He does not find good wife here.'

Calista is puzzled. 'Do you mean nobody is good enough for him?'

Eva brightens. 'Yes! No woman good enough.'

Calista grows more curious about Yiannis. She wonders what sort of a man he is. Alexandros had been stung that his eldest brother had not attended their wedding.

'Isn't he in Asia somewhere?' Calista had asked. 'It's a long way to come, at such short notice.'

But Alexandros would not be appeased.

When Ari and Spyros return to Athens with their families, Calista misses their noisy, welcome distraction. Alexandros is gone from early morning until late in the evening: all day, every day.

Maroulla is occasionally kind in that casual, offhand way she has, once the two women are alone together. But she, too, has her own life, with friends and family and comings and goings that do not include Calista.

By the end of September, Calista feels that she is the only one *without* a life of her own. And she still has at least four months to wait for her baby to arrive.

During the long afternoons and the restless nights, Calista dreams of the cool, familiar rooms of her Dublin home.

When Philip's letter arrives, Calista cries for a full morning. Her twin is a good correspondent. He writes regularly, affectionately, and his news is lively and witty:

Oxford is astonishing. I can't believe my luck. I'm settling in well, and Michaelmas term begins in a week or so. I've already met some of my lecturers, and I'm in the college residence with a couple of guys who seem decent enough. They tease me about my Irish accent, but I suppose that's only to be expected. I can't wait to dive headlong into philosophy – I feel as though I have found my way at last.

I miss you, Cally – and I know that the parents do, too. But we will come and see you as soon as the little one is born. I find it hard to believe – but happily so – that I am about to become an uncle!

Don't forget to send me photos – I think where you are is a lot warmer and sunnier than where I am.

Love always from your 'better half' – you once called me that. But no more, I think: I am so happy that you now have Alexandros in your corner.

Write very soon.
  Philip

Her twin's letter makes Calista feel suddenly suffocated. No longer by the heat, but by the oppressive smallness of her life. She feels hemmed in by her parents-in-laws' house. She needs to escape with her own new family to a place that is theirs: a home just for her and Alexandros and their baby. But Alexandros gets impatient with her every time she brings it up. After the last time, she doesn't mention it again.

'Not yet, Calista. I keep telling you. My father says I must prove myself before I can have a house.' Alexandros had looked at her then, and something in her face seemed to make him relent. He sat at the table across from her, took her hand. 'You have to try, too, you know? It upsets my mother to see you so sad all the time.'

'I know,' she said. 'I just can't help it.'

She misses having Philip for company during these long and empty days; she keeps seeing his face at the airport on that July afternoon as they'd all said goodbye. Calista even misses having her parents to fight with, and she misses Maggie. Maggie, that fund of information and conversation; that knowledge of a world way beyond Calista's horizon; all that easy, familiar companionship. But above all, she misses a life she is unable to define, a life suspended somewhere beyond her reach.

Maroulla speaks some sentences of halting English, Calista has little Greek, and sometimes the strain of day-long silences drives her to the bedroom that she and Alexandros share, immediately after lunch, pleading exhaustion. It is easier than trying to make herself understood.

As Calista lies on her bed during these slow afternoons, windows shuttered against the sun, the air heavy with heat, she begins to wonder if this is what her mother meant.

If this is to be her bed for the rest of her life, the bed she's made for herself, after all. The bed she now must lie on.

Pilar

Madrid, 1966

SISTER FLORENCIA HAS SAID SOMETHING, but Pilar hasn't heard her. The young nun's eyes are troubled, the words she speaks sound soft and compassionate, but Pilar has no wish to understand what she's saying.

'I'm afraid there is no doubt, Pilar. You are pregnant. Perhaps fifteen or sixteen weeks – have you not felt any quickening?' Sister Florencia places one hand on Pilar's abdomen. She looks anxious.

Pilar takes her hands away from her ears. It's no use trying to pretend any longer. Petros told her so many times not to worry, that he knew about such things. That he would never let this happen. What is she going to tell him? What will he say?

At first, Pilar has denied the evidence. Periods can be erratic for all sorts of reasons, as she knows from her experience in the past. Perhaps she is run-down again, tired, anaemic: it happens. And it has been a particularly busy few months, with some changes of tenants, some unpleasantness about a flood, the need to call the police to intervene in a loud and bitter domestic dispute. So yes, that's probably all it is. Overworked, exhausted, lacking in iron. Her mother had always been a great believer in iron.

'Quickening?' she asks now, uncertain. It feels like an ancient word, as old as life itself. Although Pilar cannot remember having heard it before, she suddenly understands exactly what it means.

Sister Florencia nods. 'Yes – just very faint movements, like fluttering.'

Pilar rests her head in her hands. She cannot look Sister Florencia in the eye. Perhaps three weeks ago, at the cinema with Maribel on one side and Alicia on the other, Pilar had felt faint, but discernible, tremors deep inside her somewhere: a sense of the flapping of tiny wings. Given where she was seated, she could not show panic. Instead, she sat still, rigid, her eyes on the screen, oblivious to the comedy that so delighted the audience. Pilar can't even remember the film's name anymore. All she remembers is that it was one of those nonsensical comedies about love triangles, the sort of film so beloved of Maribel and Alicia. Something about love's enchantment, Pilar realizes now, bitterly.

Even then, she knew. And the past week or so has confirmed it. The growing tautness of the skin on her breasts; the tiny appearance of fine blue veins; the annoying swelling of her ankles. And then there were those tiny shiftings, always increasing in intensity, that kept her alert and restless at night as she waited for them to happen again, needing to be sure that they were real. With each agitated hour, her terror grew. It was desperation that drove her, eventually, to seek out Sister Florencia's clinic. At least there, she knew, she would be treated with kindness.

Petros has not been to Madrid for more than three months. His business has taken him elsewhere, he says. He telephoned Pilar once, recently; his voice was soft, apologetic.

'I am sorry, truly I am. I have some pressing business matters to deal with at the moment. I don't know when I'll be in Madrid again. I will let you know immediately, of course, if things change. But right now, there are some difficulties that demand my attention.'

What about me? she wanted to cry. There are some difficulties here, too. What about me?

Pilar could feel her panic grow, its fingers closing steadily round her throat. She couldn't tell him her suspicions, not over the phone. In all their time together, Petros has never once told Pilar that he loves her. Despite her resolve, Pilar has told him, many times, but has promised herself – and Petros – that she will never make any demands.

The rational, adult part of Pilar understands whenever Petros reminds her that he is, after all, a married man, a family man, that he is not free to love Pilar in the way that she would wish.

But she had hoped. God, how she had hoped.

Pilar clutched the receiver to her ear, trying not to panic. Then she was angry – not so much at him as at herself. Just another stupid woman, she raged. How could she not have taken her mother's words to heart? To live her life unbeholden to any man.

She knew that she must not make Petros angry with her now. If she made him angry, she might never see him again. Her voice, when she heard it, was both strained and shrill. 'For how long do you think? I mean, how long will your business take to fix?'

There was a silence. When he spoke, Pilar could hear the disapproval in her lover's tone. 'It will take as long as it takes,' he said.

There was another, lengthy silence. Then Petros spoke again, his voice kinder this time. 'I know you are disappointed. So am I. I will come back to Madrid just as soon as I can. In the meantime, you have my private number. I should be back in Cyprus at the end of this month. Call me then and we'll see.'

'Pilar?'

She looks now into the kind eyes of Sister Florencia. 'Yes.' She can hear the heartbeat of defeat that pulses low and steady beneath the surface of that single word.

'I can find you somewhere, a place where you can have your baby.' Sister Florencia takes her hand, grips it firmly. 'I will help you find the courage. Afterwards, there are many good families looking for children, Catholic families who can give your baby a good home.'

Sister Florencia is offering Pilar a solution of sorts. A solution that is still some months into the future, a very different future from the one Pilar has been imagining, but nonetheless, she can feel the flood of relief that it brings with it. Perhaps, just perhaps, her life might not be over forever because of this. She might be able to survive, after all.

But for one fractured moment, Pilar wavers. A baby. Perhaps a baby – *his* baby, after all – might sway Petros. He had spoken often to Pilar about duty, about responsibility and loyalty. Might his own child – albeit one born out of wedlock – be enough to lure her lover back to her?

And what if she were to keep the child, anyway, Petros or no Petros? Pilar imagines the sudden, defiant shape of the baby in her arms, the sweet weight of its downy head, the warm softness of its skin. She shakes herself, wrenching the thought away. A sob struggles at the base of her throat, smothered in something gritty, like sand. No. Impossible. Completely. Impossible.

Señor Gómez. The tenants, the neighbours, the people at the market. The priest. Maribel and Alicia. Petros. Even her family. The shame of it all. Pilar shudders.

She will tell none of them. Not ever. Particularly Petros. She will plough her own furrow, just as Mamá had always told her.

'What do you think?' Florencia is waiting.

'Will I be able to keep on working in the meantime?'

'Of course. You are tall; you are very slim – your clothes can help to hide it for months. But there is a clinic you must go to right away – I'll give you the address. It's for—'

'Fallen women,' Pilar says grimly. And she remembers Sister María-Angeles, her face on the day that Pilar had stormed out of the hostel. Won't *she* be pleased? Pilar thinks. Another arrogant, sinful, wayward girl finally brought to book by God. Pilar no longer believes in God, but nonetheless, she is impressed by His capacity for revenge, or punishment, or whatever it is that brings a small life such as hers to a sudden full stop.

Sister Florencia looks at her. 'No. Please don't think of it like that. The clinic is for you – for your health and the baby's. This will be the greatest gift you can give your child.'

Pilar's eyes fill at last. Baby. Child. Yours. Pilar doesn't know if she can bear it. She fights for control. When she speaks, her voice is steady. 'I don't want anyone to know,' she says. 'Nobody at the hostel. I'll go to the clinic and I'll go wherever you say to have the baby, just not there. You have to promise me.'

Sister Florencia nods. 'I promise. I promise that I will keep your secret for you. Come to me for help at any time. I will never turn you away.' She hands Pilar a piece of paper.

Pilar wants to thank her, but she can't. She feels that if she opens her mouth, she will howl. Instead, she glances down at the address Sister Florencia has handed her. An address in one of Madrid's poorest barrios. A piece of paper that has been many times folded, just like the one Mamá had given her almost ten years ago, its surface ghosted with flour. How long ago all of that feels, that day when she'd fled Torre de Santa Juanita for Madrid, in search of a better life.

A life that was not to be an echo of her mother's. A life constructed only by Pilar. A life that was not to be defined by any man.

Pilar puts the piece of paper in her handbag. She does not want to think about Mamá right now, or about her escape to Madrid, or about Señor Gómez. She most particularly does not want to think about Petros, about all the parallels that are looming up at her, like the hard, straight tracks of a railway.

Her life has not been an escape after all, she thinks. Just the same old journey as her mother's, begun at a different station but ending up in the same place.

Right now, those metal tracks are bars that have constructed a cell, a prison of Pilar's own unhappy making.

At the end of September, Pilar summons the courage to call Petros's private line. She knows that he is never at the office in August. He retreats – his word – to his family and his home in the mountains, somewhere called Platres. Pilar prays that he will answer his phone.

He does, and his voice is confiding and regretful: 'I have to tell you, Pilar, that my youngest son, Alexandros, got some young girl pregnant. It was not wholly unexpected, but my wife and I are most unhappy with the situation.'

Pilar hears the click and hiss of a cigarette being lit, smoke being drawn deeply into the lungs.

'They are married now and living here with us. We had to do the honourable thing. I'm sure you understand. My family needs me now. I will speak to you again, when I can. But I want you to know—'

Pilar slams down the phone. Petros's words feel as though they have chiselled their way into the air around her before hammering themselves into her skull.

My youngest son got some young girl pregnant.

So has his father, she screams, silently. So has his father. But she is the only one who can hear the pounding of blood in her ears, the taste of fear in her mouth.

At that moment, Pilar knows, bitterly, that she is on her own.

In February 1967, the child is born.

His eyes are pools: brilliant sea-green eyes. His hair is black, and stands up in a comical series of tufts on the crown of his head. His face seems to Pilar like that of an old man, wrinkled, careworn, wise. For a newborn, he rarely cries.

Sister Florencia is with Pilar again this morning. She has wrapped the baby in a soft blanket and hands him to his mother. 'Just for a few minutes,' she whispers. 'It is important to say goodbye.'

Pilar feels that her insides have turned to stone. Numbness is preferable to the two days since his birth: raw hours of endless, blunt pain, knowing she will never see this child of hers again.

Pilar brings her lips to the baby's forehead. 'His name is Francisco-José,' she says. 'After my eldest brother – but he is not to be called "Paco".' She looks at Florencia, her eyes are fierce. 'This boy will have his full name, his full life. Will you tell them that?'

Sister Florencia nods. 'I will tell them of your wish, of course,' she says. 'They are a nice young couple. Your son will have a good life.' Her hands are gentle. 'Let me take him, Pilar. If you hold on too long, it will become all the harder to let him go.'

Suddenly, she is gone, Francisco-José along with her. Her black habit swishes round the open door; it closes immediately behind her. The last glimpse Pilar has of her boy is the trailing end of his baby blanket, a bright exclamation of loss against the dark serge of Sister Florencia's habit.

Pilar wails. It is a sound that carries her along on its swelling tide. It is something that exists independently of her, bigger than she is, more alive than she is. She feels a pair of arms around her, the warmth of a woman's voice in her ear.

'Be strong,' the woman whispers. 'You will get over this, I promise you. Just as I did.'

Pilar looks up, startled. The woman smiles. 'My name is Enrica,' she says. 'My baby was born here ten years ago. I survived. You will, too.'

'How.' It is not a question. Pilar's voice is flat and dull. Tears pour down her cheeks and she doesn't bother to wipe them away. The world is empty now.

'Work. Family. Friends. Keeping busy.' Enrica places a tray on the table beside Pilar's bed. 'I've brought you some soup and bread. Eat, just a little. And we'll talk.'

When Enrica leaves at last, summoned sharply back to work by one of the nuns, Pilar becomes aware of the other girls who now come to surround her, their hands, their words, their meaningless, flapping attempts at comfort.

Pilar bats them all away, her arms flailing, her body thrashing around the bed.

Then she turns her face to the wall.

Calista

Extremadura, 1989

CALISTA STRUGGLES INTO STANDING AT LAST.

Her legs have begun to feel stiff and sore, and one of her feet has gone to sleep. There is no point in sitting here on the hall floor any longer. She needs to get a grip. To do nothing is dangerous.

Calista pauses for a moment and massages the sole of her foot, feeling the blood begin to circulate again, its sudden, tingling return to life almost painful.

The shattered perfume bottle still lies on the floor where it fell. Calista steps over it carefully. She'll deal with it tomorrow. She'll deal with everything tomorrow.

She climbs the stairs, one hand on the banister, and makes her way towards the living room. It is not her usual time of evening to have a drink, but Calista no longer cares. She pulls open the cupboard door and pours herself a large measure of whiskey. She paces the room, glass in hand, and lights one cigarette after another. She is far too restless to sit. She glances out of the window and sees what usually soothes her: the evening light is softer, kinder, as the air acquires its end-of-day stillness. The landscape has not yet shaped itself for night.

As Calista pauses at the window, her eye is caught by a small figure in the distance, its busyness in direct contrast to the tranquillity of the fields and the olive groves that surround it. Calista stops for a moment and looks more closely.

It is a woman, an elderly woman in black – no doubt a

widow who has dressed in this way ever since the death of her husband, possibly decades before. Calista doesn't know her, but she knows who she must be: knows of the extensive Domínguez family to which she clearly belongs. The elderly woman below her now begins sweeping outside the house with a concentrated vigour. The brush arcs around her with an efficiency that is the product of a lifetime of cleaning. A lazy veil of dust rises and the woman becomes only partly visible. Just as suddenly as she began, the woman stops her busy sweeping. Then she shrugs, as though answering some inaudible command. She turns stiffly and disappears inside the house, closing the door behind her.

Of course, Calista thinks. The concentration, the vigour, the energy, despite the stiffness in the knees. They all remind her, suddenly, of Maroulla, of her tirelessness leading up to the day of Imogen's christening. It was a lavish affair. Petros and Maroulla spared no expense.

Their large garden was transformed into a flower-filled, shady expanse with what seemed like hundreds of people coming and going, pressing gifts into the new parents' hands.

It was also, of course, the time when Calista first met Yiannis. That momentous week in July 1967.

Yiannis arrives home three days before the christening. He is to be Imogen's godfather and he comes laden with all the traditional gifts: clothes and jewellery for the baby, a gold bracelet for Calista.

Calista is in the shadiest part of the garden, playing with Imogen now that the evening air is cooler. She looks up as Alexandros calls her name. He is walking towards her, away from the house, and there is another man at his side. Instantly, Calista knows who he is.

Maroulla has been fussing for days. Everything inside and outside the villa has been prepared for Yiannis's return. Watching their approach, Calista is struck by the ways in which this man is different from Alexandros. It is clear that the two are brothers: Yiannis is as tall as Alexandros; his build is similar, but his physical presence feels calmer, quieter. Nor does he have Alexandros's brilliant green eyes. His face is kind, Calista thinks.

She wonders now whether Alexandros has at last forgiven him for not attending their wedding. She stands up at once, gathering Imogen into her arms. She holds out her hand. 'You must be Yiannis,' she says, smiling.

'Yes, indeed, my big brother, another important man,' Alexandros grins, slapping Yiannis on the back. Calista is not convinced by the show of affection. Alexandros has lingered a little too long on the word 'another'.

'Calista,' Yiannis says, bowing his head and taking her hand in his. He bends as though to kiss it, but stops just short, reminding Calista of Alexandros's similar gesture on the day that they'd first met. It startles her: not so much the gesture as the feeling that that first meeting now seems like centuries ago.

Yiannis leans towards Imogen, his face already broad with smiling. The baby responds, her eyes locking on to his. Her normally serious expression softens at last and she smiles back. 'And this is my new niece.' Yiannis looks up at Calista. 'Imogen, isn't that her name?'

'Yes – and you are privileged. She doesn't smile at just anyone!'

'A beautiful name,' Yiannis continues. 'It is good to remind children of their heritage. And a beautiful little girl, too, of course,' he adds hurriedly.

'Well, you'd have to say that, wouldn't you? You're going to be the doting godfather and I'm the new mother. It would be rude of us not to think her beautiful.'

Alexandros laughs. 'I can see that the two of you are going to get along,' he says. 'I will leave you here to get acquainted. I must go to my father. He needs my help.'

Yiannis nods and Alexandros walks away, quickly. As he leaves, the air seems to thicken with something other than the fact of his departure. Neither Yiannis nor Calista says anything. It is he who breaks the silence at last.

'Come,' he says, 'let us sit down. I was very sorry not to be able to attend your wedding, but I'm afraid I was in the middle of some serious negotiations and I simply could not get away.'

Calista likes the way he acknowledges this. 'Well,' she says, surprised at her own archness, 'it was all rather sudden, you know.' And she grins at him.

He laughs again, nods his head in a kind of quizzical agreement that makes him look much younger. 'So I've heard. Nothing wrong with that. I'm a great believer in youthful passion.' He looks around. 'I think you could do with a glass of champagne. I certainly could. May I get you one?'

Calista nods. 'Please.'

'Back in a moment.'

Calista watches as he walks back towards the house. She hears the sound of laughter inside and is grateful for the excuse that the cool garden gives her. She prefers to be here.

'So, now you're home again in Cyprus,' Calista says lightly, as Yiannis returns to the table. She accepts the glass he hands her, nods her thanks.

'Indeed.' Yiannis smiles at her. 'Home at last. I've missed it. It's not easy being so far away from everyone.' He raises his drink to her; Calista tips hers to meet it. There is the muted chink of glass on glass.

Home indeed, Calista thinks. I wonder do you know, Yiannis, what your parents are hoping and planning for? She has already overheard several conversations between Petros and Maroulla about their hopes for their eldest son's future.

Calista also knows that Imogen's christening party will be an opportunity to gather together all the young, eligible, well-connected women that her parents-in-law regard as suitable daughter-in-law material. Calista has heard the names, has been able to put two and two together. It has made her angry, the way that they stop discussing the subject whenever she, Calista, is present. It's as though she is the mistake that they wish to avoid repeating.

'It must be difficult for you, to be so far away from home, particularly at a time like this,' Yiannis says.

Calista is surprised at his directness. And grateful: Alexandros has never acknowledged her homesickness. He becomes impatient when she speaks of Dublin as home. 'Yes,' she says. 'It is difficult.' She turns her face away for a moment. 'Imogen makes up for so much, but –' and she shrugs. 'I never really understood what home was until I left it.'

Yiannis smiles. 'I am familiar with that feeling. Sometimes it is a physical ache.' He looks at her. 'Negotiating another language can be difficult, too. Alienating, even.'

He understands, Calista thinks. He really understands.

'Yes,' is all she can manage.

He leans towards her. 'If you feel that there is anything—'

Maroulla has suddenly appeared beside them. Calista is startled. She has not noticed her approach. She speaks rapidly to Yiannis, and Calista knows by her tone that she is displeased.

Yiannis stands up. He smiles at Calista. 'We must go in. Some guests are arriving. All are anxious to see Imogen. Come, we'll talk later.'

Calista is reluctant to move. She regrets leaving this conversation, almost before it has begun.

'Who *are* all these people?' Calista asks on the day of the christening, bewildered, looking around at the groups of well-dressed strangers sipping champagne, laughing and devouring canapés.

Alexandros sighs. 'Calista, you must concentrate, try harder to remember.' He gestures around him. 'These are all friends of the family, cousins, neighbours, many business associates of my father. My father is an important man, you know.'

Calista does indeed know. Calista cannot help but know. She is reminded of this fact, the fact of Petros's importance, all the time. Today, there are businessmen, everywhere, talking business. There are women, too, of course, but they float around the edges: they revolve round the centre, bringing drinks, smiling; taking care of children, smiling. Stepping carefully across the grass in their high, expensive shoes. And smiling, always smiling.

For one sharp, intense moment, a moment with bitterness biting at its jagged edges, Calista wishes she was not surrounded by quite so much importance. She longs, instead, for the presence of her own family, a family that now feels loving, ordinary, unremarkable. A family that is, above all, hers.

Philip's frequent letters have helped to keep Calista company during the past year; she is happy that their closeness has continued, nourished by the words they write to each other. Philip's new life in Oxford feels oddly familiar to Calista, sometimes as familiar as their shared past life in Dublin. He helps her to imagine his days: days crammed with friendships, with studies. *'And as for the sense of freedom,'* Philip wrote to her recently, *'I can be myself here in a way I never could in Ireland. That is the biggest gift of all, Cally. To be able to live my own life in my own way.'*

María-Luisa and Timothy telephone her each week. Ever since Imogen's birth, Calista has felt a sea change in her relationship with them, particularly María-Luisa. 'Now,' her mother had said to her, shortly after Imogen's birth, 'you have your own daughter; now you will understand.'

All three of them have arrived this morning. Calista loves showing off how much Imogen has grown since they last saw

her as a tiny three-week-old baby. A baby who even then had a
serious gaze and a mind of her own.

On that occasion everyone, including María-Luisa, had been
charmed. Calista was happy that day, watching as her mother
thawed. Philip grinned over at his sister and gave her an emphatic
thumbs-up.

María-Luisa was shocked, though, at the prospect of such a
long delay between Imogen's birth and her christening.

'You cannot wait for another five months, Calista, surely!'
She did not attempt to hide her agitation. 'The child needs to
be baptised at once. Such a delay would be unthinkable in Spain,
even in Ireland. What is this about?'

María-Luisa often got upset around her children's religious
observances. Back in Dublin, as young teenagers, Calista and
Philip would often avoid Sunday Mass together, each swearing
the other to secrecy. They knew their parents trusted them: to
disobey filled them both with a mix of guilt and defiance. Here,
in Limassol, Calista had fainted, on two successive Sunday mornings, at the lengthy Greek Orthodox services. '*Three hours long*,'
she'd written to her twin. '*Can you imagine? And we thought half
an hour was bad!*'

Maroulla had decided that Calista should be excused from
the services, at least until the baby was born. To Calista's relief,
Alexandros had agreed. Calista was still hoping to use her small
daughter as an excuse not to attend for another few months.

'It's the custom here, Mamá. We will wait for the summer
to christen her, when Yiannis returns, and the weather is fine.
He's to be her godfather: that's the tradition. Imogen was born
in Cyprus: we must follow Cypriot customs.'

María-Luisa did not look convinced. Timothy intervened and
the conversation was not pursued any further.

'Besides —' Calista smiled at her '— it means you will all have to come back again and share the day of the christening with us. That can't be bad, can it?'

She feels relieved when the christening party is over and all the guests have gone. The day has been crammed with people. Now, Calista relishes the silence. She likes the still evening air that has settled over the garden. Her parents and Philip have just gone back to their hotel.

Calista sees Alexandros at the other end of the garden, deep in solitary conversation with his father. She hopes that he will not do anything to spoil what remains of today. His temper is getting shorter. Calista believes that she is not the only one to have noticed. From time to time, she sees the sharp glances that Maroulla throws at Alexandros, the quick frown, the abrupt shake of her head when she manages to catch her youngest son's eye.

Yiannis comes to sit with her. 'A lovely day,' he says, smiling at her. 'But you must be tired by now.'

'A little.' Calista waits for him to speak again.

'I'm sorry that we were interrupted the other night. I was enjoying our conversation.'

He pauses and Calista has the sense that he is weighing his words.

'You know that my father is retiring in a few months' time.' It is hardly a question. The whole island knows. The preparations for the three-day celebration are already well underway.

Calista nods.

'I am the eldest,' Yiannis goes on. 'I am just about to turn forty. My father finally thinks I'm adult and experienced enough to take over the business.' He glances over to where Petros and Alexandros are sitting.

'I see,' Calista says. She already knows this. Everybody knows this.

'His age and pressure from my mother have meant that my father has finally agreed to retire. She is concerned about him. He has been travelling far too much recently, and she worries about his health.' Yiannis looks at Calista now and there is a question in his gaze. He waits for her to speak.

'I understand that,' she says, at last. 'Of course. It's natural that you would take over the business. But there *is* something that I should like to ask you.'

Yiannis inclines his head. 'Please, ask me anything at all.' Again he waits, and Calista is unsure how to phrase her question.

I am now a father, Alexandros had ranted to her recently, his face alight with anger, *and still my brothers treat me like the office boy.*

'What about Alexandros's future?' Calista asks.

Yiannis looks at her, measuring her. 'What do you mean?'

'Isn't there a place for him?'

'Of course there is a place for him. A very specific place, already with his name on it. He knows that. But before he can call it his, Alexandros must learn the ropes, just as I had to.' Yiannis pauses. 'This is how we do things, Calista. Alexandros needs to learn patience.'

He leans towards her and she sees that Yiannis's brown eyes are kind. They regard her keenly. He lowers his voice, even though there is no one close enough to them to hear. 'We are very conscious of Alexandros's new responsibilities. He will not have to wait for long; but he needs to learn more . . . tactful ways of doing business, both within the family and outside it.'

Calista lowers her eyes. There is nothing she can say.

'I have offended you. I am sorry,' Yiannis says quietly. 'I shouldn't be telling you even this much, but it is difficult . . . May I be honest with you?'

Calista nods, looks up at him again, quickly. 'Yes, of course, please do. I'd like you to be.'

'I have taken this opportunity to speak to you, when perhaps I shouldn't, but I understand that it has been very difficult for my mother and my father to see you and Alexandros so . . . unsettled. We are doing everything we can – perhaps it is Alexandros himself who needs to do a little more.' Yiannis is speaking more quickly now.

She feels her eyes fill, but she will not turn away from him. 'I know,' she says, at last. 'I know that Alexandros needs to do more. Thank you for telling me.'

Calista has begun to walk more softly around her husband in the last few months, particularly since Imogen's birth. She is wary of giving his anger a chance to ignite. Sometimes, it ignites anyway, and Calista never knows what word of hers, what look, what gesture has lit the fuse.

And there was one time, just the one. . . but Calista doesn't want to think about that now. Besides, Alexandros was so sweet, so remorseful afterwards. It will never happen again, she knows that. She has Alexandros's word.

Yiannis takes a business card out of his wallet. 'Here,' he says. 'Have this. This must be a confusing world for a young woman not schooled in our ways. I will help you navigate the waters in any way I can.'

'Thank you.'

Once the days that surround the christening are over, Calista escapes more and more. Haridimos, the sweet, elderly driver who has worked for Petros and Maroulla for decades, takes Calista and Imogen under his wing. He speaks to Calista in slow, patient Greek, and takes the time to teach her the words for simple, everyday things.

'Would you like to go to the beach with Imogen?' Alexandros asks her, at the beginning of the blessed cool of October. 'My mother has suggested that Haridimos drive you. It is beautiful at Evdimou and Pissouri at this time of year. You will like it.'

'Yes,' Calista says at once. She is keen to leave the house, to feel the sea breeze on her skin. To breathe easily again.

Haridimos takes Calista to the turquoise-coloured waters of Evdimou on that first day. The beach is almost deserted: there are only a few, scattered families with small children along its silky sands. Haridimos makes sure that the parasol is secure, that Imogen is sheltered and comfortable.

From him, Calista learns the words for 'sea', for 'sand', for 'swimming'. She tries them out, over and over again. *Thalassa. Ammos. Kolimbo.*

'Good,' Haridimos keeps nodding. He smiles at her. 'You learn good. You learn very good.'

Imogen loves the water. She shows no fear. For a full, freedom-filled month, Calista goes wherever Haridimos suggests. He drives a little further each time. Once, he takes her to Kakopetria, right in the middle of the island. 'My village,' he tells her.

Calista meets his cousins, his elderly neighbours, the local priest. High in the foothills of the northern Troodos Mountains, Calista learns that the village name means 'the Evil Rocks'.

'Life very hard,' one of the villagers tells Calista. Rocks had to be cleared from the harsh land before crops could be planted. In many ways, the village reminds Calista of the more desolate parts of Connemara in the west of Ireland, a place she had visited while still a schoolgirl.

Once, as Calista sits reading in the living room, Imogen asleep beside her at last, she hears Maroulla's approach. Her mother-in-law's high heels clack across the tiled floor; Calista has come to dread the sound. She glances at her own bare feet and feels immediately guilty. She puts down her book. What has she done wrong now? Calista can see the determination on her mother-in-law's face, in the purposeful way she puts one foot in front of the other. In the way her hair lifts away stiffly, blackly, from her pale, broad forehead.

Calista sighs. She should be familiar with the feeling by now: that of always falling short. Earlier, Imogen gave in and finally slept in the cradle at her mother's feet. Calista has, all along, resisted the idea of a nanny. She wants to look after Imogen herself, she says, at least for the first year or so. She has not won that battle, not yet, but she senses, for now at least, Maroulla's indulgence. The truth is that Calista is afraid to let her baby go. She has no one else. As long as she is responsible for everything about Imogen's life, she has someone to hide behind.

The last several months have been exhausting, and although Calista tries really hard, it seems that Alexandros does not understand. They spent the whole month of August in Platres, in Petros and Maroulla's house in the Troodos Mountains, escaping the cruel heat of Limassol. Ari and Spyros, along with Eva and Dorothea and all their daughters, came and went with bewildering frequency. They were all casually kind and welcoming and busy and absent: it was a dance, and Calista felt that she would never learn the steps, never move with grace and freedom through all these unspoken relationships and obligations and fallings-out and -in again. She was drowning in family. Ever since their return to Limassol, Alexandros has been working a lot, and Calista has sunk gratefully into the silence and serenity of his many absences. Instead, she reads. Philip sends her parcels of books: *The Complete Works of Shakespeare*, the plays of Oscar Wilde and, recently, novels by Iris Murdoch.

Now, as her mother-in-law reaches her, Calista is aware of the book in her lap and the way the words still burn behind her eyes. She hopes that Maroulla will go away: the fictional waters of *The Unicorn* in which she, Calista, has been floating are much more startling and compelling than her real life. But Maroulla looks even more determined. Calista can see that her mother-in-law is stitching some sentences together before she speaks.

'This morning,' she says finally, and Calista can see that she is struggling to explain. 'You go, Hristina. She come now, for you.'

Calista is at a loss. 'What?'

Maroulla becomes impatient. 'Hristina, good friend. Daughter. You go.' And she starts to shoo Calista off the sofa.

Calista has no idea what is expected of her. But now Maroulla is smiling. She's waving her hand in the air, apparently at the black helmet of her recently waved hair. 'For hair,' she says. 'For hair.'

For her? Calista thinks and then the light dawns. 'Hairdresser?' she says.

'Yes!' Maroulla looks triumphant.

She wants me to go to the hairdresser, Calista thinks. What on earth . . . ? 'But Imogen—'

'I stay, I stay,' Maroulla insists. 'You go. Have coffee. Some shopping. Go.'

At that moment, the doorbell rings and the maid, Agathi, ushers in a tall, elegant young woman. Hristina's white suit is faultless. Her eyes are warm as she greets Maroulla. She kisses her on both cheeks, and there is a rapid exchange in Greek, none of which Calista is able to catch. As long as the conversation is slow and pedestrian and deliberate, Calista manages to understand and to make herself understood. She spends a long time getting her questions right, can even ask them with confidence, but she is all too often dismayed by the speed and complexity of the response.

Now Hristina turns to face Calista. 'Hello,' she says in English. 'We have met once, perhaps twice before – but always too many people.' She smiles. Calista can see that the smile does not reach her eyes. 'I am Hristina, a friend of the family. I come to spend this morning, this afternoon with you.'

Calista knows exactly who she is. She is one of those elegant females that Maroulla would like as a daughter-in-law. Calista begins to bristle. She doesn't want to spend the morning with Hristina. What she'd really like is to spend some time with María-Luisa, or Maggie. Or Philip: particularly Philip.

Why can't all these people just go away and leave her alone?

At that moment, Imogen shifts in her cradle, murmuring in her sleep, her small thumb making its way towards her mouth. Hristina glances down at her. 'Such a lovely baby,' she says. 'You must be so proud.' She looks away almost at once, her gaze resting on Calista's face.

'Thank you.' Calista begins to soften, as she always does when she looks at her baby, this new and magical being that has suddenly arrived and taken over her life. A life that seems to have shrunk in size even further: a life defined by feeds, nappies, cries, whole nights of disturbed sleep. This young woman dressed in white has brought something else from the outside along with her: the air of a larger universe, one that Calista has barely thought about.

And then she thinks: Why not? Maybe Hristina is nice enough, and it might be good to get away from the house, just for a little while.

Maroulla is now beaming. 'You go, yes?' Her eyes are kindly, Calista realizes. She feels this kindness as an almost physical shock. The woman is trying to help. 'Thank you, Maroulla,' she says. 'It is very good of you.'

But Maroulla waves her off.

In the car, Hristina says: 'Maroulla worries that you spend too much time alone.' She glances across at Calista. 'The baby is now eight months, no?'

Calista nods. 'Well, nine,' she says. 'It has all been so fast, I can hardly count it. To be honest, it feels like a bit of a blur.'

Hristina pulls out onto the main road. 'You must do other things, too,' she says. 'I am very happy to show you around, to take you to the hairdresser and, afterwards, perhaps some shopping? And some friends of mine will meet us later. Perhaps we will take an aperitif together.'

She glances at Calista's dress and Calista sees herself just then as others must. The realization startles her. Her cotton dress is cool and easy to wear, but it now looks dull and shapeless. She feels embarrassed when she compares herself to Hristina's cool, tailored whiteness. No wonder Maroulla has decided that enough is enough. For a moment, Calista wonders what María-Luisa would say, and she's sure she knows the answer.

'Shopping?' she says. Calista hopes that she doesn't sound stupid, but there is something missing here. Shopping means money, and Calista does not have any money.

'Yes, of course, shopping.' Hristina smiles, but she doesn't look at Calista. She keeps her eyes on the road ahead. 'I will take you to Aggelopoulos in Agiou Andreou Street – and then we can charge whatever you choose.'

'Charge?'

Hristina looks surprised. 'To Alexandros's account.' She glances towards Calista. 'Perhaps,' she says carefully, 'perhaps Maroulla did not have enough English to explain. You buy whatever you need in the shops. I will show you where. When you decide what you want, all you have to do is sign in Alexandros's name – you do not need to have any money. Do you understand?'

Calista nods. Of course. The memory of María-Luisa's weekly trips to Switzer's and Brown Thomas in Dublin comes back to her. She is angry at herself.

'But first, we go to Agni's in Agia Zoni. It is the best hairdresser's in Limassol.'

'That would be great, thanks,' Calista manages. And then, in a rush: 'Have you known Alexandros and the family long?'

Hristina takes a moment to answer. Calista feels that there is something happening here. It is a ripple, an eddy, an undercurrent of cool water that has washed through her words, trailing silence in its wake.

'All my life,' Hristina says. 'Our two families have always known each other. Alexandros and I grew up together.' She indicates, turns right and drives towards the city centre. Her face is a mask, Calista thinks. Beautiful, with dramatic dark-painted eyes, but unreadable.

'How do you like Cyprus?' Hristina says. Calista knows that the subject has been changed.

'It's beautiful,' Calista says. 'It's very different from home, and I think I'm still getting used to things. Sometimes it's difficult.' She is surprised at the unexpected honesty of her admission. She doesn't allow herself to think about all those things that are difficult. Calista feels her eyes begin to fill and she turns away, looking out of the window at the bright, fashionable shops that line this Limassol street.

'It will take time, I am sure,' Hristina says. 'But you have Alexandros to help you, and his family are very kind.'

Do I? Calista wonders. Is Alexandros helping me? Kindness is occasionally in the house: it usually rests with Maroulla, sometimes with Petros, but Calista rarely feels that it is directed specifically at her.

'Here we are,' Hristina says, pulling up outside Agni's hair salon.

Through the large, plate-glass window Calista can see a man – tall, bearded, animated – place a black cape around a young woman's shoulders. He leans forward for a moment, listening to something the woman is saying. Then he takes the woman's long hair in both his hands and pulls gently backwards, as though measuring its length. Dark hair, just like Calista's; long and shiny, just like hers.

Calista freezes. She cannot help it, cannot stop the memory from breaking the surface of her willingness to forget. It suffocates her. She tries to breathe; her fists clench in her lap of their own accord. Her hair, hurting. The way her head jerked backwards, the pressure of his fingers, strong and cruel on her throat. And afterwards, Alexandros's sobs. His kisses. How he had never meant to hurt her.

Forgive me, forgive me, he cried. *I don't know what came over me. It will not happen again, not ever.*

And then, the exquisite calm that had descended. Alexandros loved her once more. And Calista had forgiven him, of course she had. They faced forward together, filled with future. It would be their secret. A secret to be put behind them at once, never to be mentioned again, even to each other.

'Calista? Are you all right? Can you hear me?'

But it is not Alexandros's voice. Confused, Calista looks round. Hristina's brown eyes are puzzled; they search hers. 'Are you all right?' she repeats.

Calista tries to compose herself. Of course, she is here, in a car, outside a hairdresser's on an ordinary November morning. She is embarrassed. 'I'm sorry,' she says, 'I just got distracted. I'm fine.'

'Are you quite well?' Hristina asks. 'Would you like some water, some coffee, anything at all?'

'No, really, I'm fine,' Calista says, hurrying to open the passenger door. As she steps out onto the solidity of the pavement, she remembers her honeymoon. She remembers the streets of Lefkara where she and Alexandros walked in the evening, their life stretching before them, a bright wave of promise. But another life has taken its place and Calista is frightened. She feels words gathering and has to fight the temptation to blurt them out.

At that moment, Hristina turns, holding the door of the hairdresser's open for her. 'Let's go,' she says. 'Let's make you even more beautiful for Alexandros.' She smiles, touches Calista lightly on the arm. 'You are the envy of the whole island, you know,' she says. 'We all adore Alexandros.' She gestures towards the interior of the salon.

And so the moment passes. Calista walks by her, watches the approach of a blonde woman in a salmon-pink overall. There are greetings, kisses, nods and smiles, and Calista thanks María-Luisa's God that she stayed silent.

What was she thinking? Of course such confidences were not possible. There are standards to be maintained: some things must never be shared.

Besides, it was just the once. Only once. And never to be repeated. Alexandros has promised. Calista will do what is asked of her: she will help him keep his promise. She will wait and she will be patient.

Above all, she will hope.

Calista remembers how this day set the scene for many more that were to come. The hairdresser, the manicurist, the dressmaker. Over the coming months, she learns to slip into the routine that has already been shaped and prepared for her. It is another new dress, of sorts, tailored whitely to perfection.

Maroulla greets her daughter-in-law's transformation with delight, that first day: claps her hands together as Calista returns wearing a new pink silk dress, her hair waved and glossy, her nails painted. She is able to show the swatches of material that Hristina has helped her choose: fabrics selected after much discussion at Pafitis, delivered to one of the many tailors that line the streets around Agiou Andreou. Calista has been measured, discussed, dissected, nodded and smiled at.

On his return that evening, even Petros signals his approval. When Alexandros sees her, he is wide-eyed. He takes Calista to bed and it is as though nothing has changed since those early days in his Dublin flat. Calista is dizzy with relief. Alexandros loves her again.

This is the answer, she realizes. Of course it is. How could she have been so stupid? It is up to her, now, all of it. She must keep things right. She must fit in, adapt, be beautiful. If only she had known it was something as simple as this.

And so time passes.

Calista organizes fundraising lunches with Hristina and her friends Thegnosia and Evradiki. She shops. She begins to pick up more and more phrases in Greek. She agrees, finally, to a nanny for Imogen. She even bows to Maroulla's choice in this: Eleni, a woman in her early forties, small, dark, not at all attractive to men. Calista meets her mother-in-law's eyes that afternoon, the afternoon when the choice is finally made, and nods her agreement.

She understands. Her mother-in-law is a wise woman.

The days are filled. Calista approaches contentment.

Nonetheless – she can't help it – although she faces forward, she cannot resist from time to time and glances back over her shoulder.

Pilar

Madrid, 1968

Señor Gómez leans across the desk and shakes Pilar's hand. 'Congratulations,' he says, 'you are now part-owner of a most prestigious apartment building on Calle de Alcalá.' He smiles at her. 'What an impressive property portfolio you're putting together!'

Pilar pushes the signed documents towards him. 'Not bad for someone from the wilds of Extremadura,' she says softly. She replaces the cap on Señor Gómez's elegant fountain pen and hands it back to him. 'I want to thank you once again for all you have done for me.'

Señor Gómez waves away her thanks. 'I admire all you've achieved, Pilar. Your mother would have been proud of you.'

Pilar doesn't flinch. She can still feel the tender weight of Francisco-José in her arms. Ever since she let him go, there is an ache that never fades, a dull-edged longing that seems to be the same size and shape as that small, firm body. Pilar thinks of her mother, of her gentle eldest brother, and there is the bitter taste of irony in her mouth as she looks at the man who is, even now, speaking to her. He never knew about Paco; of course he never knew.

'Now go celebrate,' Señor Gómez is saying. 'I'll treat you to lunch later.' He stands up and escorts Pilar to the door, one gentlemanly hand under her elbow. 'Usual place, at two thirty?'

'Usual place, two thirty.' Pilar shakes his hand, gravely, as has become their custom. She wonders how much he knows about her. He has never mentioned Petros; she has never permitted an occasion to develop when he might. Neither has he ever alluded to Pilar's sudden return to the family farm in January and February of last year, other than to ask occasionally after her father's health. He accepted her explanation that Miguel had been taken ill, that she had to go home and help out for as long as she was needed. Still, the man is no fool.

Pilar walks out of the office and onto the Madrid streets, which are already thronged at this early hour. People spill out of the Metro stations, clutching bags and briefcases, faces filled with hope, despair, boredom.

Francisco-José will have celebrated his first birthday already. Pilar tries to imagine what that might have been like, what her son might now be like. Sometimes, these imaginings torment her. Other times, the images are gentler and she takes comfort in the belief that she has done her best for him. He now has a father, a proper father as well as a mother, a proper family – something that she could never have provided.

And her secret is safe, she is sure of that. Sister Florencia has been unwavering in her support. With her help, Pilar had disappeared from Madrid for the month leading up to Francisco-José's birth, when even the most shapeless of sweaters and the baggiest of skirts were having difficulty in hiding her condition. She stayed with a kindly family in Calle Jaime Roig, in Valencia.

Maribel and Alicia, too, understood that there had been a recent catastrophe in Pilar's family in Extremadura. They had been sympathetic, happy to look after the building, grateful for the generous amount that Pilar paid them.

'The owners insist,' Pilar told them. 'They are very happy to take my recommendation and wish to compensate you for the short notice.' Pilar still follows Senor Gómez's advice, to keep her cards close to her chest. Maribel and Alicia had no idea that

Pilar was a woman of such substantial means. When she returned to Madrid, a week after Francisco-José's birth, Pilar picked up the threads of her daily existence again as though nothing had happened.

But the loss of her child has created a chasm in Pilar's life that needs to be filled, over and over again, something that is both restless and relentless. Pilar has found a couple of ways to feed it, to still its ravening demands. One is to increase her visits to Calle Catalina, to Alcocer Antigüedades.

She makes her way there now, knowing that Señor Bartolomeo is always pleased to see her. This time, at her request, he has put aside for her some nineteenth-century jewellery: an emerald and pearl necklace, with matching earrings and bracelet. He has promised an emerald and diamond ring, too, to complement the set. It will take him a little time, he says, to find the perfect one. This week, Pilar has already bought some new and elegant evening wear – black, tailored, severe – and she will dress up again for her visit to the opera at the Teatro Real on Saturday night.

Pilar loves this anonymous visibility. The power to turn heads, to see and be seen and yet remain unknown.

She loves the power that money brings.

The longing that it stills.

The bell above the door jangles discreetly as Pilar enters. She is surprised to see two other people there before her. She cannot remember the last time that the shop in Calle Catalina served more than one person at a time. But she is happy to wait. There is so much to look at here.

Señor Bartolomeo is giving his customers his quiet, undivided attention. 'The frames are art nouveau,' he's saying, 'dating from approximately 1906. Sterling silver, of course. Beautiful objects, sir, and these are quite rare.' Bartolomeo is speaking in perfect, accentless English.

Pilar glances at the couple standing to her right. For an instant, she is shocked. The man is tall, dark; an imposing physical presence. Pilar is becoming accustomed to this sensation of startled familiarity. So many men she sees seem to bear an imprint of Petros, as though they are shadows, paler, ghostly versions of the man she still loves. But she has learned not to hope.

Nonetheless, she sees his ghosts everywhere – in the theatre, at the opera, sometimes strolling around the market on a Sunday. Pilar looks away quickly. The woman who is with this man is slender, fragile somehow. She wears her long, dark hair up, and her face is partly obscured by large sunglasses. Jackie Onassis sunglasses: Pilar has never liked that style.

'I'll take them,' the man says. He puts the last of the silver frames down on the counter and reaches into his inside pocket.

Bartolomeo inclines his head. 'A wise choice, sir. These will increase greatly in value over the years. And in the meantime –' he smiles '– you can enjoy displaying your family photographs.'

Pilar can see that Bartolomeo directs this last comment towards the young woman – much younger than the man who must be her husband: they are both wearing similar wedding rings – but she does not respond. Pilar is intrigued. She is no more than a girl, but in her silence, there is the air of someone already defeated.

'Are you enjoying Madrid?' Bartolomeo asks politely, as he wraps up the frames.

'Yes, indeed. April is the perfect month to visit the city. I come in springtime, whenever I can.' Impatience lurks beneath the surface of the man's reply.

'Cyprus must also be beautiful at this time of year.' Bartolomeo hands over the parcel, smiles at each of the customers in turn.

Pilar feels the shock of his words. She half turns. She looks again at the couple, more carefully this time, trying not to stare. Other than Petros, Pilar has never come across anyone from Cyprus. For a moment, she feels the urge to speak; but what on earth would she say? Do you know the city of Limassol? Do you know a man called Petros Demitriades, the man I used to love – the man I still have the misfortune to love? How absurd that would be.

The man nods now at Bartolomeo, a curt, dismissive gesture. 'Indeed,' he says. Then: 'Thank you for your help. Good morning.' And he makes to leave, hesitating for a moment as he looks in his wife's direction. 'Come, Calista,' he says.

She turns towards the door and then, even through the sunglasses, Pilar sees it. The young woman's left eye is almost completely closed. Pilar can see a bruise, the size and shape of a perfect rose. For a moment, she cannot move.

On the day before Pilar's First Communion, Mamá's face had looked just like that. The house that morning was silent, a brittle, explosive silence that made even Pilar's brothers quieten. After breakfast, Abuela Loló appeared suddenly at the door, slamming it back against the wall as she made her entrance. That was odd: Abuela Loló never called that early. And she never made an entrance like that.

Pilar remembers how Mamá stretched out one hand, as though she wanted to halt her mother's advance. Seven-year-old Pilar was puzzled: Abuela Loló was always welcome in their house. Mamá said so, many times, as though expecting someone to defy her. Papá stood up from his breakfast, taking a long time to come to his feet. And still nobody said anything.

As Pilar watched, she became astonishingly aware that Abuela Loló was carrying something that looked like a long, shiny stick. It took her a moment to realize that it was Abuelo Edelmiro's shotgun, the one he always kept wrapped in an oiled blanket, safe in the locked cupboard in the barn.

But now it was in Abuela Loló's hands and she raised it to her right shoulder, squinting as though the light suddenly bothered her eyes. 'You lay one hand again on my daughter,' she said, 'and I will blow your brains out.'

And then she fired. The shot whizzed and zinged well above Papá's head; but still he ducked. The pellet lodged with a dull thunk in the brick wall behind the kitchen table.

Pilar's ears started to sing, and she did not hear what else was said, or shouted, among the grown-ups. All she knew was that from that day on, Papá took his rages out on things, and not people. He destroyed books, broke shelves, threw plates and saucepans. But, as far as Pilar knew, he never touched Mamá again.

Some men use their fists as a weapon, Mamá used to say, *but other men use love*.

Pilar watches now as the young woman walks towards the door of the shop. She raises one hand, pushes her dark glasses more firmly into place. Then she leaves, closing the door behind her. She follows her husband down the crowded street.

Pilar stands in the glittering shop, watching as the young woman disappears into the distance.

Bartolomeo waits. Pilar doesn't know whether he has seen what she has just seen. She knows of no way to ask him. She knows of no way that he could offer a reply.

'Señorita Pilar,' he smiles, 'how good to see you again.'

Calista

Extremadura, 1989

THE DOORBELL RINGS.

Calista is at her desk, dealing with the morning's post. The sudden pealing startles her. People do not arrive unannounced at her home. She makes her way quickly from her study to the living-room window and looks out. There is a police car parked right outside.

For a moment, Calista panics. She considers not answering the door. Is this how she is to receive the news? Is this how Omiros chooses to tell her? She breathes deeply, trying to calm the hammering of her heart.

She knows that she can't hide: her car is outside; it is clear that she is at home. When the bell sounds again, Calista runs downstairs and composes herself before she opens the door, smiling.

'Good morning,' she says. Enrique, the local Guardia Civil, is on her doorstep.

'Good morning, Señora McNeill,' he says, bowing slightly.

'What can I do for you?' He is on his own: the passenger seat of the police car is empty. So it's unlikely he is the bearer of bad news. Calmer now, Calista can hear her voice above the beating of her heart.

Enrique looks uncomfortable. 'I am very sorry to tell you that there have been some break-ins recently in the nearby villages. Not in Torre de Santa Juanita, of course,' he adds, hurriedly, 'but we are visiting all of the more . . . isolated houses, to make sure that you are happy with your security.'

Calista knows that instead of 'isolated', Enrique means 'wealthy', but she is grateful for the information, nonetheless. 'Thank you, Enrique. I have an alarm, and it's been serviced recently. I think everything is secure.'

'Windows?' he asks, looking up.

'Yes, I lock them at night.'

He nods. 'Good. Too many . . . strangers around these days.' He looks embarrassed. 'We must be careful. Call us if you have any concerns.'

'I will, thank you.'

Calista watches him leave. She knows that he wanted to say 'foreigners', but hesitated in case he insulted her. She also knows that he means immigrants – a debate that has been growing in recent months even in the smallest bars and tavernas of Extremadura.

Calista goes back upstairs. As she watches from her living-room window, she thinks of Alexandros, of that moment of surprise, of terror, as a stranger entered his home. What did he think? Did he have time to resist, or was it all over too quickly?

Calista stands, motionless, as the police car makes its way back towards the village. She must make sure to lock and bolt all the windows and doors, even during the daytime. The policeman's visit has stirred something, a sense of vulnerability that has taken her by surprise.

As she turns round, ready to go back to her study, the morning sun catches Imogen's portrait and the child's face seems to shimmer in the bright, brittle light.

Her gaze alights on her mother, follows her as she makes her way slowly across the landing.

*

It is midsummer 1968.

Imogen is sixteen months old, a swift and curious toddler. It is evening and Calista keeps watch for Alexandros's arrival. She practises nonchalance before the mirror above the buffet. First she tilts her head to one side, then the other. She smiles. Alexandros has told Calista recently that she is no longer attractive when she does not smile.

She walks round the dining-room table, touching the cutlery, moving the crystal a fraction to the right, a fraction to the left. She stops herself when she realizes what she is doing, presses her hands to her sides and smooths the fabric of her dress. 'I'm turning into my mother, Imogen,' she says; 'that's what I'm doing.'

The child smiles up at her. She is playing, an array of toy boats around her, Monkey clutched tightly to her chest. From time to time, Imogen slaps the shiny surface of the coffee table with delighted hands. Sometimes, she follows her mother around the room. She often walks too quickly and topples over. But she gets up again at once. Calista loves her determination.

Calista kneels on the floor beside her now. 'Clap hands,' she says. 'Clap hands till Papa comes home.' Imogen laughs. 'Now,' Calista tells her, 'we must get ready to meet Papa at the door: he'll be here very soon.'

Tonight, she and Alexandros will be alone. Petros and Maroulla always go out for dinner on Thursdays, and Iliada, the housekeeper, has the evening off. Calista stops for a moment and hears the scrunch of tyres on gravel. She checks her reflection once more, quickly, smooths her hair, allowing it to fall over one shoulder. She applies a little more lipstick. She holds Imogen as close to her as she can.

Calista reaches the door just as Alexandros enters. He throws his keys on the hall table, his jacket and briefcase on the antique chair that Maroulla has placed over to the right. Calista pretends not to see. Maroulla has asked her son, sharply, on several occasions, not to leave anything on that small chair: it is a family heirloom – too delicate to support any weight. Calista will move Alexandros's things later, when he isn't watching.

'Welcome home!' Calista says now, taking a step towards her husband. She settles Imogen on one hip and lifts her face to be kissed.

'Hello,' Alexandros says, although whether to her or to Imogen, it's impossible to tell. The baby holds out her arms to her father and Calista silently thanks her. Perhaps this will be one of the good evenings, after all.

'Hello, sweetie,' he says, kissing Imogen on the cheek. She smiles at her father, one small hand reaching out towards his face. Alexandros kisses her again and turns to Calista. 'We are alone tonight?' he asks.

'Yes,' she says. 'We have the whole evening. Dinner's ready. I'll put Imogen to bed in a few minutes. Let me get you a drink first.' Calista makes her way swiftly towards the drinks cabinet.

Imogen has begun to wriggle, her eyes searching for her mother. 'She's getting tired,' Calista says quickly. Alexandros does not like Imogen to cry.

Without a word, he hands the baby back to Calista and takes his drink from her. Imogen has now begun to grizzle.

'I'll just run upstairs with her. Then we can have dinner in peace.' She flees.

After dinner, Alexandros smiles at her.

'I have something for you,' he says.

'Really?'

Alexandros nods. He lights a cigar, taking his time to roll it between his fingers, to observe the way the flame catches the tip and makes it pulse and glow. He likes to indulge in this ritual:

one that Calista hates. It has been used too often to make her wait. Then he exhales slowly, watching the way the smoke curls bluely towards the ceiling.

'Get me my briefcase from the hall,' he says.

My photographs, Calista thinks. She hangs up Alexandros's jacket, retrieves the briefcase and comes back to the table. 'Shall I take these out of your way?' She gestures towards the plates and dishes that are scattered over the table.

Alexandros nods, all of his concentration now focused on his cigar.

When Calista returns, there are two fat envelopes in front of him. She recognizes at once where he's had the prints developed: Anastasios Papadopoulos, the island's most famous photographer. Then he smiles at her again.

'Anastasios says that these are quite good.' Alexandros nods at her approvingly. 'Not of a high standard, of course, but not bad at all.' He pauses. 'I am glad you have made such good use of my camera.'

'I'm pleased you like them.' Calista keeps her voice steady, casual.

Alexandros pushes one of the envelopes towards her. Slowly, with fingers that want to tear it open, to spill the eager photographs across the table, Calista pulls out a bundle of glossy black-and-white prints. Her fear subsides at once. The photographs are good: very good. She has captured something fleeting, something elusive. There is almost a gentleness to Alexandros's face in some of the images, a vulnerability that is seldom there in reality.

He had sat for her patiently one night, allowed her to move around him, obeyed her requests that he look this way and that. It had been one of their better evenings: one where tenderness continued, where they had even laughed together. She has captured those moments of intimacy, too: there is a palpable connection with her, the photographer, although she is invisible. Even beyond the frame, her presence is a potent one.

Calista feels as though something inside her has taken flight.

Alexandros liked having hobbies. They rarely lasted more than a month or two. Painting had been one such passion, brief, fleeting, until it became apparent that he lacked both talent and patience.

Then he became obsessed with classic motorbikes until Maroulla put her foot down. And then the photography started. Alexandros arrived home one evening with two bags stuffed with lenses, tripods, light filters. He spent weeks poring over manuals, taking photographs, experimenting with timers. Calista had been fascinated from the beginning.

She reaches now for three of the portraits, sets them out before Alexandros on the table. She stands beside him and begins to pull each of the images closer, one by one. 'You look so hand-some,' she says softly. 'I love your eyes in this one. And here –' she draws the second one towards him '– your expression is strong and kind at the same time.'

Alexandros nods, allowing Calista to place one hand on his. He does not pull away from her.

'I'd love to have these enlarged, to have them framed. They will look wonderful on our own wall, someday.' Calista holds her breath.

Alexandros finishes his whiskey. 'We can arrange that,' he says, and Calista thinks he is pleased. 'I will speak to Anastasios.'

'Oh, please, let me do it,' Calista says quickly. 'Let me choose the frames and have everything done in time for your birthday. Please, I'd like that – to be able to give you a gift that I've made, something unique.'

Calista wonders if she has gone too far. But Alexandros smiles at her. 'All right,' he says. 'I will arrange for Haridimos to drive you there. Let me speak to him in the morning.' He puts his arm around Calista's waist. 'Let's go to bed,' he says. 'You can clean all of this up –' and he waves one hand, dismissing the table '– in the morning.' He stands up and Calista follows.

One of the good nights, she thinks. If only she can keep this mood, if only Imogen doesn't wake. If only, if only.

Maroulla will not be impressed to find her dining room in disarray, but Calista no longer cares. Another evening has passed, quietly. The camera is still hers. The portraits are a success.

And she has the result she was looking for. She has now earned the exquisite opportunity to leave this house on her own, even for a couple of hours, and to learn how to breathe again.

Other than some day trips with Imogen to the beach, and a couple of visits to Ireland when her daughter is still a small baby, Calista's daily routine is unfulfilling and unbending. She is aware of a growing restlessness: a need to do something with her life that feels solid and significant.

'Like what?' Philip had asked, on her first trip back to Dublin. He'd flown home to meet her and they were having lunch together in the Gresham Hotel. Imogen was in the delighted care of her grandparents. Timothy and María-Luisa were captivated by their granddaughter's small, busy presence.

'I don't know,' Calista confessed. 'I just have this sense that doing the rich-woman charity stuff and looking after Imogen is not enough. Besides, we'll be hiring a nanny soon. Maroulla insists. It's as though it's some kind of status thing. Then what will I do with myself?' Calista was aware that she was not being wholly truthful with her twin. It saddened her: she didn't like keeping things from him, but she couldn't share Alexandros's darker side with anyone. She felt an obscure sense of shame, as though her husband's rages were somehow her fault.

Philip grinned. 'Have another baby, why don't you?'

Calista looked around for something to throw at him.

Alexandros followed her to Dublin at the weekend, as he usually did, but Calista had had almost a full week to catch up with Philip, to chat with Maggie, to watch her parents enjoy Imogen.

'She's so like you used to be,' María-Luisa said, smiling at her daughter. 'Headstrong. Determined. Full of adventure.'

Together, they watched as Imogen played in the back garden, climbing up onto the creaky swing, whose seat Calista and Philip used to share. She slept in Calista's old bedroom, sat at Calista's former seat at the dining-room table. 'Holding court,' Timothy commented. 'Just as you used to do.'

One afternoon, Calista came back to discover that her daughter had dived into a box containing some of Calista's childhood books and dolls. 'Where did these come from!'

'Your father brought them down from the attic,' María-Luisa said proudly, as though Timothy had performed some feat of astounding valour.

Calista grinned at her father, who was looking both embarrassed and pleased with himself.

'It's not often your mother has her grandchild to dote over,' he said. 'Just doing whatever I can to help.'

María-Luisa turned quietly to Calista, her dark eyes alight with mischief. 'Yes,' she said, 'as you can see, your father himself is quite indifferent to my grandchild.'

Later, just before Alexandros arrived, María-Luisa surprised Calista. They were washing up after dinner. Imogen was already asleep, Maggie was at the cinema, and the house had descended into a friendly, contented silence. It was the sort of silence Calista recognized instantly. She wished she could fold it away somewhere and take it back to Cyprus with her.

'You are happy, you and Alexandros?'

The abruptness of her mother's question took Calista aback. She kept her eyes down, looking at the soapy water in the basin, seeing the way the bubbles clung to her arms. 'Yes,' she said. 'Of course.'

María-Luisa nodded. 'Good. I ask because you are young, and because a new husband and a new country and a new baby all at once are a lot to deal with. I know this myself. You must come to me if you are not happy. You must not endure alone.'

Calista looked at her mother in astonishment. What else was there about this woman that she couldn't predict? It felt as though a stranger was standing beside her, speaking calmly and directly, her familiar hands busy with the drying of dishes.

'I'm fine. Everything is fine.'

'Good,' María-Luisa said. 'I am happy to hear that. You know where we are if you need us.'

When her weekly escapes begin, when her photography lessons become a reality, Calista is struck by the elderly kindliness of Anastasios, right from the start. He prepares coffee for her on each of their mornings together, on a tiny gas stove in the corner of his studio. This is a task he undertakes each time with his slow, unfailing courtesy. He is eager to share with her the secrets of the darkroom. In that bright and cluttered studio, Calista feels her small world finally begin to expand.

'You have talent,' Anastasios says to her on that first day. 'Real talent. I tell you now that you have the makings of a first-class photographer.' And he smiles. 'You will not be like me, taking pictures of children on their birthdays, or the occasional wedding and christening here on the island.' And he shrugs, spreading his hands. 'You are already better than that.'

Calista is not sure what to say.

Anastasios nods his head, as if Calista has spoken. 'This, I think,' he says, his tone thoughtful, 'this will be our secret. I will teach you what I know; you will learn and practise, practise, practise.' He gestures towards the far wall of the studio. 'I have hundreds of rolls of film in those cupboards – many will soon be out of date. We will start with those. And you,' he says, 'you will repay me by helping me to remember my English. My sons tell me it is important to speak English.' And he shrugs again, as if to say English doesn't matter to him: what matters is the respect of his three sons.

Calista feels a sweet swell of gratitude. Anastasios waves away her thanks. 'This makes an old man very happy,' he insists. 'My sons are not interested in the business. Now at least I know my skills will live.'

As Calista watches her photographs ghost into life for the first time, she is immediately reminded of María-Luisa and her Polaroid camera on the day of Mary Peters's ninth birthday. She can see the three pink-bowed girls at the party, watching as their own likenesses become shiny, vibrant, living things. And then there are Anastasios's books: shelves and shelves of books. He and Calista look through them frequently together: large glossy volumes on Henri Cartier-Bresson, on Annie Leibovitz, on Dorothea Lange. Calista cannot get enough of them.

'I will keep these safe for you,' Anastasios says. He does not look at her as he speaks. But as he turns the pages, Calista feels certain of something.

He *knows*. Anastasios knows what she is hiding.

They will never speak of it, of course. But for the first time since her arrival in Cyprus, Calista begins to feel at home.

During the months that follow, Anastasios feeds what has become almost a physical need within Calista, a need like thirst or hunger.

The images she has so recently captured with Alexandros's camera often startle her as they emerge through the waters of their chemical wash. The process is an absorbing one: it becomes an addiction. Developing her own work is something that gives Calista a separate existence, one beyond the tentacles of anxiety that define her daily life.

This new work becomes a creative focus that makes her alive and free again. She almost holds her breath; as the months go by, Calista prays that Alexandros will continue to allow her these mornings with Anastasios. She has been careful to take dozens of portraits of him, of Petros and Maroulla, of Imogen.

Maroulla, in particular, is delighted with the results. 'We will get Yiannis, and Ari and Spyros, and all the girls – you will take family photographs of all of us, Calista, yes?'

Calista agrees. She will do anything to make sure that Alexandros continues to grant her this precious measure of freedom.

On their mornings together, Anastasios travels the island with Calista. He takes her back to Lefkara. Calista does not tell him she has been before, that its magic has long since faded. They go on to Omodos and Lakki: the villages are populated with fishermen, with farmers, with lacemakers. Anastasios watches as Calista takes photographs of men and women at work, of the boats, the nets, the sowing and the reaping, the weathered faces and sinewy hands that inhabit all of these ancient tasks.

'The world is changing,' Anastasios says quietly. 'Even here. We need a record of how things are now. We need to protect our heritage as much as we can.' He teaches Calista to be a quiet, unobtrusive presence; she learns about light, angles, perspective. 'Above all,' he tells her, 'a photograph is a moment of stillness, of silent insight. You can learn all the technical stuff. It is the eye that is paramount: the eye of the soul.'

The old man's face is intent now as he develops the series of black-and-white portraits that Calista has taken. His gnarled fingers tremble as he pegs the shiny sheets of photographic paper onto the makeshift line that stretches all the way across the studio space.

Calista waits. She is watchful, tense, hopeful. She does not rush him. Anastasios is a man who cannot be hurried.

Finally, he sits, and lights a cigarette. He shakes his head.

'They're not good enough,' Calista says. Her voice is flat, a dull surface that stretches over the open ground of her disappointment.

'No, they are not.' He looks at her, his gaze direct, unfaltering. 'They are not "good enough".' His voice becomes so quiet that Calista has to strain to hear him. 'They are wonderful.'

'What?' Calista is startled. 'What did you say?'

The old man's smile broadens. His eyes are lively, mischievous. 'Wonderful. I say they are wonderful!' And he is shouting, delight carved into all the planes and angles of his face.

And then Anastasios stands and pulls Calista into a mad dance around the studio, his feet stamping and crossing, lifting and jumping as though he has suddenly shed fifty years.

After a few moments, both of them breathless with laughter, Anastasios releases her. He pats his chest. 'Too much,' he says, 'too much excitement for an old man in his seventies. Now,' and his tone becomes abruptly serious, 'we are going to sell your work. There is a market for portraits like these, and that market is the private galleries of London. Trust me: I worked there for many years – I know what I am talking about. There is an agent I know. He will not cheat you; he knows his job; he will take twenty per cent of everything you earn.'

Calista feels her happiness drain away. Dismay takes its place. 'Anastasios, I cannot possibly—'

'Wait,' he says. 'I have not finished. You will take my grandmother's name – first name and surname both. You will become Katerina Pontikou: a mysterious, anonymous photographer from somewhere around . . . Nicosia. A recluse, I believe. I will keep the money safe for you. Nobody needs to know.' He wags one imperious finger at Calista. 'And I mean nobody. Do you understand?'

Calista can finally speak. 'Yes,' she says, her voice hoarse with emotion. She wants this. Wants it so badly she can taste it. But she must not cry. Anastasios has often told her how much he loathes weeping women. 'I understand. Are they really that good?'

'Yes,' Anastasios says. '*You* are really that good.'

The richness of the old man's praise, his faith in her, the possibility of a future of her own: all of these things fill Calista with an optimism that makes her feel she can bear anything now.

And she will, above all, work to earn her own money.

She exults in that secret sense of independence and all that it will bring with it.

Calista is brought abruptly back to the present when the telephone rings. Its shrillness pulls her away from that grainy black-and-white borderland between past and present where she seems to exist most fully these days.

Quickly, she leaves her study and goes downstairs. She lifts the receiver, interrupting her own mechanical voice on the answering machine. 'Hello?' she says. She sounds a little breathless, but still calm and quiet. As though this is just a normal day, any old Wednesday, with nothing at all out of the ordinary.

She is just a woman, answering the phone as she prepares to go to lunch with friends.

As she speaks, Calista sees something glint on the tiles, just out of reach. A sliver of glass from her shattered perfume bottle. She must make sure to clean up any dangerous shards that still remain. It wouldn't do to step on them in bare feet.

'Ah,' a voice says, in English. 'Good afternoon. I wonder if it would be possible to speak with Calista McNeill – Calista Demitriades, please?' A man, who sounds unsure.

'This is Calista McNeill,' she says. 'How can I help you?'

'Miss McNeill, my name is Alexios Apostolou. I am a lawyer, based in Cyprus. I am calling you on behalf of your son, Omiros Demitriades.' The voice pauses.

'Is everything all right? Is my son all right?' Calista allows a sprinkling of anxiety to pepper her words. She has practised this often enough. She thinks the tone is just right.

'Omiros is fine. Please, allow me to reassure you of that. However, I'm afraid I have some bad news.'

'What?' Calista says. Her tone rises, just a touch. 'What sort of bad news? Why can't Omiros call me himself? What's wrong?'

She hears the man draw one, deep breath. Calista feels almost sorry for him. She wonders how old he is, what he looks like, whether he has ever had to deliver bad news such as this before.

'Your son has left for Madrid in the care of his uncles, Ari and Spyros Demitriades. I'm afraid there seems to have been a dreadful accident involving his father, Alexandros, and his step-mother, Cassandra.'

'What sort of an accident? What's happened to them? Are they badly hurt?' Calista can see herself, standing in the hall-way of her Spanish home, speaking calmly on the phone. It is as though she is two people: a casual outsider and a reluctant participant. So far, her performance is just as she would have wished it to be.

'I'm afraid we have very few details. Other than that this is a dreadful tragedy.'

'What do you mean, tragedy?' demands Calista, as though the gravity of the situation is only now becoming clear to her.

'I'm very sorry to tell you that your former husband is dead, Miss McNeill, along with his wife, Cassandra. I'm very sorry indeed.'

Calista allows a long silence to develop. She counts the beats.

'Dead?' she whispers. 'Are you sure?'

'Yes. We have been contacted by the Spanish police. I'm afraid there is no doubt. Omiros and his uncles left Limassol for Madrid as soon as we received the news. He asked me to call you.'

'How is my son?' This is not in Calista's script, but she can no longer help herself. She begins to cry, sobs of bitter relief, of rage, of revenge long postponed and finally delivered.

'He is, naturally, grief-stricken. But he understands his duty. He has gone to take care of his father's arrangements. He wants you to know that.'

'We were estranged, Alexandros and I. We have not seen each other in some years. Does my son wish me to be with him? May I go to him?'

The reply is gentle – Calista knows that she has made it easy for him. 'I'm afraid he does not wish you to be there, Miss McNeill. He is quite adamant. The family asks that you do not travel to Madrid. We will contact you again, as necessary.'

'I see.' Calista pauses. She allows her voice to crack. 'Please let my son know that I love him. That I am always here if he needs me. Please tell him that. I must go now.'

'I understand. May I ask if you have someone with you?' The man's tone is delicate, probing.

'No. I am alone.'

'Is there perhaps someone—'

'No,' Calista interrupts him. 'No one at all. Thank you for your kindness. I must go now.' And she hangs up.

Omiros. Her son. The last time she spoke to him, he lashed out at her. He wanted, above all, to punish her. Calista can still see the rage on his unformed features. Eleven years old, still vulnerable, still a small child struggling with all the past hurts of his fractured family.

'I had no choice, Omiros,' Calista told him. 'I had to leave. I've tried to explain that to you. Perhaps you'll understand better when you're older.'

It was on one of Calista's visits back to Cyprus, the time with her children carefully orchestrated by Alexandros. Imogen sat quietly in the armchair in the hotel foyer, reading her book. Listening, Calista knew; children were always listening, no matter what their age. But Imogen created the illusion of being occupied while her brother made another one of what she called 'his scenes'.

Omiros drew himself up to his full height. He was so physically like his father that Calista's words faltered as she looked at him.

He would not allow her to speak. 'I am old enough now,' he said. 'I don't want to be here. I prefer to be with Papa. I can't go sailing today because of you.'

Calista felt as though something was slowly crumbling inside her all over again. Somewhere inside this angry boy was the small child she had once played with, joining in his delighted laughter as she read him nursery rhymes, played 'peep', sang to him.

But now he was glaring at her, his hands clenched by his sides.

'I won't stop you if that is what you want to do.' Calista spoke quietly. She could already see where this conversation was going. They had travelled together to its familiar destination too many times already.

'You came back; I know you did. Papa told me. But you only saw Imogen. You never came to see me.'

Calista nodded. 'You were too small, Omiros. You would not have been able to understand. I'm sorry if that hurt you.' She stopped. There was no point. Those earlier visits back to Cyprus should have remained secret, always. Calista would never forgive Alexandros for turning her son against her.

'Why don't you just leave me alone,' Omiros said. His voice cracked on the last word and Calista held her breath.

'I can't leave you alone because I love you. You are my son. I want to get to know you properly, little by little. That's all I want.'

'Take me to Papa,' he said. 'That's all I want.'

Too many of her visits ended like that. Calista regrets, bitterly, that she cannot change the past. But there it is: a past that leaches continually into the present; a past that is even now playing out its final act.

Calista glances at her watch. It would not be good, if things were ever to come to light, to be seen out and about after a telephone call such as the one she has just had. She must be careful to do what appears to be the correct, the appropriate thing. People who have just received news about their murdered spouses do not dress up and go out for lunch. Calista will stay at home and shut herself away. She will call Rosa and make some excuse.

Afterwards, Calista climbs the stairs to the living room, waiting for the hollowness inside her to fill. Waiting for the elation to flood her veins and arteries with satisfied righteousness.

Instead, she sees her children's faces. She sees Alexandros's face when he loved her, once. She sees herself, her empty home.

But above all, she sees Imogen. Her daughter: beautiful, precious, talented. Then the anger begins to seep.

I hope you suffered, Alexandros, Calista thinks. I hope you were in agony and that your death was painful and savage. I hope you died long after your slut of a wife, so that you knew what was coming to you. Above all, I hope it was lonely. And in your final moments, I hope you thought of me, of how I must have done this.

Calista sits and looks out at the Extremaduran countryside, watches people go about their daily tasks, imagines what might have been.

She pulls her packet of cigarettes towards her and lights one. She inhales, sits back and waits for whatever comes next.

Pilar

Madrid, 1970

PILAR GOES WALKING. That is what Pilar does, these days. She is reminded of her earliest days in the capital. Back then, she mapped the city streets in her head as she walked. Making her way around in the early hush of Sunday mornings, Pilar's sense of being overwhelmed had slowly ebbed away. She came to enjoy the wide, tree-lined avenues, the imposing buildings, the elegant elderly ladies walking their dogs after Mass before stopping off at one of the many pavement cafes for an aperitif. Pilar loved the buzz of conversation, the drifting cigar smoke of the loud, suited men, the sense of all that peacock-display that went hand in hand with the weekly *paseo*.

She had enjoyed above all her place as an outsider: Pilar could own these streets in the same way as everyone else and stop for a coffee wherever she chose. She could observe and make judgements and watch the comings and goings of the affluent citizens of Madrid. She could even get happily lost among the meandering side streets and nobody would stop her; nobody would exclaim at her presence, or ask what right she had to be there. Back then, the freedom of it all had been heady, exhilarating.

These days, the walking has become a reflex, a way to fill the emptiness, a way to still the steady seep of disappointment at what her life has become. Ever since the loss of Francisco-José, Pilar's days have become filled with meaningless hours. With whole weekends of Maribel and Alicia. And so Pilar walks.

She has tried many times over the past three years to change the contours of her life. She has tried to mould its shape into something that might fit her better, might chafe less against the tender flesh of her grief. But it is as though she has been handed some fixed pattern, some immutable laws that hem her in, that stitch and sew the fabric of her existence in a way that she is powerless to change. Everything she does has the familiar force of old habit. Once, she threw out all the furnishings of her *portería*, believing that new surroundings would help her meet the world in a new way. But even the newest of objects seemed to adapt themselves to the shape of whatever had been there before. Within weeks, her new *portería* felt just the same as her old one.

Pilar travelled then, secretly and compulsively. She went to Cuba, to New York, to London. Once, she almost went to Cyprus, but her courage failed her at the last minute. Each time, she bought new clothes, had her hair styled in a different way, stayed in new and apparently exciting places.

But always, each optimistic setting out, each longing for adventure became nothing more than a package holiday of same-ness: routine, tired, predictable, sometimes even squalid. And after each journey, Pilar returned home to the inevitability of her life. To the inevitability of her remorse.

And so Pilar walks once more.

This morning, she has made her way towards the Church of San Andrés. She discovered it by chance some years ago. Once inside, she had been soothed by its hushed and ancient tranquillity. Its flickering, candle-lit silence and its peace have drawn her back many times since. As she approaches the main door, Pilar stops. To her right, a few hundred metres away, a line of children make their way towards the church. They seem to shimmer as they walk. Their small hands are joined together in prayer, their faces luminous, their white suits and dresses brilliant in the May sunshine. At the head of the line, and at the end, a nun walks. Their black habits are dark punctuation marks to the sentence that is the children. Pilar looks and waits, unable to move. All of her strength has deserted her.

First Holy Communicants. She will never see her son become one of these seven- or eight-year-olds, walking in solemn procession towards the main door of the church. Pilar waits until the last child has stepped over the threshold, finally forcing herself to move. She follows them inside and slips into one of the pews at the back. The church is almost empty, apart from the children and the two nuns, one young, one elderly, who are speaking now, but Pilar cannot catch what they say. And then, at the older nun's signal, the children begin to sing.

An elderly woman pushes her way into the pew beside Pilar. She nudges her after a moment, one bony elbow digging into Pilar's side. She looks like one of the market women that Pilar sees every day, her grey hair scraped back into a bun, her dress black and dusty. Her fingers are dirty, knuckles swollen and twisted into the strange roots of arthritis. Pilar sees that rosary beads are wrapped round both hands, the small crucifix swinging free as the woman lifts it to her mouth to kiss the figure of a tiny Christ. '*Angelitos*,' she whispers, as she nudges Pilar for the second time. Her eyes glitter. *Little angels.*

Pilar feels a lump in her throat. The children rehearse their hymns, their voices high and sweet in the incense-filled air. Her eyes cannot help themselves: they seek out all the small boys with hair so black it sheens blue.

'Those angels are the same little bastards that thieve from my stall every week,' the old woman hisses now, nodding her angry head in the direction of the altar. A thin thread of drool clings to one corner of her down-turning mouth.

Pilar looks at her. She has no answer. She glances once more towards the children and sees only questions. And she cannot bear it any longer. She stands up and flees, pushing her way past the hissing woman, not caring if she topples her, not caring any longer if she hurts her.

Old women like that terrify Pilar. They bring with them the bitter air of Torre de Santa Juanita everywhere they go.

Calista

Extremadura, 1989

THE AFTERNOON IS COOLING NOW. The light in the living room is green and wavery, a tranquil underwater world. Calista leaves the blinds down as she sits, replaying the lawyer's phone call in her head, over and over again. Apostolou's call is one of the final steps in the complicated dance that Calista has choreographed from afar.

First, the anonymous messenger. Then, the transaction that was Alexandros and Cassandra. Now, Omiros, on his way to Madrid with his uncles – perhaps they are there even now.

Calista doesn't much care what happens next, to her, or to anyone else. Earlier, she had gone downstairs and swept up the remaining glassy splinters of her perfume bottle. They had lain in wait, glittering on the hall floor, hiding in corners and crevices. But she'd managed to winkle them all out and the sense of one last clean-up had satisfied her.

Calista remembers, all these years later, the power of the hook of hope.

She remembers how Alexandros reeled her in, time after time: a willing fish. He would lure her with his bright promises that he would never hurt her again; dazzle her with his words that he loved her; soothe her with his earnestness that he would change. Their new house, he said: where everything would be different.

His green eyes were brilliant with future that day, the day he told her. They would turn everything around, she'd see. A new beginning.

Their own place, their own space, away from all the pressures of living with others. A place where they could each be themselves.

A proper home. Their own family home.

Calista looks around her. It is summer 1972.

She is unable to conceal her delight. She can feel tears begin to well for the first time in months and she half sobs, half laughs: a strange sound that echoes around the empty room. Her five-year-old daughter looks up at her at once. Such a serious face, always: concerned, curious, watchful.

'Mummy,' Imogen says, frowning now. 'What's wrong?'

Calista clutches the child's hand tightly. 'Nothing, sweetheart. I'm just so happy to be here, happy that we have our very own new house. Imagine! A house just for us – you and me and Papa and the new baby. You'll have a big room all to yourself. What do you think of that?'

Imogen smiles and her small face lights up. 'Can it be pink?'

Calista laughs. 'It can be any colour you like!' She bends down, kissing her daughter on both cheeks. 'You can choose the paint and the bed and the furniture and the rugs . . . all of it! Now, let's look around downstairs first and I'll tell you where everything is going to be. Careful, now – mind the wet paint.'

Alexandros has warned her that the painters aren't finished yet, and Calista has promised to make sure that their little girl's curious fingers will be kept in check.

'Stay close to me, Imogen,' she says now. 'I want to take some photographs.'

'Can I be in them?' The child hops from one foot to the other, her eyes bright, her expression pleading. 'Please, Mummy?'

'Of course you can,' Calista says, pulling Alexandros's Nikon out of her bag. The villa is beautiful. Even with its renovations unfinished, light floods the three huge interconnecting rooms. One flows into the other, drawing the eye onwards and outwards, towards the wide paved space that will eventually be the terrace. There are plans for a swimming pool, too, and a large play-area for the children.

Children: this new baby will be here in less than three weeks, and when he arrives – Calista is convinced that it is a boy, this time, although she hasn't told Alexandros this – they will all move, together, into this villa, several blocks away from Petros and Maroulla. Calista doesn't know which gives her greater pleasure: the move into their new home, or the move away from Petros and Maroulla.

Our house, she thinks; our home. Our own family home. She can hardly believe it. She takes several photographs, quickly: she can feel her small daughter's growing impatience.

This villa is the long-awaited seal of approval on Alexandros's career, on Alexandros's family, maybe even on Alexandros's wife. Calista has worked hard to be accepted over the past five years, throwing herself into the roles of wife and mother and daughter-in-law. She has had some success, she thinks, although it can be a difficult thing to measure. Sometimes, she wonders whether people's disapproval has simply acquired a mask of acceptance, that their true feeling is still there, underneath the polished surface of the things they say. Other times, she doesn't care.

Imogen tugs at her hand, pulling her towards the staircase. 'Let's go now, Mummy. You promised to show me my bedroom,' she's saying. Calista smiles at her. 'We'll go up straightaway,' she says, 'but you must keep to the middle of each step. Otherwise, we'll ruin the paint and then the painters will be cross.'

Imogen nods, her serious face absorbing this. 'I know, Mummy,' she says. 'You told me already.'

Calista smiles gravely. 'You're right. Let's go. I'll be right behind you.'

She feels happy, this day. Mainly thanks to Yiannis – although Calista will never let her husband know this – Alexandros has recently got his promotion, a bigger office, his name on the door. He seems to have expanded to fit his new role: he has grown larger, more imposing, his now bald head making him look uncannily like Petros. Calista hopes that Alexandros will soon begin to find contentment, that he will feel, finally, that he has emerged from his brothers' shadow, particularly the larger-than-life shadow cast by Yiannis.

Yiannis takes his role of godfather seriously and never fails to visit Imogen at least once a week. Calista looks forward to his arrival; Imogen adores him. Over the past year, he has used these occasions to take Calista into his confidence.

'I think my father is ready to give Alexandros more responsibility,' Yiannis told her, several months back. 'There's a couple of things he could do, though, a few initiatives he could take himself, that would really help his case.'

They were sitting by the swimming pool in his parents' garden, keeping an eye on Imogen as she splashed up and down.

'A real water-baby, this one, isn't she?' Yiannis said, amused.

'Yes,' Calista smiled. 'She has no fear.' After a moment, she said: 'What sort of initiatives, Yiannis?'

'Look, Uncle Yiannis! Watch me swimming!'

Yiannis waved at Imogen, laughing. 'You're brilliant! You'll be able to catch me soon!' He turned to Calista. 'There are some accounts that need to be managed more carefully than others. An English firm that we're courting at the moment. Personal attention from Alexandros would go a long way in securing their buy-in.' Yiannis paused. 'If I suggest it, Alexandros will just bristle.'

Calista nodded. 'I can do that,' she said. 'He's so keen to get this promotion; work is all he talks about.'

Yiannis looked away from her. 'Are you OK?'

'Yes,' she said. She kept her voice bright, optimistic. 'A little tired, but that's to be expected.'

He looked at her, quickly.

She smiled. 'I'm pregnant. Imogen will have a baby brother or sister in about six months.'

'That's wonderful! Congratulations,' Yiannis said. He touched her hand lightly. 'I'm very happy for you both.'

'Thank you.' Calista glanced towards the house, but there was still no sign of Maroulla. She often joined them when her son visited, her broad face lighting up at the sight of Yiannis. Now, in her absence, Calista decided to seize her opportunity. 'Yiannis, I need to say something to you.' The words sounded more urgent than she had intended.

He looked at her, surprised.

'I really want to have my own home. Alexandros and I need a place for ourselves and the children. I'm struggling here.'

Yiannis nodded, still looking at her. His eyes were kind. 'I understand.'

'I'm not criticizing your parents. Please, I just . . .'

'I didn't think that you were,' he said quietly. 'I will do all in my power to help you. Don't worry: we'll make it happen.'

Each week, Yiannis updated her, quietly, sometimes in just a few snatched sentences. Calista knew that Alexandros was steadily becoming more confident, more authoritative.

And now, with their new home finally a reality, Calista is sure that she and Alexandros are on the threshold of a new life: that they can, finally, put the last few difficult years behind them.

*

When Calista meets Mirofora, she thinks immediately of Maggie. She hires her as her housekeeper and they have an animated conversation on that first day. Calista's Greek is fluent at last: she's been taking lessons for the past four years from Alexia, a young woman, a university student. Learning to speak Greek was a challenge: Calista had no landmarks, no known territories. Greek did not behave in the same ways as Spanish or schoolgirl French: Calista had felt adrift, unanchored among the oceans of its words. At times, it had felt like drowning.

But now, Calista is afloat and she moves about her new kitchen, putting away everything she's bought at the market. Imogen is playing in the garden, under Mirofora's watchful eye. Omiros is asleep upstairs. Calista has noticed how her son's eyes follow his father as soon as Alexandros enters the room. She points this out to Alexandros, over and over again. It pleases him: the way the baby's face creases into a delighted, gummy smile every time his father approaches.

María-Luisa and Timothy had travelled to Cyprus to meet their new grandson.

'Felipe will be here on Friday,' María-Luisa said, at the end of their first week. 'Your brother is really looking forward to seeing you, and to meeting Omiros. He has good news.'

Calista looked at her mother quickly. 'What sort of good news?'

María-Luisa smiled. 'I will let him tell you himself. I just wanted to prepare you.'

'Just tell me this – is there a woman?'

Her mother's smile faded. 'No,' she said, 'not that sort of good news. Just be ready.'

'Of course. I can't wait to see him.' Calista wished that she hadn't asked. Her mother's disappointed face had been eloquent.

She looked over at Imogen, forever making sandcastles. Omiros was nestled contentedly in her arms. Calista bent and kissed his forehead, glad all over again that she had produced a son.

And then she felt ashamed for having allowed herself to place the value of one of her children above the other. She remembered, guiltily, María-Luisa's casual certainties about Philip's greater value – in the family, in school, in the world. Boys' education was what mattered, boys' friendships, even boys' hobbies; but above all, boys' futures. She'd looked surprised on the few occasions that Calista had challenged her. 'But, my dear girl,' María-Luisa would say, her expression more puzzled than irritated, 'you will one day marry, have children of your own, be there as a support for your husband: that is your job in life. It is the natural order of things.'

She glanced over at her mother now. She saw María-Luisa's hesitation, could read it in the way she placed her hands in her lap.

'What is it, Mamá?' Calista asked gently.

'Is all well with you? I worry, you know.'

Calista smiled. 'There is no need, Mamá, really. Alexandros and I are fine. The first few years were difficult, and you already know that. But with his promotion, this house, Omiros's arrival – we've come through. Don't worry. Things have never been better.'

María-Luisa nodded. 'I am glad,' she said. 'I am so very glad.'

Pilar

Madrid, 1973

PILAR TAKES THE METRO, as usual, to her meeting with
Señor Gómez. She arrives at precisely seven thirty; she expects
that he will be there waiting for her. For sixteen years, this has
been their ritual. These meetings quickly became one of the fixed
points on Pilar's personal compass. They were the safe place from
which it was possible to make out the direction of her life and
feel the certainty of her place in the world. The only exceptions
to this monthly event were August and December, when Señor
Gómez allowed his family to insist on the holidays that Pilar
was sure he would rather not have taken.

As she approaches his office, Pilar gets ready for all the usual
politenesses of this September conversation. Did you have a
nice holiday? How is your wife? Did your son and grandchildren
visit as usual this August? Señor Gómez will, in turn, ask Pilar
about her two weeks in Asturias, or Galicia, or wherever she
chooses to tell him she has been. And then they will get down
to business.

This morning, however, Señor Gómez buzzes Pilar in from
the intercom by his desk. He is not standing waiting in his outer
office to greet her. Instead, he calls out to her from his 'inner
sanctum', as he calls it, and Pilar pushes open the door.

What she sees shocks her. The man behind the desk is Señor
Gómez, certainly, but it is a man who has changed almost beyond
recognition. Pilar gasps; she cannot help herself. Quickly, she

calculates that it is seven, possibly eight weeks since they last met in July, and the man has withered to a gaunt, yellowish shadow. Pilar knows that Señor Gómez is not yet sixty. The man who now speaks to her looks two decades older.

'Good morning, Pilar,' he says, and his smile is weak, tremulous. His teeth suddenly look too large for his mouth. 'You are very punctual, as usual.'

Pilar tries to gather a response from the scattering of words already racing around in her head. 'Good morning . . . It is good to see . . . Are you quite well?'

He gestures to Pilar's familiar chair. 'Please, sit,' he says. 'We don't have too much time. My son Ignacio will be joining us shortly. There are some things I need to say to you.'

Pilar nods. She can sense the man's urgency and she waits, quietly, for him to speak.

'I am dying, Pilar. There is no easy way to say it – so that's it. As blunt and as forthright as we have always been with each other.'

All the things she would like to say well at the base of Pilar's throat. She cannot speak, cannot peel her eyes away from the shape of Señor Gómez's skull, now clearly visible underneath the tight sheen of his skin.

'Well, perhaps not always forthright,' he says. 'But that has been my fault.'

The room fills with an intensity that shreds the air. Pilar wants to raise one hand to stop him, but she finds that she's not able. She does not want this man to speak the words that will allude to Petros or the baby: not now, not when everything is already too late. Pilar's body has been shocked into immobility – her face, her voice, her limbs have all frozen.

'Today, you must listen and not interrupt.' Señor Gómez looks at her with that familiar, affectionate, mildly interrogative gaze.

Pilar nods, again.

'I have the deeds to our first property here. The mortgage has been discharged in full. The building in Calle de las Huertas is yours. Completely.'

Pilar begins to move now, a slow, tentative reaching out, but Señor Gómez stops her.

'No. No words.' He pauses and his ravaged face fills with emotion. 'I loved your mother once, many years ago, Pilar. Perhaps you didn't know that.' He does not look up. 'She would not come with me to Madrid, but the truth is, I did not try to persuade her. I listened to my family, more than I should have, and I left.' He drops his head further. Pilar can barely make out the words. 'I have regretted that every day of my life. My own lack of courage. My abandonment of her and of our son. I regret that bitterly.'

Pilar feels her anger blaze: at him, at Petros, at the world. She can hardly begin to unravel the knots of emotion that tighten the air around her. So he did know. For all these years, he's known. Pilar wills him to meet her gaze. They look each other, finally, in the eye.

'I cannot undo it, nor can I even make proper recompense. I have tried, over the years, to look after you. But it is not enough. Never enough.'

Pilar's words are clamouring now. Words that careen from anger to pity to grief and back again. She cannot articulate any of them.

'Look after Francisco-José for me,' he says. 'I know that your brother grew into a fine young man.'

The outer door opens then and Ignacio enters. 'Right, Papá,' he says. 'That is enough. Time to take you home. Half an hour: you agreed.' He turns to Pilar. 'Good morning, Señorita Domínguez. My father has been most anxious to keep his appointment with you. I trust your business is completed?'

Pilar nods, speechless, the deeds to her building hastily stuffed into her handbag.

'Then we will say goodbye.' Ignacio's hand under Pilar's elbow is firm as he begins to guide her out of the room.

'Wait a moment, please,' she says. She may never see Señor Gómez again. Pilar is flooded with the sudden, pitying certainty that she cannot leave him burdened like this. Her mother would never forgive her. She remembers Mamá's face, filled with love as she spoke of this man. She would not wish him to suffer needlessly. Pilar crosses the room, stands in front of Señor Gómez's desk and places her hand on his. 'I will do as you ask,' she says. She keeps her voice low. 'I will look after your son for you now. Some things are never too late.'

He gazes up at Pilar, his eyes filled with tears. 'Thank you for that kindness,' he says. 'Thank you. You are just like your mother: a fine woman. Ignacio will take care of your affairs when I'm gone.'

Ignacio escorts Pilar to the outer door. She knows she is being hurried away. His eagerness to have her gone makes Pilar wonder.

She removes her arm from his, glances back over her shoulder at Señor Gómez. 'May I come and see him another day?' she asks, although she feels that she already knows the answer. 'I would really like to see him again.'

'I'm afraid not,' Ignacio says. Pilar can discern no regret in his voice. 'This is now family time. My father has very little left.' He doesn't look at Pilar. His gaze is directed back towards his father, now slumped over his desk.

Pilar nods. There is nothing to be said to that. 'Will you please be sure to contact me when . . . ?'

'Of course.'

Pilar steps out onto the busy Madrid street. There is the

screech of traffic, the rumble of the Metro, the heaving crowds of constant, rushing people.

For a moment, she cannot move. Mamá's life, Pilar's own life, countless other lives pulse around her. She sees mothers hurrying their small children to school; mothers pushing babies in their prams; pregnant women negotiating their careful way across the street.

Pilar stands there, allowing the crowds to part around her. She is the only fixed point in a sea of moving bodies.

Calista

Limassol, 1973

CALISTA AND ALEXANDROS are having a dinner party to celebrate their new life in their new home.

Nothing too large: Alexandros does not like more than six people at a time round his table. Calista has left the guest list up to him, of course; but she has already chosen a weekend when she knows that Petros and Maroulla will be away. Alexandros has invited two friends from his university days: men who have recently moved back to Cyprus from the United States with their brash Californian wives. That is Alexandros's word: 'brash'. It has taken Calista by surprise. She wonders what he means by it, but decides not to ask.

'Charalambos is a lawyer, and Evagoras is a tax consultant,' Alexandros tells her. 'They could be useful to me in the future.'

Calista says nothing. It seems that friendship is something Alexandros does not understand: your friends, your allies, your supporters are your brothers and your sisters and your cousins. Outside of that army of family, you have no need of others. Others will take every opportunity to betray you; others will show themselves eventually, and when you least expect it, to be the enemy.

Calista hears Omiros crying. She calls out to Mirofora. 'I'm going upstairs to feed the baby. We'll get started on tonight's meal as soon as I come down.'

Imogen looks up at the sound of her mother's voice, waves at her from the terrace, from her moat surrounded by sandcastles with tiny Cypriot flags pushed into their crenellations. An entire fortified city lies at her feet. Calista watches as her six-year-old daughter sails her fleet away, her small hands making the toy boats rise and fall, rise and fall on the sea's invisible swell.

At first, the evening is a success.

Calista looks beautiful and she knows it. She wears a long, sky-blue dress, with a daring neckline, a dress that emphasizes the new curves that baby Omiros has brought along with him. She wears her dark hair up, a gold rope round her neck, matching earrings and gold-coloured sandals. Alexandros smiles his approval when he sees her.

'You are beautiful,' he says. 'You will be the most beautiful woman in the room.'

It is over the main course that things begin to go wrong. The Californian women, Cindy and Zoe, are by now loud with wine. They are criticizing Cypriot men, talking over one another, arguing with their husbands about something called 'women's lib'. Calista has no idea what they're talking about: even the language they speak is not familiar to her. She knows each discrete word, of course, but she cannot follow the conversation. The context is missing. Cindy and Zoe are throwing around words like 'oppression', 'patriarchy', 'equality', 'liberation'. Calista is worried. One half-glance at Alexandros shows her that her husband is not pleased.

She can feel the turn the evening is taking. She can sense it in the atoms of air around her. The top of her head begins to thrum, faintly but persistently: always a bad sign, her own internal thunder. She tries to shift the evening's focus, but it feels hopeless: like trying to stop the tide coming in.

'God,' says the one called Cindy, except that it sounds to Calista like '*Gaad*'. 'I think it's just disgusting the way Cypriot women serve their men. I mean, it's 1973 and this is *still* such a *traditional* society – I keep telling Charlie I don't know if I'll ever adjust!' She blows a thin stream of smoke upwards, and keeps pulling at her blonde hair with one hand.

Calista glances in Charalambos's direction and sees him grimace. *Charlie.* Her eyes meet Alexandros's fleetingly and she can tell that his anger is growing. Please, she prays silently; please let him be mad at her, at them, and not at me. Please.

Zoe's husband, Evagoras, jumps into the conversation, protesting, and Calista feels immediately grateful. He is funny, Evagoras, and he manages to make the two women laugh. 'We've had plenty of feisty women over the years in these parts,' he says. 'Look at Helen of Troy, at Clytemnestra and Cassandra for starters, and what about Lysistrata? You can't say that women here are under the thumbs of men – far from it!'

Calista is not so sure about that. She recalls a story she once read about Agamemnon, king of Mycenae, who seduced Clytemnestra, killed her children, abandoned her in order to fight a war that lasted ten years and then carried home another woman as a prize. It seems to Calista that the women in that tale did not get much opportunity to be feisty. Not until they became hell-bent on revenge. Then, it was a different story.

Calista cannot hear any longer what Cindy and Zoe are shouting in reply, because her heart has begun to speed up. All she can hear is the bluntness of the blood pounding in her ears. The evening has begun to take a particular turn and Calista is frightened.

'Don't you agree, Calista?' Evagoras is saying, looking kindly in her direction.

'I'm sure you'll settle in, just as I did,' Calista says, smiling at her guests. She hopes that her contribution is bland enough, flexible enough, so that it can mould itself around whatever it is the Californian women have just said. Instead, there is a short, strained silence, before Charalambos and Evagoras begin speaking again, this time about business opportunities in Cyprus. It is clear that they have changed the conversation because of her. Calista catches Cindy's surprised glance; she sees Zoe make a face; and she feels Alexandros's eyes burn into hers.

Mirofora enters the dining room and begins to clear plates. Calista chooses her moment to escape. She excuses herself and murmurs about seeing to dessert and Irish coffees. When she closes the door behind her, Calista leans against it for a moment, just to catch her breath. Then she hurries to the sink, turns on the cold water and allows it to flow over her wrists, willing the force of the water to calm the heady racing of her pulse.

Calista knows that the evening is over.

All she has to do now is endure the agony of waiting until it ends.

When Alexandros closes the door behind their guests, Calista says quickly: 'Omiros is awake. I'm going up to him before he disturbs Imogen.' Alexandros nods curtly and Calista flees.

Omiros's cries would never wake Imogen: she sleeps like the dead. But either Alexandros doesn't know this or he chooses to ignore his wife's fiction. It gives Calista time to gather her forces, time to *think* about how to handle what will inevitably come next.

She changes Omiros and settles him for the night. She steps into Imogen's room and pulls the sheet out from under the tangle of her daughter's sturdy legs. Then she goes slowly back downstairs.

Even though Calista expects it, she doesn't see it coming. Alexandros's fist catches her on the left side of her jaw, sends her reeling across the living room until she crashes into the arm of the sofa and falls to her knees, stunned by the suddenness of it all.

Then, oddly, she is coming to standing again, with no effort of her own. A burning sensation across her scalp tells her that Alexandros has her by the hair. He pulls her up off her knees, makes her stand, facing him. His face is much too close to hers. Calista flinches, pulls back from him. She can smell his breath, a mix of garlic and wine and coffee.

'What is wrong with you?' he asks. His tone is soft, reasonable, as though he is making a genuine enquiry, a thoughtful one. Calista wonders where Mirofora is. But it is as though Alexandros can read her mind, at times like this. 'I sent Mirofora home. I told her she was looking tired, that she could come back and clean up in the morning.'

Slowly, deliberately, Alexandros lets her go. He chooses and lights a cigar. Calista waits as he goes through the whole long ritual while the tension in the room grows like a headache. Alexandros draws on the cigar, rolling it thoughtfully between his fingers. Then he blows a cloud of smoke into Calista's face.

But something about tonight has made Calista defiant. 'There is nothing wrong with me, Alexandros. Why are you doing this to me?'

Her husband looks at her as though he cannot believe what she has asked him.

'Why?' he says. He grabs her hair again, more fiercely this time. 'Why? When you make me look stupid in front of our guests? When you cannot even follow a *simple* conversation in *English* – it is *you* who are doing this to *me*.'

The rhythms of Alexandros's speech suddenly remind Calista of her mother: of María-Luisa's emphases, of her insistence on the polish and the practice of social skills – as though nothing were more important than surface.

'These men are necessary to me,' Alexandros says. Then he pushes Calista away from him. His face is filled with disgust. 'Get away from me,' he says. 'You have made any kind of relationship impossible.'

Calista's whole body feels filled with too much substance. It is difficult to carry it with her up the stairs. She is not sure whether she will manage to reach the bedroom before her legs give way. She needs to soak a towel in cold water, to stop her face from swelling: her hair will only cover so much. And Calista is not sure what Alexandros means: his words go round and round inside her throbbing head.

Is a relationship with these necessary men made impossible by her, Calista, or has she made any relationship between herself and Alexandros impossible?

Calista no longer knows.

Right now, tonight, Calista no longer cares.

Pilar

Madrid, 1973

LOOK AFTER FRANCISCO-JOSÉ FOR ME. *I know that your brother grew into a fine young man.*

Pilar cannot excise these words of Señor Gómez's, no matter how hard she tries. For months now, they have kept her awake at night; they refuse to allow the memories of *her* Francisco-José to leave her alone. And she'd been doing so well: practising how to forget. She'd become good at it over the years: finding those small distractions that would take her by the hand and lead her willingly away from the centre of her memories.

But after Señor Don Alfonso's death, nothing could console Pilar; nothing would keep the past from fuelling her dreams. All of her daily tasks became infused with memory. Even Señor Bartolomeo failed to distract her.

'Are you unwell, Señorita Pilar?' he'd asked her recently. His eyes were concerned as Pilar turned away from all the treasures he had displayed before her. She had stood, listless, as he rolled out the familiar black velvet cloth. Pilar watched the way the bright lights of the shop made the jewellery glitter, the way the fire in the stones came alive, calling to her. But she could no longer hear them. They no longer warmed her.

'I'm fine,' she replied. 'Just a little tired. I think I'll leave it for now.'

'Of course.' And Bartolomeo smiled. 'Please, rest and take care of yourself. We hope to see you soon again.'

'Yes,' she said. 'Soon again.'

As Pilar leaves Alcocer Antigüedades, she hears the tiny bell jangle behind her. It has the high, pure note of finality, although Pilar has no idea why. For a moment, she hesitates, glancing up and down the street. She really shouldn't, not in her home city. It is not anywhere near her own neighbourhood, of course, but still: it could be dangerous. Holiday encounters are one thing. Home territory is quite another.

Finally, she shrugs and makes her way down the street, turns left and right and left again, and enters the first bar she finds.

'Whiskey,' she says.

It is late afternoon and the bar is almost empty. Pilar takes off her jacket and sits at a table in the corner. Someone has left yesterday's copy of *El País* behind them and Pilar sees page after page of a smiling Pinochet, waving to his people in Chile. She is reminded of the day she spent with her father in Badajoz, all those years ago, and is filled with sudden revulsion. Pinochet and Franco, she thinks, cut from the same cloth.

The barman arrives with her whiskey and a jug of water. 'No water,' she says. The young man looks startled. He takes the jug away without a word.

Pilar spreads the newspaper on the small table and makes sure to look absorbed.

Four whiskeys later – or maybe five, perhaps even six – Pilar decides, somewhat unsteadily, that it is time to find a taxi and go home. She tries, and fails, to come to standing.

Out of nowhere, a man materializes beside her. He has another whiskey in his hand. His face is friendly, open. He is young; much too young.

This much-too-young man sits down beside Pilar. Afterwards, she has no recollection of their conversation. The only thing she recalls is the last question he asks her, his voice soft, his breath whiskey-tainted as he leans his smooth face closer to hers.

'Wanna fuck?' he says.

Without a word, Pilar drains her glass.

They both stand. Pilar concentrates on putting one foot in front of the other. The young man offers her his arm and she shakes her head.

He leaves the bar, holding the door open for Pilar.

Without a word, she struggles into her jacket and follows him out into the deepening evening.

Calista

Extremadura, 1989

ABOUT A YEAR AFTER HER house was finished, some four years ago now, Calista got a phone call from Rosa. She can still remember the young woman's excitement.

'You told me I could call,' Rosa said, 'and I hope I'm not disturbing you.'

Calista could hear Jaime's voice in the background, but couldn't make out what he was saying. Rosa shushed him.

'Not at all. It's lovely to hear from you. Is everything OK?'

'You have to come,' Rosa said. 'Fernando is here, but he has to leave soon. Please, come and say hello to him and join us for dinner. We all insist.'

Calista was intrigued. 'I'd love to,' she said. She had become fond of Jaime and Rosa, energized by their energy and optimism.

Besides, her evenings on her own had become much too long.

Calista was surprised to see that the bar was closed. The blinds were drawn. There was a scribbled notice in the window in Rosa's handwriting: '*Sorry! We're closed this evening. Open at ten tomorrow morning, as usual.*'

Calista knocked and the door was opened at once. Jaime grinned at her. 'We've been waiting for you. Come on in.'

José and Inmaculada greeted her warmly. Rosa kissed her on

both cheeks and handed her a glass of cava. 'We're so glad you came!'

Fernando stood up and shook Calista's hand. 'Good to see you again, Calista.' Then she saw that three of the bar's tables had been pushed together in the middle of the room. Large sheets of paper were spread out over their surface. The visible folds reminded Calista instantly of Maggie's spotless aprons, all those years ago. It took her a moment to realize what she was seeing. Jaime took Rosa by the hand. They both waited, expectant.

Calista looked from one shining face to the other. 'What are you building?' she asked at last, smiling.

Jaime said: 'We wanted you to be the first to know. Well, after Fernando, of course. He had to draw up the plans.'

Rosa clapped her hands. She couldn't contain herself any longer. 'Come and look,' she said. 'Look at what Fernando has designed.'

'You started something, Calista,' Fernando said. 'I think your house has given the village hope. You've made it think more highly of itself.'

Rosa tugged at Calista's sleeve. 'Sit, please. Fernando has to go. Jaime will talk you through it all while Inmaculada and I get dinner.' She pulled out a chair for Calista. 'We knew that you would understand the drawings.'

Calista listened as Jaime talked her through the plans. She liked how earnest he'd become, how adult he now was. Watching his face, Calista missed her own two children with the sudden intensity of an ambush. Something in her face must have changed, because Jaime stopped for a moment, looked closely at her.

'Calista, are you all right?'

'Yes, yes, of course – sorry, just remembering something. These are wonderful drawings, Jaime. Fernando has done an excellent job.'

Jaime nodded. 'We'll keep this original, central area, but these two new wings will extend to either side. Then the whole bar will surround this outdoor courtyard, which can be covered, if necessary, by the sliding roof.' He sat back. 'Do you really like it?'

'I love it,' she smiled. 'And given how Rosa's cooking is coming along, I've no doubt that she and Inmaculada have plans for outdoor catering?'

'Yeah. But the focus of the courtyard is not just the food.'

Calista could see Jaime's mounting excitement. She sat back, sipped at her cava. 'Tell me,' she said. 'I can see that it is something momentous.'

Jaime leaned forward, resting his arms on the table. 'Music,' he said softly. His face became even more animated. 'I want to host traditional music here. So many musicians around Extremadura, so few opportunities like this. I want to make Torre de Santa Juanita a centre for all sorts of music – mostly folk, because that's my passion, but we want there to be something for everyone.'

Calista remembered the melancholy songs that she'd heard when she first arrived in Extremadura. They had reminded her of Ireland.

'Look.' Jaime handed her an artist's impression of the courtyard: a large, paved space with a small, raised stage at one end. Folding doors led out from the bar's main area. It looked intimate, inviting.

José and Inmaculada emerged from the kitchen then, their trays laden with plates and cutlery, glasses and bottles. 'What do you think, Calista?' José asked.

She looked up from the sketch that Jaime had given her. 'I think it is absolutely wonderful,' she said. 'I can't wait for the opening night.'

'Not too ambitious, then?' Inmaculada glanced at her as she set the table for dinner. Calista could hear the concern that underpinned the question.

She shook her head. 'Absolutely not. I think it's pitched just right. And you'll have the best part of a year to market the idea.' She paused. 'I have a lot of promotional experience from my work in London. I will help in any way I can.'

Inmaculada's face lit up. Calista was struck by how much younger she looked. She wondered if something was wrong. She and José were quieter than usual.

'Thank you,' Inmaculada said. 'That makes me feel a lot better.'

'Still worrying, Mamá,' Jaime teased her. He kissed the top of her head. 'Even after all these years! Don't you trust us?'

'Of course,' she said. 'But all mothers worry.'

'I'm also a photographer,' Calista said, quickly, seeing the way Inmaculada's eyes had filled. 'Let me do a brochure for you. I'll have it printed and distributed to all the villages around. It would be my pleasure.'

Rosa appeared, carrying platters of tapas. 'What would?' she asked. 'What would be your pleasure?'

Calista had not used her camera in a long time. She had put it away, as she had put away so many other things, soon after her arrival here. She hoped she had not made a mistake by offering to help.

Something about Inmaculada and José that night was not right. Jaime was attentive to them, and Calista saw him squeeze his mother's hand more than once.

Inmaculada watched her son all evening, her eyes rarely leaving his face. At times, Calista thought she had looked almost fearful. And José, in turn, had watched his wife. His attention to her was subtle, tender. He, too, looked preoccupied. Both had been grateful for Calista's offer of practical help.

As she drove home, Calista felt filled with misgiving. Taking out her camera again would not be easy. So much of her life was contained behind that lens.

She wondered if she was ready to face it.

It is early April 1974.

As Calista looks in the mirror this evening, she sees what she has become: a beautiful woman, not yet twenty-five, married to a well-connected businessman who is, in his own words, going places. She, Calista, is simply the wife, mother of his two children.

The more visible Alexandros becomes within his family, his society, his business world, the more Calista feels herself disappear. Above all, she misses her photography lessons with Anastasios; she misses the electrical charge that used to light up her life on those mornings. Alexandros, finally, put a stop to them once Omiros was born.

'Your family duties come first,' he said. 'You don't have the time to dabble in photography.' He looked at her, his eyes cold. 'I will have nothing that interferes with your new responsibilities here.'

'I would never allow anything to—'

But Alexandros wasn't listening.

'Enough!' he said. 'I will not change my mind.'

Dismay overwhelmed her at Alexandros's words. Her portraits of fishermen, of lacemakers, of small barefoot children and their mothers, all of these had made Calista feel intensely visible herself, fully present within the frame. It was as though she, too, became a focus; she no longer felt like the tolerated outsider. The cloak of anonymity that the long-dead Katerina Pontikou had gifted her gave Calista the freedom to take risks, to push the boundaries of her skills as far as she could. She learned that she was good at what she did. And the money she earned made her proud. When she told Anastasios that she could no longer come to the studio, he smiled sadly and shook his head. 'I can teach you no more,' he said. 'But I am sorry that this freedom has been taken away from you.'

When Calista left the studio for the last time that day, she saw how Anastasios's eyes filled with tenderness, with grief, as though he was bidding farewell to one of his own children.

Calista poured her heart out to Philip when it happened. She wrote pages and pages, secretly, terrified that Alexandros might find out.

'I feel as though something essential has been ripped away from me,' she wrote. *'Photography is not just a hobby, not just a pastime; it helps me feel alive. I am lost without it, Philip, and I don't know what to do.'*

At the same time, she was aware of her twin's career, and all that he had achieved. A first from Oxford, followed by a master's, followed by a PhD at the University of California. Philip had gone to live in San Francisco, and although his letters to Calista arrived less frequently than before, she knew that her brother had never been happier.

The loss of Anastasios, Philip's stellar career, the trappedness of her life with Alexandros: Calista knows that she is close to drowning.

Alexandros walks into the bedroom now, just as Calista has finished dressing. She smiles at him. He smiles back and she feels hope coil itself round her once again. He is in a good mood.

'Ready?' he asks.

She nods. 'I'll just go and kiss the children goodnight,' she says.

Alexandros frowns, shakes his head. It is like the sun going in, Calista thinks. Hope loosens its grip. 'Leave them,' he says. 'Eleni has just put them to bed. There's no need to disturb them.'

It doesn't disturb them, Calista wants to say. It's our nightly ritual – what will disturb them is if I *don't* go and kiss them goodnight. But she stays silent. She nods instead, smiles again. 'Of course. You're right,' she says. 'Let's go.'

Alexandros barely speaks on the drive to the city centre.

As they enter the restaurant, Calista sees the way the social fabric unfolds once again, all around her husband, its bright colours glittering in welcome. Alexandros smiles his brilliant smile, shakes hands, jokes and laughs with his father's guests. He says the right thing to everyone, stepping across the surface of politeness with an ease and grace that makes every eye in the room follow him.

He becomes solicitous towards Calista, affectionate, introducing her to others with pride: here is my trophy, my beautiful, much-younger wife. Are we not the golden couple?

Calista nods and smiles at the United Nations of businessmen assembled before her. She catches names only briefly. What she hears is nationalities: the Frenchman, the American, the Spaniard, the Englishman. When Jemal, the Turkish Cypriot, shakes her hand, Calista hides her surprise at his presence.

There have been some rumblings, recently. Archbishop Makarios, president of the Republic of Cyprus, has been turning up the temperature of political discontents. His demand for *enosis* – political union with Greece – has alienated the growing Turkish-Cypriot population. The increasing tension between the Greek and Turkish Cypriots, particularly in the north of the island, has been the subject of many a heated dinner-time conversation round the table at Petros and Maroulla's weekend gatherings. Petros has family in Nicosia still. The divisions that are escalating between the Greek and the Turkish Cypriots trouble him.

These conversations have made Calista nervous. Back in February, she'd been surprised to receive a late-night telephone call from her father.

'I don't know how they report the news over there,' he said. 'Or whether they make any distinction between the North of Ireland or the South, so your mother and I just wanted to let you know that we are safe, that nothing has happened in Dublin.'

Calista had been mystified. 'What are you talking about?'

'There's been a bomb,' Timothy said. 'In Dungannon. It's all over the international news. We just wanted to reassure you that we're both OK.'

Calista had been aware, of course, of 'the Troubles' in the North – although the news that reached her was sketchy at best. Besides, she felt no connection to that part of Ireland: Dublin was what she knew. Dublin was what she loved.

But this looming strife in Cyprus makes her fearful. If war has happened in her own country, then it could also happen here.

That was one of the few occasions that Calista found herself warming to Petros, the day he expressed his concerns about his sisters and brothers. 'I fear what is happening,' he'd said to Calista, shaking his head. 'We have always got on well together. The two communities have done business, seen our children marry, welcomed our grandchildren together. My family has lived there for generations. And now, there is a wedge being forced between us all. I don't know where it will end. But I fear it.'

Calista makes sure to be especially warm and welcoming to Jemal; they chat for a moment or two about his children, his wife, his travels. She is careful, very careful that night. She makes sure to speak to Petros, to Maroulla. 'You look lovely, my dear,' Petros says, as his eyes slide over her head almost as soon as she has greeted him, watching the door for more important guests. Calista kisses her mother-in-law on both cheeks, exchanges some pleasantries with Yiannis. She makes sure to be charming to everyone. Alexandros will not find fault with her, not tonight.

He takes her back to the sidelines, then, back to where the

other women are chatting. He brings her champagne, makes sure she has a comfortable chair, kisses her on the cheek when he goes back to his father's side. Alexandros will return for her when dinner is about to be served.

'Such a handsome man, your Alexandros,' one of the women remarks. 'And he clearly adores you.' Someone else makes a joke about Irish sirens and how sweetly songs must have been sung and spells woven in order to snare the unwary Cypriot sailor. All the women laugh and Calista smiles politely.

She sits, her hands clenched round her glass of champagne, her mouth clamped shut.

As they leave the restaurant, Alexandros holds Calista's hand, puts one arm around her shoulder. He stops walking, just for a moment, and stands facing her while he pins her wrap in place. 'It's a little cool, my dear,' is what he says. Calista will always remember that. She thanks him, says what a lovely time she's had, walks on with her arm in his.

They enter the lift in the underground car park and Calista watches as Alexandros presses 'level two'. And then he punches her.

She is thrown backwards, her shoulders connecting painfully with the stainless-steel wall behind her. At first, she doesn't know what is happening. The lift, she thinks, puzzled: something's wrong with the lift. Why has it jerked like that?

Then Alexandros brings his face close to hers, so close that the pores of his skin seem huge. That is all Calista can focus on: they fascinate her, those pores, their size, their oily blackness.

She knows better than to ask, but she asks anyway. Shock makes her brave. 'What have I done, Alexandros? Why are you so angry with me?'

He pulls away from her. 'You need to ask?' He seems puzzled.

'Yes. I need to ask. What did I do to make you angry?'

The lift comes to a halt; the doors part smoothly. Alexandros turns his back on her and begins walking towards the car. Calista runs after him, begging for an explanation. She hates herself, but she begs nonetheless. 'Alexandros, please, speak to me. Please, Alexandros.' She is suddenly terrified that he will drive off and abandon her.

He finally comes to a halt and looks at her over the roof of the car as he opens the driver's door. He points his finger at her. 'The Englishman,' he says. 'You should be ashamed of yourself.'

Calista freezes. What Englishman? Her husband is mad, she suddenly thinks. Quite mad. Before she can reply, there is a squealing of tyres against the synthetic floor of the car park and Alexandros accelerates, away from her. Calista watches as the car speeds up the ramp, brake lights red for an instant, before they disappear into the night.

She doesn't know how long she stands there, shivering. She cannot think, can only feel where the side of her jaw has begun to throb. She touches it, her fingers trembling. It hurts. How is she going to get home?

Calista hears voices in the distance, laughter. Instinctively, she hides behind one of the concrete pillars. She hears people call goodnight, cars starting; there is the shriek of tyres again and then she sees Yiannis. He waves after a couple of the departing cars, then stops to light a cigarette. He is only a few yards away from her. Relief makes Calista suddenly weak. She holds on to the pillar and calls his name, softly, so as not to startle him.

His eyes widen when he sees her. 'Calista! What's wrong? What are you doing here? Where's Alexandros?' He looks around him, confused. Then he throws his cigarette on the ground and walks towards her, quickly, his face filling with concern.

'He's gone,' Calista says. She cannot look at him, so she looks at the ground instead. 'Alexandros has gone.'

'Gone?' he repeats.

'Yes – we . . . had a bit of a misunderstanding.' Calista raises her head, looks directly at her brother-in-law. She makes sure that her hair falls across her left cheek, hiding her jaw. She hopes that admitting to a misunderstanding with Alexandros will be enough, that Yiannis will not ask any more. All couples have rows, after all. Believe what I'm saying, she thinks, and just take me home. And soon: she can feel the ground begin to sway and lurch beneath her feet again. She clutches at the pillar and Yiannis reaches out to her. He takes her arm.

'Come with me,' he says. He walks her towards his car, opens the door and eases her gently into the passenger seat. Then he reaches into the back and hands her a bottle of water. 'Here, drink this,' he says, and then: 'Lean forward, put your head down for a moment. You're very pale.'

When she can finally speak, Calista says: 'Thanks, Yiannis. I'm fine now.' Then it strikes her. Alexandros will be furious if Yiannis drives her home. It would mean that his eldest brother knew what he had just done, and she would suffer for that. She sits up straight. 'I must be going, really. I should get a taxi.'

'Nonsense. You'll do no such thing. I'll take you,' Yiannis begins, but Calista stops him.

'No, please. Alexandros wouldn't like it if . . .' She trails off.

'If what?' Yiannis says. And then, immediately: 'Calista, what on earth has happened to your face?' Quickly, too quickly, he has reached out and his hand brushes against the side of her jaw. Calista shivers: his touch is ice against the hot ache that simmers underneath the surface of her skin. She tries to turn away from him, but he won't let her go. He is silent for a moment and then, in a voice filled with disbelief, he says: 'Alexandros hit you.' It is not a question.

Calista says nothing.

'My God.' He sits back in the driver's seat, his face aghast.

In the cold artificial light of this sudden underworld, his features look almost green.

'Please,' Calista says, her voice much calmer than she feels. 'Just put me in a taxi, Yiannis, please. I don't have any money with me, but—'

'Stop,' Yiannis says. He raises both hands in the air. 'Money is not an issue – please do not even mention it. If that is what you wish, I will of course find you a taxi.' He lowers his hands and grips the steering wheel again, although he is not about to drive anywhere. His knuckles show white against the dark leather. Calista risks a sidelong glance at him and sees the grim set of his face. She is afraid that she has just made everything worse.

'Sit until you feel better,' Yiannis says quietly. 'Then I will take you across the road to the bar. They will call us a taxi from there.'

As Calista sips at the water, something strikes her. 'Who is the Englishman?' she asks. 'The Englishman who was there tonight?'

Yiannis looks at her, surprised. She can see that he thinks it an odd question. 'David Wright,' he says. 'We'll be doing a lot of business with his firm in the future. Alexandros brought him on board.' Yiannis stops, suddenly understanding. 'He admired you,' he says quietly. 'He said so to Alexandros – I was there. Is that what this is about?'

Calista lifts her head, looks at Yiannis. 'I must have shaken his hand,' she says. 'I don't even recognize his name. Jemal was the only one I spoke to.' Then she covers her face with her hands and she sobs. Calista no longer cares that Yiannis knows, no longer cares what the family might say. It isn't her family, after all. Nothing on this island is hers except her children and this shame. She wants all of this grief, all of this helplessness to end.

'Calista,' Yiannis says. He goes to place his hand on her shoulder. Without meaning to, Calista flinches. She moves away from him, pressing herself against the passenger door, poised to escape.

'I'm sorry,' he says. He raises his hands again, this time in surrender. His voice is quiet. 'Forgive me. I will, of course, respect your privacy.'

Calista nods without looking at him. 'I'm better now,' she says. She opens the door of the car and steps out, the smell of tyres and heat and rubber suddenly making her nauseous again. She stands up straight. Hang on, she tells herself. Just get a grip, get yourself out of here and home.

Home. The thought of it fills her with sudden yearning. Her Dublin bedroom, crammed with cumbersome furniture and the smell of familiarity. Philip's room down the hallway. Maggie's blunt affection.

Calista is all at once overwhelmed by the memory of her last visit to Dublin, during the summer of 1973.

They were on Killiney Beach, she, her parents and the two children. It was one of those glorious sunny days, a surprise event in any Irish summer. María-Luisa had brought a picnic, Timothy came laden with buckets, spades, a fishing net for Imogen and deckchairs. Calista laughed at their enthusiasm.

'You used to love your fishing net,' Timothy insisted. 'We'd stand at the water's edge for hours. You'd never catch anything, of course, but that didn't seem to matter. Having the possibility was the point.'

Calista watched them – her father with Imogen, paddling, her mother cuddling Omiros. She remembered the stolen, secret day on Killiney Beach with Alexandros and her eyes filled. Horrified, she turned away from her mother. She couldn't let her see; she mustn't let her see. Nothing must spoil this beautiful morning. Calista tried to control the tears, but memories of that awful dinner party a few weeks back, with the American women, Cindy and Zoe, were suddenly too much for her.

María-Luisa touched Calista on the shoulder. 'What is it, my dear? What's wrong?'

Calista shook her head, half tearful, half smiling. 'I miss home,' she said. 'I miss you and Dad and Philip. I wish I didn't live so far away.' She bit her lip. Enough.

'I know. We wish it also. I know how hard it is.' María-Luisa took Calista's hand and squeezed it. 'We are so happy to have you. You must come to us if we can help to make things easier. Ask for anything you need, anything at all.'

That is what home is, Calista thinks now. The unwavering affection of her parents. A sanctuary for her and her children. Somewhere she can breathe.

That's what Calista wants.

She wants to go home.

Alexandros never speaks of that night afterwards. He doesn't even ask how she got home. Calista never mentions it. But it is there, between them, afterwards. A solid edifice of change. It is the night that Calista makes her decision and she still remembers the exact moment at which she did.

Yiannis pays the taxi driver to take her back to Alexandros. The man's face lights up at the generous tip. Yiannis turns to Calista to say goodnight and his face is troubled. She sees that his eyes are filled with questions that she cannot answer. For a moment, she thinks he is about to say something to her and she cuts him off. She can't bear to have his sympathy, his words of comfort.

'Goodnight, Yiannis,' she says quickly.

'Goodnight, Calista.'

She can see his reluctance in the way he steps away from the taxi. Calista leans back her head. The interior of the car smells of pungent air-freshener, and she can feel her stomach begin to shift again. She fumbles at the handle and opens the window, just a crack, and allows the cool night air to wash over her, to cleanse her. Then she closes her eyes and asks herself: What am I doing?

Calista is no longer sure how she has ended up living a life that was never meant for her. She cannot pinpoint the precise moment when her future had fallen away from her and another had taken its place.

The only thing she is certain of is that she has become a refugee, fleeing from a present that is not of her making.

And, perhaps more than anything else, she is tired of feeling ashamed.

Pilar

Madrid, 1974

WHEN PILAR WAKES, she does not know where she is. The
room smells of sweat and sex and something else that she cannot
name, not yet. Her mouth is dry and gritty. Her head has started
to pound. She begins to ease herself into sitting and feels the
cheap quality of the nylon sheets underneath her naked legs.
Light has begun to filter through the badly fitting curtains, but
not enough to give her an idea of what time it might be.

The body in the bed beside her stirs and suddenly Pilar
remembers. The bar. The night before. The young man with the
whiskey. Oh God.

He wakes now and in the grey dimness of the early light,
Pilar makes out his shape as he props himself up on one elbow.

'Good morning,' he says.

Pilar comes immediately to standing. 'Good morning.' She
hears him fumble at the lamp and pulls her clothes towards her,
dressing as quickly as she can.

'Hey, what's your hurry?' he says.

Pilar hears the sharp click of a switch and light pools abruptly
around his bedside table. She sees the glasses, the cigarette butts,
the remains of a cheap bottle of wine. The young man turns to
look at her, his eyes hopeful.

Nausea clenches a fist at the base of Pilar's throat. 'I'm late
for work,' she says, and smiles at him.

He frowns, looking at his watch. 'It's not even five,' he says.

Pilar leans forward and kisses him lightly. 'I start at six,' she says. 'I'm a nurse. I have to fly.'

'When can I see you again?' The young man – what was his name? – is already struggling with the sheet, his feet seeking the floor. He grabs a piece of paper and a pen, thrusts them at Pilar. 'Will you write down your number for me?'

'Of course.' Pilar takes the pen and paper from him. Past experience has taught her to be cautious in these situations. You never know when a man might turn nasty. She scribbles a fictional number, hands the piece of paper back to him. 'Call me tonight,' she says. 'I should be home by eight.'

He grins at her. Pilar feels the lightness of relief settle around her. It's OK. He's not going to make any trouble. She has no memory from the time they left the bar together last night. But she's not telling him that. Her nausea increases.

'I'll call you, then,' he says. 'That was great. Let's do it again soon.'

Pilar flees.

Outside, the day is struggling towards dawn. Pilar needs a coffee, badly, but she is afraid to linger in the neighbourhood in case Eduardo – that's his name – tries to pursue her. She hurries down the steps of the Metro, already planning her journey home: she'll take a detour or two, just in case.

She'd been followed only once before: just once, but that man's silent tenacity had frightened her. She'd spotted him on the Metro, pursuing her, then again on the bus, and finally in El Corte Inglés, where she had taken refuge. She'd hidden in the women's changing rooms for over an hour, finally slipping out through a fire door that someone had left carelessly open. At the time, Pilar had promised herself: never again. She'd spent days looking over her shoulder afterwards. At night, she dreamed of being trapped, or being held captive. The dreams paralysed her and she would wake, sweating, her heart hammering.

But three, maybe four months later, she broke that promise to herself and the whole cycle started all over again. The thrill of the unknown, the sharp, jagged edge of danger, the satisfaction of the conquest. It all helped her to forget; it helped to fill that place where her courage should have been.

Where her son should have been.

Pilar buys her ticket now and boards the first train. It is almost empty: just some sad-eyed men and women on their way to, or from, some dead-end job, the kind that the night city specializes in. Nobody speaks. A few people smoke. The train rattles its way towards the next stop.

Suddenly, Pilar cannot breathe. It is as though she has a stone in her chest. Somebody's fist is round her heart, squeezing. The light in the carriage turns blue and grainy, everything slows down, and Pilar is afraid she is going to be sick. She tries to stand, but her legs no longer work. The last thing she sees is a startled, unshaven face that looms over her, the mouth making soundless words of comfort, or blame, or anger: Pilar cannot be sure.

And then, all the rest is darkness.

The hospital doctor looks to be about fourteen. Pilar is shocked. How can she trust the diagnosis of a child? She struggles into sitting. She's not sure how much time has passed since they brought her here. One day? Two? The residents of her building won't be pleased to find her missing.

The doctor doesn't bother with the formalities. 'You had a panic attack, Señorita Domínguez,' he says. 'Your heart is fine. Your bloods are fine. When you feel up to it, you can go home.'

'Panic attack?' Pilar looks at him blankly.

'Yes. When you are under a lot of stress, the body can often mimic the symptoms of a heart attack. Very frightening, but essentially harmless.' He pauses, looks at her more kindly. He flips over a page on his clipboard. 'What age are you, señorita?' he asks.

'Thirty-five.'

He frowns, looks at her more closely. 'Have you been under a lot of stress lately?'

Pilar thinks about that. 'Yes,' she says slowly. 'Yes, I have.'

'I can prescribe something for you, if you like. Or we can try to arrange an appointment with the hospital psychiatrist.'

Pilar looks at him in horror. 'No,' she says. 'No, I'll be fine. I know what I need to do.'

She isn't going near any psychiatrist. Nor is she going to succumb to Valium or any of its sisters: she has already seen what that did to Señora Ochoa – third floor right – last year. The woman had become listless, vacant-eyed, hardly able to carry on a conversation. No, Pilar isn't having any of that.

She starts to get out of bed.

'Just a moment,' the doctor begins, but Pilar holds up one hand.

'You said I could go.' Her voice is firm, steady. 'I am going home. As I say, I know what I have to do.'

The young man shrugs. An even younger-looking nurse helps Pilar to her feet.

'There is still some paperwork . . .' the doctor begins.

'Fine,' Pilar says. 'Where do I sign?'

Calista

Limassol, 1974

IT IS 10 JULY 1974. Seven o'clock in the evening.

Calista watches until Alexandros's car is no longer visible, until the dust of his departure has settled, until the tail lights have disappeared off into the distance. He has a meeting, he said. He will not be back before midnight. Calista waits for a few more minutes, just to be sure.

Then, she moves. She runs to the stairs, taking the steps two at a time. She stumbles halfway up, banging her shin against the hardwood edging. Her hands try to save her; the outstretched palms make stinging contact with the tiles. The pain brings tears to her eyes, but she does not stop: she must not stop.

At the top of the stairs, Calista turns right, into Imogen's bedroom. Imogen is in her pyjamas. She has just had her bath and she's sitting on the floor, flicking through her colouring books, a bunch of pencils in one hand. Calista kneels on the floor beside her. She brushes the long, soft hair out of her daughter's eyes, feels the familiar blade of guilt, slicing her. It is intense, almost blinding.

'I need you to stand up for me, sweetheart,' she says. 'We need to get you out of those pyjamas and into your dress.'

'Why?' Imogen is unwilling to move.

'Remember I told you we might have an adventure, just you, me and Omiros? That we'd go off somewhere together on a mystery tour?' Calista's hands are trembling; she can hear the crack in her voice. 'Do you remember?'

'No,' Imogen says, her tone suddenly belligerent. She twists away from her mother. 'I don't want to go anywhere. I want to do my colouring.'

Calista feels a sob catch at the back of her throat. She can barely breathe. Something akin to gravel has lodged where her breath should begin, making her gasp and struggle for air. She grabs Monkey and thrusts the soft toy into Imogen's arms. She cups her daughter's face in her hands.

'Mummyneedsyourightnowtobe*areallygoodgirl*,' she says. The vowels and consonants are flowing too fast; the words are waves crashing into each other, pummelling the shore that is her daughter. Calista is horrified that she is capable of reducing her child to tears. She forces herself to slow down. She manages what she hopes is a smile – although Imogen has never been one to be easily fooled. Her ability to see through to the heart of the matter has always startled Calista. She is a watchful child; not much escapes her green, level gaze.

Calista helps her into her dress. Her fingers shake as she tries to do up the seven buttons. 'I need you to wait here, sweetheart, until I come back for you. Will you do that?' Calista hates herself all over again, hates what she's about to put her children through.

Something odd about her mother – the strangled sob, the urgency, the trembling hands – suddenly seems to reach the little girl and she quietens. 'Yes, Mummy,' she says, her eyes huge. 'Don't cry. Please don't cry.'

Calista kisses the top of Imogen's head. She gives her one more hug. 'You're the best,' she says. 'Now, you and Monkey stay right here. I'll be back in a flash: I have to go and get Omiros.'

Once inside her son's bedroom, Calista wrenches out the

lowest drawer of the chest and turns it upside down. She has taped a plastic wallet to the wooden base and she now rips it free. The wallet contains her passport. The airline tickets are already in her handbag in an envelope: just like an ordinary letter, innocently stamped and sealed and addressed to her mother, in case Alexandros went rummaging again. Calista had caught him going through her handbag a few weeks back. He was startled when she walked in on him, then aggressive.

'What are you doing?' she asked.

'My car keys are missing.' He continued to take things out of Calista's handbag: her purse, her lipstick, some letters from her mother. The casual deliberation of his movements was defiant, a loudness in the air between them: his shrug a portcullis that slammed suddenly shut, dividing them into their separate silences.

'Why would your car keys be in my bag, Alexandros?' Calista asked eventually, knowing she shouldn't, knowing that this was provocation. She kept her voice quiet, calm.

He shrugged. 'You tell me,' he said. 'You forget things; you move things around; maybe you take things that are not yours.' He shrugged at her, daring her. 'I have the right to look in *my wife*'s handbag if I so choose.' His eyes were cold, his face closed to her, the way it so often was these days.

'Your car keys are not in my bag,' Calista said. She struggled now to keep her tone even. She must not push him. 'They are on the hall table, where you always leave them.'

He threw her handbag across the table, knocking over the small vase filled with iris that Calista had picked earlier in the evening. Calista filled the house with flowers as often as she could; their perfume was an antidote to the toxic air that continued to build up around her.

Now, the small vase shattered and the water pooled across the surface of the table, reflecting the delicate blooms. Calista watched its rapid progress across the polished wood, keeping her eyes averted from her husband's. It was always best not to look directly at him, at times like this. Best, too, never to move in his presence to clear up whatever mess he had just created.

'Don't think I don't know,' he said, on his way past. He paused, thrust his face into hers. 'I am not a fool. Don't think I don't see what you are up to. I have eyes.' And he pushed her out of his way. Not too hard: just enough to make her stumble a little, enough to catch her off-balance.

'Alexandros,' she pleaded. She could hear the despair in her voice. 'Please, why won't you talk to me? Why are you treating me like this? I am not "up to" anything at all. Please, talk to me.' Calista had already spent countless hours trying to figure out what she was doing wrong; days trying to gauge a mood, to tiptoe around her own shortcomings. Years trying to make her husband happy.

But Alexandros didn't answer. Instead, he walked away from her, as though he had forgotten her existence. Down the long hallway he went, his back resolute, his steps steady and regular. She watched him as he made his way out to the carport. Calista waited, praying he might come back this time. He had done, on so many occasions in the past, full of remorse and kisses; although those times were long gone.

That day, Calista watched her husband's retreating form, heard the closing of the front door, the gunning of the car engine. It was an almost animal rumbling. Alexandros kept pressing the accelerator as though he couldn't wait to be gone, out of there, away from her. His urgency made Calista suspicious, all over again.

Lately, Alexandros seemed to come and go at odd hours, his routine changing without warning. It had made her wonder who the other woman might be. There would be no shortage, Calista knew – there were always too many young women waiting in the wings for Alexandros to notice them. Good luck to you, she thought, whoever you are.

Calista saw her husband's hands on the steering wheel. She imagined his fingers tapping impatiently as he waited for a car to pass. And then he was gone, clouds of yellow dust in his wake.

Calista stuffs the passport into the pocket of her dress and gets ready to wake her son. Omiros has begun to mooch and grizzle under his cotton blanket.

'Hello, darling,' Calista says cheerfully. She bends down and lifts his small body into her arms, kisses him on the forehead. 'Good boy,' she says, 'good boy.' There is no need to dress Omiros: his sleeping suit is perfect for a two-year-old. And unlike his older sister, he needs no explanations.

On the way out of the bedroom door, Calista reaches in and pulls a suitcase from the top shelf of the wardrobe. It is already packed with their things. She moves Omiros over onto her right hip and glances at her watch. She needs to get going.

Back in Imogen's room, she hands the child a pink rucksack, filled with her favourite belongings – some books, a sturdy cassette player, her colouring books and pencils. 'OK, Imogen, let's go.'

Omiros is still silent, sleepy. Calista makes her way down the stairs, careful not to rush. She holds Imogen's hand firmly in hers. The last thing she needs is for the child to stumble and fall. Once outside, the noise of the crickets is shrill: a warning that vibrates in the velvety evening air. Calista opens the door of her car and lifts Omiros in, lies him down on the back seat. He is sleeping again. Imogen climbs in beside him.

'Where are we going, Mummy?' Imogen asks. Her small face is serious, her eyes big with questions. But there is no fear in her voice. She sounds, above all, curious, interested.

'We are going to see Abuela María-Luisa and Grandad Timothy,' Calista says. 'We're going to pay them a visit in Ireland.' She hopes that the enthusiasm in her voice is convincing. 'Now,' she says, 'I need you to mind Omiros. He should sleep all the way to the airport. But if he wakes, you must take him on your knee. We have to get going if we're to catch our plane to Dublin.'

'Is it a surprise?' Imogen loves surprises.

'Yes, sweetheart,' Calista says. 'It is indeed a surprise.'

'Is Papa coming, too?'

Calista doesn't hesitate. 'Later, sweetheart. Papa will follow us later, just as he always does.'

She hurries back inside the house and grabs her handbag. She pulls the front door shut behind her and runs back to the car, where her children are waiting. She needs to hurry.

Lately, Calista has felt as though Alexandros has been testing her, as though he hopes to catch her out doing something she shouldn't. Each time he arrives back early, Calista senses his disappointment when he finds her quietly with a book, or watching television, or writing letters, the children in bed, the house orderly. She watches as he tries to find fault. Either way, it can be dangerous: he becomes angry when he finds evidence of her shortcomings, angry when he can't. When he can't, it's as though Calista has cheated him out of his entitlement to punish her.

She pulls carefully away from the kerb. This is the street that Petros and Maroulla live on, too, although they are several blocks away. The street, Ark Kyprianou, is filled with the beautiful, exclusive homes for the wealthy of Limassol. The houses are all large, set back from the street, surrounded by well-tended gardens. All are painted in bright, immaculate colours; their arched facades gleam in the sunlight; the wrought-iron balconies are stark and simple against the ornate plasterwork.

Calista wonders what secrets might be hiding behind such perfect walls.

The airport is buzzing. There are plenty of people around, something that makes Calista feel safer. She pulls a luggage trolley out of its station and manages, with difficulty, to place her suitcase on it, along with Imogen's rucksack. Omiros is heavy. His weight makes Calista hunch forward. Perspiration trickles down her face. She is trembling and everything takes twice as long. Her hands refuse to obey her, and her feet don't feel steady on the ground.

Imogen is quiet, and her eyes never leave her mother's face. Calista smiles at her. 'Omiros is getting to be a very big boy,' she says. 'It's a good thing Abi María-Luisa keeps a baby-buggy at her house, otherwise we'd never manage to get him around, would we?'

Imogen nods gravely.

Calista looks around. There is no sign of Alexandros anywhere. She begins to breathe. Maybe, just maybe . . .

Calista sees the check-in gates in the distance. She pauses for a moment, retrieves the passport from her pocket and pulls out the envelope with the plane tickets inside. She has bought them with cash – cash that she has earned from the sale of her photographs. Anastasios has been as good as his word. Calista rips open the envelope, pulls out the flimsy tickets.

'May we help you?'

Calista looks up. Two men, one on either side of her. Almost mirror images of each other, but one is slightly taller. They each have walkie-talkies; each man is completely bald; their heads glisten. Airport officials, Calista thinks. She smiles back at them brightly. 'We're managing fine, thank you.'

'May I see your tickets?' the taller one asks her.

Calista hands them over. 'We're going to see my parents in Ireland,' she offers. 'Isn't that right, Imogen?'

Imogen nods. 'Yes,' she says. 'Abi María-Luisa and Grandad Timothy. They live in Dublin. It's a surprise.'

The official scrutinizes the tickets, turning each thin page, one after the other, as though there is something new to be discovered underneath. 'May I see your passport?'

Calista hands it over. Her insides are churning. An innocent visit to grandparents: what possible reason could they have to stop her?

'Come with us, please.'

Already, the second man has begun to push the luggage trolley, away from the departure gates, all the way across the terminal.

'Wait!' Calista cries. 'What is going on?' She starts to run after the trolley, stops, turns back again to the taller man. He looks at her, his face impassive.

'What are you doing?' Calista pulls Imogen closer to her, places a protective arm around her daughter. She holds on to Omiros as firmly as she can. 'Why are you stopping me? You have no right! I demand to be taken to the police!'

Curious knots of onlookers are already gathering, staring. Calista appeals to them. 'I want to take my children to see their grandparents,' she says, desperation making her shrill. 'And these men are trying to stop me!'

'Lower your voice, madam,' the taller man says, his hand already firmly under Calista's elbow. 'You are creating a disturb-ance.'

Calista wrenches her arm away, angry now. 'Leave me alone!' she cries. 'I insist you call the police.'

'Madam,' the taller man hisses, his hand on her arm again, his mouth at her ear, 'we are the police.'

And then Calista sees Imogen's face, her mouth like a huge 'O', the tears streaming. And Omiros wakes, howling.

And Calista knows that it is over.

The office is small and hot, despite the air conditioning and the fan turning constantly in the corner. Calista sits on one side of the desk, the taller policeman across from her. The passport and the tickets are spread out between them, like an accusation.

Calista sticks to her story. 'I want to take my children to Ireland to see their grandparents. As you can see, I have booked return flights. I don't understand the problem.'

'The problem.' The policeman considers this for a moment. 'The problem is, Mrs Demitriades, that you have been attempting to remove your children from this jurisdiction against the wishes of your husband. Child abduction is a very serious matter.'

Calista stares at him. 'Abduction? These are *my* children! We are going to Ireland for a holiday, to see my parents! How can that be abduction?'

He bows his head, waits for her to stop, as she knows she must. 'These are also your husband's children, and in the circumstances, he does not wish you to take them out of the country.'

'The circumstances?' Calista's mouth is dry. She sips at the glass of water in front of her. She knows that somehow Alexandros has beaten her, as she should have known he would.

The policeman spreads his hands, a gesture of apology. 'We understand that there are some difficulties . . .' He shrugs. It is a movement eloquent of all that it symbolizes. The room is very quiet. Imogen has been standing at her side throughout, leaning into her mother, refusing the chair that was offered her earlier. Omiros is fretful, wriggling out of Calista's arms, making his unsteady way around the room before coming back to her again, struggling onto her knee and then beginning the whole process again moments later.

She has to stop this. She cannot let it go on any longer. 'What happens now?' Calista asks. She doesn't even try to hide the defeat in her voice.

'The children's father is on his way. I understand that Mr Demitriades is accompanied by his mother. They will make arrangements for the children until all of this can be settled.' Calista feels the terror that has begun to grow inside her. She grips Imogen's hand tightly.

'Where are they taking them?'

'That's not for me to say.' The policeman shakes his head at her. 'You, however, are free to continue to Ireland, should you so wish. Your husband will not press charges.'

Calista looks at him, unable to form the words. Leave? Without her children? She scoops Omiros up into her arms, places one hand on her daughter's head. She struggles into standing, realizing all at once that her legs have no power.

Finally, she says: 'I am not going anywhere. My place is with my children.' She feels full of rage now, a rage that she knows is impotent, but she will not please any of them by showing it. She straightens, looks him right in the eye.

'As you wish.' The policeman stands, gathers up the tickets and nods curtly in Calista's direction. Then he stops, puts Calista's passport on the desk in front of her and leaves without another word.

That's it, then, his departing back says to her.
You're on your own now.

Calista sits there, in that small office, as her mind tries to grapple with what has just happened. She feeds the children with rusks, pieces of fruit and insists that they drink water. She does all of these things mechanically, locked into the tiny, repetitive tasks of automatic mothering. She doesn't want to think about the enormity of the future.

She is twenty-five years old, the mother of two small children, with little money and no escape. She isn't stupid: she knows the power of her husband's family on this island. She has engaged in a battle she could never win.

Alexandros arrives within the hour, with Maroulla in tow. He is surrounded by an air of aggrieved innocence. His arrival is so swift that Calista is taken aback. How has he had the time to go and collect his mother? And where was he when they telephoned him?

Suddenly, Calista has the bitter taste of betrayal in her mouth. Who is it? Mirofora? Haridimos? Or has Maroulla been spying on her? Or – and here Calista feels shock ripple through her – Alexandros must have had her followed.

Now he enters the airport office, Maroulla at his heels. He looks at Calista, and even then she believes that he doesn't really see her. Omiros toddles across the room and hurls himself at his father's legs, squeaking in delight. Imogen moves closer to her mother, slips one sticky hand into hers.

'I hope you are satisfied,' Alexandros says. 'I hope you know that you are responsible for breaking this family apart.'

Calista tries to speak. Her words are faint, trembling, but she summons strength from somewhere. She turns to Maroulla. 'Can you leave us, please, for a few moments? I should like to speak to my husband.'

She has the benefit of surprise. Before Alexandros can stop her – and he tries – Maroulla leaves the room, closing the door behind her.

'How dare you—' he begins.

'Listen to me, Alexandros,' Calista says, urgency finally giving strength to her voice. 'I needed time to think: you will not speak to me; you are angry with me all the time; we have stopped . . . loving each other properly.' She hesitates. She will not accuse him of anything else, otherwise she will lose her children. 'I wanted you to know how serious this is. I needed you to listen to me.'

'And you do this by betraying me? By going behind my back, by stealing my children from me?' Alexandros's voice is rising steadily. His face is tight with rage. But Calista is no longer frightened: there are other people around; he will not harm her here.

Besides, the worst has already happened.

'I was not betraying you,' Calista says. 'I needed your attention. If I intended running away with the children for good, why would I buy return tickets? I'd always intended coming back, Alexandros; but we need to fix this marriage.'

'There is no marriage,' he says. His tone is curt. 'I should have listened to my father. You will never be one of us. And if you think, for one moment, that you will ever take my children from me, then you do not know Alexandros Demitriades.' He turns and barks words at the door. He summons his mother, demands that she comes back into the room and does her duty as a grandmother.

'Go back,' he says to Calista. 'Go back to where you came from. You do not belong here.'

Maroulla comes in and Alexandros hands Omiros straight into her arms. Then he walks towards Imogen, his arms outstretched. Instinctively, the little girl hides behind her mother, her hands clinging to Calista's dress. Alexandros makes a grab for her, and Calista can't bear it any longer.

'Don't! Please!' she cries. 'Don't take her from me!'

But Alexandros is not listening. He pushes Calista away. 'Go home,' he hisses. 'You can never win.'

He lifts his daughter easily into his arms and Imogen wails, her hands clutching at Calista. It is all too quick, and Alexandros is too strong and too sure. Before Calista has time to respond, they are gone, all of them, and the door to the office swings shut behind them. Calista falls to her knees and howls, paralysed by defeat. The animal, wounded sound that seems to be coming from her fills the small, stifling room.

When she comes to, what seems like hours later, the room is dim and she is huddled with her back to the wall, a tear-soaked Monkey clutched to her chest.

Imogen

Limassol, 1974

IMOGEN IS SILENT ALL THE way back to Aiya's house. She is too scared to cry. Aiya Maroulla tries to hug her, but Imogen struggles free again and again until, finally, Papa shouts at her. She and Aiya and Omiros are in the back of the car. Papa is driving: angry-driving. Aiya tries to quieten him from time to time, saying things like 'Alexandros, the children . . .' or 'Alexandros, slow down' or just 'Please, Alexandros . . .', but Papa doesn't listen. Instead, he shouts at her, too, and waves his hands around, even though he should always keep them on the steering wheel, just like Mummy says.

Imogen wants Monkey. She cries for him. His furry absence has made her chest ache. She asks for Monkey, over and over until Aiya whispers: 'Monkey is with Mummy, Imogen. He'll take care of her. Don't cry.'

And so, finally, Imogen quietens. Aiya is right: Monkey will take care of Mummy; Mummy will take care of Monkey.

When they get home, Papa sends Imogen straight up to bed with Aiya. He carries Omiros up the stairs himself. As Aiya tucks her in, she whispers: 'I'll explain everything to you tomorrow, my sweet. Mummy and Papa have had a misunderstanding, that's all. It will all be sorted out, you'll see. You're not to worry.'

Imogen is not sure what a misunderstanding is. She knows the word 'understand' because her English teacher uses it a lot. Misunderstanding sounds like its opposite – and they learned all about English words and their opposites last week, things like loved and unloved; fortunate and unfortunate; happy and unhappy. Misunderstanding hadn't been one of them, though. But even when the children say 'no' to something, even while they're telling Teacher that they *don't* understand, nobody ever gets upset, not even Teacher. Nobody ever *cries*. Not like Mummy cried tonight. There must have been a lot that she didn't understand.

'Everything will be fine,' Aiya is still whispering. 'You and I will chat tomorrow. Keep your questions until then, and don't make Papa cross when he comes in to say goodnight. Can you do that?'

Imogen nods. Yes, she can do that. When Papa is angry, his face goes all black and his eyes are no longer kind. Imogen has already seen that tonight and she doesn't want to see it again. Not ever. She shivers.

Aiya pulls the blanket more closely around her. 'Are you cold? Do you want another blanket?'

But Imogen isn't that kind of cold – the kind that a blanket will send away. Instead, she feels shivery and loose, as though someone has scooped out all of her insides and left her empty.

'That's enough, Mother. It's time she went to sleep.' Papa is in the doorway. His face isn't black anymore, but he still doesn't look like Papa.

Aiya gets up off the bed. She frowns, as if something is hurting her. Perhaps it is her knees. Aiya talks a lot about her knees. 'Is Omiros asleep?' she asks.

'Yes. No need to disturb him.'

'I wasn't intending to disturb him. I just want to look in on him.' Aiya's voice is sharper now. Is she cross with Papa, too? Is everyone cross with everyone else?

Papa doesn't answer. Instead, he bends down and kisses Imogen on the forehead. But he doesn't really look at her. Instead, he seems to be looking at the wall behind her head. 'Sleep, now, there's a good girl.'

Imogen is afraid to ask, but she thinks that she and Omiros will not be going to see Abuela María-Luisa and Grandad Timothy after all. Mummy isn't here anymore and she has taken the surprise away with her.

Imogen also wants to ask, but doesn't dare, when Mummy will be coming back. She glances at the doorway, where Aiya Maroulla is now standing, her finger to her lips, her dark eyes warning Imogen. It's funny – although Aiya cannot hear what Imogen is thinking, Imogen knows that Aiya is telling her not to ask Papa anything about Mummy. Maybe because that would make another misunderstanding and Papa would get angry all over again.

'Goodnight, Papa,' Imogen says instead.

And Aiya Maroulla smiles at her.

It's hard to sleep without Monkey. The bed feels hot, and then cold, and Imogen can't find her usual comfortable spot. That's because this isn't her bed, and her own bed is the one that she sleeps best in – Mummy always says that. Besides, there is a rumble of voices from downstairs, the kind of rumble that won't go away. Imogen hears Papa, then Bapi Petros, then Aiya Maroulla. Sometimes they speak separately and the noise is quieter. But then they all talk together and the noise rumbles louder and louder. She can't make out any words, though, which is funny. Just noises, banging into each other, as if they are trying to find their way around in the dark.

After a while, they become calmer. Imogen hopes that the words have all found their way home.

She sleeps.

Calista

Limassol, 1974

CALISTA MAKES HER UNSTEADY WAY around the car park. The airport is suddenly unfamiliar, filled with shadows, strange noises, shapes that startle her with their gleaming suddenness.

They are cars, Calista realizes. Just cars. She must find hers; she must try to remember where she's parked it.

And then she will go to Yiannis. He is her only hope.

Calista keeps her finger on the bell. He has to be home: please, please let Yiannis be home.

Finally, she hears his voice across the intercom. 'Yes?'

'Yiannis, it's Calista. Let me in. Please, I need your help.'

The buzzer sounds instantly and Calista lets herself in, allowing the heavy metal door to swing shut behind her. She takes the lift to the third floor, where Yiannis is waiting in the hallway.

'Come in,' he says. He closes the apartment door behind her.

'Is there anyone here?' she demands, looking around her.

'No,' Yiannis says. He looks perplexed. 'I am alone. Calista, you look like death. What has happened?'

'You don't know?' she asks, angry at him as well. 'Are you sure you don't know, or are you just keeping it from me?'

Yiannis shakes his head slowly. 'I don't know what you're

talking about. If I knew, I wouldn't ask. Sit down. Let me get you a brandy.'

Calista shivers.

'What happened?' Yiannis asks her. He pours some brandy into a glass and hands it to her. 'Wait, let me get you a blanket.'

When he returns, he looks at Calista closely. 'Something bad has happened. What is it?'

Calista tells him.

When she finishes, Yiannis says, his voice so quiet she can barely hear him: 'Where are the children?'

'Alexandros took them. Along with your mother.' And now Calista can't help herself. 'Why do you all protect him?' she cries. 'He is a bully and a liar and a wife-beater. You knew that! You knew that Alexandros beats me!' Calista tries to stand up, but she falls back onto the sofa again.

Yiannis puts one hand on her forearm: restraining her. His fingers are warm and firm, even through the fabric of the blanket.

'I understood that Alexandros had struck you once,' Yiannis says quietly. 'I did not realize it was habitual – forgive me.' He stops, and Calista knows what he is going to say next. 'If you remember, you did not wish him to know that I had discovered this . . . side to him. I kept silent for your sake.'

Tears well and fall and Calista lets them. She doesn't even attempt to brush them away. 'What am I going to do? I can't bear it. How can I bear it?'

Yiannis drags one hand through his hair. He looks years older. 'I will try to find out what is happening,' he says. 'But there is nothing more we can do tonight, and you are exhausted. Come, there is a room where you can sleep. We'll speak again in the morning.'

*

When Calista wakes just before seven, it takes her a moment to realize where she is, a moment before the full horror of the night before floods her. She cries out.

Yiannis knocks on the door at once. 'Calista? Are you awake? Don't worry – you are safe.'

Frantic, Calista pulls on her clothes and stumbles out of the bedroom to where Yiannis is waiting. Her whole body feels bruised and battered; even her scalp feels tender, although this time Alexandros has not laid a finger upon her.

Yiannis's face is white, strained. The remains of breakfast are on the table; a diary is open beside the telephone. Calista wonders briefly if he has been to bed. He pushes his glasses up, and they rest there, at the top of his forehead. His eyes look tired, circled by dull, dry flesh.

'What?' she says. 'What is it? Tell me, what have you found out?'

'Sit, please.' He pours coffee. Calista cannot bear the waiting, and she knows by Yiannis's face that he has something to tell her. Something that is not good.

'I called my father at five thirty,' he says. 'He has a private line, a separate number that only he and I have access to. I use it in emergencies. We spoke for a long time.'

'And?'

'He is unhappy – both he and my mother are very unhappy. Alexandros has told them that you are having an affair, that you have been unfaithful to him for some time. They say he has evidence to prove it.'

Calista looks at him. It takes her several seconds to find her voice. '*What?*'

Yiannis looks at her, his gaze level. He places both hands on the table in front of him, his fingers interlocked. 'Is it true?'

'*No!*' Calista shouts. 'Jesus Christ, no! How could you even *think* that of me?' She stands up from the table, knocking over her chair as she does so. It clatters backwards onto the tiled floor. She feels as though anger has split her in two; she is beside herself. 'I have *never* been unfaithful to Alexandros! I have *never* broken my vows! I've been a good wife, a good mother. I have even put up with his beatings. Do your parents know that their son beats his wife?'

Yiannis sighs, looks downwards.

Slowly, Calista understands. 'God Almighty,' she says, taking a step back from him. 'What sort of people are you? Is it OK for Alexandros to beat me if he thinks I've been unfaithful? Is that what you and your parents believe?'

Yiannis looks at her. His expression is guarded. 'It is not a question of what I believe. My parents are concerned for my brother's honour and his reputation.'

Calista almost laughs. 'His honour and his reputation? What kind of honour might that be, I wonder – a man who uses his fists on his wife? And what about me? Do I count for nothing?' She stops, looks again at Yiannis. 'I thought you were different. Tell me the truth. Do you believe me? Do you believe that I have been a faithful wife to your brother, a good mother to his children?' She slams both fists on the table, hurting them with the force of her anguish. 'You know that I have!'

Yiannis stands up. He looks helpless. 'This is difficult for my family, Calista—'

She shakes her head at him. 'No,' she says. 'No, it is not difficult. It is very simple. It is the difference between truth and lies.' She grabs her handbag, pushes her way past Yiannis. 'I am going. I was a fool to expect any help here.' She turns back to look at him. 'You're all the same. You all protect each other. The foreigner must always be the liar, the enemy. You have no honour, any of you.' Calista makes her way towards the door.

'Wait,' Yiannis says. He looks unhappy. 'I have told my father that you came to me for help. I have said that natural justice demands that he see you, that both he and my mother see you.'

Something strikes Calista then. 'By the way, what evidence does Alexandros say he has?'

Yiannis looks at her. He seems wary and Calista's anger flares again, but she keeps it under control.

'My father gave no detail.'

'That's convenient.' Calista allows the silence between them to thicken.

'Do you know Hristina . . . ?' Yiannis begins at last.

Calista feels the impact of her name as a physical blow. 'Hristina Emilianides?' Hristina, who took her shopping and to the hairdressers's. Hristina, who pretended to be her friend.

He nods.

'She has accused me of having an affair?'

'Apparently so. Yes.'

Calista shakes her head in disbelief. Hristina. How clever Alexandros is. She shivers.

Yiannis looks at her, concerned. 'Are you all right?' he asks. 'I mean . . .'

Calista shakes her head. 'No,' she says. 'I am not all right. How could I possibly be all right?'

'Sit down, please,' Yiannis says. 'Please don't go. Let me see if I can find you somewhere to stay. Allow me to help you.'

A little later, Yiannis says: 'I have booked you into the Asteria Hotel for the next five nights. It would compromise you to stay here any longer. It is not appropriate.'

Calista nods. Not appropriate, she thinks bitterly. I'm the one who has to be appropriate and I've done nothing wrong.

Yiannis taps his pen a couple of times on the open pages of his diary. 'My parents are very old-fashioned, very traditional people,' he says. 'But they are also good people, people of their word. My father would be most unhappy if Alexandros was violent. Let me go to him right away.' Yiannis pauses. 'May I now tell him all that you have told me? Do I have your permission?'

Calista shrugs. 'I've nothing left to lose, have I? He will either believe me or he won't. But I would like the opportunity to face him, to tell him the truth, even if he doesn't believe me. I'll do whatever it takes to get my children back.'

Yiannis stands up, reaches for his car keys. 'I will go to him now,' he says. 'And I will find out where the children are and let you know. That much I can promise you. Now, let me take you to the Asteria Hotel. You can have breakfast and wait for me there.' He glances at Calista's dress. 'Have you everything you need?'

'I'll get my case. It's in the back of my car.'

'Let's go.'

'What about your mother?' Calista asks suddenly.

'My mother can often surprise me,' Yiannis says. 'She chooses her battles – my father is a very strong-willed man. She knows how to get around him. I have often gone to her for help when my father was being . . . stubborn.'

'How can they possibly believe I was unfaithful?'

'Alexandros is their son,' Yiannis says, shrugging. 'I'm sorry, but it's as simple as that.'

Calista wonders if she would feel the same way about Omiros: would she still protect him, believe in him, love him, no matter what?

Calista thinks she already knows the answer to that, and wishes that she didn't.

Pilar

Madrid, 1974

PILAR IS AT HER LOCAL fruit and vegetable market by six thirty. Mornings in late September are kind: the fury has gone out of the sun. There will be some heat later on, of course, but for now, the air is balmy. There is even a pleasant breeze. Pilar's favourite stallholder, Nacho, greets her.

'What's good this morning, Nacho?' she asks.

He grins, spreading his hands wide, lifting his expressive shoulders at the same time: all his produce is good. 'Only the best for you, Señorita Pilar,' he says, 'and at a very special price.'

'Yeah, yeah,' she says. 'You've given me the same line every day for two years.' She consults her residents' lists. 'Right,' she says. 'Let's get started before the crowds arrive.'

Pilar makes her way back to Calle de las Huertas, several bulging plastic bags in each hand. For several months now, she has found that repetition, the routine accomplishment of mundane tasks, the familiarity of ordinary daily friendships have all helped. She is proud of what she has achieved: a bland, quiet, ordinary life.

No more random men, no whiskey-drinking alone in bars, no more self-destruction.

Her panic attack on the Metro earlier in the year had been the catalyst for change. When Pilar told the young doctor that she knew what she needed to do, she meant it. After she left the hospital, she slipped back into the *portería* late that morning, distributed the post as usual, carried out her residents' instructions, supervised Rufina's cleaning and polishing. Pilar was glad of the careful – they would have called it respectful – distance that she had always maintained from her residents. It seemed that nobody had even noticed she was gone.

The following morning, she phoned Maribel and Alicia and invited them to dinner. Then she wrote to her brother, Francisco-José, telling him she would visit Torre de Santa Juanita before the end of the month. Pilar kept her letter light, affectionate, full of fictional good news.

Change is necessary, Pilar reflects now, as she approaches her building, the bulging bags of fruit and vegetables evenly distributed between both hands. Change is good. Not because of any moral imperative: not because she feels guilty or remorseful about the past. Not even because that awful panic attack frightened her into submission, into making a fearful inventory of her life.

No. Pilar is quite certain of that.

Change is imperative if Pilar is now to pursue her decision, no matter how long it takes, no matter how much money it costs.

After seven years, Pilar has now made up her mind.

She is going to do whatever it takes to get her boy back. Already, in a fat new diary, Pilar has listed all the places she intends to visit: the hostel, the clinic, the bishop's palace, if necessary. She has dates, names, times, addresses, telephone numbers. All waiting.

She has taken a year to prove to herself that she can change, to show herself, above all, that she has the courage, the tenacity, the will to follow Francisco-José to the ends of the earth.

And she is ready to start now.

Calista

Limassol, 1974

CALISTA WAKES. Her thin, dream-filled sleep is pierced by a great commotion that has just filled her bedroom in the Hotel Asteria. It takes a moment for her to come to, to realize that the ruckus is coming from the street below.

Car horns are sounding, engines revving; men are shouting: the roar of traffic is all at once deafening. Occasional words float up to her bedroom window, but she cannot make sense of what they mean, once she puts them together. She tries to concentrate, but the garbled phrases, the short, jagged sentences continue to crash against each other, their sharp edges blunting all meaning.

Calista throws back the sheet and makes her way cautiously towards the window. She is frightened. The atmosphere outside has become charged. The car horns, the noise, the incessant movement of traffic lend an urgency to the voices below her window. And inside, there is not enough air to breathe. The July heat is already stifling, and the air conditioning hasn't been working properly for days.

Calista glances at her watch. Two o'clock: she must have been asleep for over an hour. Yiannis is now two hours late. That's either good news or bad news. Calista has given up trying to call it. The slow, steady leaching away of hope over the past few days has left her trembling on the brink of exhaustion. Without her children, she cannot think, cannot plan. It is as though the onslaught of grief has abruptly retreated, leaving her numb and empty in its wake.

Yiannis has told her to hold firm, to wait in her hotel room until he has news from Petros. As she'd suspected, Alexandros had fled with his mother and Imogen and Omiros to the Troodos Mountains, to the house in Platres. They had gone there the day after Alexandros had swifted her children away from her. Calista has no way of reaching him there. The car she used to drive was gone. It had vanished without trace the day before yesterday. And even if she had found a way to follow, her husband's door would be locked and barred against her.

Calista leans forward cautiously to try and see what is going on in the street outside her hotel. For a moment, she wonders whether something has finally spilled over politically: the last few days have been stalked by an escalating tension that has been vented on radio, on television, in the national newspapers. Calista has not engaged with it. It has been background noise, static on the airwaves of her own personal plight. But she cannot ignore it any longer. Like a wilful child, it has been plucking at her sleeve for some time and refuses to go away.

She sees men gathered together in tight knots in the street below, in sprawling groups, in crowds whose contours continue to shift and change as she watches: a whole undulating sea of people, washing up in waves on the pavements. Most have transistor radios clamped to their ears; some are scanning newspapers. All are intent, gesticulating wildly, smoking, shouting news to one another.

Calista watches, listens, tries to piece it all together. The cars are now barely moving: they block all the streets leading onto the square and Calista suddenly panics. What if Yiannis cannot get to her? What if something has happened to the children, to him, and he is unable to reach her?

Calista moves back from the window, not wanting to be seen

in case being seen is suddenly the wrong thing to do. As she makes her way towards the telephone, there is an urgent knocking at her door. She hesitates. She puts her ear to the wooden surface and hears: 'Calista? Open the door. It's me, Yiannis.'

Washed with relief, she unlocks the door. Her brother-in-law is standing there, perspiration running in rivulets down his face. His hair is matted, plastered to his head. Dark circles bloom on the underarms of his shirt. And his brown eyes are alight with something that Calista thinks is fear.

'Quickly,' he says, pushing his way into the room. 'Take your handbag and your passport and follow me.'

'But—'

'Now!' he barks. 'If you ever want to see your children again, you must trust me right here, right now. We must go. I will explain on the way.'

'On the way where?'

'Quickly,' he says, pulling her out into the corridor. 'Not the lift: the stairs. Be quick.'

Calista follows, her shoes making an anxious, clacking sound as they descend the tiled steps to the basement.

There is a taxi waiting there, its engine humming. Yiannis opens one of the doors. 'Get in.'

Calista obeys.

When they start to move, she turns to Yiannis. Her head is pounding; she knows that her face must be as white as his.

'What's happening?'

'A coup,' he says. 'President Makarios has just been deposed. All hell has broken loose. Eoka-B are in control. That's all I know for sure.'

Calista tries to remember what she can, but her brain has seized in terror. Eoka-B: Colonel Grivas's men, the men that Petros condemned over and over again as extremists in their demands for *enosis* – political union with Greece. Calista knows that the organization was banned by Makarios, as recently as three months ago, in the midst of growing unrest. And now they have deposed the man they regard as a traitor.

My children, is all that Calista can think. How can I keep my children safe in the middle of all of this?

'Where are we going?' she asks Yiannis.

He turns, looks at her. 'To the airport,' he says. 'You are going home. I have got you on a flight to London. From there, you can get to Dublin if you wish. It was all I could manage.'

'No!' Calista cries. She raises her arms. Yiannis grabs both her fists, makes her look at him.

'Listen to me,' he says. 'There is talk of a Turkish invasion. I do not believe it is mere talk: I believe it is real, that it will happen in a matter of days. When it does, you might not be able to leave. They will close the airport. You must go now.'

'But Imogen—'

'Imogen is safe. Omiros is safe. I saw them last night with my own two eyes in my parents' house in Platres. They are both well; they are both fine. But you must go now.' He pauses, leans closer to her. 'For now, you *must* go, Calista. There is no other choice. When things calm down, you will come back.'

He reaches into his pocket, then, and pulls out an envelope. 'Take it.' He lowers his voice. 'There's three hundred pounds in sterling here. And an address in Palmers Green in London for Aristides, an old friend of mine. Go there. You can trust Aristides and his wife. I will get in touch with you as soon as I can.'

'What about my babies?' Helpless, Calista clutches at Yiannis's arm.

'They are in no danger – trust me. But I cannot look after you and them and my father's business and my father's family in Nicosia – I simply cannot. Go until it is safe to return. I will bring you back, and you will see your children again. I swear it. But now you must go.'

Calista turns her face away from him, looks out of the window. She can no longer speak. The streets are heaving with people. News is spreading: people cluster everywhere around radios. They congregate on the pavements outside local shops. Nobody seems to have stayed indoors. It is as though this is news that can only be absorbed in the company of others: it is too much to deal with alone.

Yiannis is right. Calista no longer has a place here.

He touches her elbow. 'You have your passport?'

'Yes.' That and the clothes I stand up in, Calista thinks. 'Yiannis, how will you keep in touch?'

The taxi pulls up at the departures area. Yiannis pulls some drachma notes out of his pocket; at the same time, he nods towards the envelope he has just given her. 'My friend's address, in there,' he says. 'I will telephone Aristides at home, every week. Make contact with him as soon as you arrive. He will help you. Now put that money away. Keep it safe.'

Calista puts the envelope in her bag, zips it closed. 'Thank you.'

'It is family money,' he says, somewhat curtly. 'You are entitled to it. I will send more when I can. Open an account with the Cyprus Popular Bank in Green Lanes – Aristides will help you. I can transfer money to you there.'

They run from the taxi into the chaos of the departures area. Terrified faces are everywhere, children screaming, baggage piled high and treacherous.

'Quickly,' Yiannis says, pulling her by the hand. He stops for no one. He has donned authority like a suit of armour. He is untouchable, Calista thinks, filled with a bitter gratitude.

They arrive at the gate and Yiannis takes the ticket from her, waves it in the air, has himself called forward to a check-in desk. Calista has no time to think about the last time she was here, the two bald policemen, her children by the hand. Then, she had been stopped when she wanted to leave. Now, she leaves when she wants nothing more than to stay. Her passport is approved, her boarding card issued.

'Go now,' Yiannis says, giving her a gentle shove. 'Do not linger.'

She turns to say goodbye. Yiannis kisses her briefly on both cheeks and she fights to keep her tears under control.

'Don't ever doubt it,' he says. 'I promise you that you will see your children again.'

It is too much. Calista sobs and throws her arms around Yiannis. She is about to move away, to say a last goodbye, when he pulls her closer. He says nothing, but his embrace is a powerful one; he puts one hand on Calista's hair, presses his lips to her forehead.

Calista takes a step back. She cannot speak. She looks at Yiannis, her eyes searching his. She sees her own shock, her own confusion, reflected there. She wants to stay, to continue the conversation he has just started, but it's impossible. She is waved along, impatiently, and the force of the crowd moves her towards the door that leads to the plane.

The last thing she sees before she has to face forward once again is Yiannis, watching her. He raises one hand, and stands there, the only solid, unmoving body in a throng of swarming, fearful people.

Pilar

Madrid, 1974

PILAR HOPES THAT SISTER MARÍA-ANGELES is not on duty this evening. Perhaps she'll have moved on from the hostel and the laundry, and someone else will be in charge. It's been seven years, after all, and people do move on: even at convents. Pilar would rather face anyone other than Sister High and Mighty herself.

She steps into the hallway of the hostel and is immediately overwhelmed by all the familiar smells of the past. Top notes of beeswax and disinfectant, with an unpleasant undertone of onions cooking. There is also that peculiar smell that cold weather brings with it: an austere, hostile scent that reminds Pilar all too painfully of Torre de Santa Juanita. With an effort, she gathers her courage around her like a coat and marches towards the office.

God could prove his existence right now, Pilar thinks. He could make sure that Sister Florencia herself sits behind this office door. Pilar knocks, twice. And holds her breath.

The door opens and Sister María-Angeles stands before her. It takes a moment before her eyebrows shoot up. She glares at Pilar, her pale cheeks colouring.

'Well,' she says. Then: 'Well,' again. 'So you're back.' Her words seem to say that she had never doubted it; but Pilar can see her surprise.

It is the first time she has ever seen the woman on the

back foot. Good. Keep her there. Time to seize the advantage. 'Good evening, Sister. How nice to see you again.' And Pilar smiles.

'Is it indeed, Señorita Domínguez. I seem to remember that you couldn't wait to shake the dust off your feet as you left us. I seem to remember your ingratitude above everything else.' Pilar watches as the nun begins to warm to her theme.

She fixes her smile in place. 'That's all a very long time ago, Sister. A lot of water under the bridge since then.'

'What do you want?' The nun's posture is stiff, alert to insult. 'I presume you do want something, given that you have graced us with a visit. I'm busy. Make your request.' She half turns towards the desk, shuffling the busy papers that lie there.

Pilar keeps her irritation in check. 'I'm actually looking for Sister Florencia,' she says.

'May I ask why?' Sister looks taken aback.

No, Pilar thinks. No, you definitely may not. 'It's delicate,' she says. 'I understand that Sister Florencia helped some families to adopt babies in the past. My brother and his wife are, sadly, without children . . . and so I thought of her. I was hoping – my whole family is hoping – that Sister Florencia might be able to help them adopt a child.'

The nun's face fills with suspicion. 'Who told you that?' she says. 'Who told you that Sister Florencia would be in a position to help you with that?'

Pilar's answer is careful. 'I can't remember. I'm here, Sister, only because I wish to help my brother and his wife. They will make good Catholic parents. I promised them I would make enquiries on their behalf. This seemed the best, the most natural place to start. I don't wish to cause any trouble.'

Sister María-Angeles smooths the skirts of her habit. She does not look at Pilar. 'Sister Florencia serves God elsewhere,' she says finally. Her voice is flat. 'She is no longer in Madrid.'

Pilar feels hope fall away from her. 'I understand,' she says. 'I thought that that might be the case. And so I've come to you, a woman in authority. I hoped you might be able to help me find her.' Perhaps a little flattery might not go astray, in the circumstances.

But Sister María-Angeles shakes her head. Pilar can see the undertow of triumph in that movement, in the expression that crosses the woman's face. 'I'm afraid I cannot possibly give out that sort of information.'

Pilar nods. 'Then perhaps you might be able to ask her to contact me instead? If I leave my name and address? My brother and his wife are most anxious to have news.' She sees something struggle across the nun's face. Duty, Pilar reckons; duty doing battle with revenge. Revenge wins.

'Why should I? Why should I do that? Why should I help you?' She's warming up again.

Pilar meets the older woman's gaze. 'It's not about helping me,' she says. 'It's about helping a young and unhappy childless couple. But I might have known. No kindness, no compassion, no understanding.' Pilar prepares to leave. 'You're consistent, at least, Sister – I'll grant you that. The bishop will be keen to hear about how you treat good Catholic families.'

Pilar turns and walks steadily out through the door.

But at least she now knows. While Sister María-Angeles would not meet her eye, she, Pilar, had time to glance quickly at the weekly duty roster that was always displayed on the back wall of the office. Sister Florencia's name was nowhere to be seen.

It was worth a chance, but Pilar is sure that Sister María-Angeles is telling the truth. She will have to look for Sister Florencia elsewhere. It is as Pilar has expected. She refuses to be defeated.

She has her list. She has her names, her addresses, her

telephone numbers. Pilar will continue to work her way through all of them. This is a setback: a small, anticipated setback.

She is, after all, just beginning.

Calista

London, 1974

CALISTA HESITATES, moves closer to the street light. She checks the number again. Thirty-seven: a large, Edwardian house, solid and comforting. It reminds her for a painful moment of home, Dublin home. Right now, there is no other. Home and family are a concept that has gone missing, a longing, an empty space waiting to be filled. Their absence is like a breath intaken, a stilled heartbeat of loss. She must telephone Dublin as soon as she can.

Calista moves towards the garden gate and waits for a moment. She watches the way the light filters through a chink in the curtains of the downstairs bay window. It's almost midnight. Somebody is still up; but shouldn't she wait until tomorrow? Find a hotel somewhere? Who needs a stranger calling at midnight?

The front door opens and a tall, slender woman steps out. A small dog yaps, dashes past her ankles, hurtles through the garden and flings itself at the gate, tail wagging, barking furiously. The studs on its collar glint with malice. 'Be quiet, Raffles,' the woman says, hurrying to his side. She leans down to put a restraining hand on the dog's collar. Raffles growls.

The woman looks up. Green eyes, Calista notices, luminous in the light of the street lamp. Her mouth goes dry and she is unable to speak. The woman speaks first. 'May I help you?' she asks. Her voice is low, pleasant. English. Calista falters. She must have got the wrong house.

'I'm sorry,' she says. Her voice sounds odd: it is a hollow echo inside her head. It is the first time she has heard herself speak since she left Yiannis late this afternoon. On the plane, she had turned her head away from all conversational assaults, feigning sleep. She didn't want to talk about politics, about war, about the future of Cyprus.

It seemed that the whole world was filled with bitter people fighting each other. Just two short months ago, Calista's heart had stilled when the TV screen in her own kitchen had erupted with images of Dublin and Monaghan, their centres ripped open by massive explosions. Horrified, she'd watched the streets she knew, the places she loved, all filled with screaming people, with mutilated bodies, with thick palls of smoke. She'd sat through the night, Maroulla at her side, and tried over and over to phone home. The lines were jammed; meanwhile the news kept getting worse: ten dead; twenty; then twenty-three. A baby about to be born. Hundreds injured. It was four in the morning when Calista finally got through to María-Luisa. Maroulla had held her as she wept for hours, terrified that somewhere out there, someone she loved had died. Someone whose loss had yet to be revealed to her.

And today, travelling to London, Calista had not wanted to talk about war – that war, or the war she was now fleeing. Above all, she hadn't wanted to talk about the life that she was leaving behind. 'I'm sorry,' she says again. 'I think perhaps I have the wrong house.'

'What number are you looking for?' the woman asks. She has lifted the dog up into her arms and Raffles has finally quietened under the firm pressure of her hands.

'I'm looking for number 37 Broomfield Close. For Aristides Michaelides.'

The woman looks surprised. 'Then you've found us,' she says. 'That's my husband. May I ask—'

But she gets no further. Calista breaks, grief and relief unravelling her at last as she stands in this suburban street, undone by a kindly voice. For an instant, she wonders what this woman must be seeing: a grubby, distraught stranger. A stranger clutching a well-worn leather bag, wearing a thin cotton dress and sandals, with hair that has worked loose from its combs several hours earlier. Calista has no interest in brushing it. She longer cares what she looks like.

She rubs one hand across her eyes, fighting to compose herself. 'Please,' she says, 'forgive me. I've come from Cyprus. I arrived late this evening.' She stops, knowing that not much more will be possible: she must choose carefully. 'Yiannis Demitriades sent me.'

'My dear,' the woman says, opening the gate. 'Do come in – let me get you a glass of water – come in and sit down and take your time. Please, come with me.' All the while, the woman has one hand under Calista's elbow and she is steering her towards the open front door. Once inside, she leads Calista into a formal drawing room, gestures towards a deep, sea-green armchair. 'I'll be back to you in just a moment.'

Calista sinks into the chair and leans back, exhausted. She's made it. She's here. She breathes deeply. Behind her eyes, there is a parade of images that she is powerless to halt. Scenes from Imogen and Omiros's earliest months and years unfurl before her.

She cannot see her children's faces; instead, she sees images of their childhood. She sees beaches fringed with blue water; picnics with ice cream and lemonade; small, sturdy bodies tumbling down a grassy slope. But it is as though all of this has been recorded with a silent, shaky cine camera, like the one her father used to have, the one he wielded at family celebrations, First Communions, Christmas dinners. There was no hiding from him. But Calista can no longer be sure what it is she's seeing: her and Philip's childhood, or the childhood of her own son and daughter?

There is a noise at the living-room door. Calista's eyes snap open. A man stands before her: big, barrel-chested, with thinning dark hair and a luxuriant moustache. His hands are in his dressing-gown pockets. He looks wary.

Calista stands up. She extends her hand. 'Mr Michaelides,' she says, 'my name is Calista Demitriades. Yiannis is my brother-in-law. I had to leave Cyprus suddenly and he told me to come to you.' She hands him the piece of paper on which Yiannis had written the London address and a hastily scribbled greeting. 'He said that you would help me.'

The man glances down at the piece of paper and smiles. 'Aristides, please,' he says, shaking her hand. He turns back towards the doorway, where the kindly woman and her dog are standing. 'And this is my wife, Anne.' Then he clicks his fingers and the dog comes trotting over to lie at his feet. 'Raffles I believe you have already met.'

Calista nods. The warmth of his handshake has already begun to make her feel a small seep of optimism. The living-room door closes with a click.

'Please, Calista, sit down. My wife has gone to make us some tea.' He regards Calista gravely. 'Although I think you could do with something stronger. Give me a moment.' He stands up and leaves the room, Raffles at his heels.

Calista fights to control the sob that clutches at the underside of every breath she takes.

Aristides returns and stands at Calista's elbow. 'Here, take this,' he says, and hands her a glass. 'My best Metaxa.' He smiles.

'Thank you.' For a moment, Calista is unable to meet his eye.

'The situation is indeed very bad,' Aristides begins. 'But somehow I don't believe it is politics that has driven you away from Cyprus.' He settles himself into the armchair opposite Calista and waits.

Calista looks over at him. At that moment, Anne comes back in, angling a tray round the door. Calista is struck by how familiar this is, and how distant: the china teapot, the floral cups and saucers, matching milk-jug and sugar-bowl. She has a momentary vision of María-Luisa. She feels suspended between two worlds and can belong in neither: the war-torn territory that has been her more recent life, and the land of bone-china cups and cucumber sandwiches. She is now a stranger to both.

'You're right,' she says. 'That is not why I left. I would let nothing keep me from my children, if I had the choice.'

Anne offers her the plate of thin sandwiches. 'Eat something,' she says. She glances at her husband as she does so. 'Can't this wait until the morning? Calista looks exhausted.'

'No, please,' Calista says quickly. 'You deserve an explanation and it's a relief to talk.'

Aristides's gaze never wavers. Calista feels that she is being scrutinized, summed up, weighed and measured.

'Yiannis is my oldest friend,' Aristides says quietly. 'You are welcome on that account alone. No explanations are necessary.'

Calista manages to smile. 'You are very kind.' She pauses, pushing aside images of her children's bedtime, of babies fragrant and warm with sleep.

'I married Alexandros, Yiannis's youngest brother, eight years ago. I met him at home, in Ireland. I was seventeen; he was thirty. We have two children. For the past six years, he has been violent towards me.' Calista sips at her brandy. She needs to wait until the wave of shame recedes; it washes over her and makes her words falter somewhere beneath her voice. 'It became unbearable and I tried to leave, with my children. He had me stopped at the airport and took Imogen and Omiros from me. I have not seen them in almost a week.'

How neat it sounds, this narrative, Calista thinks. How empty of despair and hope and denial. It sounds like a life belonging to someone else.

'And Yiannis?'

'He tried to get permission for me to see my children, but he couldn't. The last thing I knew, Alexandros had taken them to Platres, where Petros and Maroulla have a house. I wanted to follow them there, but then everything changed. Makarios was deposed and life became . . . volatile. Everything was dangerous and I had nowhere to go, nowhere to live and no money. Yiannis insisted I leave Cyprus, for now. He was afraid the airport would be closed and that I'd be trapped. He told me to come to you, that he trusted you.' She stops. She can see that Aristides has begun frowning.

'Petros is involved in this? I know Alexandros hardly at all, but I have always found Petros to be a man of honour. Stubborn, mind you, but decent and fair.'

Calista can hear the question in what he says. 'I believe that he is all of those things,' she says, 'but Alexandros has convinced him that I was unfaithful.'

Calista sees Anne glance towards her husband. But neither of them will ask.

'I was not,' she says firmly. 'I know now that I put up with much more than I should have from Alexandros, but I stayed for the sake of my daughter and my son. I would never have done anything to risk losing them.'

A silence settles over the room.

After a moment, Aristides nods. 'I believe you,' he says. 'And clearly Yiannis does, too. I have never had any reason to doubt him.' He takes his wife's hand in his.

'And you've been friends for over forty years,' Anne adds, smiling back at him. 'Ever since they were tiny children,' she says to Calista. 'Their two families grew up together.'

Calista feels grief grow again, a bewildered, physical ache as she watches the way Anne's hand lies in Aristides's. If only Alexandros had been kind. If only.

Aristides nods, almost to himself. 'It's good that you have managed to get out. We will help you, of course, Anne and I. You can stay with us until everything is –' he waves one hand in the air, an almost embarrassed gesture '– clearer, that much at least.'

Anne stands up. 'Come with me, Calista. Let me show you where you can sleep. That's enough for one night. You're done in.'

Aristides stands up at once. 'Goodnight, Calista,' he says. 'We'll talk again in the morning.'

'Goodnight,' Calista says. 'And thank you.'

She follows Anne up the stairs, conscious that there is only one more thing she needs to do tonight.

Just put one foot in front of the other, one in front of the other, until she reaches the top.

Then, at last, she can sleep.

Imogen

Platres, 1974

IMOGEN WAKES EARLY. This house feels strange: it is not her house, not even her room; everything here belongs to Aiya Maroulla and Bapi Petros. Imogen usually likes to come here to the mountains during the summer, and sometimes at Easter, because the cousins from Athens are here then, too, but she doesn't want to sleep over again. It's been three whole nights. She wants to go home. The bedclothes smell funny, and her room isn't pink. It's a big person's room, and big people usually don't like pink all that much, or so Mummy told her, but Imogen doesn't really understand why that is. How could a big person not like pink?

Imogen hears the sound of a car starting. At exactly the same moment, Omiros begins to wail. Imogen struggles into sitting and pulls up the blind above her bed. She looks down and sees Papa's big black car drive out through the gate. Omiros's cries become louder, as though he knows Papa is driving away from him, although he can't, not really, because the room where Omiros is sleeping is over at the side of the house, where the terrace is, and the swimming pool. So he can't see Papa's car, and he probably can't hear it either.

Imogen hears Aiya Maroulla's voice getting closer as she comes up the stairs. She is nearly there: Imogen can even hear the way she is breathing, louder than she usually does.

'Aiya's here, Omiros. Aiya's here. Don't cry, my love.'

Aiya Maroulla goes in to Omiros first. That's OK – he's the

one who's crying, after all, and Imogen is older, so she doesn't cry as much – hardly at all, if you don't count that night when the bald men were mean to Mummy and Papa shouted at her in the car. It must be time very soon for Mummy to come back home.

Imogen runs out onto the landing and sees Aiya Maroulla with Omiros, still in his pyjamas with the dancing elves on the front. He is sucking his thumb again, and his free hand is holding on to Aiya's.

'Good morning, sweetheart,' Aiya says, and smiles at her. 'Did you sleep well?'

Imogen nods. 'Is Mummy back yet?'

Aiya's face changes; it's as though her mouth can't make up its mind whether it's OK to smile. 'Come downstairs, dear, and we'll talk about it.'

But Imogen feels mutinous. She doesn't want to come downstairs. And she doesn't want to wait. She's already waited three whole nights, and that's enough for anybody. She shakes her head. 'I don't want to,' she says. 'I want my mummy.' And then the tears come back and there is nothing she can do about it, nothing at all.

They just fall and fall without making any noise. Imogen wraps her arms around herself and hugs her body close; she's not nearly as soft as Monkey, but she'll have to do.

Aiya bends down and Imogen sees that she is nearly crying as well: her eyes are too shiny; even the cracks and lines underneath look all wet. She wraps one arm around Imogen, the other holding Omiros close. He looks at his sister, his eyes wide and staring.

'Oh, child, child,' Aiya says. 'I don't know what to say to you, truly I don't.'

But Imogen feels that she is talking to herself, and not to Imogen at all. She pulls away from Aiya, pushing back her grandmother's hand, the one that wears all the heavy gold rings.

Imogen understands that a misunderstanding must be a huge thing: something big enough to make even someone as old as Aiya cry. And she no longer wants to know what that is.

Imogen backs away, into the bedroom where she has just slept. Before Aiya can move to stop her, or even say anything to her, Imogen pushes the door closed. With both hands, she turns the big metal key in the lock, the key that looks like a stick-man with a big round head.

She hears the lock click to. She walks over to the bed, lies down on top of it and closes her eyes.

Like Monkey: she wants to be like Monkey.

She will stay here until her mummy comes back to fetch her.

Calista

London, 1974

A COUPLE OF DAYS after her arrival in Broomfield Close, Calista is woken in the early hours of the morning. She hears the urgency of voices from downstairs, and the insistent noise of a radio. Its volume has just been turned up. She gets out of bed and dresses hurriedly. Something has happened.

In the kitchen, Aristides and Anne are sitting at the small table, a pot of tea between them. Aristides is smoking, and the ashtray in front of him is full to overflowing. Both of their faces are white, tense. It looks to Calista as though Anne has been crying.

'What is it?' she asks.

'The Turks have invaded,' Anne says quietly.

Aristides holds up one hand, demanding silence. Calista sits at the table beside him. He turns to her for a moment. 'They have bombed Nicosia,' he says. 'Thousands upon thousands have fled their homes. There is rumour and counter rumour, but that much is true. The airport is closed. It is good you left when you did.'

Calista doesn't reply. She feels sick. For a moment, she is almost grateful that Alexandros has stolen the children away to Platres: at least they will be safe there.

'President Makarios?' she asks.

'Safe, in London.'

She nods. Just like her. How is she ever going to get back? Now Calista can see her children's faces: vivid with love and terror. She forces herself to be calm. The two people in front of her are distressed enough. Calista owes it to them to sit and listen quietly, to wait.

Much later that day, Yiannis calls. He had phoned the day after Calista's arrival, but they did not speak. Now, Calista hears Aristides's raised voice. She creeps out onto the landing and listens. She can follow the conversation with ease: it is clear that Aristides is made unhappy by whatever news Yiannis is giving him.

'How many refugees do they estimate?' he asks. 'What! In the *hundreds* of thousands?' The hallway fills with his incredulity.

After a moment, Calista hears her name being called and she runs downstairs, not caring that her eavesdropping will be obvious. Aristides hands her the phone.

'Quickly,' he says. 'It is Yiannis. The line may go dead at any moment. He wants to speak to you.'

Calista takes the receiver, her hands already clammy, her heart pounding.

'I haven't much time,' Yiannis says. 'I just wanted to let you know that today I have been to Platres and the children are perfectly safe. I know it is not what you want, but trust me, right now the fact that Alexandros took them there is a blessing. Limassol is in complete chaos, trying to cope with the numbers of refugees.'

'Are the children all right?' Calista wants to ask if they missed her, if they called out for her and feels immediately ashamed. Her war, her suffering, now seems small in comparison to others'.

'They are fine. My mother is looking after them. She sends her love to you, Calista. She does not believe that you have dishonoured anyone. She has asked me to tell you that she will help you, but that right now, it is impossible. Do you understand?'

Relief spills. 'Yes,' she says. 'Yes, I understand and tell her thank you.'

'You will need to be patient and wait until I can work something out. I will come to London as soon as I can. Do you have everything you need?'

For a moment, Calista is unable to answer that. Then she says: 'Yes. Your friends are very kind to me.'

'In the meantime, I will do what I can,' Yiannis says.

'And you? Are you all safe? Are your father's sisters all right?'

'In our house in Limassol, yes,' Yiannis says. 'Nicosia is a war zone. My aunts have lost everything, but they are safely here with my father. Every house in Limassol is bursting at the seams. It is a disaster, such a disaster.'

Calista hears his voice break. The line crackles then and she cannot hear what else Yiannis is saying.

'Do you want to speak to Aristides again?' Calista is aware that he has opened the living-room door and is standing almost at her elbow.

'Yes,' she hears, but the rest of what Yiannis says disappears into static. She hands the phone to Aristides.

'Yiannis?' he says. 'News of our families? Your aunts in Nicosia, my brothers?'

She sees him pass his hand over his eyes. All at once, the man seems smaller. It's as though something vital continues to leach away as he stands in the hallway, the receiver grasped in one hand, knuckles showing white.

'I can't hear you,' he says.

A moment later, he replaces the receiver in the cradle and stands there, looking at it, one hand still resting on it, as though reluctant to let it go.

Calista is afraid to speak. Anne comes out into the hallway. Without a word she walks up to her husband, puts her arms around him and pulls him close. His sobs are startling, a deep wracking sound that chills the air.

'Mamá?'

'Calista! Oh, thank God you've phoned! We've been out of our minds with worry. Where are you? Are you safe? Are the children safe?'

'Yes. I'm in London, Mamá. I have something I need to tell you.'

As soon as she can, Calista flies back to Dublin.

María-Luisa and Timothy are waiting for her at the airport. When she spots her daughter, María-Luisa opens both arms wide and Calista walks straight into them, sobbing at last despite the steeliest of resolves.

'Child, child,' María-Luisa murmurs, 'we are so happy you have come to us.' She draws back and looks at her daughter. She holds Calista's face in both her hands. 'News of the children?' she asks.

'With Alexandros. They are safe.'

Back home, Calista says: 'Things are bad. I need to tell you both what has happened.'

Afterwards, Timothy pats his daughter's back. 'We will fight Alexandros,' he says. 'We will help you get the children back. That's a promise.'

Philip is due back from San Francisco in two days' time and Calista begins to feel the tight circle of family embrace her once more.

*

On the day of his arrival, María-Luisa says to her: 'We have a surprise for you. Some guests are joining us for dinner this evening. We'll welcome Philip home together.' She smiles at Calista. 'We thought it might help to distract you.'

Calista meets her twin at the airport. She remembers the last time they were here together: the day after the wedding, when she and Alexandros left for Cyprus. On that occasion, she'd had the most vivid of memories of their shared childhood: of how Philip had taught her to roller-skate, patiently, doggedly, when she was nine.

'You can do it, Cally!' His words, his voice, still ring clear in Calista's head, almost two decades later. The memory makes her smile all over again.

Now, as she sees Philip emerge into the arrivals hall, she realizes how much she has missed him. 'Cally,' he says, pulling her into a bear-hug. 'So happy you're safe. So happy.'

That evening, Calista answers the door to a young man. He stands in the porch and looks at her shyly. He wears an ill-fitting suit, and his hands are clasped in front of his waistcoat, as though he is not quite sure what else to do with them. Calista is puzzled at the way he stands there, waiting.

'Yes?' she says, once she realizes he is not going to speak. 'May I help you?'

From behind the rhododendron bush in the front garden, a figure suddenly emerges. It takes Calista a moment. 'Maggie!' she shouts. 'Maggie!' She runs towards her, almost knocking over this unknown man in her haste to get to Maggie. The man grins, looking at them both in amusement.

Maggie hugs her. 'Welcome home, Calista,' she says. 'You look wonderful – more beautiful than ever.' Her broad face is filled with delight. She gestures towards the unknown young man. 'This is John, my husband. We are so happy to see you.'

'Come in, come in! It's wonderful to see you both!'

Calista takes to John at once. It is good to see Maggie, so proud and smiling. To see her and her new husband share such everyday happiness.

'What now?' Philip asks, as soon as Maggie and John have left and Timothy and María-Luisa have gone to bed.

'I'm going to stay on in London. Aristides says he has work for me in his gallery. I might even make a go of my photography again.'

'What about Alexandros and the kids?' Philip is watching her keenly.

'We're working on it,' Calista says. 'Yiannis is helping – trying to get Alexandros to agree to some sort of access. But things are too chaotic in Limassol right now – I'll have to be patient. I miss them so much.'

'Let me know if there is anything I can do to help, OK?' Philip takes her hands in his. 'I have money. I have time. I can do whatever you need me to do. Just ask.'

'I will.' She smiles. 'What about things with you? How is San Francisco? And your work at the university?'

'Great,' he says. 'All good.' He stifles a yawn. 'Sorry, Cally – that'll have to keep till tomorrow. I'm still on San Francisco time – I really need to hit the hay.'

'Of course,' Calista says. 'I forgot. It's just such a treat to be in the same house with you again.' She kisses him goodnight.

Silence fills the room on Philip's departure. It is not uncomfortable. Calista is reminded of all the things that she has missed about her native city: those things which she hardly ever thought about while living there. The cool, open spaces of St

Stephen's Green. The sea at Killiney: the majestic sweep of the bay. The cry of the gulls in Howth, swooping down to follow the fishing boats as they leave the harbour. And the tailored, symmetrical elegance of the city's Georgian squares. She'd love to photograph them some day. She climbs the stairs, reluctant to let the day slip away from her.

Calista sleeps in her old room that night. Philip is just down the hallway. Her parents are close by.

Home. At last, Calista feels safe. But she dreams of her children. She sees them before her, at play in some strange, underworld garden. As she reaches out to them, they move further away from her, their small bodies elusive and insubstantial. Calista tries to cry out, but her voice is paralysed somewhere in her throat. When she wakes at last, she is cold, trembling, the bedclothes in disarray all around her.

Pilar

Madrid, 1975

THE CLINIC WAITING ROOM is just as Pilar remembers it. Crammed with pregnant women, with toddlers, with screaming babies swaddled in blankets. Some of these tired young mothers are no more than girls, Pilar thinks. Children having children of their own. Some are coughing; some look ill, worn out, as though their lives have already defeated them. As though they have nothing to look forward to but this.

It is what Pilar has expected. Why should anything have changed? Why should anything be different?

She turns away, unable to quell the pool of bitterness that gathers in her throat. She would have done better. She'd have been able to offer more to her son. Pilar should have got the courage from somewhere. She should not have let him be taken away from her and given to strangers.

A sudden movement to the left makes Pilar glance in that direction. She sees, with a jolt of familiarity, a woman whom she recognizes. Her grey hair is swept up into a neat bun. Her blue overall is pristine, ironed, just the way it was when Pilar had seen her last. She moves a mop swiftly, methodically, across the floor, taking care of spillages. Pilar freezes. Enrica, that was her name: Pilar remembers the woman's moment of kindness to her and she looks away quickly. It would not suit to have Enrica recognize her now. Pilar averts her eyes and makes her way purposefully towards reception.

She looks up at the strip of wall above the hatch where the name of the doctor on duty used to be displayed. It still is; but this time, it's a name Pilar doesn't recognize. Hardly surprising, after more than eight years. She approaches the window. Behind it, a young postulant is filling out forms, her face a study in concentration.

'Sister?' Pilar says softly. She half turns, making sure her back is towards Enrica.

The young woman looks up, frowning. 'Yes,' she says. 'Can I help you? We are very busy this morning – an appointment may not be possible until sometime tomorrow . . .'

'I'm not here for an appointment.' Pilar smiles. She lowers her voice. 'I'm here to make a donation. My friends and I have always admired the work that the clinic does in this area. It's so important.'

The young woman stares at her.

'I was wondering if I might speak to the person in charge, just for a moment?' Pilar tries to make sure her expression is open, innocent.

'Doctor González-Arías is very busy – he's running behind . . . There's so much—'

'I wouldn't dream of disturbing Doctor González-Arías,' Pilar interrupts. 'I meant the sister in charge. Perhaps I could speak to Sister Florencia or Sister Magdalena or even Sister María-Angeles?' She hopes, whatever else happens, that Sister María-Angeles is not here today. Her name should be enough. And it is: Pilar's apparent familiarity with the nuns who run the clinic makes the young postulant relax.

'I'll see who I can find,' she says. She hurries out into the corridor behind her, leaving the door open.

Pilar remembers that corridor well. The small, cramped consulting rooms. The all-pervasive smells of disinfectant and poverty and desperation.

'May I help you?'

Pilar looks up, disappointed. That voice is not the voice she had hoped for. It is not the voice of Sister Florencia. An older nun stands before Pilar, her expression curious.

'Yes,' Pilar says brightly. 'I'd like to leave a donation with Sister Florencia. She helped a friend of mine once, some years ago, and she has never forgotten. I wanted to pass on her thanks to Sister Florencia myself.'

The nun smiles – a faint, knowing smile that makes Pilar angry. 'I'm afraid Sister Florencia no longer works here. She has moved on.'

Pilar nods. 'I see. Of course, it has been some time. I wonder might you know where I could contact her? I'm happy to leave the donation with you, naturally, but I should like to speak to Sister Florencia myself.'

The nun holds out her hand. 'That's very generous, and on behalf of the clinic, I thank you.'

Pilar hands over the envelope. She waits while the nun turns it first one way and then the other, as though she has never seen a white envelope before. Pilar has the impression that the woman is considering something. She seems to hesitate, and in that hesitation, Pilar allows herself a tiny moment of hope.

'But I'm afraid I can't help you with that,' the nun says, at last. 'I am new here – and I have no idea where Sister Florencia has been moved to. I'm sorry. Perhaps if you contact our Mother Superior—'

'Thank you,' Pilar says abruptly.

Mother Superior has been less than helpful, she wants to say. As has everyone else I've tried. You were my last hope.

Pilar is suddenly at a loss. How could she have been so foolish as to come here, hoping for an answer, after all these years? She might have known that they would all close ranks against her.

She sees the nun look at her, her expression expectant. Pilar says nothing.

'Very well, then. I must get back to work. Thank you for the donation. Good morning to you.'

Pilar watches as she swishes away, her long black habit a poignant reminder of the way Sister Florencia had left the hospital ward that day, with Pilar's baby in her arms. Her eyes fill again as she remembers. That bright, sterile space where she saw Francisco-José for the first time, and for the last. All those other girls crowding round her, spilling their meaningless words of comfort.

Pilar walks to the door and steps outside. She stays there for a moment, trying to quell the disappointment. Another dead end.

She feels the door open behind her and moves to one side, to let whoever it is pass by. She rummages in her pocket for a handkerchief. 'Señorita?' she hears.

Pilar turns.

'I recognize you, señorita.'

Pilar stares at her. She has no idea what to say.

'Don't worry,' Enrica whispers, glancing over her shoulder back towards the waiting room. 'I will tell no one.' She pauses for a second. 'You are looking for Sister Florencia, yes?'

Pilar nods. 'Yes. I'd like to contact her.'

Enrica begins to speak more quickly. 'Sister Florencia has left the order – there was a big scandal here, about a year, year and a half ago.'

'A scandal?' Pilar is dubious.

'She ran away,' Enrica says. 'Sister Florencia did. With a man, a doctor here . . .' She glances over her shoulder again, clearly nervous.

'Who?' Pilar is alert now. 'What doctor?'

'Doctor Antonio Suárez – he worked here for about five years. They left together. That's all I know. I have to go now.'

'Wait!' Pilar says. 'Do you know anything else about him – or about her, her real name?'

Enrica shakes her head. 'No, that's all. I really have to go or I will be in trouble. Doctor Suárez is from San Sebastián – that's all I know. He used to talk about going back there.'

Through the small pane of glass in the clinic door, Pilar sees the elderly nun approach the hatch. 'Go, Enrica – she's back. Thank you. Take care of yourself.'

Enrica's face fills with surprise. 'How do you know my name?'

Pilar smiles. 'I remember you, too. You were kind to me. You brought me my lunch on a tray and held my hand while I cried. You and Florencia. I have never forgotten.'

Enrica nods. 'I'm glad,' she says. 'Such a small thing. There is not enough kindness here.'

And then she is gone, back through the door that leads to the waiting room.

Slowly, Pilar steps out onto the street. She has a man's name now. And even more important, she has a profession. And she has a city.

The next step is Telefónica. She will consult all of the directories for San Sebastián. If that doesn't work, then Pilar will consider going north herself. She will visit all the doctors' surgeries she can find in the city and in its surroundings.

And if that isn't possible, then she will hire a private detective.

Resolute again, Pilar makes her way towards the Metro and home. No matter how little, progress is being made, step by step, bit by bit, day by day.

She will never give up.

Calista

London, 1974

SHORTLY AFTER HER ARRIVAL from Cyprus, Aristides took Calista to see his gallery in Mayfair. The name, in both Greek and Roman letters, was painted above the large, plate-glass window in a bright cerulean blue. *Aphrodite*, she read.

Calista was startled when she saw the name. Alexandros had told her a story in Limassol, once: the ancient myth of Aphrodite and Adonis. Aphrodite, married to Mars, the god of war, had betrayed her husband. She gave herself, secretly, to the most beautiful of all human men, Adonis.

'To punish his unfaithful wife,' Alexandros continued, 'Mars changed himself into a wild boar. He chased Adonis and killed him – right here, on the island of Cyprus. Adonis's blood was spilled all over the field, and wherever those drops fell, Aphrodite made poppies bloom.'

Calista remembered that scarlet image, and Alexandros's passion in the retelling of the story.

'That's why there are still so many poppies all over Cyprus,' Alexandros went on. The way he looked at Calista as he spoke had chilled her. She knew that he was telling her something other than a story. 'You do know, don't you, that Aphrodite spent the rest of her life weeping for her lover? And everywhere her tears fell, anemones grew.'

'Calista, are you all right?' Aristides had taken her arm on that morning, concerned at her sudden reaction. She realized that she had unconsciously taken a step back, away from the door, almost stumbling on the kerb.

'Sorry, yes – it's nothing.' She turned to him and smiled. 'What a beautiful gallery.'

Aristides inclined his head in thanks, held open the door for her. 'Wait until you see inside.' His voice was filled with pride.

Calista stepped into a large, hushed space. Polished cedarwood floors, white walls: a whole ocean of serenity. She saw large, vibrant canvases displayed everywhere. There were pieces of sculpture by artists still unknown to her, but she felt the intensity of their impact. They drew Calista towards them: she wanted to reach out and touch their textured strangeness. 'It's lovely, Aristides,' she said. 'Such a strong sense of tranquillity. You must be so proud.'

He nodded, pleased. 'My life's work,' he said simply. 'Come with me. I want to show you my newest venture. Anne insisted on it, a few years back. She believes that photography is the next big thing.' He looked at Calista, his gaze shrewd. 'You have told me of your own keen interest. My hope is that we can work together. I need this aspect of the business to grow, now more than ever.'

'Why now more than ever?' Calista felt the tingle of anticipation. This could mean real work for her, significant work. She followed Aristides up the stairs.

He paused as they entered the upper storey. 'Because all profits from this gallery will now be repatriated.' His voice faltered. 'Anne and I, we have enough. We are fortunate. I can retire soon. Whatever we make from now on will go back to Cyprus. To help all those families who have lost everything in the war.'

Calista touched his sleeve. His words moved her. 'I promise you I will work hard to make that a reality. I will do my very best.'

He nodded. 'I trust you, as my oldest friend trusts you. I have never known Yiannis to be wrong in his judgement of people.' He waved Calista inside. 'Come and look,' he said. 'Anne is convinced that these photographers show great talent. I agree.' He walked into the room. 'As yet, it is not too expensive to buy from these artists – they are mostly unknowns. But they are already achieving an excellent price among some of the collectors I deal with.'

Calista followed him towards an entire wall of black-and-white portraits. There, among the work of six up-and-coming photographers, Calista saw the name of Katerina Pontikou. She stopped. The air around her seemed to still.

'Do you like the work? Do you think highly of it?' Aristides was at her shoulder at once and Calista found it hard to speak.

'Yes, very,' she managed at last, not able to take her eyes off the images. These portraits were her work: her own stark, narrative-fuelled portraits of fishermen. Of lacemakers. Of bare-foot children and their mothers. She remembered all the mornings she had spent with Anastasios: his patient lessons, the way the developing photographs acquired a ghostly life of their own.

At that moment, Calista knew what she was going to do. She would tell Aristides, of course: not now, but later, once she had carried out her plans. She listened as he deconstructed the images before them, one by one. She absorbed his praise, the accuracy of his eye, the subtlety of his insight.

She felt like a drowning woman, able to reach upwards at last, to punch through the surface of her life.

In October 1974, Calista is ready. Anne and Aristides are curious. Calista has asked for some space in Aphrodite for a temporary exhibition that she would like them to see.

'I don't want to give you any detail,' she's said. 'I want to see how you respond to the work. I've promised the photographer that I will report back faithfully.' And that is all she will say.

She's been here since five this morning, arranging the portraits and the lighting as Aristides has already taught her to do. She's taken Shakespeare's 'Seven Ages of Man' as her theme, and she is exhilarated by the powerful black-and-white images that now hang on the gallery wall.

Calista has spent weeks among the Irish immigrant communities of Kilburn and Cricklewood. She has got to know their community centres, their churches, their schools. She's spent Saturday nights with them in the dancehalls that they frequent with such enthusiasm: the Galtymore, the Round Tower, the Garryowen. The names are all redolent of the Irish landscape that these men and women have left behind. Their sense of loss is stitched awkwardly into the fabric of a new and uncomfortable life.

Like a badly fitting suit, Calista thinks. She is reminded of her own going-away outfit, the blue suit that made her feel ill at ease, just like her new life.

Calista is surprised at how readily these men and women have agreed to be photographed: her Irishness has made her one of them, without question. So many of the faces she sees are as rugged and impenetrable as the west of Ireland from where they come.

And there is a vulnerability to all of them that Calista soon learns to recognize. It is, above all, the longing for home. She has attended christenings and weddings at Quex Road, the huge congregations spilling out onto the church grounds afterwards. She has learned to sense the complex mix of community and displacement that is a silent presence among them.

Once, a nine-year-old boy in short trousers had posed happily for her, his satchel slung over one shoulder as he waited, scowling, outside his school gates. Calista had captured him as the morning light glanced across one side of his face, giving him a strange, luminous beauty.

And then there are the hands that fascinate her: hands that build roads and bridges; hands that bake cakes and soothe children; hands that care for the elderly.

She is nervous now as Aristides and Anne make their way round the room. The waiting is unbearable. Calista can hear them murmur to each other as they move from image to image, but she cannot make out what they are saying.

Finally, Aristides approaches. Anne, she notices, is still studying the final portrait, gazing at it intently.

'Calista, these are superb. I don't believe I have ever seen anything quite like them. Is the photographer known to you?'

'Yes.'

Aristides gestures over one shoulder. 'They tell the entire story of a community. Some of them are almost painfully intimate.'

'Particularly *The Wake*.' Anne is back now by her husband's side. 'The tenderness of the women as they prepare the old man's body is quite extraordinary. Where did you get them?'

It takes Calista a moment before she can speak.

The silence is intense. It fills with sudden understanding.

'They're yours, aren't they?' Anne says.

Calista nods. 'I'm sorry for the secrecy, but I needed your gut response. This is no time for politeness.'

Aristides looks from Calista to his wife and back again. 'Your work?' he says, excitement colliding with disbelief. 'This is you?'

Calista smiles. 'The photographer is Kate McNeill, otherwise known as Katerina Pontikou.'

'Calista Demitriades in a past life,' Anne says. She takes Calista's hands in hers, looks archly at her husband. 'You're promoted,' she says. 'Gallery manager and contributing artist. Congratulations!'

Aristides can't stop smiling. 'Champagne,' he says. 'This calls for a celebration!'

Thank you, Anastasios Papadopoulos, Calista thinks, as she and Anne and Aristides discuss her plans over dinner.

Thank you. Somehow, the knowledge that her work is good fills Calista with a new and powerful sense of optimism. She can do anything: she can work, she can survive, and despite what Alexandros says, she now feels that she can win. She will get her children back, and soon.

'Come as early as you can,' Maroulla said, over the phone. 'I will keep Imogen home from school. No one must know that you are coming. Limassol is still in turmoil – so many refugees. With any luck, that will mean you can come and go unnoticed.'

And now Calista is there, and she is careful. When she arrives at the airport in Limassol in early January 1975, she puts on a long blonde wig and her Jackie Onassis sunglasses. Her jeans are old, her blouse shapeless. She has slung a well-worn rucksack over one careless shoulder. She glances at her reflection in the mirror of the ladies' room and hardly recognizes herself. Calista steps out into the arrivals area and walks briskly towards the exit. Nobody gives her a second look.

She takes a taxi to the outskirts of the city. When she speaks to the driver, she speaks Greek haltingly, with a British accent. She makes all the usual grammar mistakes of the hesitant learner – mistakes she had struggled so hard to overcome all those years ago. They come in handy now.

She pays for her moped in cash, tucks her hair into a scarf and makes her way by the most indirect route possible towards Maroulla's house.

'I've told Imogen I have a surprise for her,' Maroulla had said, 'and that she won't be going to school. I've bought her some new books that she's asked for, in case you can't make it. Please be careful, won't you?'

Calista hides the moped as best she can, in between two oleander bushes. The sudden memory of their pink, fragrant blossoms makes her breath catch. Pink: Imogen's favourite colour – the colour of her childhood, of safety, of family. Calista turns away and walks the couple of streets back to Maroulla's house. She makes her way there quickly, hands stuffed into her jeans pockets, her eyes looking straight ahead.

Maroulla opens the door before she knocks. She puts a finger to her lips.

'Omiros isn't here, is he?' Calista whispers in alarm.

Maroulla shakes her head. 'I told Eleni to take him away for the day.' She points to the kitchen door. 'Go,' she says. 'Your daughter is waiting.'

Calista opens the door quietly. Imogen is standing at the window, looking out over the garden. Calista wonders what she sees. Out of nowhere, she remembers the day when Imogen played with her boats, surrounded by sandcastles. She'd pushed tiny Cypriot flags into their crenellations, and an entire fortified city lay at her feet. Calista had watched as her daughter sailed her fleet away, her small hands making the toy boats rise and fall, rise and fall on the sea's invisible swell.

'Imogen,' she says softly.

The child turns. When she sees her mother, her mouth opens in that huge 'O' that reminds Calista of the night at the airport. The memory of it bruises her and despite herself, she sobs. She runs towards her daughter, now, her arms open wide, her face streaked with tears. 'Sweetheart, darling girl,' she says, over and over again.

'Mummy!' The child's voice is high and clear: terrified by joy.

Calista pulls her daughter to her, rocking her back and forth, back and forth.

Imogen pulls away for a moment; her eyes search Calista's face, as though she cannot believe what she is seeing. She brushes the tears away, pinching her mother's cheeks to see whether she is waking-time real: *really* real, not just dream-time real. She strokes Calista's hair, the same way Aiya strokes hers, kisses her and nestles into the warm, downy comfort of Calista's neck, breathing in the scent that is as familiar to her as daylight.

'Mummy,' she whispers, over and over again. 'Mummy.'

'We don't have all that much time,' Aiya is saying. 'I've phoned the airline and the next plane is due in at four. I've told Iliada to take her time, to go and see her mother after she does the shopping. But I can't be certain when she'll be back. It's almost eleven now, Calista; you need to be gone by three, just to be on the safe side.'

Calista stretches out her hand. 'Thank you, Maroulla. Thank you so much,' she says.

Maroulla pats the back of Calista's hand. 'I'll leave you alone.' Then she frowns. 'Did you come by taxi?'

Calista shakes her head. 'No, I hired a moped – and I paid for it with cash. I've hidden it a couple of hundred metres up from the main road, a few streets from here. I was careful. I spoke to no one.' She gestures towards the table, where her sunglasses sit, along with the wig and the brightly coloured scarf.

Imogen is puzzled. The wig looks like a small, discarded animal. And the scarf has none of the colours Mummy likes.

'And I covered up.'

'Thank you.' Maroulla looks at her and pauses for a moment. Calista can see her struggle with something. 'Alexandros is my son. And his father is my husband. I don't need to tell you what will happen if—'

Calista raises one hand. 'I understand, Maroulla. And Imogen understands, too. This is our secret. It will not be shared with anyone, I promise. You have my word.'

'And I promise, too,' Imogen says. She is eager to be a grown-up. 'I won't tell anyone. Cross my heart and hope to die.'

Calista hugs her. 'Don't say that,' she whispers. 'Don't ever say that. A promise on its own is good enough.'

Aiya says: 'We must all try to do what we believe to be right.'

And she turns and walks away, slowly, pulling the door closed behind her.

Calista sits on the kitchen chair and pulls her daughter onto her knee. She puts both arms around her and holds her close. Then, remembering, she cups Imogen's chin in one hand and says, smiling: 'I almost forgot.' She reaches into a big green rucksack and pulls out something dark and furry. Imogen recognizes it instantly and her face lights up.

'It's Monkey!' she says.

Calista laughs. 'Monkey and I have become very good friends,' she says. 'Look – I even bought him a new jacket and bow tie. I wanted him to look smart when we came to visit.'

Imogen rubs Monkey's soft fur against her cheek. 'Aiya said that he would look after you,' she begins. 'Did he?'

'Absolutely. We looked after each other.' Calista pauses. 'I'll have to take him away with me again, but I'll bring him back, the next time I come to see you.'

Imogen is dismayed. 'Can't you stay?'

Calista shakes her head.

Imogen is afraid that she – that both of them, she and Mummy – are going to cry again.

'No, darling, not this time. I can't. But I really, really want to. Do you believe me?'

Imogen nods. 'Is it because of the misunderstanding with Papa?'

Calista nods. 'Yes. Yes, that's what it is. The misunderstanding with Papa. It is taking a long time to clear up. But we're doing our very best.'

'Are you going to wait and see Omiros?'

Calista takes both of Imogen's hands in hers. 'Not this time, sweetheart. Maybe on my next visit. And you know that you must keep this a secret, don't you?'

Imogen sighs. 'Yes, Mummy. You told me already. And so did Aiya Maroulla. I know how to keep a secret. But Omiros doesn't. He's too small.'

'Exactly,' Calista says. 'That's exactly right. That's why we've got to be careful.'

'So that Papa doesn't make another misunderstanding?'

'Yes. We don't want another misunderstanding.'

'Do you live far away now?'

Calista nods. 'Yes. I live in another country, but I really hope to come back here someday. And until I do, I will come and visit you as often as I can. If I can't visit, I'll send you lots of letters and photographs. Aiya Maroulla will keep them for you.'

Imogen's eyes are wide and solemn. 'Do they have to be a secret, too?'

'I'm afraid so. Not a forever secret, just until we get everything cleared up.'

'Why can't I come and stay with you?'

Calista grips her hand more tightly. 'That's not possible right now, sweetheart. It's what I would love above anything, and someday we'll make it happen. But right now, you'll just have to trust me. Can you do that?'

Imogen nods, and at the same time she says: 'Can it be soon?'

'I hope so, darling. I really hope so. It's all I'm working for. It's all I ever think about. Don't ever forget that. One day, we'll make it happen and we'll be together in the same house again.'

Imogen wants to ask: 'What house?' but Mummy has started to look sad again, so she doesn't. Instead, she says: 'Do you want to see what we're doing at school?'

Calista smiles. 'I'd love that. Show me. Show me everything.'

The hours disappear into a sunny haze of drawings, of books, of stories about playtime. Soon, too soon, Aiya Maroulla comes tapping on the door. 'Calista,' she says, 'it's nearly time. Do you want something to eat before you go?'

'No, thank you, Maroulla. I'll have plenty of time at the airport. Ten more minutes here and I'm gone.'

Aiya Maroulla smiles. 'She's a wonderful girl. Imogen is a very good student. Teacher says so, all the time.'

'Yes,' Calista says.

Imogen looks at her quickly. Her voice has cracked on the 'yes' and her chin is all trembly again. Imogen goes to her at once. 'Don't cry, Mummy.' She hands Monkey to her, smoothing down the bow tie, which has got a bit ruffled from all the hugging. 'Here, take him with you. I promise I'll be good until the next time you come. Really, really good. And I'll help Aiya look after Omiros.'

Mummy almost crushes her with the hug she gives her – Imogen can barely breathe. 'I know you will,' she says. 'I know you will.' She bends down and kisses Imogen's forehead hard. When she pulls away, Imogen tries not to show any tears. She understands that Mummy would prefer to stay, but she can't.

She watches as Mummy puts Monkey back into her rucksack, throws it over one shoulder and puts her arms around Aiya Maroulla. They both stand still for a while. Imogen can't hear what they say – or if they say anything at all. The room is strangely quiet.

Then Mummy puts on her wig, ties the scarf under her chin and slides on the big sunglasses. She pulls open the kitchen door, turns, blows a kiss.

The front door opens quietly, closes quietly a moment later, and then she's gone.

Aiya Maroulla holds out her arms. 'Come, child,' she says.

And Imogen goes to her.

Pilar

Madrid, 1975

PILAR DOESN'T LIKE THE MAN, but that hardly matters. She has chosen him for his anonymity, above all. The more respectable private detectives she has met have seemed too smooth, too polished, too *visible*, in her opinion. Nevertheless, she dislikes the way this man is unshaven, his clothes sloppy, his shoes unpolished. That first morning, in his shabby backstreet office, he sees the way she looks at him.

'Don't worry, señorita,' he says. He gestures towards himself, then brushes the flakes of cigarette ash and dandruff off his waistcoat. 'Think of this as my disguise. It helps me disappear into the undergrowth, as it were,' and he grins. 'I'm a chameleon – I can don the appropriate fancy suits whenever I need to.' He pauses for a moment, looks at Pilar with frank admiration. 'Foolish man, I say, your Doctor Antonio Suárez.' He lights a cigarette and regards Pilar through the blue fog of smoke as he exhales. 'I wouldn't have let you get away from me.'

Pilar ignores the bait. 'I just want to know where he works,' she says. 'I don't care about a home address. Just search every-where: hospitals, private clinics, public clinics. Start with the poorest areas of the city.'

The private detective looks at her. Disbelief is written all over his face. 'Are you serious? Is this all you can give me?' He waves his hand in the direction of the piece of paper Pilar has handed him earlier. 'Just a name? No date of birth, no previous address, nothing?'

'That's it,' Pilar says. 'Just the name of the clinic here in Madrid where he used to work. Look, are you going to take the job or not?'

The man – 'Call me Juanjo,' he'd said earlier. 'No need for formalities' – shrugs. 'Sure, I'll give it a shot. I'll telephone you when I have news.'

Pilar shakes her head. 'No,' she says firmly. 'I will come back here in two weeks' time. I'd prefer to speak to you personally.'

He sighs. 'Suit yourself.'

'What about your fee?'

'Cash or cheque?' he asks.

'Cash.'

'My retainer, plus travel expenses to San Sebastián, plus daily rate – we can work out all the details later – a deposit of ten thousand will do for now.'

Pilar counts out the notes. 'There will be a bonus for you if you find this man quickly.'

Juanjo counts the notes slowly, deliberately. 'And when I do?' He doesn't look at Pilar.

She wonders what he is thinking. Then she decides that she doesn't want to know. 'I only want to speak to him – to him and his wife,' Pilar says firmly. 'I wish him no harm.'

Juanjo nods, considering this. 'OK, then.' He folds the notes over carefully, then stuffs them into his trouser pocket. 'I'll see you in two weeks.'

Pilar waits.

'What?' he says.

'A receipt for the ten thousand pesetas. Please.'

Juanjo grins. He pulls a sheet of notepaper towards him and scribbles on it. 'Will this do?' He holds it up for Pilar to see.

'Date and sign it, please.' It's no protection at all, Pilar thinks, but at least it's something.

Juanjo hands it over to her with a flourish. '*Hasta la vista*,' he says, and salutes.

It has taken six months and Pilar is still no closer to finding Florencia or Doctor Antonio Suárez.

Juanjo has been to San Sebastián, followed by Bilbao, followed by a useless, expensive three days in Santander. Each lead has proved to be fruitless. 'It's as though they don't want to be found,' he complained. 'Could that be the case? Are they hiding from someone?'

'You're the detective,' Pilar said coldly. 'That's what I pay you for. Why don't you go and find out?'

Frustration made her slam the phone down on that occasion. It took six weeks before Pilar spoke to Juanjo again. Perhaps he was evading all his clients — if he had any others — but he seemed to have a sixth sense as far as Pilar's calls were concerned.

Now he has called her. Pilar feels hope leap inside her as she answers the phone in the *portería*.

'I think I've found them,' Juanjo says, without preamble. He sounds excited. 'Or at least, I've found where they've gone to.'

Pilar sighs. She can hear the triumph in his voice. He's going to make her work for this. 'Congratulations,' she says. And she waits.

'Don't you want to know?' Now he sounds offended, as though his innocent best is no longer good enough. Pilar is clearly one of those demanding clients for whom nothing is ever good enough.

'Yes,' Pilar says. 'Of course I want to know.' She pauses for a moment. 'That is, after all, what I pay you for.'

Juanjo clears his throat. 'I've tracked them down to Peru.'

Pilar thinks she has misheard. 'What?'

'Peru,' he repeats. 'You know, in South America.'

'I know where Peru is,' Pilar snaps. 'And it's a pretty big place, for Christ's sake. Is that all you've managed to come up with, after all this time?'

'No,' he says. 'Not quite. My contact is pretty sure that the doctor and his wife went to Lima. But she doesn't know other than that.'

Pilar breathes. 'Lima. That's a pretty big place, too. Can we narrow it down a bit, do you think?' Pilar is determined to keep the spikiness in her tone. If she relents, she knows that she will cry. All this time; all that hope; all the anxiety of waiting and not knowing, of longing and not having. 'And who was your contact this time, by the way?'

'A nurse,' Juanjo says. 'Someone who worked with your doctor guy a few years back and heard him making plans to work in the slums of Lima. He got a job in a clinic somewhere in the city, she thinks, but she doesn't remember the name.'

'So what have you got, then?'

'I have the names and addresses of three strong possibilities – all public clinics, all in the poorest areas. That's the best I can do. Addresses and phone numbers, so you can call them yourself if you want. Or maybe even write to them. I presume you don't want me to go to Lima?'

Pilar thinks she hears optimism in his voice: whether he wants a paid trip to Lima or he's hoping that Pilar will fire him right now, she cannot tell. She decides that their professional relationship has come to an end. 'No,' she says, weary. 'I don't want you to go to Lima. I'll follow things up myself. I'll take it from here, thanks all the same.'

He does not demur, not even for the sake of appearances. 'I'll drop the addresses round to you,' Juanjo says, 'along with my final bill.'

Nice try, Pilar thinks. 'I will come to your office,' she says. 'Tomorrow morning at eight thirty.'

'But I don't start until—'

'Be there,' Pilar says, and hangs up.

Calista

London, 1975

IT IS EARLY MARCH 1975 and Calista and Yiannis are sitting at the window of her flat, looking out onto her tiny London garden. They watch as the sun begins to go down. They are planning her next secret visit to Limassol.

At first, Anne and Aristides resisted her moving out. But in December, Calista had insisted. 'You have more than enough to deal with,' she said. 'Your house is full of refugees. You pay me well; my portraits are selling; your commissions are more than generous. It's time I found my own place.'

They helped her find her new home. 'This is how the Cypriot community works,' Aristides said. 'Through a friend of a friend. You can find anything you want: it is important we all look after each other.'

Right now, Calista's eye rests on the warm yellow bricks of this London garden. She has weeded the overgrown flowerbed, already planted the poppies and narcissi and anemones that will remind her of the garden in which Imogen used to play, sailing her toy boats over the swelling seas to Troy.

'Omiros is still way too small to be trusted,' Yiannis is saying. 'He wouldn't understand the need for secrecy. I'm sorry, Calista, but I don't think you should see him this time either – if we can, we'll arrange for you to see him at a distance, but I feel wary of involving anyone else.' He pauses, his tone becoming more gentle. 'And maybe by the next time, we'll have got

Alexandros's agreement. Sometimes I think we're getting closer, but he always pulls back at the last minute.'

Calista knows the games that Alexandros plays. She understands how he uses hope to hook Yiannis and Maroulla in, time and time again. She had once been that willing fish herself. 'Seeing Imogen is wonderful,' Calista says. 'I miss Omiros terribly, of course; but I don't want to jeopardize anything. I hate all this secrecy – it is so unfair on a little girl. The sooner we can get Alexandros to meet us even part of the way, the better.' She looks over at Yiannis. 'I am so grateful to you and to Maroulla.'

He nods. 'Maroulla is her own woman,' he says, with his sudden smile. 'My father would be furious with her if he found out – he'd see this as a betrayal. He'd feel that my mother was disobeying him. Never mind what's good for the children.'

'I understand.' Calista becomes aware that Yiannis is regarding her closely. 'As for me,' he says, and his words are slow and deliberate, 'no gratitude is necessary. None at all. I thought you already knew that.'

The room fills with silence as Calista's eyes search his. Yiannis's gaze does not falter. It is full of questions. This is the first opportunity they have had to be alone together since that day at Limassol Airport when Yiannis had pulled Calista into his arms. She has never forgotten that embrace, and she knows that he hasn't, either. Until now, the war in Cyprus and his family's needs have consumed Yiannis. He and Calista have met, hurriedly, in Anne and Aristides's house on several occasions. They have always been surrounded by dozens of urgent people. Until now.

'You know that I would never do anything to endanger your relationship with your children, Calista. But I need you to know how I feel about you. I cannot keep silent any longer.'

Calista allows a moment to elapse before she speaks, before she is able to speak.

'I don't care about Alexandros for himself,' she says, struggling to find the right words, 'but I do care about you. And your mother. It could be so dangerous . . . Alexandros would never let me see my children again if he thought . . . The whole world would crucify us if they found out, Yiannis,' she says softly. 'You must know that: you, his brother; me, his wife. It would be beyond betrayal, beyond humiliation, in Alexandros's eyes.'

Calista waits. Waits for what she hopes Yiannis will say, needing him to say it. The last seven months have been filled with a bitter loneliness. The soft evening air around them is suddenly suffused with her longing.

'I love you, Calista,' Yiannis says. His eyes never leave her face. 'From the first moment I met you in my parents' garden, I have loved you. Had my brother behaved as he should, I would never have told you.' He reaches out, takes Calista's hand. 'I will understand if you say no.' He strokes her fingers. 'But I hope you will say yes.' He pauses. 'You are worth the risk. We will be careful. We are among people I trust. And London is very far away from Cyprus.'

Calista closes her eyes, overwhelmed at the tenderness of his touch. This is something she has never known with Alexandros. The light pressure of fingers; the gentleness; the freedom to say yes or no.

'I am all too aware,' Yiannis says, 'that I am more than twenty years older than you are, and that has given me pause. But I have weighed everything up and down a thousand times, and argued with myself over and over.' He shrugs. 'No matter what I do, the answer is always the same. I have tried to keep away from you, but I have not been able.'

Calista turns to face him. She understands all that this might mean, and she has already lost so much. But he is right: this is worth it. Despite everything, loving this man is worth it. She waits until she can breathe again. 'I say yes, Yiannis. Yes, with all my heart.'

He stands up, pulls Calista into his embrace. They stand,

looking out on the bright spring garden, arms wound tightly around each other, not speaking.

In the months that follow, they are careful. They rarely appear together in public. If they do, they leave Palmers Green separately, meeting up in Greenwich or Richmond or Kensington. Occasionally, they have dinner at home with Anne and Aristides. Sometimes, Calista has caught Anne's eye as she watches them, and she wonders. But if either of their friends suspects, they say nothing. They are, like so many others, distracted by larger events.

Love and war, Calista thinks.

It seems that each can make the other flourish.

Imogen

Limassol, 1977

ONE MORNING, AIYA MAROULLA does not come to wake Imogen. This is very puzzling: the first sight every day is Aiya's smiling face at her doorway. First she comes to Imogen's room; then she crosses the landing to Omiros's. Omiros doesn't need to be visited first anymore: he stopped his howling a long time ago now. He's almost five, and Imogen is ten. Aiya says that they are both quite grown-up. After they get washed and dressed, and Aiya changes out of her dressing gown and into her street clothes, they all go downstairs and have breakfast together.

This is what Aiya calls their routine: it only changes during the school holidays, when they don't have to go anywhere early, and on the weekends. It also changes, of course, on the days when the secret happens and Mummy comes to visit, or Imogen is taken to visit her. Either way, the routine only changes for Imogen: never for Omiros. Omiros would never be able to keep such a secret.

But today is neither of those special days. Today is a Monday in February and Imogen and Omiros have to go to school.

Imogen gets out of bed and makes her way across to the bedroom door. It is open, just a crack. Ever since the time she locked herself in, Aiya has insisted that Imogen leave her door open at night. Imogen does; besides, in all the houses, every single key that looked like the stick-man with a big head had been taken away a long time ago. Imogen couldn't lock herself in even if she wanted to. And she doesn't want to: Mummy's secret visits, and her letters and her photographs, have made it easy for Imogen to leave doors open. She wants to be ready to welcome whatever reminder of Mummy might come to visit her.

Already, Imogen can hear Iliada clattering around downstairs in the kitchen. Aiya has told her that Iliada is a little deaf and so she can't hear the amount of noise she is making. Sometimes Aiya smiles when Iliada drops things and bangs about; other times she sighs. It depends on what sort of a day Aiya is having – something that Imogen has learned to gauge by the look on her grandmother's face. Some days she looks as though something is hurting her, and Imogen has asked a few times whether her knees are giving her trouble.

And Aiya has smiled in response and said: 'Yes, sweetheart. That's it. My knees are giving me trouble today.' Imogen has wondered why Aiya often puts her hand to her chest if it is her knees that hurt. But she has learned not to ask. Sometimes, Imogen thinks that grown-ups are very strange: they say one thing and mean another.

Or else they don't say anything at all, and that's the kind of silence that is louder than any of the words they *could* use.

Bapi Petros and Papa left last night to go to London. Aiya showed Imogen where London was on the map, and also showed her how close London was to Dublin. Mummy lives in London, and Imogen hopes that she goes often to visit Abi María-Luisa and Grandad Timothy, even if Imogen can't, at least not yet.

She taps gently now on Aiya Maroulla's door. No answer. Imogen waits a moment, presses her ear to the wooden surface, taps louder. Then she calls Aiya's name.

Omiros comes out of his room. 'Where's Aiya?' he says. He's already looking fretful. Omiros doesn't like it when the things around him change.

'She's getting ready,' Imogen says quickly.

Something is wrong. Imogen doesn't know what it is, but the air in the house is strangely still this morning. She wants Omiros to go downstairs so that she can find out what it is. She knows that it is part of her job as his big sister to look after him, to explain those things to him that he cannot understand for himself.

'Can you ask Iliada to make breakfast? Tell her me and Aiya'll be down in a minute?'

'Why can't you ask her?' Now Omiros is frowning, looking downwards and sideways in that way he has when he doesn't want to do as he's told. It always makes Aiya cross.

''Cos Aiya wants me to help her get dressed, that's why.' Imogen takes a deep breath.

'Can I play with my cars?'

Then she exhales. Playing in the morning is only allowed at weekends, but Imogen can see that Omiros is not going to move unless she says yes. She nods. 'OK – but go to Iliada first and tell her Aiya says we're on our way.'

Omiros runs downstairs, his dark hair standing up every-where. And he's still in his pyjamas. Imogen hopes that Aiya won't be cross that their daily routine has so suddenly changed on a day when everything should stay the same.

She pushes open the heavy wooden door. She can see that Aiya is still in bed. She lies on her side, facing the window. The white woven counterpane outlines all the curves of her body. She looks deeply asleep.

Imogen approaches quietly. She doesn't want to startle Aiya, but she needs to wake her or they'll be late for school. So she coughs, once, twice, waiting for Aiya to turn over sleepily and say: 'Good morning, sweetheart.' But she doesn't. She doesn't move at all.

Imogen reaches the bed and stretches out one hand. She taps

Aiya on the shoulder, gently. 'Aiya?' she says. She comes closer and rests one hand on Aiya's cheek, the way that sometimes Aiya does to her. Imogen sleeps very deeply, Aiya has always said that, and sometimes it takes a while to get her to wake up. Imogen presses her palm into Aiya's cheek now, then her forehead, puzzled at how cold she feels. The window is not yet open, and the air in the bedroom is warm. Why is she so cold?

Imogen decides to try something different. She runs round to the other side, Bapi Petros's side, and climbs up onto the bed. Aiya's face is so white that Imogen feels afraid. She looks as though she is here but not here; it's as though she has gone away from herself. Then Imogen begins to understand; it is an inside understanding, one that comes without the right words to name it. Frantic now, she pushes at Aiya's shoulder with both hands. She kneels facing her grandmother and, with all her strength, shakes and shakes and shakes her, crying to her to wake up, wake up, wake up.

But even as she does, Imogen has already begun to know that nothing is going to make Aiya Maroulla wake up ever again.

On the day of the funeral, lots of people come and go. Imogen has never seen the house so full. Everyone is dressed in black, and the ladies are all wearing hats. Bapi Petros has got smaller in the last few days. Imogen thinks that he has somehow grown downwards. His back has become stooped, and his hands have begun to make her feel afraid: they are suddenly so very different from the way they used to be. Once soft and big and generous, they now look as though the fingers have grown longer. Veins stand out on the back, like thin, tight, blue-coloured ropes, and the fingernails look sharp and yellow. It's as though Aiya Maroulla has taken all of Bapi Petros's fleshy bigness away with her.

'I loved her,' he keeps saying. 'I never loved anyone else the way I loved her. What am I going to do without her?'

Papa's eyes, too, are red with crying. Imogen has not been able to cry, not yet. Secretly, there are times – whole hours, even – when she doesn't believe that Aiya Maroulla has gone away forever. Imogen remembers how she once thought that Mummy had gone away forever, too, and then she came back again, although that's still a secret. Imogen will keep her door open and her heart open, just like Aiya Maroulla always said she should. You never know what might happen.

'She's gone from us, sweetheart,' Papa had said, shaking his head at her. 'Do you understand? Aiya has been taken away from us.' He and Bapi had arrived late that afternoon, the day Aiya died. They got home after the doctor had been and after Iliada had put clean sheets on the bed and candles and flowers all around Aiya. Imogen had never seen Papa cry before – him or Bapi – and the deep, tearing sound of their sobs had frightened her, but there were no arms to run to, except Iliada's, and Imogen did not feel like running there. Iliada always smelled of fish and garlic and kitchens. She didn't have Aiya's soft, soapy smells, or Mummy's clean, lemony perfume.

Imogen let Papa talk to her that night, even though he said the same things over and over again. It was as though he was talking to himself and she just happened to be standing beside him. Imogen already knew how huge the thing was that had happened: she was the one who couldn't waken Aiya Maroulla after all, who ran down to tug at Iliada's sleeve, who told Omiros he could play with his cars and his toy garage all that morning. There was no misunderstanding that day: Iliada's tears and Doctor Simon's sad shake of the head told Imogen that Aiya was not coming back to them.

That had been the first of several busy days, with everyone coming and going. Aiya had never liked that sort of day: a day of too much coming and going. The house always seemed to be full, Iliada and Mirofora were always there, Bapi and Papa never stopped talking to people. Uncle Yiannis, Uncle Ari and Uncle Spyros were all there too, along with Aunt Eva, Aunt Dorothea and some of the girl cousins.

Imogen knew that she had to be very careful, with all these people in the house, never to speak about Mummy. Above all, she could never speak about their secret meetings or Papa would be very angry indeed. It was her secret, hers and Mummy's alone, and Imogen knew she could not be the one to let the cat out of the bag.

Mummy had had to explain that to her and Imogen remembered how she and Mummy had laughed and laughed at the notion of a cat, struggling and spitting and scratching and mewling and wanting to be let out of its bag, just like their secret.

And so, on the days that surrounded Aiya's funeral, Imogen spends lots of time in her bedroom, because sometimes it feels as though all that knowledge, all those secrets, are fighting with her. She is afraid that they will somehow explode their own way out into the air and then Papa would be cross as well as sad, and it would all be her fault.

Uncle Yiannis came to her, though. He sat on the side of her bed and told Papa he could go back downstairs if he liked, to see to all the people who were still everywhere, all around the house.

'Are you sure?' Papa hardly ever read Imogen a bedtime story, but he said he would on that night, the night of Aiya's funeral.

'Certain. Imogen is a brave girl. She looked after Aiya very well. I'd like to thank her in person.' And Uncle Yiannis smiled.

Papa just nodded. He kissed Imogen on the forehead and left the room, closing the door behind him.

Then Uncle Yiannis did something that Imogen did not expect. He took an envelope out of the inside pocket of his black jacket and handed it to her. He kissed her cheek and took one of her hands in his: warm, comforting hands. He had kind eyes; warm, brown eyes that smiled at her too.

'This is part of your secret,' he said. 'Your mummy asked me to give you this. She is sad she can't be with you tonight, but she will be very soon.'

Imogen looked at him without speaking. The whole room seemed to freeze. Even the walls were bewildered.

Was this a trick? Was Uncle Yiannis trying to get her to say something that she shouldn't?

Uncle Yiannis seemed to read her mind. 'Your mummy has sent you something to show that, from time to time, I can be part of your secret too. We want to make it easier for her to visit, now that Aiya can't be with us. Do you understand?'

Imogen was afraid to nod, in case that would let the cat out of the bag.

Uncle Yiannis took a small photograph out of another pocket and handed it to Imogen. It was a picture of Monkey, sitting on Mummy's knee. She had one of Monkey's paws in her hand, and was making him wave at Imogen out of the photograph. Across his chest, Monkey had a sticker that said: '*Lots of love to Imogen. Mummy and Monkey.*'

'Can I keep it?' Imogen asked. Her voice sounded strange, as though it wasn't really hers.

Uncle Yiannis nodded. 'Of course. It's yours to keep,' he said.

'Another secret.'

He nodded. 'For now,' he said. 'But your mummy hopes that you won't need to keep secrets for too much longer.'

Imogen thought that Uncle Yiannis's face looked sad. Even sadder than before. Whenever Aiya looked sad, Imogen would ask for a story. It usually worked. Aiya would sit on the bed and use funny voices for all the different animals and people in the story. She'd forget to be sad for a while.

'Will you read me a story, Uncle Yiannis? The one Aiya liked best?'

And he smiled. 'I'd be happy to,' he said.

Imogen pulled *Jungle Book* from the pile beside her bed. She thought that she was much too grown-up for *Jungle Book,* but Aiya always loved reading it to her. And Imogen didn't really mind: she had a sneaking fondness for King Louie. He reminded her of Monkey.

Uncle Yiannis sat, just where Aiya used to sit, and he began to read.

It worked, Imogen thought. He looked happier.

Grown-ups were funny creatures. She'd never get to understand them.

Weeks later, when everything is over and Papa and Bapi move around the house like ghosts and Eleni comes to take Imogen and Omiros home from school, something happens.

Imogen is not sure what it is, except that she has been waiting for something like this without knowing what it might be. The moment she steps through the front door, Imogen feels that the air has become charged with something that feels both light and dark and dangerous.

Papa comes out of Bapi's study, the one that Bapi disappears into at night or at weekends when he doesn't want to go to the office with the big desk and the swivel chair. 'Imogen?' Papa says. Omiros runs towards him, but Papa stretches out one hand, stopping him. 'Not now, Omiros,' he says. 'I need to speak to your sister. I'll be out to you soon.'

'But you promised to take me to—'

'I said not now.' Papa's voice is sharp, the way it used to be at night when Aiya Maroulla argued with him.

Omiros's face falls; his chin crumples. Slowly, he turns away, dragging his rucksack across the floor instead of carrying it. Aiya always used to tell him not to do that.

'Come inside, Imogen. I need to speak to you.'

Imogen leaves her rucksack in the cupboard under the stairs and hangs up her school jacket. She is aware of time passing slowly. She does everything that Aiya taught her to do, hoping that this will somehow take away the sad tightness that has taken over her father's face, as though it belongs there for good. She steps into Bapi's study and Papa closes the door behind them.

Across Bapi's desk, photographs are strewn and pages and pages covered with Mummy's writing — handwriting that Aiya used to call 'distinctive' — all loops and curls, big letters that Imogen had begun to find easier and easier to read for herself, with just a little help from Aiya.

'I'm not angry at you,' Papa begins. 'I just need to know . . .'

But Imogen hears no more. Papa's bald head reminds her of the horrible men on that horrible night who stopped them going to visit Abi María-Luisa. And Imogen can't help herself. Sobs arise from deep inside that heart-place which has been feeling numb since Aiya died. Imogen sees her mother; she sees her aiya; she sees the secret visits to the villa. She cries and she cries and doesn't even care that she can hardly breathe and that Papa has discovered her secret and will be angry with her all over again.

'Don't,' Papa says. But his face isn't black. It looks weak and sorry, and its shape keeps changing as though it doesn't know what kind of a face it's supposed to be anymore.

From nowhere that she can name, something pure and clean and angry rises in Imogen and spills out of her mouth before she can stop it. 'Mummy wrote those letters to me,' she cries. 'They're mine! Aiya promised they were our secret. Hers and mine and Mummy's.'

She watches as Papa moves back from her, as though she has slapped his face, or is about to. 'You are right,' he says. 'I am profoundly sorry – very sorry indeed.' His face is calm, serious. 'I did not go looking for your secret. But I have the task of looking after Aiya's papers. I found these without meaning to.'

And then something astonishing happens. Papa gathers together all the pages and photographs and puts them back into Aiya's secret box and hands the box to Imogen. 'These are yours to keep,' he says.

Imogen does not know what to say. It's as though all of her words are locked up in the box in her hands, along with the letters and the photographs. Papa kisses her on the forehead. 'It seems that Aiya knew best. Aiya was the one who did what was right for you.' His voice trembles and he stops. Imogen thinks he is finding it hard to say all the words. But she doesn't break the silence because she knows it is still his turn to speak.

Then Papa sighs and pinches his eyes shut with his thumb and middle finger. It makes his nose look really big. Imogen hears him swallow a sob that is trying hard to escape. 'I think . . .' he says, 'I think that it's time we arranged for you and Omiros to spend some proper time with Mummy. What do *you* think?'

Imogen clutches the box of secrets to her chest. It feels as though her inside-place has finally blown wide open. Her heart has started to beat again. She looks at her papa's face, and it has a bright shadow of something that she saw once before, a long time ago, on that summer day when he'd taught her to sail.

Then she's laughing and crying all at the same time. 'Promise?' she says.

Papa crushes her to his chest. 'I promise,' he whispers. 'I promise. Cross my heart and hope to die.' And he smiles.

Calista

London, 1977

YIANNIS COMES TO FIND HER AT APHRODITE. Calista is surprised to see him. It is shortly after Maroulla has died, and the brothers – Yiannis, Ari, Spyros and Alexandros – have all had their hands full trying to manage Petros.

'My father has just given up,' Yiannis tells Calista over the phone, a couple of weeks after his mother's funeral. 'He says he doesn't want to live without her. He doesn't sleep, barely eats. We're trying to invent ways to keep him busy. I think it'll be another month or so before I can get back to London. Will you be OK?'

Calista smiles at that. 'Of course. I miss you,' she says. 'But Petros needs you. I'll be fine: just come when you can.'

And so she's surprised to see Yiannis cross the threshold of the gallery, little more than a week later.

'Close early,' he says. 'I've cleared it with the boss.'

'But how?'

Yiannis takes both of her hands in his. 'I'm taking you to lunch, at Alexandros's request. We can go wherever you choose. I have some good news.'

Calista is almost too terrified to hope. 'Tell me,' she says, her mouth suddenly dry. She can feel her hands start to tremble. 'I'm not moving one more step until you tell me. Can I see my children, both my children?'

Yiannis's smile tells her everything. 'Yes. Yes, you can. Your daughter gave Alexandros a piece of her mind. My father

294

supported her. Alexandros has agreed that you can come to Limassol and spend a full week with them. He will take them to you. Let me tell you all about it over lunch.'

At the end of April, Calista flies to Limassol. She has booked into the Asteria Hotel, her room there crowded with memories. Alexandros drives Imogen and Omiros to meet her on the afternoon of her arrival. Calista is nervous. She knows that she must give Alexandros no reason to change his mind.

All the power in this situation is his. All the power must remain his. His territory, his rules of engagement.

She watches from the hotel foyer as Alexandros's Mercedes pulls up outside the main door. She remains seated: he will bring the children to her; that is the agreement. Calista waits, her heart full as she sees Omiros step carefully out of the back of the car. How tall he's grown, she thinks, but she shouldn't be surprised: it's been three years. Her son is now a sturdy five-year-old. Imogen bounces out, her eyes already searching for her mother.

Alexandros turns off the engine, opens the driver's door. He says something to the children and they move closer to him. He locks the car, puts the key in his pocket. Everything is done with a careful deliberation that tells Calista he knows she is watching him. And that he will make her wait.

He hasn't changed, Calista thinks. As smooth and as imposing as ever. The hotel's glass doors part obediently and Alexandros comes in with the children. He nods to Calista. His greeting is stiff and formal. 'Good afternoon, Calista,' he says. 'I hope you had a pleasant journey.'

Calista is polite, reserved in turn. She cannot help but feel astonished that this is all he says, that this is all she will say:

'Hello, Alexandros. Thank you for bringing the children to me.' She waits for a moment, turns to him quietly. 'Please accept my condolences on the death of your mother.'

He nods. 'Thank you.'

It feels surreal. This is a man she once loved, a man who once loved her. A man whose family was once entwined with every detail of her daily life. Calista waits in silence. All the things she wants to say must remain unspoken.

Alexandros has both of the children by the hand. Calista sees how watchful her son and daughter have become. They will not move without permission. She looks at Alexandros, her face a question.

He nods.

In the middle of the hotel's foyer, Calista bends down, holds her arms out and says softly: 'Omiros, Imogen. How wonderful to see you both. I've missed you so much.' She keeps her voice low: she must not overwhelm them, particularly Omiros.

Imogen runs to her at once, but Omiros hangs back. Calista watches as longing and hostility battle their way across his features.

Alexandros touches his son on the shoulder. His voice is stern. 'Go to your mother, Omiros. Do as we have discussed.'

The small boy makes his way towards Calista, step by reluctant step. She feels emotion gather, but she will not let it show. Instead, she smiles, smooths his dark hair away from his forehead with one hand. 'It is good to see you,' she says. 'You have grown very tall. I am so happy to be with you.'

Finally, the child moves closer. Calista puts one arm around him, gently, and presses him to her. Imogen has already folded herself into her mother, both her arms around Calista's waist.

'Come,' she says. 'Let's sit down and have something to drink, and some ice cream. Do you still like honey ice cream?'

Omiros nods, his expression shading from shyness to

uncertainty. He continues to glance back over his shoulder, to where Alexandros still waits.

I'm a stranger to him, Calista thinks. A stranger to my own son. She wonders how much he remembers, how much he has absorbed since her leaving. 'Let's sit over here, shall we?'

Both children move obediently towards the seating area with the low glass coffee table.

'I'll be back for them at nine o'clock sharp,' Alexandros says now. His tone is brisk, businesslike. 'Tomorrow, Saturday, you may keep them with you all day and overnight. On Sunday, they will come to church with me. Afterwards, we'll discuss the rest of the week.' He gets ready to leave.

Imogen and Omiros are already seated, their legs dangling over the cushions of the deep leather couch. Omiros's feet do not yet reach the floor. Calista is struck by how small they both look. In the grown-up surroundings of an anonymous hotel, how small and vulnerable. She turns to Alexandros.

'Thank you,' she says. 'I want you to know how grateful I am for this.'

His answering nod is curt, dismissive. 'I will see you later.'

He turns and walks away from her. Calista sees the way Omiros's eyes follow his father, the way Imogen smiles at her brightly, eagerly.

It will always be like this, Calista thinks. I will always have Imogen.

But Omiros will never forgive me.

Pilar

Madrid, 1981

PILAR OFTEN WATCHES THE STUDENTS as they make their way to and from school past her building on Calle de las Huertas. She watches them again this morning, as she waits for some prospective tenants to come and view her vacant apartment on the third floor.

Pilar is amused by the antics of the young people outside her door. She sees how they travel in packs, the girls shrill and emphatic, the boys loud and awkward. Their bodies have not yet caught up with their sophisticated image of themselves, despite the cigarettes they smoke, the words they hurl at one another, the pushing and the shoving as the boys jostle loudly for position.

From time to time, one of these teenagers makes Pilar take a second look. His hair stands up in dark spikes: a line of fine, upright trees growing from the front of his forehead to the nape of his neck. He is clearly popular. Girls crowd round him; boys follow in his wake.

Pilar watches him, and she wonders. From time to time, she still allows herself to dream. In the absence of certainty, fantasy brings a comfort of its own.

The doorbell peals and Pilar starts, her daydream dissolving. It is Jorge, with his sack of mail over one shoulder. Pilar is irritated by his grin: he clearly believes he has caught her napping. But she mustn't annoy him. Jorge's local knowledge is immeasurable. You never know when you might need someone like Jorge. She opens the door.

'Good morning,' Pilar says. She hopes he isn't angling for coffee: she hasn't the time this morning.

'How's it goin'?' he replies.

Pilar waits for him to hand over the bundles of letters. She can see them in his hand, already neatly bound together with string. But he hesitates. Pilar grows impatient.

'I've a bit of a favour to ask,' he says.

'Yes?'

Where is he going with this? Pilar wonders.

'My young lad collects stamps, particularly foreign stamps. He has whole albums full of them. I was wondering . . .' He starts fumbling at the bundles of letters.

'Spit it out, Jorge: I've some tenants arriving in a minute – just let me know what you want. I'll help if I can.'

'It's just that on one of these envelopes here, there's some stamps I've never seen before. I haven't been prying, Señorita Dóminguez, but you have a letter from Peru and . . .'

Pilar doesn't hear any more. She yanks both bundles from Jorge's hand. She wants to run to the sanctuary of her *portería*. She begins to turn away, her mouth dry, her hands all at once clumsy and hesitant. It's from her. It has to be.

'Keep them for me, won't you?' Jorge calls. 'My boy would love to have those stamps. All those different-coloured stone heads. OK?'

Pilar doesn't look up. 'Yes, yes,' she says, 'I will. I'll keep them for you, of course.' She wants to rip the envelope apart, to devour the words. Florencia's words about her son. At last. After all these years.

But she has to wait. A middle-aged man and his wife are just now stepping into the entrance hall as Jorge is making his exit.

'Señorita Domínguez?' the man asks. He looks anxious.

Pilar folds the letter in two and slips it into her apron pocket. She must hide her agitation. 'Yes,' she says. 'Good morning.'

She notices that the woman's coat is not the best quality. Her shoes are worn, and her gloves have seen better days. It's highly unlikely that these two have the kind of money to rent an apartment in a building such as this. But right now, Pilar doesn't care about that.

She extends her hand. 'You're very welcome. It's a pleasure to meet you both. Please, follow me and let me show you around. Then we'll have coffee and I'll answer any questions you may have.'

Just get rid of them, as soon as possible. She leads them towards the lift and they follow.

Pilar can hear the rustle of the envelope as she walks. She can feel the heat of the paper against her skin.

Imogen

Limassol, 1981

IT IS THE MORNING OF Omiros's ninth birthday. Imogen, his big sister of fourteen, is looking after him for the day. Papa has given her money to take Omiros and some of his friends to lunch. Later, Papa will come to meet them both at the yacht club and there, he will present his son with his very own Mermaid sailing boat. Imogen has been trusted to keep the secret.

'You ready, Omiros?' Imogen calls.

He comes running out of his bedroom. Bapi Petros is in the hallway, waiting.

'Happy birthday, Omiros,' Bapi says, as Omiros jumps down the last three steps, landing just shy of his grandfather's feet. Imogen notices that Bapi is getting more and more unsteady these days, that he has to use his walking stick a lot.

Eleni comes fussing over, hurrying her way out of the kitchen towards him. Imogen and Omiros don't need a nanny anymore, of course, but they have allowed the fiction to continue that they do. They are willing conspirators with their father.

'Petros needs to be looked after, now,' Papa had said, recently. 'But he doesn't like the idea. Eleni will stay on here with us and help him – but you must never say anything about that, do you understand?'

Imogen had sighed to herself at that. Sometimes, adults could be very stupid. Why would either she or Omiros say anything that might upset Bapi Petros? Often, the only person who made him unhappy is Alexandros himself. Particularly now that he had a new woman in his life.

When Papa introduced Sandra, he'd been all smiles. But Imogen wasn't fooled. She knew by the way he tapped his fingers on the tabletop that he was nervous.

'This is Sandra, everyone,' he said, leading this tall, fair-haired woman into the living room, where they all had to sit, politely, waiting to meet her. Sandra had the kind of beauty that so many of Imogen's friends admired, but she didn't. The peachy, freckled skin, the blue eyes that always looked cold, the severe, tailored elegance of her expensive clothes.

'Well, Cassandra, really,' she'd said, with her bright painted smile. 'But everyone calls me Sandra. Much more modern, don't you think?'

Bapi had said something that sounded like a grunt. He didn't get up out of his chair, although he did shake hands with the foreign woman. Imogen had had to stifle a giggle at the rude noise he'd made. *What's wrong with a good Cypriot girl?* Imogen had heard him demand one night. *Why do you keep bringing all these foreigners home?*

For a moment, Imogen felt indignant on her mother's behalf, angry at Bapi Petros. Afterwards, though, she was pleased that Bapi disliked Sandra just as much as she did. Omiros didn't seem to care either way, as long as Sandra didn't take up all of Papa's time, which she didn't, not yet.

Mummy knew about her. She said so, the last time she was here. 'I've heard about her, yes,' she said. 'Uncle Yiannis told me when he was last in London. I understand that they are engaged to be married.'

'I can't stand her,' Imogen blurted. 'She's so fake.'

'Sweetheart, you have to make an effort.'

Imogen didn't want to make an effort. She didn't want any new woman, any Sandra, taking her mother's place.

'Listen to me,' Calista said, sitting beside her on the bed in her hotel room. Imogen thought that her mother's face was suddenly serious. It was the way she always looked when she had something important to say. 'People are entitled to another chance if their marriage doesn't work. If Sandra makes Papa happy, that can only be good for you and for Omiros.'

Imogen decided to change the subject. 'Why can't I come and live with you in London?'

She already knew the answer to this, but that didn't stop her asking, again.

'Your father won't hear of it, so there's no point in us even discussing it. Not just yet. Maybe when you're sixteen,' Calista said. 'Things should be easier then.'

'But that's two whole years!' Imogen protested.

'It won't be long in passing, I promise you. In the meantime, we'll just have to take every chance we can get to be together, and you have to help me not to make your father too mad, OK?'

Imogen nodded and managed a watery smile.

And now Imogen is seated at a long table with seven nine-year-old boys. They are all eating and shouting and being disgusting. Seven nines are sixty-three, she calculates: I'm surrounded by sixty-three years of mischief. Some of the boys are even throwing food at each other, and Imogen has to yell at them to stop.

Omiros hasn't wanted Mummy here for his birthday, and Imogen feels sad about that. She has seen the way her mother's face closes over each time Omiros tells her to go away. She's tried to comfort Calista.

Maybe next time, she says. *Maybe next time.*

Next time, Imogen hopes she will be one year closer to going to London. One year closer to leaving Papa and Sandra behind.

One year closer to freedom.

Pilar

Madrid, 1981

BY THE TIME THE NEW tenants finally leave, Pilar has become a fever of impatience. She's waved away their bank statements, their letters of reference, their identity cards. *Next time*, she's said: *Next time you're passing will be fine.*

She locks herself into the *portería* and pulls the crumpled envelope out of her apron pocket. She opens it carefully, seeing that Sister Florencia has written her return address in Lima across the flap at the back. Pilar takes care not to damage it.

Inside, there are two closely written pages, flimsy airmail pages that feel to Pilar much too insubstantial to carry the weight of the news that they surely must contain.

'*My dear Pilar*,' she reads, '*what an extraordinary thing to hear from you.*'

Pilar's eyes devour the words, quickly scanning the lines to find what she is looking for. She will reread the letter in its entirety later, but for now, all she cares about is finding out where Florencia sent her son.

'*I kept my own diary in those days*,' Florencia writes, '*in which I noted the mother's name, the child's date of birth and the names of the adoptive parents. Addresses of adoptive parents are less reliable – couples came from all over Spain, staying with relatives in Madrid, going home when the babies were born.*'

Give me whatever you have, Pilar thinks. Just tell me.

'*I always felt uncomfortable with the secrecy, the lack of documents, the way children just sailed off into the unknown, citizens of some shady underworld. Now that I have two babies of my own, I understand all too well what your grief must have been.'*

Pilar skips to the final paragraph. She cannot bear the agony of waiting any longer.

'We have another eighteen months here in Lima. I want my children to go to school in Madrid, to know their cousins and their grandparents. I hope that by the time we come back, my own parents will have learned to forgive me.'

Pilar feels her dismay begin to grow.

'I will of course meet you on my return. I have none of my personal papers from the convent with me – I left them in a safe place in Madrid. Here, in Lima, my husband and I – what a strange word! I never thought to write it about my own life: Antonio is a good man, a loving husband and father – we run a clinic together for mothers and babies. Our aim is to support the young women to keep their children, not give them away to strangers. It is a struggle: the concept of sin is still a strong one.'

Pilar begins to weep with frustration. Another eighteen months. A whole year and a half. Francisco-José is already fourteen years of age.

'Please feel free to write to me again. I will help you in any way I can on my return. But please remember that these things, as Antonio and I have learned, must be treated with delicacy. I will try to contact the adoptive parents on your behalf in the first instance. We must remember that they have raised your son for many years: we cannot descend upon them like some avenging angel from the past. We must respect their needs too. But have courage, my dear – and believe me: we will do all we can to find your son. God is good.'

Is he? Pilar thinks bitterly. Is he really? He hasn't been all that good to me.

She folds the letter and places it in the drawer of her dressing table. She will read it again, later, and many times over.

For now, she has read enough. For now, she must do what she has learned to do so well over the years.

Pilar will wait. She will work; she will save; she will find ways to fill all the empty days until Florencia's return.

Pilar will watch, and Pilar will wait.

Calista

Extremadura, 1989

CALISTA LOOKS OUT OVER THE midday landscape of Extremadura. The heat of noon has begun to haze and shimmer above the surrounding fields.

She is thinking about Yiannis. About the ten years they had, the love they shared. Recently, she'd gone looking for a box of photographs from the early 1980s, a series of colour prints from the weekends she and Yiannis spent together. She had stored them on a high shelf in the study, unable to bear looking at them before now.

Calista will never forget his face as they stepped out of Prague Airport to hail a taxi. His eyes were dark with shock. He looked at her in amazement. 'You never warned me it would be this cold!'

'You're the one who's the seasoned traveller!' Calista laughed. 'What else is the middle of Europe going to feel like at Christmas?'

'Must be why I never travelled here in December,' he grumbled.

'Come on: follow me.' Calista took him by the hand. 'I know where we can get the best mulled wine ever.'

Yiannis looked at her in surprise. 'I thought you'd never been here before,' he said. 'I thought that was why we chose this city together.' He looked crestfallen.

'I haven't,' Calista grinned. She waved her guidebook under his nose. 'I just believe everything I read. Let's go – here's our taxi.'

She remembers how they'd walked the city in the snow, how they'd visited the castle and the museums and listened to music in all the concert halls dotted across the city. To Yiannis's own surprise, he'd loved the ballet. *Swan Lake*, Calista remembers. That was probably one of the happiest nights of her life, sitting in that darkened, magical space, watching dancers glide across the stage. Yiannis held her hand throughout, turning to smile at her when something in the music moved him. Calista remembers how loved, how safe, how privileged she felt.

It is Yiannis who comes to tell Calista what has happened in the summer of 1983 – six long years ago now.

He travelled from Limassol to London on the last flight, arriving well after midnight.

The sound of a key in the door puzzles Calista at first, then frightens her.

She puts her book face down on the table and stands up from the sofa, tying the belt of her dressing gown more tightly round her. It is as though she is girding herself: she feels an alertness that is like a warning.

A moment later, he steps into the room. He looks crumpled; a rucksack sags across his shoulders.

'Yiannis,' Calista says, almost laughing with relief. 'You startled me! I wasn't expecting you.' She begins to move towards him, then stops.

Something is not right. He has brought a strange feeling with him into the room, something that has not been there previously. The air seems to have stilled all around him, and he has not yet spoken. He looks at Calista, and she sees how grey his face is, how strained the flesh around his eyes.

She feels a great surge of love for this man, a rush of sympathy for how suddenly tired and worn he seems. For the first time, Calista thinks how old Yiannis looks. She wants to comfort him, to care for him, the way he has so often cared for her.

But Yiannis stands there, facing her, his hands by his side. How odd, Calista thinks. He has no luggage with him.

'Calista,' he says, and his voice breaks.

In two steps, she is at his side. 'Sweetheart, you look exhausted. Come and sit down.'

'Calista,' he says again, almost raising one hand, but letting it fall again at once. She sees, to her horror, that his eyes have filled.

Instantly, Calista backs away from him. Somewhere, deep in her gut, she knows.

'What is it?' she says. 'Tell me. Something has happened to my children. Tell me. Has something happened to my children?' She hears her voice become shrill; she hardly recognizes it as her own.

Yiannis nods, unable to speak. Calista sees the sweat on his forehead, although it is not warm.

'Tell me!' she screams. 'Tell me! Tell me what has happened to my children!'

'Calista . . .' He moves towards her now, his arms open.

But Calista is beyond fear. She steps back further, her hands warding off whatever news he is about to tell her. 'Is it Imogen?' she asks.

Yiannis nods. 'Yes,' he whispers. 'My darling—'

'Don't,' she says. 'Don't try and soften it! Tell me. Tell me!' Her voice fills the room and Yiannis flinches. She keeps her arms extended against him. She cannot bear comfort. All she wants is to know what it is, this news he brings with him.

'There has been an awful accident,' he blurts. 'At sea.'

'It's Imogen, isn't it?'

Yiannis nods, wordless.

'Is she dead?' The word is blunt, brutal and Calista feels the dull weight of it on her tongue. It hangs in the room between them, a remorseless, heavy presence.

Yiannis nods.

Calista does not hear any more, although she knows that Yiannis keeps speaking. She can see his lips move.

But she is howling, an unearthly sound that is high and deep and filled with despair, and she clutches at her hair and she falls to her knees and she wails and wails until she cries herself to quietness in the useless shelter of Yiannis's arms.

Pilar

Madrid, 1983

PILAR SETTLES HERSELF comfortably into the hire car. Four hours along the motorway from Madrid to Badajoz, if she doesn't stop. She will, though, in Trujillo. She's always had a fondness for Trujillo. She likes its ancient air, its wide plazas, the way the bell towers at evening are conquered by flights of swifts, swooping and chittering as dusk leaches into darkness.

Pilar is filled with optimism these days. Florencia will soon be back and Pilar's final search can begin in earnest. She knows that every day brings her closer to her son. She can feel it. And she has kept herself busy while she waits.

In the past year, Pilar has concluded some very satisfactory negotiations on another apartment building. Something for Francisco-José, for his future, for the children he may have someday. Pilar is pleased with herself. No more poverty, Mamá, she thinks. Not for the next generation, either.

She has installed Maribel and Alicia as the *porteras* of her new building. Pilar was truthful with them about her ownership. She'd watched as a mix of gratitude and envy washed across their faces; they had always been so transparent, those two. But Pilar did not reveal to them the full extent of her property portfolio; instead, she followed Señor Gómez's advice about playing her cards close to her chest. Never let the right hand know what the left hand is doing. Business is business.

Pilar has also kept her promise to Señor Gómez. She has

visited Paco a couple of times each year. Despite her urgings, he will not come to her in Madrid. His duty to the land and to his father, he tells her, must come first.

The first time she went back, Paco's joy at seeing her brought tears to Pilar's eyes. He was waiting for her, as she made the final turn into the farm. She wondered how long he'd been standing there: she was at least an hour later than she'd hoped to be.

'Pilar,' he said, coming towards her as she stepped out of the car. They hugged and Pilar was grateful for the few moments this gave her to hide her face. Although it had only been a couple of years since she last saw him – four, he later corrected her – Paco's physical resemblance to Señor Gómez had grown stronger with each passing year. A life on the land had not coarsened him. His features had all the elegant refinements of his father's.

Pilar's father, Miguel, did not seem at all pleased to see her. He was distant, monosyllabic, turned his face away from her whenever she entered the room. She ignored him.

For the next few days, Pilar helped Paco around the farm. She went with him – only because he had begged her – to visit her brothers Javier and Carlos, and their bitter wives, Mercedes and Paquita.

Once, she went with him to Bar Jaime. She had never been there before, but Paco insisted that she visit with him. 'It belongs to José Martínez,' Paco told her. 'He owns his family vineyard now. He and his wife are really nice. Do you remember him?'

'I remember the name,' Pilar says. 'If it belongs to José, why is it called Bar Jaime?' She is curious.

'It's named after José and Inmaculada's son, Jaime. He's away at school. The bar is for him when he finishes university – and the vineyard, too, I suppose, eventually.'

'Assuming he wants to come home,' Pilar said. 'I wouldn't

bet on it, if I was his parents.' She grins at Paco. 'Torre de Santa Juanita for a twenty-something-year-old man? I don't think so.'

'Ah, but he has a lovely girlfriend called Rosa,' Paco says. 'That would make a difference to any man.'

Pilar glances at her brother. She sees the sudden loneliness etched across his face. For a moment, she is tempted to tell him about Francisco-José, but she stops herself. You'd never know where such a conversation might lead.

That evening, as they enter the bar, Pilar immediately feels its warmth, its lightness, its air of welcome and optimism – something unusual for the village – or, at least, for the village as Pilar recalls it. But then, she supposes, things can change.

'You remember José and Inmaculada?' Paco says, introducing Pilar to the smiling couple behind the bar. They shake hands.

'Yes,' Pilar says, surprised at herself. 'I do remember your names. It was your parents who used to own the vineyard, isn't that right?'

'That's right,' José beams. 'You have a good memory.'

'I left for Madrid twenty-six years ago,' Pilar says, 'but some things about Torre de Santa Juanita remain unforgettable.' Everyone laughs.

'I would have been in my mid-twenties then,' José says. 'I was tempted by the bright lights myself; but I took over the vineyard around that time.' He nods towards his wife. 'So I stayed. And that's when we got married.'

'And I was a child bride,' Inmaculada jokes, 'as you can clearly tell.'

It's an evening that Pilar still remembers with pleasure.

Before she returned to Madrid that first time, Paco asked her to accompany him to Badajoz. He had some business there, he said, but he didn't like driving on the main roads. Pilar can still see her father's sour expression as she and Paco drove off. He refused to go with them. He refused to waste his time, he said. Pilar did not encourage him to change his mind.

She wondered if her father still remembered – as she did – the last time, the only time, they visited that city together. Miguel took her there just the once, when Pilar can have been no more than seven. 'She has reached the age of reason,' he insisted, when Pilar's mother tried to prevent him from taking her. 'It is time she knew.'

Pilar had looked from one face to the other, bewildered, afraid that she was the unknowing cause of yet more trouble between Mamá and Papá. The house was filled with something uneasy, all over again – something that felt heavier than air and might fall to the ground at any moment, bringing her father's rage with it.

'She's a child,' her mother said, warning her husband with her eyes.

But Miguel shrugged and took Pilar by the hand anyway, none too gently.

They arrived at the *plaza de toros* in Badajoz; all she remembers is being there, and her father's words as they stood together, sharing an awkward closeness, looking out over what seemed to Pilar to be a vast, sandy wasteland.

'You asked me,' her father said, not looking at her, but at something in the middle of the *plaza* that Pilar could not see, no matter how she strained. 'About your grandfather and grandmother. Did you not?'

Pilar nodded, feeling guilty. Should she not have asked? The grim set of Papá's face made her wish she hadn't. Somehow, she knew then that she didn't want to know more. She didn't want to hear whatever it was that was making Papá look the way he did at that moment. She preferred his angry face, not this black and twisted one that looked, astonishingly, as if it might collapse into tears at any moment.

'They were murdered,' he said. His tone was cold, blunt. 'My parents were both murdered. Think how lucky you are to have yours.' His arms were folded, held tightly against his chest, although it was not cold, not that day.

But it was, however, silent. No birdsong. No wind. No movement that created a rustling of any kind. The stillness made Pilar suddenly afraid. She wanted to go home, but her father had not finished yet.

'The fascists shot them,' he said, and something about his tone sounded almost curious, wondering, as if he still couldn't quite believe it himself. 'And then they burned their bodies. Four thousand of them. This is what people do to one another.'

Pilar began to cry. She didn't know who the fascists were, and she didn't like this story.

The sound seemed to remind Papá of her presence. 'What are you crying for?' he demanded. 'Nothing bad has ever happened to you.'

Pilar had no answer for that. She remembers feeling that in some way that she did not understand, her escape from suffering must have been the cause of Papá's, maybe even the cause of her grandparents'. She felt guilt settle itself around her, a thick, hairy blanket that chafed against her skin every time she moved.

'Come,' her father said at last. 'It is time to go home.'

Pilar does not remember the journey back to the farm, either. But that afternoon, the silence of the bullring, her father's face, his tightly folded arms, these have all stayed with her. The Butcher of Badajoz, she learned later. One of Generalísimo Franco's henchmen: one of the many atrocities of the civil war. And Juan Yagüe had done his butchering a mere three years before she was born. Pilar wonders now, as she has often wondered in the intervening years, what happens to people when all that brutality seeps its poisonous way through the generations.

As she drives the final few kilometres to the farm now, Pilar promises herself, once again, that she will try to be kind and tolerant towards her father. If not for his sake, then for Paco's. That day in Badajoz has come back to haunt her more than once.

This is what people do to one another.

Pilar does not forgive Miguel; she can never forgive him for the life he gave her mother. But she has often asked herself what drove him to become the man he was. His fists, his boot, his rage.

In Carlos and Javier both, Pilar has seen some of her father's darkness. She thinks of their wives, Mercedes and Paquita, and she wonders.

You never know what goes on behind people's front doors, she thinks. All those gleaming surfaces hiding something.

Imogen

Limassol, 1983

IMOGEN MAKES HER WAY DOWN the jetty towards where Alexandros's yacht is moored. The *Cassandra* is a thing of beauty. Imogen has always felt this, despite its having been named for her stepmother. The arrival of Sandra into her father's life, into all of their lives, is something that Imogen prefers not to think about. She prefers to remember other things instead, such as the summer her father taught her to sail: the summer she was eight. Three whole years before British Sandra made her appearance.

Imogen remembers the Mermaid, her own tiny sailing boat: remembers the solid heft of the wave, the slap of the canvas, the sheer slick saltiness of flying before the wind. She remembers, too, the day she finally grasped what her father had been trying to teach her, patiently, almost doggedly, for months.

That is a day that stands out above so many others, something Imogen can still see and hear and feel with a bright, brittle clarity. Learning how to master the wind and the waves was only one part of the exhilaration she felt. Knowing that her mother would visit again, as soon as she could, was the other. Imogen hugged that secret knowledge to herself, storing up her memories until the next time.

'Well done, Imogen!' Her father's face was filled with pride. 'You've done it: you're a sailor!' He lifted her into his arms and strode hugely towards the beach. The Mermaid bobbed and ducked along behind them.

Old Karolis came running towards them. He was panting, anxious. 'Is everything all right, Mr Alexandros?'

'Yes, Karolis: everything is fine, just fine!'

The older man relaxed at Alexandros's jovial tone. He grinned, years falling away from his face, smoothing out his weathered skin so that he looked just like his son, twelve-year-old Young Karolis.

'I'll take care of the Mermaid,' Old Karolis said, already reaching for the painter.

'Which one?' Alexandros rocked with laughter. 'Which mermaid? That Mermaid there or –' and he swung Imogen round, dipping her scarily towards the sand and then scooping her back up into his powerful arms again '– this one, my lovely daughter!'

But it wasn't really a question and Old Karolis seemed to know that because he didn't answer. He just nodded and smiled and took the rope from Alexandros. He pulled the Mermaid smoothly up onto the sand, where it sat, becalmed. Imogen thought that the little boat looked relieved to be there, as though it had fulfilled some secret purpose of its own and could rest now.

Alexandros strode up the beach to where the car was parked. As he walked, he patted Imogen's back from time to time, murmuring endearments. He kissed her wet and salty cheek.

Imogen rested against his shoulder, could hear his voice rumbling away beneath her.

She, too, felt becalmed.

At last.

Today, as Imogen approaches the end of the jetty, she has time to admire the sleek lines of her father's yacht, the white sheen of the hull. She can already imagine the smooth warmth of its varnished wood under her bare feet.

Young Karolis is already there, hosing down everything above the water line. Alexandros is very particular about the appearance of the *Cassandra*.

Imogen watches Young Karolis now, sees the way he coils up the hose and places it round the base of the tap that is dedicated to the *Cassandra*'s mooring. All the lines are similarly coiled: they lie neat and flat on the jetty. Everything is ready for an afternoon departure.

He looks up, finally, at Imogen's approach. And he smiles. '*Kalimera*,' he says.

Imogen is glad that she has her sunglasses on. Without them, Young Karolis might be able to read what he should not be able to read in her eyes. Alexandros had caught her looking at the boy once, late last summer, watching him as he unloaded the crates of supplies for the *Cassandra* – food, wine, bottles of beer and lemonade. She watched as he moved with an unconscious grace, a loping ease that made her breath catch somewhere towards the back of her throat. She was fifteen then, Karolis an unattainable nineteen; but a girl could dream, couldn't she?

And then her father's hand was on her shoulder. 'You are *my* daughter,' he'd said, almost as though he had heard her. His voice was quiet, but Imogen immediately understood his meaning, although she pretended not to.

'*What?*' she said, backing away from the porthole as if she'd been stung.

'You are my daughter,' Alexandros repeated, 'and you will behave in an appropriate manner. I see how you look at him. I will not have it.'

Imogen had slammed her way into her cabin, locking the door behind her. She'd refused to come out for hours. When she did, it was to her father's repeated mantra of his duty; his authority; her safety and security above all else.

'Good morning, Karolis,' Imogen says now, her voice friendly, cheerful. 'All done?'

'Yes, Miss Imogen, everything is ready. I charged the fridge battery last night and put the food away. The icepacks are frozen, and the drinks are in the second cabin – use the blue coolboxes first, then the red.' He flicks the butt of his cigarette into the water. Imogen feels a shivery thrill at the gesture. Karolis is so grown-up. Sexy. 'Mr Alexandros and Madam Sandra will be here within the hour.'

Imogen looks at him. She can feel the way her mouth has opened and she closes it again, quickly. 'What did you say?'

'Your father called the office,' Karolis says. He looks puzzled, as though this, surely, is information that Imogen must already have. 'He told my father to put supplies on board for the three of you, that you had had a change of plan?'

Imogen says nothing. She does not acknowledge the interrogative lift at the end of Karolis's sentence. *I* have not had a change of anything, she fumes. Anger towards her father vies with what Aiya María-Luisa calls 'breeding'. And Imogen remembers her father's warning about loyalty: never, ever to discuss family business in front of servants or employees.

Loyalty.

Fuck loyalty, Imogen thinks. *Fuck* it.

Fury makes tears spring to her eyes. Omiros is away, taking part in a junior regatta; Sandra is supposed to be in Athens. This was to be Imogen's day in charge of the *Cassandra*, under the supervision of her father. Skipper for the day, he'd promised her. You are more than ready. I've taught you all that I know.

'That's fine, thank you,' Imogen says to Karolis now.

'Do you need any help at all on board?' he asks.

Imogen can hear the hope in his voice. She hesitates, but only for an instant. 'Thanks, Karolis, but I don't think that's a good idea.'

His smile collapses. 'Of course,' Karolis says. 'I understand.' He nods abruptly. 'It would not be appropriate.' He touches two fingers to the imaginary peak of the cap he is not wearing – an ironic salute, a mock-servile gesture – and then he's gone, walking briskly away from her up the jetty. He does not turn back.

Imogen watches his departure, dismayed. She wants to call out, but she doesn't know what to say. She wishes she could just walk away from this: from the yacht, from the prospect of her father and his wife for twenty-four hours. From her life.

She climbs on board and opens the hatch in the forward cabin. The heat is stifling. It will be so much better once they get underway. Karolis has left clean sheets and pillowslips on the double berth and Imogen ignores them.

Let Sandra make her own bed.

She crosses to her cabin and throws her rucksack onto the top bunk. Quickly, she pulls off her shorts and T-shirt. She'll sunbathe in her bikini while she waits for the two of them to arrive. And if Alexandros objects, he can just go to hell.

He can take the *Cassandra* out of the marina himself today. Imogen has no intention of sharing the cockpit with her father and Sandra while they fawn all over each other.

Sitting up at the bow is the part Imogen loves best. Particularly once they get underway. The heat disappears; the breeze ruffles and cools; the engine noise makes conversation impossible.

She scrambles up to the bow, taking her book with her. She has, maybe, twenty minutes' peace before they arrive.

Imogen hears voices, sees the dip and swell of the jetty as Alexandros and Sandra approach. She hears her stepmother's high, clear laughter and her father's deeper tone underneath.

She looks up. Alexandros waves. Imogen does not wave back.

He says something to Sandra out of the side of his mouth and they both laugh.

'You ready to take her out?' Alexandros asks Imogen as he reaches the yacht and helps Sandra on board. He's looking pleased with himself.

'I'd rather you did it,' she says, without lifting her eyes from her book. Her tone is cold. 'The marina is very crowded today.'

'You're more than capable,' Alexandros begins. Imogen raises her eyes to his and sees the way Sandra quickly touches her father's arm. He stops. 'Well, if you're sure that's what you want,' he says, his voice conciliatory.

'I'm sure.'

'Gosh, it's hot,' Sandra says. She fans herself with her ridiculous straw hat. Her freckled skin is already pink. 'I'm going to have a beer. Imogen, would you like one?'

Why not? Imogen thinks. Why not take advantage of the situation? 'Thanks,' she says, reaching back as her father's wife hands her a bottle from the coolbox.

Sandra thinks giving her a beer is a big deal: Imogen is amused at her stepmother's attempt to be cool.

If only she knew.

Imogen's mood begins to improve as they reach the open water. She already knows where her father will slow down, knows the exact spot where he will cut the engine, the time when he will expect her to unfurl the sails. This knowledge, this unchanging routine makes something rebellious stir inside her: Imogen's familiar, bitter longing to make her life her own, to make it different from the one that has shaped itself around her.

As the bow rises and falls, Imogen thinks of her mother: of her mother's life. She resolves that this is the last time she will come sailing with her father and his English wife, the last time she will be treated as a child. She is not one to be bought off with spurious reassurances of adulthood. Sandra can keep her bottles of beer and her phony gestures of equality.

Somehow, Imogen will escape. Somehow, she will get herself to London and to Calista. She is, at last, sixteen and she knows how to be cunning. She'll take the time to plan her getaway; but get away she will. Imogen feels a surge of triumph, followed by a sense of relief so powerful that it feels like an assault.

She is trapped only by her own acquiescence.

A realization has been reached, a decision made.

Is there any greater freedom than that?

Imogen looks down over the side, down into deep water that is turquoise in its clarity. Small waves begin to slap at the sides of the *Cassandra*. The yacht turns lazily on its anchor. But the breeze is beginning to strengthen: you could set your watch by it in this part of the world. Always around three in the afternoon, the wind gathers force around the island. This makes Imogen happy: they will have an exhilarating sail to the harbour.

Over lunch, Imogen makes an effort to be polite, to show interest in her father's plans for the evening, once they dock. She doesn't really care what they do later on, or where Alexandros intends to treat them to dinner. Her earlier decision makes her feel calm and resolute and grown-up. She feels that she can tolerate whatever her father does today.

Alexandros drains his bottle of beer, stands up, stretches, yawns.

'I'm going to lie down for an hour or so,' he says. 'We'll give the breeze the chance to strengthen a bit; then we'll be on our way.' He turns to Sandra, much too casually. 'Coming, my love?'

Imogen thinks she'll throw up. He's so *transparent*.

Sandra hesitates. Imogen turns away, but not before she sees

Sandra's moue of embarrassment. She senses, rather than sees, her father's shrug. Without a word, Sandra gets up and follows Alexandros into the forward cabin.

Disgusting, Imogen thinks. They're just so disgusting, both of them.

When the cabin door closes, Imogen sits back into the padded seat of the cockpit, shaded from the intensity of the sun. She no longer has any intention of sitting up on the bow; no intention of feeling herself surrounded by her father's grunts and her stepmother's high-pitched cries.

Soundlessly, Imogen reaches for another beer. She has her own secret stash under her bunk. She'll use it to replace the cold ones that she intends to drink, one after the other, until her father reappears.

When Alexandros emerges, Imogen has already heard the crackle of radio static from below. 'There's a bit of a blow coming,' he says. 'It's almost upon us. Time to test your skills.' And he grins at her. There is no sign of Sandra.

'How much of a blow?' she asks.

Even as she speaks, Imogen hears the snap of canvas: a taut, angry sound. It is the skipper's duty, always, to check the weather in advance. Alexandros has taught her this, but Imogen holds her tongue. Her father will take no hint of criticism, particularly in the presence of his precious wife.

'Nothing you and I can't handle,' he says. But he moves with speed towards the bow.

Imogen watches as Alexandros raises the anchor. The chain comes up from the deep, rattling its way into the housing with an aggressive screech of steel. It's as though it's reluctant to be disturbed. Alexandros noses the bow into the wind. There is an unaccustomed urgency to each of his movements.

All at once, the rigging begins to sound as though it is struggling to break free, the metal zinging and slapping against the aluminium mast.

Imogen feels the familiar thrust of excitement as the wind gusts from the west.

'Ready?' Alexandros calls.

'Ready,' she shouts.

Alexandros grins again, gives her the thumbs-up. 'That's my girl!'

But this is no ordinary afternoon. This is not something to be harnessed by exhilarated sailors bent on the pleasures of running before the wind.

Instead, Imogen sees a storm racing across the water. She sees a grey, angry god churning the docile surface of the waves as it blasts its way towards them from the west. The yacht begins to buck and heave; the wind attacks from all sides. The rain comes in torrents.

Imogen spots Sandra's terrified face at the cabin door. The spray begins to lash the deck, wild and sharp and stinging. Sandra is screaming for Alexandros to come to her.

And then there is a moment of calm. Imogen has no idea where it has come from. There is an abrupt, eerie stillness. The spray seethes back off the deck, fingering its way over the side, disappearing into the white waves below. Imogen feels an abrupt rush of nausea. She wishes she hadn't drunk so much beer.

'Jackets, Sandra!' Alexandros is shouting. 'Throw us up the life jackets!' But Sandra cannot move. She screams something at Alexandros, but the wind whips the words from her mouth.

Alexandros is gesticulating wildly now. Imogen can see that he wants to tell her something, but she cannot hear – she cannot make out what he wants from her. The yacht heels over at an acute, sudden angle. Alexandros waves his arms. Imogen is aware of a sudden commotion behind her – has something happened to Sandra?

'. . . come about!' she hears at last.

But she's not ready to come about. She's not quick enough. As she starts to turn, something hard cracks against the side of her head. It stuns her for a moment and pain blinds her. Imogen feels knocked sideways: something has furied all the breath out of her body. The boom, she thinks in surprise. I've been hit by the boom.

The knowledge feels hazy, interesting but detached: as though it is all happening to someone else.

As she plunges into the water below, Imogen realizes she has had this feeling before. This feeling of pitching downwards, of having all her insides scooped out, of having her heart-place wounded beyond repair.

She is aware of shouts, somewhere above her. Of voices that rumble and shrill, shredding the air somewhere just out of her reach.

All Imogen can feel is how quickly she is falling, falling, falling into that deep and dark and dreaming space just before sleep. Soon, she will jolt awake and this will be over.

Night-time shapes, sinister and darting, move around her.

Imogen sees her mother in the kitchen, light shining behind her, Monkey at her feet. He's wearing his new jacket and his smart new bow tie.

She sees Aiya, warning her about something, but she cannot understand what she's saying.

Her eyes can just discern the outline of a shadowy country: a map with which she is unfamiliar. But Imogen knows where London is. She is sure that she can sail there, on her own, as she once navigated the swelling seas to Troy.

Imogen reaches out one hand to touch the city. But the image recedes; it becomes watery and distant.

Instead, Imogen sees, floating in front of her face, a pale, white hand.

Her hand.

Darkness comes.

Calista

Limassol, 1983

CALISTA SEES ALEXANDROS'S RAVAGED FACE. Eyes that are raw with weeping.

She cannot look away from the white coffin. Its surface is hidden by a calamity of red roses, poppies, anemones.

Imogen's body rests within. She waits, just below the altar.

At the house, Petros is weeping. Calista watches Alexandros. Her eyes never leave his face. There is something in his expression that she cannot read.

She waits, as people come to her and speak words.

Sometime, late in the afternoon, Calista says: 'What happened? Tell me again what happened.'

Alexandros sighs. When he speaks, his voice is hoarse with emotion. 'There was a storm. It came at us out of the blue.'

Calista sees the way his eyes flicker. She catches the glance that passes between him and his wife. She sees Sandra, watching.

'But you've handled storms before,' Calista says. 'You pride yourself on your seamanship. I've heard your stories so many times.' Her voice is even, controlled.

Alexandros weeps. He wipes away the tears with one hand. 'She wasn't quick enough when we were coming about. The

boom knocked her overboard. She would have been unconscious.' He weeps again, his last words almost pleading with
her.

Calista waits for him to compose himself. 'Was she wearing
her life jacket?'

Then she sees Sandra flinch; sees the look that she casts in
her husband's direction. A look like a stone.

The room has gone quiet. Calista is aware of Petros watching
her. His face is distraught. But she will not stop.

'What about the weather forecast, Alexandros? Haven't you
always taught the children to check the weather, no matter where
they're going?'

Nobody moves.

Calista feels Sandra's eyes on her. She turns, quickly, and sees
guilt in those polite, blue, duplicitous eyes.

Suddenly, Calista understands. 'You were fucking! You didn't
know because you were fucking!'

Petros has struggled into standing. He places one hand on
Calista's elbow. She shrugs him off, roughly. She screams at
Alexandros: 'You should have watched out for your daughter,
protected her! You should have done your duty as a father!'

And she flies at him. Her fists punch the base of his throat.
Alexandros gasps, reeling away from her. Sandra runs to his side,
shrieking. Strong, sudden arms pin Calista's to her sides. She
sobs. Somewhere in front of her, she sees Yiannis's horrified face.
He makes his way towards her, his arms outstretched. She can
see his lips move but cannot hear anything he says. The sound
of her own weeping is loud in her ears.

Before they take her away, she sees Omiros across the room. She
sees the way her son looks at her, sees the way he watches Yiannis.

And then everything becomes the darkness.

*

Old Doctor Simon is by her side. Dimly, Calista is aware of his soothing voice. She feels the needle piercing flesh and gratefully she sinks. Into the darkness again, to Imogen. To the darkness where Imogen lies.

When Calista dreams, she sees her daughter. Her lovely daughter, changed into a deer, all grace and elegance. She is escaping. Fleeing the darkness.

Fleeing the light.

Calista wakes. Yiannis comes to help her dress. She sees the shock in his eyes. She glances towards the bedroom mirror.

'My hair,' she says. 'Look at my hair.'

She touches its steely surface, her hand full of wonder.

Pilar

Madrid, 1983

FLORENCIA IS BACK.

How young she looks, Pilar thinks. And beautiful. But she's tougher than Pilar remembers. Much tougher.

'This is the way it has to be, Pilar. This family may not have told the child he's adopted. Or the child himself – now a teenager, of course – he may not wish to meet the woman who gave birth to him.'

Pilar flinches.

'There are so many sensitive issues that must be taken into consideration. I know you're disappointed, but you must trust me.' Florencia pauses. 'I might have acted differently some years back, but Antonio and I have learned a lot in Lima.' She looks at Pilar, her gaze steady, unyielding. 'This is how it has to be.'

Pilar nods. 'I understand.' Disappointment engulfs her. She sees hope slipping away, sneaking out through a back door she hadn't even realized was open.

Florencia takes her hand. 'It's hard, I know. I can't even begin to feel what you have been through.'

Pilar's eyes fill. Don't be kind to me, she thinks, or I will unravel. She tries to smile. 'I don't want to steal him away from anyone, you know, from his family. I just want to see him, to hear his voice. To know what he looks like, what his life looks like.' And then she breaks.

331

Florencia says: 'I know, I know. I will do my best for you. God is good.'

Pilar resigns herself to waiting.

She fills the days with writing: letters to her son, letters he may never see, but letters she needs to write, nonetheless.

Softly, softly, Florencia says.

She tells Pilar that she remembers the parents: remembers above all their desperation for a child. They were a lovely young couple, she says. In their late thirties at that time, they had given up hope of their own child after fifteen years of marriage.

'I have a couple of addresses in Madrid where they stayed while they tried to adopt. They'd had a number of disappointments over the years.' Florencia stops, seeing Pilar's face. 'I'm sorry, Pilar. I know how painful this must be for you.'

'Never mind. Go on, tell me the rest, please. I need to know it all.'

Florencia nods. 'The addresses go back to 1965, and they adopted Francisco-José in 1967. We have no guarantee that anybody who was living there sixteen or eighteen years ago is still around – or even alive.'

'Can you let me know the address? The neighbourhood?' It is a forlorn hope, Pilar knows, but she has to try.

Florencia shakes her head. 'No. You must leave this to me.'

And so Pilar writes, in the hope that someday, she will be able to tell her son how much she has missed him.

Calista

London, 1983

AFTER IMOGEN'S FUNERAL, Calista returns to London and pushes through the days.

Yiannis comes with her. Once, before they had left Cyprus, Alexandros had pulled Yiannis roughly aside.

'You are no longer my brother,' he said. Fury blackened his face. 'You have betrayed me.'

Calista watched as, slowly, Yiannis removed Alexandros's hand from his forearm. 'We are not having this conversation,' he said. 'Your daughter has just died. My niece. Show some respect.'

Alexandros roared: 'You are a traitor to me and to this family! You have been sleeping with my wife! You have betrayed your own brother!'

Sandra began to move towards Alexandros then, but he stopped her, with one imperious gesture.

'I am not your wife,' Calista said. 'You made sure of that. You killed anything good we ever had together. Leave us alone.'

Alexandros stepped forward and raised his fist. Instantly, Yiannis shoved him, hard. Alexandros staggered backwards and fell over, sprawling on the floor of Petros's living room. Sandra rushed towards him and he pushed her away, his rage reminding Calista of that night in their brand-new hopeful home: lifetimes ago. The night when she had listened to brash Californian women speak about those things in her own life that she did not understand.

'Get out,' Alexandros bellowed. 'Get out of here.'

Only then did Calista see Petros in the doorway. Omiros stood beside his grandfather, his face white and terrified, his eyes huge as he looked at Alexandros, sprawled, filled with impotent rage.

'Come, Calista.' Yiannis pulled her away, out of the room, out of the house, into the car. 'Airport,' he snapped at the driver.

Calista felt numbness descend. Her son's face haunted her then, and in the years that followed.

Back in London, Calista knows that Yiannis is fearful for her safety. Her despair after Imogen's death frightened him, frightens him still.

'Let me take care of you,' he says. He watches over her tenderly, holds her when she cries, takes her out of the flat, out of herself. She often resists: all Calista wants in the early days without her daughter is to curl up under the softness of her blankets and disappear.

But Yiannis will not let her disappear. He takes her for walks – short walks at first. They stop for coffee in the fashionable cafes that are springing up all over London. They spend a lot of time with Anne and Aristides, whose kindness feels endless.

Once, after several months, Yiannis takes her back to Mayfair. Anne and Aristides are waiting for them outside Aphrodite. It is one of the better days, one when Calista feels a small nub of optimism, a kind of hopeful tranquillity that her life might even continue, as long as Yiannis is by her side.

'Calista,' Aristides says, 'we were hoping you would agree to meet us.'

Anne is smiling. 'We have something to show you.'

'Come.' Aristides shepherds them away from the door of the gallery. 'Follow me,' he says.

Calista is puzzled. 'Aren't we going inside?'

Yiannis squeezes her hand. 'Just come with us,' he says.

At the end of the street, Aristides and Anne stop outside a blue doorway. Calista is puzzled by the excitement she can see on Aristides's face. 'What?' she asks, smiling at him.

He hands her a key. 'Open the door.'

Yiannis kisses her. 'Do as the man says.'

Calista is intrigued. She opens the door and steps inside, feeling the hollowness of the space around her. There is no furniture, no fittings; the floorboards are bare, and the windows have been painted over with white polish.

'It's completely empty – what am I supposed to see?' Calista says at last.

'Your new gallery,' Aristides says.

'We thought you might like to call it "Artemis",' Yiannis says. 'You know, a kind of companion for Aphrodite. They're on the same street, after all.' He smiles at her.

Calista looks at each of them in astonishment. 'My new *what?*'

'For Katerina Pontikou,' Anne says. 'And also for Kate McNeill. 'We all thought it time they began working again. They deserve their own gallery.'

Calista looks from one smiling face to the next. 'But how?' She turns to Aristides.

'Speak to this man,' Aristides says, gesturing towards his friend. 'Yiannis is the expert in overseas investments,' and he grins. 'We are equal partners in setting you up here on your own. We will still do business, of course, you and I, mutually beneficial business. But Artemis is all yours.'

Yiannis puts his arms around her. 'Congratulations,' he says. 'My very own Katerina-Calista.'

*

Calista throws herself into Artemis. Work consumes her. She has Yiannis; she has her photography; she has work that now feels new and significant. All of these things fill her with gratitude. Silently, she thanks Katerina Pontikou: the anonymous woman who has saved her life, twice.

But she is also Kate McNeill. The pull of home after Imogen's death becomes irresistible. But this time, she wants to go back to the city of her childhood.

'Will you come with me to Dublin?' she asks Yiannis.

He looks at her in surprise. 'Of course. But I thought you couldn't face your parents' grief again so soon.'

Calista shakes her head. 'I can't. Not just yet. I won't go to see them, not this time. But I need to go back. I want to photograph the city I remember, before it disappears.' She remembers Anastasios's passion about preserving what was important before it became too late.

'I'd love to,' Yiannis says. 'You know that. And you know how I feel about your work. I'd be delighted to be your assistant.' He smiles at her. 'Are you really ready?'

'Yes,' she says. 'But you'll have to pretend to be my husband.' She laughs at his expression. 'Irish hotels and bed and breakfasts are still very old-fashioned.'

'I want nothing more than to be your husband,' he says softly. 'I'm looking forward to it.'

'I've never seen you like this,' Yiannis says to her during their two days in Dublin. 'So engaged, so passionate about what you do. It's the first time I've watched you work.'

Work is like breathing, Calista thinks. 'It helps,' she says. 'It makes me feel I can recover.'

Yiannis carries her tripod, the bags with her lenses, her jacket.

'It rains here, even in July?' Yiannis is perplexed.

Calista grins at him. 'It's Dublin. It rains all year round. But this July is better than most.' She takes his hand. 'I'm glad you're here.'

She takes Yiannis to Howth. She photographs the fishermen as they unload their catch. She responds to their banter, giving as good as she gets. The pier is a loud shriek of seagulls. She and Yiannis take the newly opened DART all the way from Howth village to Greystones. He is taken aback as the train rounds Killiney Bay. 'I never knew it was this beautiful,' he says.

Calista photographs the amazement on his face as he looks out of the window. She feels proud: not even the memory of Alexandros here all those years ago can taint her happiness.

She and Yiannis walk the city streets together.

'I don't know which I like more,' Yiannis says, as they are leaving. 'The parks, or the pubs.'

They laugh. Calista's brightest memory is seeing him in St Stephen's Green, crouching down, watching the small children feed the ducks. She sees the tender way he looks at them.

I love this man, Calista thinks. More than I ever thought possible. Nothing can drive us apart now, not after all we've been through.

Yiannis stands up at last, walks back to where she is waiting for him.

'You're looking thoughtful,' he says. Calista sees the concern in those kind eyes.

'I'm thinking about us,' she says. 'About our future. We have so much to talk about.'

And Yiannis takes her in his arms.

'I'm ready, Yiannis,' she says. She looks up at him, sees the hope in his eyes. 'For us, for marriage. For a child, if we are lucky enough.'

Yiannis doesn't speak. He pulls her closer, kissing the top of her head the way he did that long-ago day in Limassol Airport.

They stand, each holding on tightly to the other, as the summer crowds part and make their leisurely way around them.

All through that long year, Omiros rejects her attempts to contact him. Calista will keep trying. She will never give up.

But one day, she knows, she may have to accept defeat.

Pilar

Madrid, 1984

IGNACIO GÓMEZ HAS JUST TELEPHONED. Ignacio is a very busy man.

Unlike his father, he does not make special allowances for Pilar. Gómez Senior was a man who always seemed to have arrived comfortably at his chosen destination. His was a still, grounded presence, filling each moment. He never rushed Pilar. She still misses him.

Ignacio, on the other hand, is constantly on the move: always going places but always too impatient to arrive. 'Some more prospective tenants for you,' he's told her just now. 'Look after them well, please.' There is no time for questions. 'Call me later.'

Pilar's doorbell is pushed smartly: one loud peal bounces off the tiles of the foyer. She hurries towards the door. This is perfect timing. Both top-floor apartments have recently become vacant. Property values are on the rise again: Pilar wants to make a killing. She also wants to make a good impression. First impressions are important. She pulls open the heavy door to the street, and then, it is as though everything begins to slow down.

Her surroundings grow still. They capture the earth's atmosphere and fold it away. Not even the most slender of sounds arcs its way out into the morning air. Pilar's movements become sluggish, her efforts at speech futile.

She is aware, too, that her mouth is opening and closing: a stranded fish on some startled riverbank. A riverbank above fast-flowing waters that lead only to the past. Almost two decades telescope into a narrow beam of light.

A beam that glints and shafts its way sharply through the glass of the front door; it illuminates the face of the man who now stands before her.

Because this man is Petros: Petros as he might once have been. A vigorous man in his fifties, when Pilar had not yet known him. That intense physical presence, the smooth bald head, dark beard, the brilliant eyes, although this man's eyes are green, not brown.

Time fractures. The years converge and dissolve. Pilar sees before her a strange kaleidoscope of lives lived and unlived.

Who is this man?

He has just spoken, although Pilar cannot hear a word he says. She forces herself to focus instead. She holds out one hand. 'Pilar Domínguez-Lechón,' she says.

'A pleasure to make your acquaintance. My name is Alexandros Demitriades. My father, Petros, and Señor Alfonso Gómez were close colleagues for many years. He always spoke very highly of him.' He smiles a brilliant smile. 'We are grateful for this introduction to you.' He turns for a moment towards the woman who has been silent all this time. 'This is my wife, Cassandra.'

The woman leans towards Pilar, shakes her hand. She is beautiful, Pilar sees. An English rose. Blonde, blue-eyed, with unlined, lightly freckled, creamy skin: the sort that has never seen too much sun. Pilar tries to pull her thoughts together. Her heart is pounding.

'I prefer to be called Sandra,' the woman is saying. 'Much more modern, don't you think?' And her mouth smiles, a crimson bow that perfectly matches the shade of her dress.

'You are most welcome to Madrid,' Pilar says. And she smiles, despite the nausea that has just begun to crawl around her stomach. 'I understand from Ignacio that you're interested in seeing the top-floor apartments?' Better now. This is surer territory. Pilar feels herself begin to quieten. A small area of interior calm has suddenly blossomed to her rescue.

'We are interested, yes,' Alexandros says. His expression is guarded.

Pilar is used to this. The negotiations have begun.

'Please,' she says, 'come with me. You may take all the time you need to look around. When you are done, take the lift back down to the *portería*. I will wait for you there and answer any questions you may have.'

'Thank you,' Alexandros says. The three of them step into the lift together.

As they ascend, Pilar makes polite conversation about Madrid, about the area, about the exciting possibilities offered by the entire top floor.

But her mind is racing.

This man is Petros's son – there is no doubt about that – and the resemblance is remarkable. This is the once troublesome Alexandros, the man who took Petros away from her: all those years ago. The man who is responsible for so many things.

And is this the young, naive girl that Alexandros made pregnant? Somehow, Pilar doubts it.

Alexandros is something more, too: something that Pilar cannot quite adjust to. He is Francisco-José's half-brother: her own son's half-brother. Pilar is shocked at this certainty. She searches this stranger's familiar face as he speaks. She is desperate to see there some shadow of her own child.

'You are very kind,' Alexandros says, as the lift reaches the sixth floor. 'We will not detain you long – we have a flight to catch. Thank you for seeing us at such short notice.'

'Not at all. It's a pleasure. Señor Gómez and I knew each other for many years. I will do whatever I can to help you.' There are nods and smiles, and Pilar opens the door to one of the sixth-floor apartments. It is looking well: the morning light makes it appear cosy and tranquil, rather than old-fashioned and slightly shabby. Pilar knows that this spacious apartment is filled with potential.

She already senses Madam Sandra's keen interest, her critical eye.

'Take all the time you need,' Pilar says now, opening the door of the second apartment, 'and I will see you downstairs when you are finished.'

Alexandros barely acknowledges her departure. Madam Sandra nods, her eye already taken by the views from the terrace.

Pilar leaves them to it, closes the heavy oak door and flees.

Yiannis

Limassol, 1985

YIANNIS HAS JUST NOW RETURNED to Limassol. It will be
for the last time. There are loose ends to tie up, company business to see to before he washes his hands of all of it. Over the
past two years, Alexandros's bitterness towards him has not less-
ened. If anything, it has increased.

'I'm not discussing it, Alexandros,' Yiannis said, the last time
his brother confronted him. 'You treated Calista badly; you were
unfaithful to her; you now have a new wife. Let it go. Let us be
happy for however long we have together.'

Alexandros had glared at him. Yiannis pushed past him and
began to organize the papers on his desk. But Alexandros would
not move.

'What do you mean, I was unfaithful?' He sounded aggressive,
but Yiannis knew his brother well enough to hear the layer of
defensiveness that underpinned his question.

Yiannis stopped what he was doing and looked Alexandros
in the eye.

'You think I don't know about Hristina?' he said softly. 'You
were sleeping with her from not long after Imogen was born.
You think I don't know that?'

Alexandros stood up straighter. Yiannis remembered how he
used to do this all the time as a small child, every time he told
an untruth. 'I don't know what you're talking about,' he said. 'If
Calista told you that, then she's lying.'

343

Yiannis threw his hands up in the air. He no longer attempted to hide his frustration. 'Why are we doing this? Why are you even bothering? Calista knows nothing – I saw you with my own eyes. Now get out of my office, Alexandros. I have work to do.'

That was the last time he spoke to his brother. There will be no further confrontations. Alexandros and Sandra spend less and less time in Cyprus. Yiannis knows that they have now acquired a base in Madrid. Good riddance to them. He hopes they stay there.

Yiannis can now go about finishing his business here in peace.

Yiannis carries some boxes down to the car. The last remaining personal items from his office. He'll be fifty-eight in a few months and he is looking forward to leaving this life behind. Yiannis thinks of Petros, sighing his peaceful way into the darkness of a winter night several months ago. He, Yiannis, wants his life to be different from his father's: slower, more intimate, more connected to the ones he loves. It feels good to be handing over the mantle of business to his brothers. Ari and Spyros are welcome to all of it, Yiannis thinks. He relishes this new freedom.

He longs for the future Calista has planned for them. Yiannis still thrills with gratitude to all the gods he no longer believes in that Calista loves him: the way he has always loved her. A few months back, with Anne and Aristides as their witnesses, Yiannis and Calista married in their local registry office. Yiannis longs for a child. Calista thinks she is ready, but Yiannis is not so sure. He will never rush her. They have plenty of time to decide. In the meantime, he yearns for the peace and tranquillity of the woman he loves by his side. A new start; a quiet life.

It is what they both dream of, after all the years of chaos.

He knows, too, that Calista has already found their new home in Extremadura, already engaged the architect to transform it. The prophetic burn and glow of a loving future together has helped Calista, he feels, helped her in some small way, to begin to bury the ghosts of the past.

Although Imogen will always be with them.

How could she not?

Spain is a part of the world with which Yiannis is unfamiliar. He has, of course, visited Madrid and Bilbao and Santander on his father's business; but the wild and beautiful landscape of Extremadura is unknown to him.

It is unknown to both of them; that is why Calista has chosen it. She has family connections there, going back many years. Her maternal grandparents used to live there, he remembers, until the horrors of the civil war drove them out of their homeplace to the teeming anonymity of Madrid.

Yiannis unlocks the door of his car now, seats himself behind the wheel. He glances at his watch. Nine p.m. Time he went home. He turns the key in the ignition. In his rear-view mirror, he sees the gleam of leather, the glint of light on a helmet. Odd, a motorcyclist in the car park, particularly at this time of night.

He pulls quickly out into the traffic and leaves the port of Limassol behind, heading towards the lights of the city and home.

Yiannis has seen the man on the motorbike several times over the past few days. At least, he's sure it's a man, the same man: tall, athletic-looking, seemingly young. It makes him wonder.

The motorcyclist is, of course, unrecognizable. He is dressed, head to toe, in black. Black leather jacket, black leather trousers and boots, and one of those helmets with the darkened visors that make the eyes invisible.

Yiannis parks in the underground car park of his building. He gathers his briefcase and his jacket, the bottle of wine and the bread and cheese he's bought earlier, and makes his way towards the lift. As he does so, there is the screech of rubber, the gunning of an engine, the stench of sudden heat. The noise is all at once tremendous in this greenish, low-ceilinged space.

Yiannis turns, knowing instantly what he will see.

The bike rears towards him, its front wheel lifting off the ground. For a moment, all Yiannis can think of is a boar, a matted, maddened, stampeding boar, making its murderous way towards him. He tries to step out of the way, but it's too late.

He feels himself tossed into the air, sailing away into the darkness. He feels a hot pain shooting across his chest. For a moment, he worries about the wine bottle breaking, scattering shards of glass everywhere.

Then the boar roars on and Yiannis hits the ground, his head cracking open.

When they find him later that night, a young man and his wife returning from the theatre, he is cold, his body already beginning to stiffen, his brown eyes open in surprise.

Around him, blood has blossomed everywhere: the colour of a thousand poppies.

Pilar

Madrid, 1985

MR ALEXANDER HAS JUST SHOWN Pilar around the finished apartment. His pride shimmers as he speaks. The living room is filled with what have to be souvenirs of the couple's foreign travels. And amid the tribal masks and glowing ceramics is a collection of small, silver-framed photographs.

Art nouveau: Pilar recognizes the style at once. Expensive. For a moment, something about the frames feels familiar: the ornate borders, the asymmetry of the design. She tries to remember where she might have seen them, to filter out other, similar memories. She knows that the knowledge is packed away inside her head somewhere, but it keeps eluding her, no matter how hard she tries.

Pilar tries not to be obvious, but Mr Alexander catches her looking. The photos are of a little girl of about seven and a toddler of around two, she guesses. Both children are dark and good-looking.

Mr Alexander quietens at once. 'My children,' he says. 'Imogen and Omiros.'

Pilar understands that this is not an invitation. She murmurs something about such lovely children and swiftly changes the subject.

*

347

Florencia is keeping in touch. Pilar is grateful and impatient: she still doesn't know which feeling is the stronger.

'The baby's adoptive parents stayed with some friends in Madrid,' Florencia said when she telephoned. 'Those people no longer live at either of the addresses I have. But I've made contact with a daughter, and she's promised to get back to me.'

'What did you tell her?'

'Something of the truth,' Florencia replied. 'I have to be discreet. I told her I had once been a nun and had met this couple many years ago. Some family matters have recently made it urgent that I contact them again.'

Pilar felt despondent. 'And if she doesn't get back to you?'

Florencia hesitated. 'Then there is one more route I can try. Don't give up hope, Pilar. We are making progress.'

Pilar put down the phone. For the rest of the afternoon, she sat in her *portería,* watching without interest the comings and goings of her residents.

Calista

Extremadura, 1985

IT IS LATE EVENING NOW and Fernando, the architect, has just left.

Calista has made sure that everything has been done according to Yiannis's wishes. He had loved the thought of this house, of their life here together. Calista has been careful to overlook no detail that might have given Yiannis pleasure.

The house has simple lines, light everywhere, breathing space. There is some small satisfaction in watching how it has all come together.

The garden, above all, is Calista's passion. She makes her way there now. This is where she most strongly senses Imogen and Yiannis's presence; their absence. Omiros is here too; but that is a different kind of grief.

After Yiannis died, Calista made one last attempt to reclaim her son. She travelled to his boarding school outside Limassol and waited for hours until he finally agreed to see her. Seeing him in a uniform that looked much too big for his still-slender teenage frame, Calista wanted to crush him to her, to kiss his unruly black hair. He resisted every attempt to reach him.

Finally, Calista handed him a piece of paper with the address and telephone number of her new home in Extremadura.

'You are no longer my mother,' Omiros said. 'You abandoned my father; you abandoned me. And then you slept with my uncle. You disgust me.'

'Please, Omiros. Take my contact details.'

'I don't want them,' he said. His eyes were cut stone. 'Why would I want them?'

'In case you ever need me,' she said.

Her son looked at her. 'I have my father,' he said. 'Why would I ever need you?'

Calista loves these quiet garden hours. She loves the way everything thrives here. It reminds her of her garden in Cyprus.

She remembers the way Maroulla had written the names of native trees and plants in Calista's diligent notebook. Calista had looked them up in the dictionary and spent hours poring over their pictures in gardening books.

Mimosa; rock roses; anemones. Acacias; cyclamen; poppies. Calista loves their names, too, the way they sound when she speaks them, their taste unfamiliar on her tongue. Asphodel; bohemia tree; camel-foot tree.

Calista puts her watering can away and makes her way back inside.

She has, she supposes, made half a life.

And tomorrow is another day.

Tomorrow and tomorrow and tomorrow.

Pilar

Madrid, 1986

'WHAT DID YOU SAY?'

Florencia is smiling. Her real name is Isabel, but Pilar cannot learn to call her anything except Florencia.

'The parents are not unwilling,' Florencia says, 'but it is difficult for them. This initial resistance is normal. We must be gentle, let them take their time. The fact that they have not said no is positive. We must build on that. The next step is to tell their son about you. They have promised to do so in the next few weeks. This is progress, Pilar, I promise you. Keep your heart up.'

'When will I know?'

'As soon as I do. The day you see me on your doorstep is the day you'll know they've said yes.'

And now Florencia is here. She is here. Pilar feels her legs weaken. She tries to hurry to the door, hardly able to believe Florencia's smiling face.

She wastes no time. 'They've said yes, Pilar. The boy has always been aware that he was adopted. They want to meet you; all the family wants to meet you.'

Pilar feels suddenly terrified. 'What if I am not what he imagines? What if I disappoint him?'

Florencia puts one arm around Pilar's shoulders. 'Your son

wants to get to know you, Pilar. This is not the time to let your courage fail you.'

Pilar feels her hands begin to tremble. Florencia is handing her a letter, but she cannot reach out to grasp it.

'Tell me,' she begs. 'Just tell me what it says.'

Afterwards, Pilar cannot speak. She hardly hears what Florencia says to her. Only the soothing refrain – the words that Pilar has never before believed, not once – words that she now hears repeated, over and over again.

God is good. God is good.

Calista

London, 1988

CALISTA WAITS AT THE ALMOST-EMPTY BAR. It is still early. Retsina cools in the bucket on the counter. The watery beads on its surface are glittering, reflecting the lights above. A nondescript young man slides onto the barstool beside her.

Go away, Calista thinks. That's meant for someone else.

The man nods in her direction. 'Wine of our homeland,' he says, in Greek. Smiling at her.

Calista ignores him, pretends she doesn't understand. She lights a cigarette. She looks towards the bar, seeing the young man's face partly reflected in the mirrors there. His features are broken up by the many images of bottles, glasses, containers of kalamata olives.

His appearance looks strangely fractured. His own glasses with their thick black frames and their magnified lenses make him look like some strange, unearthly creature.

'I miss the poppies and anemones of Cyprus,' he says. So softly that Calista is not sure that she has really heard him.

She freezes.

'I miss the poppies and anemones of Cyprus,' he repeats, looking straight ahead. His tone is low and insistent.

Calista collects herself. She stubs out her cigarette. 'I do too. You?' she says.

'Me.'

She swallows. Nods. She has not expected to feel such fear. 'Kitchen,' he says. 'In five minutes.'

'But—'

'Madam,' he says, still looking straight ahead. 'The chefs have not arrived as yet. You must trust me in this, if you are to trust me in everything else.'

Aristides would never do business with any of those people, he'd told Calista many times. Thugs, all of them. They abuse the trust of their British hosts. They are nothing other than scum, a disgrace to their nation. Aristides would cross the street from them, he said, if they ever dared to enter his neighbourhood.

Calista lights another cigarette. Her hands are openly shaking now. Yiannis, my love. I know of no other way. I cannot live half a life. My grief consumes me.

With you, I might have forgiven him for Imogen. I might have forgiven him for turning Omiros against me.

A life without you and I cannot do any of these things.

Calista waits the five minutes, smoking. Then she makes her way to the kitchen.

'Target?' the man asks, without preamble.

'Alexandros Demitriades and his wife, Cassandra.'

He frowns. 'Both together?'

'Yes.'

'Tricky.' He pauses. 'Location?'

'Madrid. That's all I know.'

'Method?'

Calista hesitates. She feels no emotion: no rage, no grief. No regrets.

'Nothing quick. I want the woman to go first. Make sure the man knows what's coming.'

He is looking at her intently now. 'Message?'

'Tell them Imogen and Yiannis sent you.'

He holds out one hand. 'Contact number for you?'

Calista hands him a slip of paper.

'We will meet again,' he says. 'Once more and not here. I will get in touch with you.'

Calista nods. 'What is your name? What do I call you?'

He hesitates. 'Call me Damiano.'

'When will we meet again?'

'When I am ready. We will meet in order to arrange the transfer of funds to Zurich. Half in advance, half once the transaction is completed.' He waits.

'Anything else?' Calista says. It feels like a strange question, but there seems to be something unfinished here.

The young man looks at her. 'No details,' he says. 'No attempts at further contact. If you do, our arrangement is terminated immediately.'

'I understand.'

'Should I need to contact you, we will use a code word.'

Calista waits.

'Aphrodite,' he says, and walks away from her.

Calista watches him disappear out through the back door into an alleyway.

Then she walks quickly to the ladies' room. Once inside the cubicle, she pulls a wig, a scarf and a pair of Jackie Onassis sunglasses out of her bag. The same ones she had worn that first time she'd travelled back to Cyprus in secret to see her small daughter.

Calista checks her reflection quickly. She sees no one as she leaves; the door to the street swings closed behind her.

Her hands are trembling. She walks away in the direction of the main road and hails a taxi. 'Heathrow,' she says.

Madrid, she thinks, as the taxi speeds her away. You couldn't have chosen better, Alexandros.

Poetic justice, after all these years.

Poetic justice.

'Come with me to Madrid,' Yiannis had said, once.

But Calista shook her head. 'I don't want to go to Madrid.'

Yiannis had read her expression immediately. He didn't speak for a moment, and when he did, his voice was gentle. He pulled her into his arms, kissed the top of her head. 'I can help to dispel the bad memories.'

But Calista was adamant. 'No. Never again. I never want to set foot in Madrid again.'

Alexandros loved Madrid. Calista always believed that he loved it because his father had loved it. He was eager to emulate everything Petros did. For Alexandros, his father's approval was oxygen.

'Wonderful city,' Petros used to enthuse. 'Great people, and great business opportunities. I have some very valuable contacts there. Particularly in property. You should look at the property market in Madrid, Alexandros. Make a killing.'

Calista and he had travelled there together, a short break when Imogen was still very small. A long weekend in April, she remembers. And she also remembers Alexandros's disappointment. He'd left it too late to make appointments; he'd been unable to reach his father's colleagues. And everything Calista said and did during those days irritated him.

His bad mood escalated. On the evening before they were due to fly back to Cyprus, Alexandros slapped her face. It was the only time he had ever struck Calista in such a public place, and she remembers the searing sense of shame. Calista felt that she was the one who had done something wrong.

The hotel foyer fell silent, instantly. Waiters stopped in their tracks.

Calista waited, frozen, certain that someone would come to them. But nobody did. All of the faces before her looked down, or to the left, or off somewhere into the middle distance, unseeing.

Alexandros took Calista by the arm and marched her towards the lift.

As they crossed the wide, hushed space, Calista could hear the foyer slowly come to life again. Waiters attended to their customers. Guests began to talk among themselves.

As they walked towards their room, Calista had to fight the urge to run. Down the stairs, out the door, into the blessed cool of the city streets.

But where would she go? Who could she turn to? How could she pay for anything?

And so she stood, trembling, as Alexandros opened the door of their room and pushed her roughly in before him.

Pilar

Extremadura, 1986

THE DRIVE TO Torre de Santa Juanita passes in a blaze of summer colour. The door of Bar Jaime is festooned with balloons and streamers.

Pilar answered the letter that Florencia had handed her that day: answered it immediately and at length. 'They are happy to know it is you,' Florencia said. 'My first letter frightened Inmaculada, I think. But the boy's response has been so loving that she is ready. Go carefully, Pilar.'

After that, there was no more need for the written word.

José Martínez telephoned her at once. 'We can't believe it,' he said. 'After all these years! You were so close! Jaime can't wait to meet you. We are so happy you got in touch.'

Pilar could hear the emotion in his voice. She recognized it as her own.

'You are welcome to our family, Pilar. Inmaculada joins me in this – please, come and see us as soon as you can.'

Pilar remembers, above all, the joy she felt. She could almost believe Sister Florencia's words: that God was good. Maybe kindness and compassion do survive, she thinks now, no matter what people do to one another.

She remembers her father that day in Badajoz and wishes that some joy, at least, had been his before he died.

*

Two young people are standing outside the door of the bar when Pilar pulls up. She is in no doubt about who they must be. She's already heard so much about Jaime and Rosa; she's even seen some photographs. She laughed when she saw her son's unruly hair, still sticking up just as she imagined. Jaime, her son. Rosa, soon to be his wife.

She parks the car and begins to walk, still hesitant, towards them. Jaime leaves Rosa's side and walks towards her. His strides are long and loping, his face open and smiling. His hair sheens blue in the light.

He is so like my mother, Pilar thinks.

'Francisco-José,' she says at last. For a moment, she cannot say more. The sight of her son fills her with pity for Petros, for Alexandros, for all that they have lost. She will tell her son, someday, about the man she loved, the man who was his father. But she will never tell him about Alexandros. He must always remain a secret.

The young man called Jaime holds out his arms. 'Mamá Pilar,' he says.

After a moment, he reaches for Rosa. 'Meet your new daughter,' he says, grinning. 'Rosa, meet Mamá Pilar.'

José and Inmaculada approach her the moment she comes into the bar. Pilar rushes to speak before they do. She needs them to feel her gratitude. 'Thank you,' she says. She takes Inmaculada's hands in hers. 'My dearest wish was to see my son, to hear his voice, to make sure he was happy. Thank you. Thank you, both.'

Inmaculada's smile is tentative. 'You are welcome,' she says. 'We look forward to getting to know you properly.'

'He was christened Jaime Francisco-José Martínez,' José says. 'We remember well what that nun told us. We hope you can see that he lives a complete life.'

Pilar looks at the man, at his shining eyes. 'He is indeed living a complete life,' she says, 'thanks to you both.'

Later that day, the bar is full. Paco is there, of course, all smiles. 'A nephew,' he keeps saying. 'How about that!'

No sign of her brothers, Javier and Carlos, or their wives or daughters. Pilar doesn't care: the shedding of this secret is such a good thing. She feels light and free and happy.

Rosa approaches. Pilar thinks she looks shy.

'I'd like you to meet a very dear friend of ours,' she says. An elegant woman with steel-grey hair stands at Rosa's side. In her late thirties, Pilar reckons, and so beautiful. She is struck by the woman's sad eyes, despite her lovely smile.

'This is Calista,' Rosa says. 'All the way from Dublin, but a native of Torre de Santa Juanita now. Isn't that so, Calista?'

Calista smiles. 'I'm certainly here to stay, no matter what,' she says. She shakes Pilar's hand, and Pilar is reminded of the similar formality of Madam Sandra. No cheek-kissing here.

'Calista lives in that beautiful house on the hill,' Rosa says. 'Still the talk of the village.'

'You're welcome to come and visit,' Calista says to Pilar. 'Anytime. I understand you're from around here? One of the Domínguez family? I think I know your cousins.'

What a small world, Pilar thinks.

Then Jaime is at her side. 'Mamá Pilar?' he says. 'Just for a moment?'

She follows him over to the counter, where José has opened a bottle of champagne. 'Our first vintage,' he grins. 'To be improved upon.'

Pilar smiles. 'I don't think it could be,' she says, looking around her. 'I don't honestly think it could be.'

EPILOGUE

Pilar

Madrid, 1989

IT WAS INEVITABLE, and Pilar knows that.

Three weeks of police interviews, of forensic intrusion into her life and her building, and the story will still not go away.

Detective Sánchez has been particularly tenacious. 'I want you to take a look at some photographs with me,' he says.

He reaches for a manila file that lies on the floor beside him. He takes out a sheaf of shiny, slippery photographs. Some of them begin to slide off his knee onto the floor and Pilar catches them, glancing down as she does so.

She sees a young man's face looking back at her. He is dark, bearded, heavy glasses partly obscuring his eyes.

'Do you recognize him?' the detective asked. 'Take a good look.'

'No,' Pilar says. 'I've never seen him before in my life.'

She is sick of photographs. Yesterday afternoon's pictures of the dead bodies had appalled Pilar, almost more than the actual discovery of them. Those black-and-white images were starker than the real thing, somehow, as though they revealed some essential truth that had remained hidden behind the shocked shadow of reality.

Their light was sharper; the surroundings lost all their softness, all their familiarity: it was like looking into another room, into the harshness of a parallel universe, one that mocked her with its superficial resemblances to this one.

And then, of course, there was the shock of recognition: in

death, Mr Alexander looked even more like his father. It was as though Petros was here, even now, haunting her from within the frames of the police photographs.

Pilar is terrified by the thought that he might arrive on her doorstep at any moment. Does he know? Will he come? Is Petros even alive anymore? Pilar has never been able to find the words, no matter how relaxed the conversation, to ask Mr Alexander about his family.

Pilar looks through the glossy photographs now, one by one. She shakes her head. 'I might have seen some of these people before, but I really can't be sure. And they all seem to be so alike.' She can feel herself getting agitated again.

'It's OK,' the detective says. His tone is soothing, reassuring. 'We can leave them for now. Talk me through your daily routine.'

And Pilar obeys, for at least the fourth time. Running errands, accepting deliveries. Supervising the dusting, the hoovering, the polishing. She's said it all before.

He nods. 'I understand.'

And so it goes for days and days, over and over again. Until she and the detective could have written the script between them.

Pilar is impatient. She wishes it was all over. It is time she was on her way to where Jaime and Rosa and her grandchild are waiting for her. To where real life now awaits her, after all these years. She is impatient to get back to it again. Soon, she will leave Madrid for good.

She's going home, at last. Back to her roots. Back to her own family.

Pilar is furious: there is an interview with a 'close friend' in today's paper and it has Juan Pablo's footprints all over it. When this is all done and dusted, Pilar will wait for the furore to die down completely and then she will fire him.

Pilar is about to sit and have her morning coffee when the bell rings. One long blast, one short. Speak of the devil: Juan Pablo's calling card.

Pilar stands up from the table. Coffee slops into the saucer as she does so. Irritated, she makes her way out into the foyer and pulls open the front door. She is about to say something sharp to Juan Pablo, but his face stops her.

'What is it?' she asks. 'What's wrong?'

'I need to talk to you.' He looks nervous.

Pilar turns on her heel. 'Come in,' she says, without looking at him. He follows her without a word.

'There's something I need to say to you,' Juan Pablo begins.

'Get on with it, please,' Pilar says. 'I have a lot on my plate today.' If he's not careful, she'll fire him right this minute for having such a big mouth.

'Back in May, it might have been early June,' Juan Pablo rushes forward, 'a man came asking for you.'

'For me?'

'Yeah. I was doing my usual maintenance stuff when he rang the doorbell. I thought he might have wanted to rent one of the third-floor apartments. I let him in and we had a chat in the hallway.'

'What did he want?'

Juan Pablo looks uneasy. 'I don't really know. He stayed for a while, chatting, and then he left.'

'You don't really know?' Pilar looks at him in disbelief. 'You let him in. You stood there, talking to him. He must have asked you something – what did he say?'

'Well, he just went on about the neighbourhood really, and

if it was easy to find apartments to rent, and then he asked if I knew of some family called Muñoz. He thought they lived on the sixth floor, somewhere along the street, but he couldn't find them. He said it was a real sign of a posh neighbourhood when people didn't have their names beside their doorbells.'

'Go on.' Where is he going with this?

'I told him it wasn't in this building, anyway – that Mr Alexander had the whole sixth floor to himself and his wife, and he definitely wasn't Muñoz.' Here, Juan Pablo grins, triumphant. 'I told him Mr Alexander's name and he laughed. Said he wouldn't be able to spell that in a fit, and no wonder it wasn't on his doorbell.'

Juan Pablo laughs again, lights himself a cigarette. He seems to be enjoying himself.

God above, Pilar thinks. What has he done?

Juan Pablo shifts on his chair. 'He seemed to know a good bit about you. Said he'd heard you ran a really good show here.'

'What did he look like, this mystery man?' she asks.

'He was youngish, tall. I don't think he was Spanish: he was fluent, an' all, but there was something a bit odd about his accent.'

'What else?'

'He had dark hair and a dark beard, and his eyesight wasn't good. He had on those glasses we used to wear as kids – you know the ones I mean. I thought they'd gone out with the dodo.'

'What kind of glasses?'

'The ones like bottle-ends,' Juan Pablo says. 'You know, the ones that magnify your eyes and make them look huge.'

Pilar nods. 'Anything else?'

'No, not really. I don't think so.'

'Are you sure?'

'Yeah,' he says. 'I'd forgotten all about him, but the cops kept prodding and prodding, and then I remembered.'

'Did you say anything to them?'

Juan Pablo shakes his head. 'Nah. I'd never be able to recognize the guy again, anyway, so I said nothing. Just wanted you to know, in case, like, they come back again asking.'

'And you're sure he was here just that one time?'

'Yeah – I only met him the once, anyway.' Juan Pablo drags again on his cigarette. He looks uncomfortable. Pilar is sure he's hiding something.

A memory begins. 'When did the door start acting up?' she asks. 'Was it before or after that?'

'After,' Juan Pablo says at once. 'I know it was after. I wrote down the date I tried to fix it, so's I could tell you.'

Pilar looks at him. 'I'm only going to ask this once. Did you leave that man alone, at any stage, that day?'

Juan Pablo shifts on his chair. 'He asked to use a bathroom. I let him into one of the empty apartments on the third floor.'

'And?'

'Then Señora de Moreno nabbed me. You know, the one with the leaking washing machine?'

'I know who Señora de Moreno is, and I know all about her washing machine. How long were you gone?'

'Not long – just a few minutes. When I came back, he was gone.'

'Is that everything?'

'Yeah, I think so. I wanted you to know. Should I say anything? To the cops, I mean?'

Pilar thinks of Petros, of Alexandros, of Francisco-José: all the ties, all the complex, secret connections that bind them together. Then she thinks of her residents. She thinks of herself: of the new life that is waiting for her. She will not have that endangered. What had puzzled Pilar before is clear to her now. Juan Pablo had let a murderer into her building. With his talk, and his absences and his carelessness, he had literally opened the door to death. Pilar makes her decision. She looks Juan Pablo in the eye and speaks softly.

'If you say anything, anything at all, I'll fire you,' she says. 'You've already said enough. Let it go.'

Juan Pablo looks embarrassed, then relieved. 'That's what I thought,' he says. He stands up. 'I'm happy to let it go. I'm sure it's not important anyway. He was probably just a random stranger.' He stubs out his cigarette.

'Yes,' she says. 'A random stranger.'

'You off on your holidays soon?' Juan Pablo asks.

'Yes,' Pilar says, feeling suddenly happy. 'Off on my holidays.'

To my son. To Rosa, my daughter. To my grandchild, María Dolores. To spend time with them and with gentle Paco.

'Right, then,' he says. 'See you the first week in September. Give my regards to Extremadura.'

Pilar lets him out and closes the door firmly behind him.

EPILOGUE

Calista

Extremadura, 2016

CALISTA IS DREAMING. All around her, poppies and anemones bloom. Their colour is startling against the dark soil, a scarlet shriek against the blankness of the midday sun.

'Imogen,' she calls. She loves the quiet intensity that her daughter brings to all of the games she plays. Right now, the girl has built sandcastles, and she's pushed tiny Cypriot flags into their crenellations. An entire fortified city lies at her feet. Calista watches as she sails her fleet away, her small hands making the toy boats rise and fall, rise and fall on the sea's invisible swell.

'Imogen?' she calls again.

But Imogen does not turn round. She turns her face away, her gaze directed towards the east.

Calista waits. All at once, the sky darkens. There will be no fair winds for Troy today, she thinks, not any longer. The ground begins to shift now, to feel less firm beneath her feet. At first, the undulations are slight: those uneasy mutterings of water. Calista feels something begin to grow inside her again, just as before: the feathered restlessness of a captive bird.

She rests one hand on the place where her heart used to be, before Imogen used it up. She looks at the hand in surprise: she no longer recognizes it. The wrinkled flesh, the knotty blue veins, sluggish rivers and their tributaries. Maroulla's hands. The heavy rings seem to slide over the knuckle, seeking escape.

'Imogen?' she calls.

Now the girl turns round. At last. Calista begins to smile. She reaches out and takes one of her hands. 'There you are,' she says. 'I knew you'd come to me.'

The flesh is warm in hers. For a moment, Calista is confused. No – warmth is not right: Imogen is no longer warm. She snatches back her hand and moves abruptly away. She presses herself against the garden wall, poppies and anemones crushed and bleeding underneath her feet.

'Calista,' she hears. 'It's me, Rosa. Are you all right?'

Rosa?

The garden disappears and now Rosa and two uncertain toddlers stand in the shadowy room where Calista sits. She waits as something shuttles back and forth across the loom of her memory. She tries to grasp it, to separate it from the warp and weft of all those other memories that have, lately, begun to weave the tight tapestry of her life. Ever since her stroke, too many things keep slipping away from her.

Calista looks from one child to the other. The woman Rosa is looking at her kindly. She reaches out one tentative hand towards Calista's shoulder, but she does not touch her. Instead, she speaks. Her voice is gentle and familiar.

'Calista? Can I get you something?'

Rosa. *Rosé with Rosa.* Of course.

Calista struggles to sit up straighter, surprised that she is no longer standing with her back to the garden wall. 'Rosa,' she says. 'You're welcome. Forgive me, I . . .'

But Rosa waves away her apology.

And then Calista remembers. Memory is an arrow, a sharp, steel broadhead. It brings with it the forgotten knowledge that the little girl is Mercedes; the little boy is Francisco-José. Rosa, Rosa and her grandchildren.

Three pairs of eyes regard Calista now, their expressions grave. Relief floods her. She has managed that much at least – to retrieve their names, who they are, who their grandmother is.

Calista does not want these children here, but she cannot say that to Rosa. Rosa would not understand, and Calista does not wish her to.

Instead, she extends one arm, a gracious movement that reminds her instantly of María-Luisa. Her mother's face is still vivid: she thinks about her and Timothy every day. Dead now, of course, along with all the others whom Calista has loved.

She must remember her manners. 'Please,' Calista says now, 'do sit down. Let us have some tea.'

She sees the way that Rosa looks at her. For a moment, Calista has the sense that something has once again begun to escape, just when she thought she had it firmly by the hand.

What is it? Is there no tea? She feels her lower lip begin to tremble. How can she have forgotten to buy tea?

Rosa leans down and lifts up the walking stick that lies on the floor beside Calista's chair. 'Don't worry,' she says. 'I will look after the tea. Perhaps we will take it on the terrace?'

Calista nods. That's a good idea. The children watch her, silently. Before she attempts to stand up, she says to Rosa: 'Did you know that even as the old trees are being felled, the birds are building their nests?'

Rosa reaches for Calista's hand, tucks it into the crook of her right arm.

'Yes,' she says. 'But it's summer now and the fledglings have all gone. Before we know it, it will be time for the birds to fly south for the winter.'

Calista walks alongside Rosa, as smartly as she can, her walking stick tapping its secret message across the terracotta tiles.

The birds are indeed gone, Calista thinks. And all my nests are empty.

ACKNOWLEDGEMENTS

THIS BOOK HAS been in my head for a long time.

It's taken even longer to make its way, finally, onto the page and certain people have been invaluable in that process. I want to say a sincere 'thank you' to all of them.

To my editor, Trisha Jackson, and all the team at Macmillan, particularly Dave Adamson, Mary Chamberlain, Laura Collins, Natasha Harding, Ami Smithson and Eloise Wood.

Writing the novel was a lovely opportunity to visit Cyprus, where I met Alexia Christodoulou and enjoyed both her company and her encyclopaedic knowledge of her native island.

Extremadura was a great adventure, shared by Fergus Murray and Davy and Joan Abernethy. Particular thanks to Davy for all the heroic driving involved and to Joan and Fergus for their valiant, though fruitless efforts to spot the black pigs . . .

Thanks to Luz-Mar González-Arías for introducing me to Carolina Amador, in whose company I discovered the many delights of the city of Cáceres and the wild beauty of the entire region. Long may Extremadura remain 'undiscovered'.

Novels only become living things when they have readers. In this regard, I owe a huge debt of gratitude to Helen Pat Hansen and Carmen Wood who read many early drafts of this book and whose observations were always informed and intelligent. Thank you both.

To my friends-in-writing Celia de Fréine and Lia Mills: a huge thank you for fun, feedback and encouragement.

And finally, but by no means least, to my tireless agents, Shirley Stewart of the Shirley Stewart Literary Agency, Nicola Barr of Greene and Heaton in London and Grainne Fox of Fletcher and Company in New York. Couldn't have done it without you.

Missing Julia

BY CATHERINE DUNNE

We all make choices.

Some will haunt us forever.

A powerful and compelling story that explores one of the most difficult decisions we might ever have to make.

One morning in October, William Harris is confronted by the shocking disappearance of the woman he loves.

Julia Seymour has vanished without trace – from his life, from her daughter's and from her own. Her sudden departure seems to be both deliberate and final.

But William is determined to find her. In the days that follow, he tries to piece together what might have driven her away. His search takes him to London, to India – and to Julia's life before he met her.

In the process, William discovers secrets about Julia's past that challenge and disturb his view of all they shared together. Secrets that illuminate the present in ways he could never have expected.

The Things We Know Now

by Catherine Dunne

A golden child. A glittering future.
And the darker truth that lies beneath.

When Patrick Grant meets Ella, he seizes the opportunity of a new life with her. He imagines the future with his beautiful second wife by his side: the years ahead filled with all that is bright and promising. When Ella gives birth to Daniel, Patrick's happiness is complete. A son at last. Patrick adores Daniel: a golden child, talented, artistic, loving.

And then, when Daniel is fourteen, tragedy strikes. Without warning, Patrick and Ella's world is shattered beyond repair and Patrick is forced to re-evaluate everything: his own life, his role as husband and father, all his previous assumptions about family. Together with Ella, he is forced to embark on a voyage of discovery. He must confront uncomfortable truths about himself and about the privileged world he and his wife inhabit.

This is the story of a family torn apart by conflict, suspicion and loss. It is also a story, ultimately, of redemption and forgiveness – and the strength of severely tested family bonds.